KISS THE
VILLAIN

NEW YORK TIMES BESTSELLING AUTHOR
RINA KENT

Cover Design: Opulent Designs.
Art: @sketchesanmin

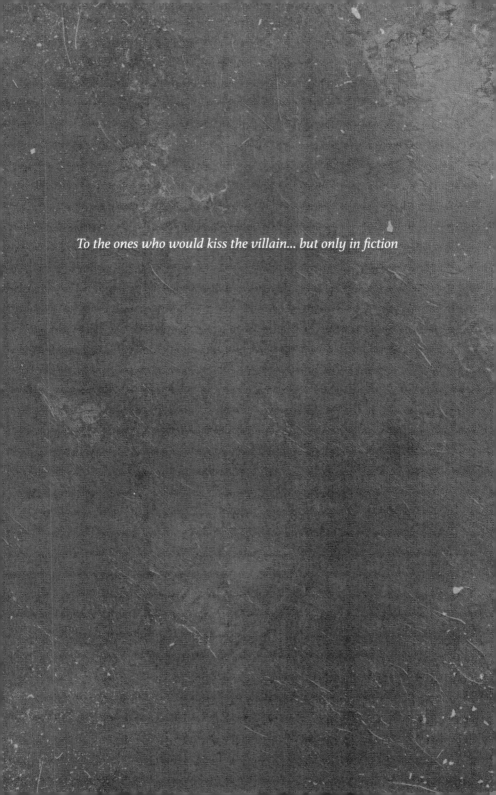

To the ones who would kiss the villain... but only in fiction

AUTHOR NOTE

Hello reader friend,

If you're new to my books, you might not know that I write darker stories that can be intense, unsettling, and even disturbing. My characters and their journeys defy societal norms and aren't meant for everyone.

The following paragraph contains content warnings and specific kinks that may spoil plot details. If you have no triggers, feel free to skip it.

Kiss the Villain includes themes of consensual non-con, dub-con, self-harm, violence, and mild homophobia. It also contains non on-page mentions of suicide, rape, child sexual assault, and domestic abuse. Specific kinks featured in this book include degradation, mild consensual feminization, mild BDSM, and praise. Please be mindful of your triggers before diving in.

For more things Rina Kent, visit www.rinakent.com

BLURB

My darkness meets a darker soul.

I'm a golden boy.
A genius law student, the heir to the Carson empire, and the
dutiful son.
Or, at least, that's what it looks like from the outside.
Deep inside, I have the urge to set the world on fire.
I keep these impulses in check, rarely indulging in mayhem.
Until one night of debauchery backfires, and I'm caught by a
villain.
I bury the entire ordeal with the rest of my skeletons.
That is, until that night walks into my classroom in the form of
my new professor.
Kayden Lockwood.
A criminal who's teaching criminal law.
I can't expose what he's done without unmasking my secret life.
What I can do, however, is force him to taste the poison he
gave me.
In the clash of titans, Kayden and I break and crumble.
And I'm starting to realize this dangerous game may have no
winners.

PLAYLIST

Power – Isak Danielson
He's My Man – Luvcat
Daddy Issues – The Neighberhood
Strangers – Ethel Cain
Apocalypse – Cigarettes After Sex
Addicted to the Wicked and Twisted – Palaye Royale
The Summoning – Sleep Token
Teacher's Pet – Melanie Martinez
Swim – Chase Atlantic
Want Me – Stephen Dawes
Bad Omens – 5 Seconds of Summer
Pain Killer – Grabbitz
Sail – AWOLNATION
nameless – Stevie Howie
Green Eyes - Coldplay
Into The Fire Acoustic – Asking Alexandria
Something Blue – VOILA
Birds of a Feather – Billie Eilish
Livin' in a World Without You – The Rasmus

You can find the complete playlist on Spotify.

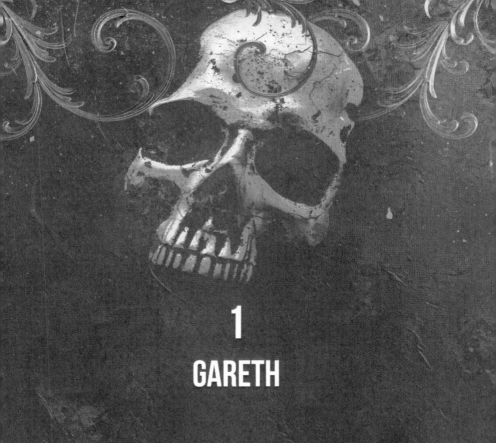

1

GARETH

Tonight, I'm going to hurt someone.

I don't care who as long as they wiggle and writhe like worms beneath my shoes.

Or more accurately, a snake.

Just kidding. I do care who.

It can't be just *anyone*. The target of my night of mayhem needs to be a miscreant who's as bad as me.

Or worse.

On paper, *everyone* is worse than me, though, so there's that, I guess.

No one would expect The King's U—or TKU—college's resident genius law student to infiltrate the Serpents' mansion during one of their grand parties.

Or to target none other than the head of the Serpents, Yulian Dimitriev.

The son of the leader of the Chicago Bratva.

But I've always been up for a little challenge.

So here I am, walking amid the overflowing extravagance of their lively mansion, sliding between hot, drugged, and drunk bodies. Despite being a Heathen—the other secret club on King's U's grounds and the Serpents' deadly rival.

We've been at each other's throats since the start of school on this godforsaken island on the coast of the dreary, dark, and depressing United Kingdom.

And while we love causing trouble, the one who actually started the war was Yulian, who was just itching to have his head bashed in and splintered to pieces.

Obviously, we returned the initial blow, and ever since then, it's been a struggle to determine who holds more power.

Just kidding again. We're unrivaled.

However, the Serpents are up there as well. Especially Yulian.

Our fights are always the talk of the campus, and the underground fights draw more crowds than intended.

Truth is, everyone loves a bit of anarchy.

A touch of chaos and violence.

A drip of blood here. A crack of bones there.

The crazier the better. The more unhinged the scene, the more entertaining it is to the audience.

But that audience is appalled about the idea of getting close, throwing a punch, tasting that blood, or touching that broken bone.

It's shockingly disgusting.

Severely deviant.

Outrageously inhumane.

Vile.

Atrocious.

Horrifying.

I chant the same mantra in public—even amongst my friends. They know me as Gareth 'The Fixer.' Gareth, who makes sure no one gets killed and that the police are taken care of.

Golden boy Gareth with the highest GPA, who had Ivy League colleges foaming at the mouth to have him join their ranks.

Gareth, who possesses the cleanest reputation and a future lined with open doors.

No one suspects that when they think I'm closed off in my room studying, I'm actually here, roaming behind enemy lines with the Serpents.

Doing what none of them, not even my brother, Killian, would ever do.

And I've been so meticulous about it, too. First, I needed to receive an invitation, and those are only issued by the upper echelon, i.e., Yulian and his gang of useless followers. But they also allow their invitees to bring plus-ones.

So I seduced one of the girls Yulian's been flirting with, pretending the book she was reading was interesting—it wasn't, just another piece of mind-numbing analytical bullshit written by a self-righteous idiot—and it got the convo going.

I was pretty sure she was Yulian's girlfriend since she was always hanging onto his arm and deep-throating him with her tongue around campus, but she sure didn't look like it when she had her foot on my crotch under the table in the library— disgusting, by the way, don't ever put your dirty shoes anywhere near me.

One incinerated pair of jeans later, I had the invitation I'd endured the urge to slit her throat for.

I've totally ignored her since I got here, though. The mask helps in keeping my preferred identity tucked away.

Invisible.

I adjust my white skeleton mask that has two large, black-painted holes where my eyes are—the Serpents' version of our neon stitch masks. While ours are differentiated by color, theirs can be distinguished by the symbols engraved on them.

Normal members, like who I'm pretending to be, wear a simple white skeleton mask.

The leaders wear black skeleton masks.

Yulian, whose movements I've been following from across the room, is also wearing a black skeleton mask, but his has engraved golden serpents shooting out from where his eyes are.

No surprise there as he always loves standing out. The freakier the better.

His mansion is everything one would expect, though. An overwhelming display of power, wealth, and control. The grand hall stretches out before me in cold, decadent shades of ivory.

The chandeliers hang from the ceiling, dripping with crystals, emitting a dim, ethereal glow over the marble floors that shine like glass. Velvet drapes line the walls, their deep-red swaths casting a crimson hue on TKU's students.

Noisy chatter and loud music fill the air, but it all feels distant, muffled, because I'm standing on the outside of something I don't care to be part of.

I move through the crowd with ease, a faceless figure among the Serpents, blending in with the rest of them. My posture straight and movements confident, I slip further between them, unnoticed.

That's what I've always been.

Invisible.

Unremarkable.

Since I grew up in the overpowering shadow of my younger brother, I automatically became smaller.

Barely discernable next to him.

Completely overshadowed by his attention-seeking habits.

You're such a good boy, Gaz.

I never have to worry about you.
I'm so glad you're this dependable, son.
Responsible.
Reliable.
Perfect.
Perfect.
P. E. R. F. E. C. T.
Those are the words I grew up hearing from my parents, my grandpa, my teachers, and my entire entourage, really.

And I *love* it.

I like that none of them caught a whiff of this side of me.

The side riddled with urges and voids, and a thirst so deep, Kill would look like a saint if they realized.

Except for Grandpa.

Grandpa is different.

So back to those urges—the reason I'm wasting my time with these people. The air is thick with perfume, alcohol, and something else, something darker, like desperation and pain. It wraps around my throat like a noose, and I suck it deep into my lungs.

Like a hit of the strongest shit on the market.

Shit I slipped into Yulian's drink earlier when I casually passed by him while he was talking to one of his goons.

I made sure to be facing away from the camera so that if they checked the security footage later, they wouldn't find anything. Sure, they could track my movements throughout the evening, but I'm a step ahead on that front as well.

Not only did I make sure to avoid all cameras, but I also wore brown contacts, so even if they managed to get a picture of my eyes, it'd be misleading.

Yulian stumbles and grabs onto the staircase for balance. None of the other drunk fools pay him any attention.

My lips pull in a smirk behind the mask.

The drug is kicking in.

Soon, he'll be losing all his strength.

Don't misunderstand. I might want to ruin the Serpents' leader, but I'm not foolish enough to think I can handle him.

Not only is he big—almost as large and tall as my cousin Nikolai—but he's also cunning and surrounded by his people and guards who'll maim me on the spot.

I had to be smart about this.

I was never that good with my fists, which is why I learned archery and use arrows to shoot people at our initiations.

Pity I couldn't slip my bow in here.

He'd look cute with an arrow between his eyes and blood dripping down his face.

What a missed opportunity.

But my plans are more wicked. I'll humiliate him in a way that will get him blacklisted, not only on the island, but even back home.

His dad might put a bullet in his head. That would be fun.

My smile widens at the thought.

With Yulian gone, the Serpents will be over. Unlike us, who have a more balanced power structure, Yulian has been carrying this entire clusterfuck on his back this whole time.

Sure enough, Yulian trudges up the stairs slowly, holding on to the railing.

I wish I had a camera to record this scene.

The guys' minds would be blown if they knew what I've done and what I'll be doing.

But then again, they won't.

No one will.

Unlike my brother, I don't like showing off my masterpieces.

I blend in with a group that's heading upstairs and then break away and slide through other partygoers who are searching for a room where they can fuck the horniness out of each other.

It's beyond me how people can be such...animals. Letting

their urges get the better of them, succumbing to dumb decisions and lackluster fucks they'll definitely regret come morning.

Don't get me wrong. Fucking is good, but only when I decide it's time to. I only get in the mood when I make the conscious decision to fuck, and never due to external stimuli.

Mostly, I love the power, the choking, seeing them writhe beneath me. I love it more when they have this little pained look in their eyes when it gets to be too much, and I wish I could keep hurting them. Turn their skin red. See their fucking tears. Blood. Their goddamn insides.

But alas, I can't have rumors that I'm a sadist going around. I'm known to be a good fuck with a huge dick who eats girls out until they come. I make sure they always come first, too. I also set the mood and ensure they stay hydrated and sleep well.

I'm the best fuck any girl can have and I come with a ten out of ten recommendation rate.

So to keep that image, I can't exactly act on instinct.

Doesn't bother me, though. I've mastered the act of wearing a mask at all times—sex included.

Even with the people closest to me.

There's an external persona and an internal one.

The main version is the genius, well-mannered Gareth who's loved by everyone and would make a perfect politician.

The secondary version, coincidentally my true self, is Gareth, who I only let loose when the void gets too wide and I need to purge some dark energy.

Yulian happens to be the fortunate scapegoat.

Or unfortunate, depending on how you look at it.

I follow from afar and watch as he stumbles into a room, whether or not it's his, I don't know.

Doesn't matter either.

I remain still near the corner for a few minutes.

Invisible.

It's a superpower I lost over the years as I grew up and became noticeable, mostly due to my looks. An accidental thing that happened because two good-looking people fell into something called love and decided to spawn some clones.

The clones were me and my brother—definitely not what my parents wanted.

They think Killian is the only anomaly with the Carson name, but that's only because they never *met* me.

Not really.

When I saw how they both freaked out about Kill's stupid harmless fun with killing mice, I stood around the corner and listened.

I listened to Dad blame himself, his genes, and that person who should not be named. I heard Mom cry and beg him to stop.

I heard the mess.

The desperation.

The impression that their perfect little family was shattered.

And I decided I wouldn't be like Kill.

I wouldn't flaunt my demons or publicize my emptiness. I wouldn't even let them figure out something is wrong or, worse, get so concerned that they take me to a doctor and have me diagnosed like they did with that idiot brother of mine.

I decided to be their unblemished boy. The picture-perfect son they actually never had and never will.

A spotless, unparalleled emulation of what I imagine a younger version of my dad would've been like.

Because that's who I would've turned out like if I hadn't been born me.

After a quick glance at my surroundings and making sure no one is paying attention, I walk to the room Yulian went into. My fingers are steady as I turn the doorknob, do a quick once-over to make sure no one is around, and then go inside.

With a small smile, I flatten my back against the door and lock it.

That was so easy, I'm slightly offended, but that doesn't stop my blood from roaring in my veins, a thunderous surge that resurrects me.

I've always loved the hunt, the way the creatures scurry in the shadows, the thrill of the unknown creeping in with every breath.

My heart booms and my demons claw at their chains, their rage spilling from the depths of the void, their bloodlust painting the room in my mind red.

My favorite color.

Yulian's room of choice is dim, the air thick with a stale, artificial chill. The walls are lined with dark wood paneling, casting shadows that stretch into the corners, making the space feel smaller than it is.

As I move closer, I catch a glimpse of a desk and shelves filled with books and knickknacks. But the only real thing that stands out is the black leather sofa in the center of the room, on top of which Yulian is sprawled. The sorry fuck probably couldn't make it to a room with a bed, too drugged out of his goddamn mind.

A mask still covering his face, he's dressed in black slacks and a long-sleeved shirt. My eyes flit to his pulse point—the first thing I notice about people.

It's beating steadily, the point throbbing against the skin in a hypnotizing view. It's silent, but I can hear the deep, rhythmic pulsating.

Thump.

Thump.

Thump.

And I want to cut it off.

To slice my knife through it and watch as it grows quiet.

Motionless.

Nonexistent.

I flick my thumb at the edge of my upper lip but quickly drop my hand before I can bite the skin and draw my own blood.

It's been a while since I got rid of that habit and I certainly won't let it rush back in now that I'm in full control of my being.

As much as I want to kill Yulian, I won't.

The one rule I have for myself is no killing.

It's not out of any moral code I mentally don't possess. In fact, I believe it'd do the human race good to get rid of the stupid wastes of space that keep diluting the average IQ.

It's the knowledge that I won't be able to stop and will eventually get caught.

Yes, I can avoid prison for a while. Not only am I a first-year law student who's studying law to manipulate it, but also, my dad's side of the family owns one of the largest and most successful law firms in the States, Carson & Carson.

My grandfather loves me more than his own son and would get me the 'not guilty' verdict no matter how many shady methods he has to use.

But how long would that last?

I'd still kill.

It would be impossible not to.

Especially after...*him.*

I know because bloodlust is the only urge I can't fully control. I watch people's pulse points and I wish I could turn them red. To see them choke on their own blood and let it fill the void inside me. I look into their eyes and I want them empty. I fantasize about dead eyes looking at me, knowing I'm the god who ended their lives.

It happens a lot during sex as they're moaning while I wrap my hand around their throats, and I want to squeeze that pulse point to nothingness.

I want their pleasure to turn into death. It'd be poetic, really. To end their lives in their happiest moment.

Unfortunately, that would ruin this whole image I've spent my entire life curating, and I do care about my image more than my need to see people die.

So, sadly, I can't kill Yulian.

I pause as I run my gaze over him again, the music thumping from downstairs barely audible.

Was he always this tall? I know he's big like that brute Nikolai, and they often go at each other in the fight club, but I thought he was closer to my 6'3" than Nikolai's 6'4".

And he's not standing, so he shouldn't look *this* tall.

With a mental shrug, I stroll toward him and pull a knife from my calf sheath.

Step one: Undress him.

But I won't be undressing a guy personally—I don't even like undressing girls—which is why I brought the knife to cut his clothes off.

Step two: Empty the vial containing lube that looks and feels like semen over him.

Step three: Take a picture of my cock in my hand as if I just came on him.

Step four: Blast it all over the internet with his face on full display.

Step five: Retreat to my public persona, knowing I'm the one who brought his ruin.

Might punch and kick him a few times after, just to release this aggression that's been bubbling in my veins lately.

I pull on the hem of his shirt with a finger, not wanting to touch his skin. Preferably at all. Begrudgingly, once or twice for necessity.

The sharp knife cuts through the fabric and I pause as the two pieces of the torn shirt fall to either side of him, revealing a muscular chest, an eight-pack, and a very *wrong* tattoo.

Due to all the fighting he participates in, I've often seen Yulian half naked. While his back is tattooed with all sorts of shit, he only has one small tattoo on his chest—a scripture in Russian.

That's not what I see right now.

The guy lying in front of me, his chest exposed, has a massive 3D black snake coiling across his abs, its scales rising and twisting like they're alive, winding down to his side with menacing grace. Its mouth is open, fangs bared, inches from his heart like it's ready to sink in and tear into him.

I take a step back.

Unless Yulian got a new tattoo in the last forty-eight hours, this isn't him.

My mind races. How?

I clearly heard his voice when I slipped him the drug, and I kept my eyes on him from then on.

Except for when he went up the stairs first.

Fuck.

If this is a trap, I'm not waiting around to find out. My legs carry me toward the door in quick, silent steps.

The moment I grab the knob, a metal barrel is placed against my temple, and a gun clicks.

A deep, unfamiliar voice whispers in my ear, "It's bad form to get a man excited and then leave. How about we fix that?"

2

GARETH

The reason I've kept my mask on for almost twenty-two years isn't due to a coincidence.

Or a lack of observation by my parents, teachers, or any of the adults in my life.

It's not an accident or something I've grown into.

It's a conscious decision I made when I was younger, and I've done everything necessary to make sure the image stays in place.

Mostly because I plot ahead.

Way ahead.

I don't move without having plans for all the variables in the equation. *Multiple* plans. So if one fails, I have several more to fall back on.

But tonight, I didn't count on Yulian being substituted.

It's not like him. At *all*. If he'd figured out I roofied his drink, he would've faced me head-on and tried to bash my head in.

He's not a coward, and he definitely loves using his fists.

So it's not Yulian who's behind this mishap. It's the guy holding a gun to my temple, his chest emanating repulsive heat at my back.

He better *not* touch me.

I consider opening the door and leaving anyway, but I only plan to die in my sixties, so being killed now would be getting in the way of that plan.

Letting my hand fall, I turn around in one swift movement and swing my knife, aiming at his throat.

A silenced shot pierces my ear and the knife flies from my hand. My wrist jerks and I let it rest at my side as drops of blood fall on the beige carpet.

Drip.

Drip.

Drip.

Motherfucker shot the handle of the knife, and while the bullet didn't hit me, it grazed me.

Pain throbs on the side of my hand, and I briefly close my eyes, trying not to get consumed with the pain. If I do, I'll have this urge to inflict it ten times worse.

"Look what you've done." Yulian's imposter's deep voice rings out like a calm mock. "That wasn't necessary, now, was it?"

When I open my eyes, he's close.

Closer than anyone should get to my person after attacking me. Because I'm staring at his pulse point, and I want to bite and rip the flesh out like a rabid dog.

My jaw clenches and I shove the demons back where they came from and stare at him.

Not at his chest or the peculiar snake tattoo, but at the mask with golden serpents that should only be Yulian's.

Was this a trap?

"Now, how about we pick up where we left off?" His breath, a mixture of whiskey and mint, penetrates my senses through my mask's holes. It takes all my control not to slam my head into his so he'll back the fuck off.

The silencer attached to his gun lifts my mask and lingers at my mouth, the cold metal brushing against my warm skin for a beat too long. It presses into my lips, the chill sinking into my flesh, but it fails to trigger any emotions.

I don't possess the notion of fear. That switch just doesn't exist in my brain. Not even when being held at gunpoint.

Anger, however? Yeah, that one I have in spades, and it's mounting the more this motherfucker holds a gun to my face.

I remain still, though, breathing as steadily as possible.

Any sudden movement could lead to my death, and due to the silencer, no one at this party would be the wiser. This fucking waste of space proved that he wouldn't hesitate to pull the trigger, and I don't want to try my luck.

The silencer leaves my lips and he flips off my mask, letting it clatter on the floor.

Here we go again.

My least favorite shit.

Unmasking.

Showing my beautifully proportionate face. Shiny blond hair and 'enchanting green eyes,' as many describe them— though they look brown right now.

I've often been called the personification of a Prince Charming with my classically handsome face, dimpled smile, and welcoming appearance.

They're all weapons in my arsenal.

The man pauses as he watches me. They all do. Men and women alike. I'm just *that* irresistible.

This one in particular doesn't look like he wants to fuck me, though. His gray eyes, the color of rainstorms and hurricanes, remain impassive as he flips my face back and forth with the gun.

As if he's looking for something. What, I don't know, and I'm not interested to find out.

Because I don't like those eyes.

Call it hate at first sight.

Why?

They lack color, and it's not only because of the cloudy gray. They truly seem dead, and he's not—dead, I mean. He should have some respect for the dead and stop those eyes from being so empty. That way, I can fantasize about turning them lifeless.

His gun lifts my chin and I struggle to continue staring at him and not the ceiling. "Such a pretty face for a grotesque personality."

Grotesque.

Did this motherfucking piece of shit call me grotesque?

Me? The best-looking person I know?

Maybe I need to rip his pulse the fuck off, after all.

"It looks like you despise my wording." A smile slips into his tone and I find something else I hate.

The deep rumble in his voice. The dispassionate, neutral, and absolutely monotonous way he speaks, as if he can't be bothered to inject any emotions into it.

It rings again as his breath skims my mouth. "But I wouldn't have used it if it weren't true."

I stare at him like he's a robot—and maybe he is.

"Allow me to elaborate. You came here with a vile plan up your sleeve. It started with drugging Yulian's drink and patiently waiting for him to break away from the others. I waited to see what you intended to do with him, but you stopped midway. So the suspense is killing me."

I start to lift my thumb to my mouth, then allow my hand to remain down.

He's been *watching* me.

While I was focused on Yulian, this fucking asshole was watching *me*.

The audacity to stalk the stalker.

The damn fucking *nerve*.

"Are you one of his guards?" I speak for the first time tonight. "You don't sound Russian."

Most of Yulian's guards, like ours, are supplied by the Russian mafia and usually have a very thick accent.

He doesn't.

If anything, he's more refined and has a slow, precise way of speaking. He also sounds and seems older than me, so he could be a retired military member turned security guard. Though his speech is a bit too sophisticated for someone with a stereotypical military background.

"Why?" That mocking edge returns to his voice. "You prefer Russians?"

"I prefer to leave if you don't mind." I smile, putting my charming persona on display, along with my seemingly irresistible dimples.

It doesn't affect the prick whatsoever. There's no loosening of his gun nor any change in those unsightly dead eyes of his.

He cocks his head to the side, leaning so close that my nostrils flood with his revolting male scent, like amber with a hint of something woodsy. "Not before you tell me what you had in mind for Yulian."

"Just some harmless fun."

"No harmless fun includes drugging and cutting clothes." His gun digs harder into my skin, the pain making me grind my teeth. "You know what I think?"

"Not interested. Thanks."

He ignores my words and steps into my space. "I think you planned something disgusting."

I peer down and pause. He's half naked. He must've discarded the tatters of his shirt and is now only wearing black slacks. He's tall with a couple inches on me and definitely broader. The snake looks menacing coupled with his mask, and I want to unmask him, too. To see the face of the man who dares to hunt *me*.

"Something that fits that grotesque personality of yours," he continues, shoving his gun against my mouth.

I let my lips fall open so that he doesn't break my teeth, all the while considering if my plan to die at sixty is that important, because I'm starting to think being shot would be worth it if I get to punch this motherfucker who called me grotesque.

Twice.

The muzzle of the gun rests against my tongue and he rams it farther until it slams against the back of my throat, and I stay calm as my breath is confiscated.

The surest way to start choking? Losing your cool—which is something foreign to me. It's not even a thing I can pretend or mask.

"No gag reflex. Interesting." His rough voice smothers the ringing in my ears.

And then something strange happens.

Those gray eyes? The ones that haven't changed and resemble a dead person's?

They're not completely empty now. Something shifts, the slightest bit, and I see a flash of light. A gleam in the darkness.

It's so fast and fleeting, I'd question my eyes if I had the ability to doubt myself.

"But do you know what's more interesting?" He pulls the gun from my mouth and taps it on my lips, smearing them with my own saliva, then thoroughly wipes it on my shirt, close to my heart.

On purpose.

To make me see that I disgust him, hence the excessive wiping, and he's doing it near my heart so that I know he could shoot at any second. He even has his finger on the trigger.

Sick motherfucker.

He's proficient at messing with people and pushing their buttons, it seems. If it were anyone else, they'd be trembling at the very least and begging to be released at most.

Too bad for him that I don't do that.

But he better watch his back after I get out of here.

"Want to know what's more interesting?" he asks again with his gun to my throat.

"I'm sure you'll enlighten me."

"Such a little brat."

"Oh my, what gave me away?"

"Watch it." He presses the gun in further, and I swallow because it's blocking my trachea.

His eyes watch the movement, mechanically, like I'm a boring game, before sliding back to mine. "You're not fighting. Why?"

"If I do, will you let me leave this tiresome event?"

A dark chuckle spills from him. "No. But it might make the event less tiresome."

"That'll only be possible if you tell me what you want."

"What makes you think I want something?"

"Surely you didn't point that gun and play a whole intimidation game for nothing? That'd be an epic waste of your time, and mine."

"Wasting both our time is the last *thing* I want." His gun skims my belt at the same time as he stresses *thing*.

I grow still.

It couldn't be.

My fingers start to wrap around the gun, but he slips it out of my hand and jams it against my head. "Touch it again and I'll spill your brains on the floor."

"It's not a shotgun. No brains will be spilled."

"You believe yourself to be funny?"

"No, I just dislike inaccurate information."

His gun slides down again, this time over my belt, and my hand twitches, but I don't reach for it.

Instead, I say in my clearest voice, "Stop."

"A word Yulian wouldn't have been able to say if you'd had your way with him."

I pause.

Was that anger?

Hatred?

Both?

It's the first time I've heard any emotion in his voice and it's because of...*Yulian?*

What is he? His boyfriend?

I didn't know Yulian swung in that direction. Maybe he plays for both teams?

"How far did you plan to go?" The man slips the gun beneath the waistband of my jeans, the tip grazing my stomach.

"I said. Stop."

"And I asked you a question." The tip of the silencer trails down to my groin.

And he's touching me now. His fucking hand that's wrapped around the gun is on my lower stomach, over the shirt, yes, but that doesn't negate the fact that this fucking piece of shit is touching me.

Putting his revolting hand that'll be broken on *me*.

"Did you plan to ram this limp dick inside him after you drugged him?" He speaks against my face, his mask almost pressing against my cheek, but at least his body is at a distance.

Except for the fucking hand, its warmth unbearable.

"So that's what all this is about?" I force a smile. "You're jealous I almost fucked Yulian, who'll never look in your worthless direction?"

He jams his gun against my cock and I grunt, pain erupting through me.

But at least my theory is confirmed. I'd find the information interesting under different circumstances.

Now, I have to bite my tongue to suppress the pain.

Motherfucker has hurt me more in the course of one night than anyone in my entire life.

I'm going to find out who he is and have him killed. I might not do it myself, but he needs to be eliminated for daring to get on my last nerve.

And touching me.

He's still fucking *touching* me.

"So you won't even pretend otherwise?" His voice darkens, deepening. "Oh, well."

He pulls the gun out and takes a step back.

Is he going to shoot me now—

"On your knees."

"I'm good. Shoot me while I'm standing."

"I'm not going to shoot you, little monster. At least, not yet." He places a hand on my shoulder and shoves me down so hard, my knees meet the ground with a thud and pain rips through my bones.

"What do you think—"

"Shh." He taps the gun on my mouth. "I don't want to hear your revolting voice."

The fuck is wrong with this asshole? My voice is deep, composed, and always gets the girls hot and bothered. I have a beautiful voice. Everyone *knows* that.

Every. Fucking. One.

So how *dare* he?

With the gun to my mouth, he unbuckles his belt with his free hand, and I stare in a rare, dumbfounded moment as he pulls out his half-erect cock.

Did this creep get hard by threatening me? Bringing me to my knees?

The veins on the back of his large hand bulge as he fists his cock.

And it's a big cock. A bit bigger than mine, to my dismay, and I have a pretty monstrous one.

The thing he has in his hand should be castrated eunuch style.

"Don't just look." He slaps the side of my mouth with the underside of his cock, his masculine smell invading my nostrils. "Make those revolting lips useful and suck."

"That'd be a fuck no. Thanks." I start to get up, but the grip of his gun hits the top of my head and I fall back down.

"I'm sorry. Did it sound like I was asking? Open your fucking mouth so I can use you like a nameless whore."

My head and knees throb, but I have a high pain tolerance, so physical discomfort has never really fazed me.

It's what he called me.

A whore.

Me, Gareth fucking Carson, a *whore*?

This bitch has pushed every limit and will now die. Thanks for coming to my show.

I open my mouth wide. The thought of letting someone use me, let alone a damn fucking man, disgusts me to my core, and it's hard not to think about throwing up.

It's physically excruciating to be in this position and allow a cock into *my* mouth.

But that's okay because it'll only last a second.

The man thrusts his dick in my mouth. "I expected more resistance, but you seem eager to suck cock like a dirty little slut."

I look him in the eye as I clamp my teeth on his girth. I'm about to bite his limp dick off when he grabs a handful of my hair and tugs me back so hard, my neck nearly breaks.

His cock slips out of my mouth as he points the gun

beneath my jaw. "Do that again and I'll fuck your ass raw. And I'll make sure you bleed before I blow your head off."

I glare up at him. "Or you can just let me go, and I'll consider not reporting you for sexual assault."

He laughs, the sound unhinged. "The same sexual assault you planned for Yulian? The one I actually have evidence for?"

"One I didn't go through with."

"But you would've if given the chance."

"Does a wrong cancel a wrong?"

"No." The motherfucker slaps my mouth with his cock as he digs his fingers into my cheeks—putting his repulsive fingers on me *again*. "But it sure feels good."

He forces my mouth open, and I let him. Mostly because his gun is now pointing at the top of my head, and I can't die and have this prick move along with his life as if nothing happened.

I also will not be fucked in this lifetime. Will never relinquish that type of control to someone else, and certainly not to him, as I'm sure he'll make it as unpleasant as possible.

Because his motive is revenge for what I intended to do to Yulian. A tit for tat. A way to make me taste my own medicine.

His cock forces its way into my mouth and I try to stay calm. That's my strongest suit, so it shouldn't be this hard.

I shouldn't have to literally boil with the need to bite him off again.

Harder.

Rip his cock off.

"Watch those teeth," he says when my teeth graze his cock. "And be a bit more proactive. Suck. Show me how much of a whore you are."

I glare up at him.

If he thinks I'm going to give him a blowjob, he's in for a rude awakening.

He must see it in my eyes as well, because he releases my

cheeks and pulls at my hair. "You don't want to? I suppose it doesn't matter because I'll be using this hole however I see fit."

I glare harder. *Just get it over with, motherfucker.*

Let's hope he's not like me and actually finishes fast like the rest of the limp-dicked assholes.

"You need to stop looking at me like that. The way you hate me makes my cock hard."

I feel it, the veins in his shaft pulsing, his size growing bigger in my mouth until my jaw hurts.

And then he does something.

He thrusts so deep inside, it hits the back of my throat, bringing my face too close to his groin.

I can't breathe.

Moisture stings my eyes and I hold on to my cool.

But I still *can't* breathe.

It's amazing how the human body is designed for survival. My hands slap on his thighs, trying to push him away, but my strength only allows me to grab onto him.

The edges of my vision blur, accompanied by a hum in my ears, and he starts developing a twin.

"That's more like it. I love the sight of those eyes dripping with tears." He pulls back, and I barely choke on an inhale before he rams back in again, my head banging against the door. "Seeing you in such a mess is a fucking turn-on."

And the sick motherfucker means it.

His dick grows thicker and heavier in my mouth as he thrusts in and out, using my tongue for friction, not caring about the saliva, snot, and tears that trail down my chin.

"You're surprisingly good at taking cock." He shoves me against his groin and keeps me there.

Choking me.

Making me *touch* him.

His zipper scratches my chin, and I claw at his thighs, my

fingers desperately clinging to the fabric, his skin, anywhere I can touch.

"Or more accurately." He thrusts, knocking my head against the door. "You're good at being used."

This bitch is going to suffocate me to death.

I'm going to die with a cock in my mouth.

With a man using *me*.

In a snap decision, I move my lax tongue, licking the underside of his cock, thinking about the blowjobs I get on the regular, then suck. Mostly how I like to be sucked but don't voice it, because girls can't or prefer not to do it.

They don't go hard and deep, to the point it hurts a little.

I think he likes it, because his violent thrusts stop.

My hands wrap around the base of his cock, smudging him with some of the blood, sucking deeper, licking with more passion, wanting to empty him of every last drop of cum.

The man whose days are numbered pulls my hair tighter. "The fuck you think you're doing?"

He doesn't like it—the way I'm giving him a blowjob. I can hear the bewildered anger in his voice. I can also hear the roughness and the masked desire.

So I squeeze his cock in my hand, jerking him and then pulling it in my mouth that's all full of saliva now, making the sounds sloppy.

The idea that I'm on my knees, sucking off a man, is enough to make any other guy spiral, but I push it down.

Because those empty eyes are narrowing, but he doesn't stop me as I deep-throat him, taking him in as far as possible and using my throat's movement to bring him over the edge.

His abs coil and contract.

A grunt falls from his lips.

His veins pulse and throb in my mouth.

That's it. He's at my mercy now, even though I'm on my knees and his cock is in my mouth.

The sense of power gets me high and I suck and lick, draping my lips along the crown in harsh strokes and a fast rhythm that I'd like if I were being given head.

I don't think about the humiliating position or him towering over me or even the gun.

I only think about the power in my hands. The way his breathing grows uncoordinated, his fingers pulling at my hair.

My spine jerks, my cock growing heavy in my jeans.

No.

I'm not getting hard due to sucking cock.

That is not fucking possible.

I never get hard if I don't put myself in the mood. It just doesn't happen.

"What a fucking natural slut." The man jams his shoe on my jeans, over my hardening cock, and I grunt against his dick. "Too much of a slut, it seems."

"Fuck you," I mumble, but it ends on a groan as he slides his shoe up and down, the friction drawing tingles down my spine.

"You got hard by being used. What a little masochist. Want a hand with that? It looks painful."

I'd rather he shoot me.

But I do something better.

As he toys with my cock, I do that swallowing thing with my throat on his crown. The one that made him grunt earlier.

And his movements stop.

He grabs my head with both hands, the gun resting against the back of my neck as he thrusts into my mouth a few more times, his rough grunts filling the space.

There's no other word for it. He *uses* me.

The wet sound of his cock mixing with my saliva and his precum is deafening. And I hate it, or I really hope I do, because my cock has grown into a full erection now.

By being face-fucked.

Am I turned on?

No way in fuck. I don't get *turned on* due to someone else's actions.

This better be a nightmare.

"You're such a natural at taking cock, little monster." His groan vibrates through me and settles in my balls. "This hot, warm mouth is dying to be filled with my cum."

I want to shake my head, but I can't, and I'm painfully hard now.

Like it's not even a joke. For the first time in my life, my erection *hurts*.

"I'm coming down this goddamn throat and stuffing you full of my cum." He jerks a few times and a salty taste explodes at the back of my throat and a sticky liquid escapes on either side of my chin.

As he pulls out and tucks himself in, I turn to the side to spit, but he grips my chin, touching me, *again*. "Swallow every last drop. Waste any and I'll move to your other hole."

I glare at him and a smirk pulls on the corner of his lips beneath the mask. "But then again, you might like that, too, considering how you're so goddamn hard beneath my shoe."

I swallow as he pushes his shoe further and I'm leaking precum. A grunt echoes in the air and I realize it's come from me.

Fuck. Have I ever been this hard before?

If he rubs a bit more, I might come in my pants.

What the *fuck*?

I should think his shoe is dirty, not want him to move it up and down.

He gathers the cum on my chin and presses his index and middle fingers on my lips. "Open."

When I do, he shoves them inside, curling them against my tongue, pushing all the way to the back of my throat. All the while applying incremental pressure to my cock.

My balls are so heavy, they'll burst, and I'm still leaking in my fucking boxers. My spine jerks as I rock back and forth on my knees.

"What a little freak. You're close just due to pain?" He pulls his fingers from my mouth at the same time as his shoe is gone.

And so is the pressure.

All that remains is damn fucking frustration and the infamous blue ball situation I've never experienced before.

He leans down and squeezes my cheeks between his tall, lean fingers. My lips part of their own accord and he spits right between them.

He spits in *my* mouth.

"Little monsters like you don't deserve to come." He pats my cheek twice. "Useful hole, though."

And then he shoves me aside as if I'm a sack of potatoes, opens the door, and leaves.

3

GARETH

The urge to see blood spill before my eyes has been constant and unshakable since I left the Serpents' mansion.

It's been throbbing beneath the wound in my hand, the ache in my jaw, and the disgusting taste I still can't purge no matter how many times I brush my teeth and gargle and even swallow mouthwash.

It's trapped between my skin and that urge for pain.

The demons in the void have been pulsing, fucking palpitating for something.

Pain, yes, but that doesn't seem to be enough no matter how many times I jam my knife into my hand wound, twisting and twirling the blade until my blood forms a pool at the shower drain.

I stare as the bright red spreads, its intensity faltering, slowly diluting to a murky, sickly hue before it's washed away by the water. It swirls around like it's trying to cling to something, but it's powerless, fading, draining into nothingness.

The constrictive feeling perching on my chest doesn't, though. Turn into nothingness, I mean. It's like a heavy burning ball sitting on my chest, a constant fucking weight I can barely breathe through.

It's spreading, the burn, to the back of my throat, my hair, my abdomen, my cheeks.

Everywhere he fucking touched me.

I scrubbed my face until it turned red. Even my shoulders, my stomach, my dick. I've been scrubbing and scrubbing and *scrubbing* everywhere he put his filthy fucking fingers—even through my clothes. And when that didn't work, I turned to my knife. Another knife, not the one he shot the fuck out of my hand.

This isn't working either, it seems, and I need to stop before I damage my nerves and can't use my hand properly.

I need it to kill that motherfucker.

Throwing the knife down, I step out of the shower, my blood mixing with the water and forming rivulets down my fingers before it drips to the floor.

Like a constant.

Drip. Red.

Drip. Red.

Drip. *Red.*

I like the view of red on the white tiles. The irregular shape of the blood droplets. The way they get darker with each drop.

It's calming, in a sense, which makes it a risk of addiction. If I get used to this sight, I'll want to see it again and again, in more significant quantities. Like a drug.

But I don't do addictions.

And I stopped one from becoming dangerous over six years ago.

So I'm stable now. I *should* be stable.

I drag my attention from the blood and stand in front of the mirror. The antifog surface shows a crystal image of water dripping down my hair, onto my impassive face, my abs, and to my half-erect cock.

It's been in this state since that piece of shit left me with blue balls, and I refuse to touch myself.

This isn't arousal due to *anything* he's done, and it's only a mere miscalculation in my fucking system.

I swear to fuck, if my dick keeps being a hindrance, I'll castrate it.

That internal threat doesn't get the little bitch to get the fuck down.

With a sigh, I throw a towel over my head, wrap another around my waist, and bandage my hand. The blood still soaks through, forming a blotch.

Maybe I need stitches.

What a fucking mess.

I pause after I walk into my room while toweling my hair.

"What are you doing here?" I ask in a detached tone, not bothering to feign annoyance at seeing my brother sitting on my bed.

He's the last person I want to engage with right now.

Killian's arms are speared behind his head as he leans against the headboard, his legs crossed at his ankles as he watches me.

He's about two and a half years younger than me but is a fourth-year med student because he loves showing off his intellect and made sure to skip ahead. I did skip one year, but that was all.

Standing out like he does is the furthest thing from what I want.

A gleam shines in his dark-blue eyes. We barely look like siblings. He has Mom's eyes and Dad's dark hair. I have Mom's blonde hair and Dad's green eyes.

And he hates those eyes—Dad's and mine, I mean. Something about not being Dad's favorite.

Well, he should've never stood out.

"I'm just checking in on you." He grins. "Saw blood on your car's steering wheel."

So I might have started the knife thing when I got into the car, using the spare one in the glove box. Now, I feel bad for Medusa—my car. I need to give her a thorough clean and apologize for putting her through this.

I raise a brow. "And why were you looking at my car?"

"So I could tamper with your brakes as I previously promised."

"I see." I walk toward my desk, not in the mood to engage in our usual conversation where he threatens to eliminate me and I pretend to be scared or that he creeps me the fuck out.

He doesn't. He's me in a different, less glamorous font.

I just don't like to be lumped in the same box as him.

At this time, I'd usually be studying or putting on the show that I'm doing so, but now I need Kill to leave so I can sleep.

"You *see*?" He jumps up from the bed and stalks toward me with a slight narrowing in his eyes. "That's all you have to say?"

Now, there's good news and bad news about Kill's presence.

Good news: my hard-on is gone. Thank fuck.

Bad news: he's suspicious of me.

"I just had a bad night." *An understatement.* "Can I get a rain check on your shenanigans?"

"Bad night in what sense?" He motions at my bandaged hand. "Who did that?"

A dead man walking. "It was an accident."

"Who was responsible for the *accident*?"

"Why are you asking?" I let my lips form in a smile. "You'll avenge my honor?"

"*Our* honor. Can't have you disgracing my last name."

I throw my hair towel at him. "Just stop being a red flag and we won't have that problem."

"You're bleeding again." He shakes the bloodstained towel in his hand. "You probably need stitches. I'll take a look if you beg me to."

"No, thanks."

He walks out of the room, but before I can release a breath, he comes back in with his medical kit.

I rub my eyes with the heel of my palm. "Did you not hear the 'no, thanks' part?"

"Nah, I'd have to care about your opinion to hear your words."

I sit down on the edge of the bed opposite him, the box between us. The quicker he's done, the sooner he'll be out of my face.

Besides, I do need stitches.

Because of that motherfucker in the Serpents' mansion.

He didn't stab the knife in the wound, but it's *his* fault.

My spine jerks upright at the thought of him, and disturbing images flash through my head.

Thankfully, Killian's voice cuts through them like an arrow as he examines the gaping wound at the side of my hand. "The fuck type of accident is this?"

"Either stitch it or fuck off."

"Getting snappy today," he says with that slight narrowing of his eyes.

I inhale deeply, because I'm losing my cool, and I don't do that.

A groan escapes me when he douses the wound with something that burns after digging his gloved finger inside. "That fucking hurts."

"Should've thought of that before you got yourself in whatever fuckery you indulged in tonight."

Indulged.

I don't like his use of that word, almost as if he has everything figured out and knows I do *indulge* in all sorts of shit he shouldn't be aware of.

"You know." He works on the sutures at an impressive speed. "My career choice has nothing to do with fixing you the fuck up. I only chose this to see inside people without killing them. Your insides bring me no satisfaction due to how ugly they are."

"Okay."

"Don't okay me. Just don't let me see inside you again and hurt my eyes with the view."

"Is this your version of being worried?"

"Not even if you die."

"Who'll handle your tiresome personality then?"

"Actually, you're right. Don't die, so I can have a punching bag at all times."

I let my lips curl in a tired smile as I stare at the ceiling. Little fucker can be effortlessly entertaining.

"Hey, Kill."

"Hmm?"

"Do you know if Yulian is into guys?"

He lifts his head. "Why?"

"I'm trying to figure out a plan to bring him down, and I heard rumors that I want to confirm before plotting."

There's nothing suspicious about what I'm saying. While I take a background position in the Heathens, I'm mostly the brain behind many of our operations.

"If by guys, you mean Vaughn, then yeah. Yulian *definitely* wants to fuck him. Or be fucked by him, I'm not sure."

"*Our* Vaughn?" I ask, honestly surprised.

"Is there another Vaughn?"

"The New York Bratva Pakhan's son, Vaughn?"

"Again, do we know another one? You hit your head or something?"

Vaughn is the fifth member of the Heathens. An absent member. He's around Kill's age and chose not to come to this island or go to this college, opting to stay in New York. It was solely his choice.

He was vehemently against studying with us, no matter how many times Nikolai and Jeremy asked him to.

But he still joins the fun at initiations, mostly to hunt people.

"That doesn't make sense," I say. "Vaughn is straight. Hasn't he had a girlfriend for years?"

"The girlfriend Yulian seduced and fucked, then sent Vaughn the video of her screaming his name while riding him? They'll probably break up. That is, if he doesn't kill her. You know how much he hates sharing."

"When did that happen?"

"Last week? Right before we got back to school."

"How do you know all this?"

"I heard it when I happened to pass by Vaughn talking about it to Jeremy and promising to kill Yulian."

Happened to pass by in Kill's vocabulary is eavesdropping. He loves gathering the most random shit about people. Big or small. He thinks it'll help him crack them open and see inside them. Figuratively or literally.

I, on the other hand, find most people depressingly dull and would rather not gather any unnecessary details.

Vaughn is anything but dull, though, especially with this latest development.

"What do you think his plan with Yulian is? He's on the other side of the ocean, so he can't do much about him."

My brother shrugs. "Not sure yet, but he's putting in a last-minute transfer request to come here next term, which is playing into Yulian's hand, if you ask me."

"Because Yulian is the reason Vaughn didn't want to study here in the first place," I say, not a question, but a fact.

The pieces of the puzzle are starting to come together.

The way Yulian always, and I mean *always*, only fights Kill, Jeremy, or Nikolai in the ring.

Those are the only three he's had any interest in fighting. He also makes sure someone is filming. I thought it was a sense of pride, but this is different.

He's probably been sending those to Vaughn.

Our friend, on the other hand, has chosen not to engage in Yulian's antics, hence the girlfriend and the staying in New York thing.

But he obviously hasn't been able to completely stay away. I've always thought it's because we're his friends, since we grew up together, so he wants to pay us a visit now and again, but maybe that's not all of it.

"Exactly." Kill finishes and releases my hand as he grins. "Not sure what type of foreplay those two are into, but shit will be interesting. The sons of the leaders of the two most notorious Russian mafia branches? I sense trouble and I'm here for it."

I say nothing and kick Kill out. As I close the door, I lean against it and let my lips pull in a smile.

This is a variable I didn't expect.

The motherfucker from tonight is such a fool. Yulian is obviously obsessed with Vaughn in some way, and that means the man who's probably a bodyguard is struggling with some form of unrequited lust, or even better, love.

I'd feel sorry for him if I knew how.

I thought I'd find him and kill him, but now, I have an upgraded plan—make him suffer.

In the most painful way possible.

I'll make him wish he never met me.

Let alone touched me.

———

"This is so fucking boring." My cousin Nikolai wraps an arm around Jeremy's shoulders as we walk to campus. "Give me something, Jer. A battle, a war, a little toy to fuck with."

"We have the initiation coming. Try to hold it in until then," Jeremy speaks in a calm, unbothered tone.

He's the Heathens' leader, the son of the New York Bratva's strategist, and has quite a few similarities with his father. Like me, he doesn't act without a plan, but unlike me, he's openly ruthless when need be.

"It's not piss, Jer. I can't just hold it in," Nikolai grumbles out loud, drawing people's attention due to his big frame and the full-sleeve tattoos peeking from beneath his T-shirt.

He's my maternal cousin—our moms are identical twin sisters—and the most chaotic person I know. He's the most violent among us and gets off on crunching people's bones, but he's also random as fuck.

While my mom is a Russian mafia princess, she separated from the organization long before I was born. Aunt Rai and her husband, however, are two of their leaders. That gives Nikolai, like Jeremy and Vaughn, a legacy to continue and his parents' shoes to fill.

Kill and I are just here for the ride. A revival of our distant Russian roots, perhaps. In my case, I need a venting outlet, which I'm sure is the same for Kill.

"Just get your dick wet, Niko," my brother says, walking on

Niko's left. "That usually takes care of the aggression, even if temporarily."

"Satan's heir, you evil genius." Niko releases Jeremy and headlocks my brother.

"Stating the obvious, I see," Kill says in his usual arrogant tone that will one day get him murdered decapitation style.

Niko keeps talking about his dick, and I'm glad we're not in the house or he'd be indulging in exhibitionism.

I fall behind to match Jeremy's steps. "Vaughn is coming to the initiation, right?"

"Is there a reason he wouldn't?"

"Just checking."

Jeremy glances at my bandage, then back at my face. "How about getting your hand properly checked? Kill said the wound is deep."

"You know he likes to exaggerate things."

"I saw the blood in the car. Didn't seem exaggerated."

"Just a little accident, Jer."

"I expect Niko and Kill to get into little accidents. Hell, even Vaughn, but not you, Gaz."

Jeremy stops and I'm forced to do the same. Since he's the oldest among us, he annoyingly takes the leadership position seriously.

Way too seriously for my taste.

"Won't happen again." *From now on, I'll be the one inflicting pain.*

"Better not. You're the only levelheaded person I trust to keep things under control."

"Don't worry." *As long as* I'm *under control, that is.*

"You won't tell me what actually happened?"

"Not important." I tap his shoulder, wearing my most charming smile. "See you later."

I let them go to their respective classes and head to mine.

Kill goes to the med school building, and Jeremy and Nikolai, who are in business school, go to that building.

The walk to my first class is constantly interrupted by students and professors greeting me, talking to me, wanting as much of my attention as they can get.

They're like sponges, sucking on and soaking up my words and smiles and empty compliments just so they'll grow bigger and more inflated.

While I usually don't mind, their constant noise is worsening the headache I woke up with today.

Sleep evaded me for most of last night, and when I did nod off, I dreamt of a man in a skeleton mask with gold serpents wrapping his fingers around my dick and squeezing until it hurt.

I remember thinking that I don't find men attractive.

And his veiny hand around my cock shouldn't make it so hard that it's leaking precum.

But then he was jerking me off, roughly, until it hurt—the way I like it but have never had it.

And I grunted, in the nightmare, about to come, but then he was shoving a pillow over my head and suffocating me to death.

I woke up in a puddle of sweat and with another fucking hard-on.

Thank God Niko barged into my room and threw a bucket of ice water on me just for fun—effectively killing the tent—or we would've had a problem.

The headache is getting worse despite the painkillers I took. My hand wound still throbs and my jaw aches so bad, it was impossible to eat, so I only had coffee and a strawberry for breakfast.

This is one of those days where I wish I hadn't chosen overachiever, A+ student as my mask, because every single person is pissing me the fuck off.

As soon as I walk into the lecture hall, I'm once again surrounded by my classmates, as if they're bees and I'm damn fucking honey. They're all buzzing and talking nonstop around me once I take my seat, and I just want them to shut the fuck up already. All their blabbering is causing my head to pound worse.

"Where were you last night, Gaz?" a guy whose name I've forgotten asks.

A brunette slides to my side, shoving her tits against my arm. Morgan. I only remember because I fucked her a few times and she always brings one of her friends to join. A booty call of sorts.

She grins up at me, her mouth too big for her pretty face, and the lack of symmetry bugs me. "I thought we'd have one of those *fun* study nights."

Fun, as in I'd fuck her and her friend while they pretend to kiss and lick each other's pussies to turn me on.

It never really works.

I only get hard on demand.

Except for last night, a demon whispers from the void, and I'm about to gag him bondage style.

I smile and slightly shift away. "Next time, beautiful."

She blushes, but she still doesn't remove her tits and even slides them up and down my arm, and I want to break her fucking neck.

I don't usually get this prickly about people touching me. Yes, I hate it, but I can manage to mask it so well, no one can tell.

Right now, however, I struggle not to shove her away. I lift my thumb to my mouth, slightly flick it at the corner, then drop it back down when my phone buzzes on the table.

CHERRY

Hi, handsome 🖤

Would you look at that. My brother's ex-fuck buddy, who sucked my cock just to continue chasing him.

She was so ready to ride my cock as well, but I happen to draw the line at sharing holes with my brother. It'd be nice to mess with him, though.

Pretty sure he has a girl he's been stalking at the neighboring Royal Elite University. Now, if both she and Cherry could make it to the initiation, how entertaining would that be?

Not as entertaining as Vaughn and Yulian—the latter of whom won't refuse an invitation if given one—but close enough.

As the others keep buzzing around me, I reply to Cherry.

ME

Hi, beautiful. Miss your face.

CHERRY

Not more than me. I get so wet thinking of your huge cock every night and I have to use this toy I got. It's not as big as you, though *pouting GIF*

Ew.

You're killing me. I'm getting hard in class.

Nope. My dick is as dead as a corpse, actually.

Yum.

Listen. You know there's that initiation coming up, right? Want to join?

OMG, really?

What a tool. She must think I'm a simp who's drooling over her and she can use me as she sees fit. In fact, Cherry has been hinting at the initiation for a while. Only an idiot wouldn't notice her blatant attempts to get invited.

> Really. Tell you what, I'll even protect you and make sure you get to the finish line. How does that sound?

> Sounds amazing! You're the best.

Don't go stating the obvious now.

"...what do you think, Gaz?"

I lift my head at Morgan's voice—who's still rubbing her tits all over me.

The shirt will be burned later.

"Depends, really," I say, even though I have no clue what the fuck they're talking about.

"I mean, he has a great reputation." One of the guys, Meyers, picks up the conversation. "And since criminal law is an important part of the core curriculum, this will be fun."

"Heard he's hot as fuck," a girl chimes in. "I call dibs."

"Get in line," her friend says.

"I'm the one who shared the information about him first," Morgan protests.

Ah. The professor.

I swear to fuck I lose brain cells whenever I listen to their gossip.

Whoever this professor is, they'll fall under my spell like the lot of them. I'm charming, smart, and an A+ student, which is porn for professors. But, like, professionally.

None of my classmates even try to beat me in grades anymore. Not even Zara Jones, Morgan's friend and the only one who's now talking about the Professor's good reputation instead of how hot he is.

Zara, like everyone, learned she'll never reach my level. What's effortless for me is something she and the others can only achieve if they study day and night.

Shuffling ensues as a tall, broad man walks into class.

Everyone heads to their seat, and the girls who were fighting about dibs squeal.

"He's drop-dead gorgeous," one of them whispers.

"Lock me up, Your Honor," the other says, and they giggle like schoolgirls.

Damn hormonal college kids.

I drag my gaze to the professor again and pause.

Because he's watching me.

Among everyone in the entire lecture hall, his gray, dead, and absolutely disturbing eyes are set on me.

My skin prickles and my wound burns.

Before he even speaks, before he opens his mouth and I confirm my suspicion, a deep premonition slashes through my skin and my demons roar in their pit, devouring each other alive.

His dead gaze remains on me as he says, "Hello, class. My name is Kayden Lockwood, and I'm your criminal law professor."

4
GARETH

Kayden Lockwood.

That's the name of the motherfucker who used my mouth to get off last night.

The man who held me at gunpoint, grazed my hand with a bullet, and called me grotesque, a whore, and a useful hole, among other things.

The asshole who humiliated me like no one else has.

I woke up today dead set on revenge, on finding him and making him bleed. I considered striking a deal with Yulian, where I provide him with an invitation to the initiation and he gives me the identity of this motherfucker.

But that's no longer necessary.

Because the bastard is looking at me.

And I'm finally putting a face to the voice of the man I've been fantasizing about stabbing a thousand times.

A sharp jaw, features carved with subtle authority, and jet-black hair that's cropped tight on the sides but long enough on top to be styled back with ruthless precision. His full, defined lips are set in a cold, impassive line as if he finds this entire ordeal bland. Faint stubble brushes his cheeks, enhancing the rough edge of his quiet confidence.

But what truly gave him away the second I saw him?

The eyes. Still dead and empty, like they've seen too much, felt too little. The deepest shade of a storm, rolling, brewing, and heightening with no intention of ever calming down.

His tailored slacks match the color of his eyes, and his white shirt stretches across his chest, clinging to the hard lines of muscle, every inch of it pulling across his body. The fabric strains around his biceps that tighten and flex with every movement like when he fucked my mouth.

When he grabbed my hair, shoved my head against his groin, and came down my throat. He's now standing in front of me as my professor of criminal law.

Professor. Not a bodyguard as I suspected.

A damn *professor*.

Why was a goddamn professor in the Serpents' mansion? Holding a gun, wearing Yulian's mask, and forcing a student to his knees?

The class seems to hold their collective breath at his introduction, the air thick with the weight of his presence. Everyone seems frozen, drawn in by the sheer force of him—his domineering, magnetic energy filling every corner of the hall.

Even *I* feel it, and I'm usually immune to the pull of other people's auras.

"Welcome to criminal law." He speaks in that same deep, calm voice that makes my skin prickle. "This is not a course about theory or abstract principles; this is about understanding the very foundation of justice in society. Through this course, we will examine how the law distinguishes between right and wrong, but more importantly, how it punishes the wrongs."

Is this bastard hearing a word he's saying? How can he talk about punishing wrongs with a straight face after what he's done?

"Gosh, he sounds so hot." Morgan trails her red nails over my arm as she whispers in my ear, and this time, I'm about to scoot away.

Or I'll bang her head on the desk for continuing to fucking *touch* me.

The prof's eyes flit to me for a brief second, and I glare back.

"You, over there." He juts his chin in my direction. "It appears you've mistaken this classroom for a social gathering. While I'm sure your companion finds your attention flattering, I suggest you remember where you are. This is a place for rigorous intellectual engagement, not an opportunity to parade your schoolboy charms."

The whole class falls into oppressive silence.

Morgan's face turns all shades of red.

I grab a pen in my hand to stop myself from jumping down there and throttling him on the spot.

He's humiliating me on purpose. In front of the *whole* class.

A class that only knows me as a golden boy.

I let my lips curl into a smile. "Of course, Professor. I'll be sure to keep my charms in check. Wouldn't want to disrupt your perfect class with any *distractions*."

I think I see a gleam amid the gray, but he directs his attention to the rest of the lecture hall. "You will be expected to think critically, analyze evidence, and confront uncomfortable truths. There is no room for leniency or weakness in this field. You are not here to make excuses for criminals. You are here to understand the system that holds them accountable. If you cannot accept that, then this course is not for you. Now, let's get to work."

The PowerPoint slides turn on and he starts the lecture, his voice making my headache pound harder, more persistently that my vision blurs. My wound pulses in annoying frequency, and I suppress the urge to rip the fucking stitches out and dig my knife into it.

The longer he talks in that smooth, slightly austere tone, as if he doesn't have a care in the world, the more murderous I turn.

How *dare* he show up in front of me?

How can he be so damn...detached?

I slide my pen on the paper back and forth, back and forth.

As if I'm summoning a demon.

The whole class hangs on his every word, falling over each other to answer any questions he asks.

Bunch of fucking fools.

They're all charmed by his looks, his eloquent manner of speaking, and the commanding way he carries himself. But none of them seems to see the monster lurking within.

Then again, I do use my looks as well, so I'm in no position to judge, but come on. The fucker is a literal criminal who's teaching criminal law.

Usually, I'd answer all questions and impress the professor, but I've just been sliding the pen on my notebook while keeping him in my sight the entire time.

There's this unfathomable itch beneath my skin, a nonsensical thought, that if I don't pay attention, he might jump me again.

Even if we're in a class full of people.

My head hurts worse the more I watch him moving effortlessly, speaking confidently.

Being all put together.

I want to ruin that.

Ruin *him*.

Break him the fuck up.

"Now, when we talk about *actus reus*, the physical act of committing a crime, it's important to remember that it's not just about the action itself, but the context in which it happens." He walks the length of the podium, speaking in a monotone voice. "Was there intent? Did the defendant have the necessary *mens rea*, the guilty mind? Without both elements, you don't have a crime. Let's take rape, for example."

My pen screeches to a halt on the notebook as he continues to address the class.

"The act of sexual penetration is clearly the physical component, but it's the mental state that determines the severity and nature of the charge. Consent—or lack thereof—is crucial here. If the accused knew, or should have known, that consent was absent, the question becomes: was there willful disregard for the victim's autonomy? Was there an intent to dominate, to exert power?

"Rape as a crime isn't just about physical violence; it's about the control, the manipulation, and the disregard for the victim's agency. And this is where it becomes complex, because consent, and whether it was freely given, is often a matter of perception, a gray area that must be examined carefully. We need to ask ourselves: did the defendant act in a way that violates the very essence of someone else's bodily autonomy?"

The pen breaks in my hand, and I let it fall on the notebook as his eyes flash toward me, deep mockery lying within.

He's *enjoying* this.

The prick is having the best time of his life reminding me of the only humiliation I've ever experienced.

He's rubbing it in, ripping open the stitches Kill sutured and thrusting his fingers inside the wound, toying and making me feel every move.

The lecture is a damn hassle. My head feels like it'll explode even after he moves on to another subject.

So when it ends, I'm ready to leave.

To gather information, form a bulletproof plan, and come back to face him in better physical and mental capacity.

Notebook in hand, I trail after my other classmates, listening to the girls giggling and whispering amongst each other about the 'hot-as-fuck' professor.

And I want to bash *their* heads in.

Stupid fucking idiots with no sense of recognizing danger or predators—

"Stay behind, Carson."

My spine prickles at the disturbingly calm voice. He's not even looking at me, his attention on his laptop, and I consider ignoring him.

I'm not in the mood for a face-off, and I'm certainly having more murderous urges this fine morning.

But then again, Gareth Carson would never ignore a professor. And I never pull away from a challenge.

With a sigh, I step to the side, letting the others filter past me.

Some of my classmates give me a fleeting look, many of them smiling inside at seeing the resident golden boy being hated by the hotshot new professor. People don't really like it when you hog the attention, especially if they're incompetent fools who could've never reached that height.

So they wish for your downfall—they fantasize about it.

As the last of the students leave, silence fills the vast lecture hall, along with the pounding in my head.

A constant fucking pressure that's clouding my vision.

Kayden doesn't move to close the door—protocol for sure. He wouldn't do anything that would get him fucked all the way to Sunday at such a prestigious university.

He sits at the edge of his desk, his hands gripping the frame with an ease that suggests control, his legs casually crossed at the ankles. I'd say he looks relaxed if I didn't know exactly what the sick fuck is capable of.

His long, lean fingers tighten on the desk, and I catch a glimpse of the veins at the back, prominent, pulsing with every flex, extending to beneath the cuff of his shirt. Those veins that tightened and tensed when he held my jaw, my cheeks—

No.

Not going there.

"You need to stop looking at me like that." His slightly rough voice is low enough that none of the students passing by can hear it.

"Like what?"

"Like you're thinking about last night. It's making me hard, and this is not the appropriate place to come down that throat again."

My fingers tighten around my notebook and the wound tingles beneath the bandage. There's nothing I want to do more than grab his fucking head and smash it against that desk.

Spill his blood.

Cut his dick off.

But then, that would be impulsive. And I don't do that.

Or *didn't*—past tense. Because, really, since last night, I've been the personification of a ticking time bomb.

I let my lips curve in a smile. "That won't be happening."

"Let's disagree agreeably."

"What's the definition of agreeably to you? A gun to my head?"

"If you want."

"I want nothing from you. Oh wait, I want you to rot in jail."

A twitch touches the corner of his lips. "Not a chance."

"Because you can manipulate the justice you preach?"

"No. Because you'd be rotting right there beside me." He

rises to his full height. "I don't have to tell you what I'd do to you in that cell, do I?"

Fucking creep.

I keep my smile in place, adopting a mocking tone. "Wow. I'm surprised you don't have a PhD in psychotic behavior. Do you often prey on your students?"

"Only little monsters like yourself." He approaches me and I remain still, refusing to give in to the authoritativeness he exudes with every step.

Like a robot—or a tank—that will smash everything in its wake.

Well, I'm the fortress facing the tank.

There will be no smashing. At least, not from his side.

He stops a few inches away, but I can still smell him. The faintest hint of wood and amber floods my nostrils and a string of memories follow.

Thrusting, gagging, choking, groaning, writhing for something, *anything*.

Stop.

"Tell me, Carson." His voice is close now and so are his eyes that are peering into my soul. "How did you manage to hide that revolting personality until now?"

I look at him but say nothing. If he believes he can ruffle my feathers, he truly doesn't know who he's dealing with. Punching down has never affected me.

And despite the massive headache and the constant screech of my demons for blood, I maintain my calm.

He cocks his head to the side, giving me a mechanical once-over, as if I'm a piece of art he finds unsightly. "The other professors can't stop singing your praises. They said you're so hardworking and loveable. The best student any professor could have. Either they're excruciatingly blind or you're just so staggeringly charming."

"You don't find me charming?" I let my lips form a mock pout.

His gaze slides down, zeroing in on the motion, and something flashes there before he meets my eyes again. "I think we've established that you have a magnificent ability to be grotesque."

My lips lift into a snarl, but I force them into a smile. "I didn't seem grotesque when you came all over my mouth. You enjoyed it so much, you kept coming on and on, I thought it'd never stop."

"Your hole is the only useful thing about you." I think I see a change of expression, but it's so fleeting, I can't read it as he continues, "But enough about that."

"And here I was *dying* to keep broaching the subject."

"Watch the way you speak to me. I'm your professor and will not tolerate any disrespect." The firm edge in his voice sets my skin ablaze. It's uncomfortable, this feeling that's making me grip the notebook tighter.

"I have no respect for you whatsoever, *Professor*."

"I'll tell you this once, so listen carefully, Carson." He stands taller, forcing me to crane my head back to look up at him. "I have zero tolerance for spoiled, rich little brats like you who believe they can rule the world through their daddies' trust funds. If you don't drop the attitude and watch your mouth, I will fuck it into submission. Are we clear?"

My teeth grind, chomping down on the demons that are trying to rush through and strangle the fuck out of him.

I'm thinking of an appropriate insult when he says, "Now that we have that out of the way. I have a proposition for you."

"As a witness to your crimes? Sure."

He narrows his eyes the slightest bit, like an authoritarian bastard who hates being talked back to, but that makes me want to do it even more.

Usually, I like meeting societal expectations of me, being on my best behavior and charming those around me into believing I am my public image.

But I don't give a fuck with this asshole. He's going to see me unfiltered and raw. And my true self loves antagonizing others and getting on their last goddamn nerve, especially when they antagonize me first.

"You believe that was funny?" he asks with that damn firm voice.

"Only slightly?"

"It wasn't, and you're just being a brat who's begging to be shoved to his knees for proper discipline your parents clearly didn't give you. Is that what you truly want, Carson? My cock in your hot little mouth again?"

"I'll never let you touch me again, you damn bastard."

That gleam appears again, like lightning in a dark night. "Never is a stretch. Besides, you obviously enjoyed yourself so much last night, you were practically begging to come."

"I was not!"

"My, getting agitated, are we?" He steps forward and I go still, my jaw locked so tight, I can't breathe properly.

This close, I can see the planes of his muscles peeking from the first few buttons of his shirt, his collarbone, the coiled muscles of his neck and that pulse point.

The one I want to bite the fuck off.

He leans close to my ear, his rough whisper setting my skin on edge. "Did you jerk off to the memory of me fucking your hot, wet mouth, little monster? Or did you get so scared you'd have your best orgasm and refuse to touch your throbbing cock?"

I step back, his breaths burning the shell of my ear. It takes everything in me to smile. "You seem to be under the misconception that I remember anything from last night. Lackluster performances don't really stay in the memory, you know."

"So it was the second option. Hmm. Interesting." His little

smile pisses me off, but before I can say anything, he continues, "On to business, the position I have for you is legal aid."

"What?"

"Apologies. I forgot you come from a legal empire and don't know what legal aid is. It's offering legal help to those who can't afford it."

"Don't insult my intelligence. I know what legal aid is. I also know I can't be a legal aid since I'm a first-year law student."

"You'll intern under me."

"No, thanks. I intern under my father or grandfather during the summer."

"Very typical." He returns to his desk. "You're free to go."

The complete dismissal leaves a sour taste at the back of my throat, and my head starts pounding harder. My wound feels hotter, pulsing with discomfort, and the bandage feels suffocating.

Maybe that's why I snap, "You expected me to work under you after you assaulted me?"

He doesn't look up as he closes his laptop and gathers his files. "I don't mix business with pleasure."

"There was no fucking pleasure."

"Language."

"I had no goddamn pleasure whatsoever."

He lifts his head, pinning me with stern dark-gray eyes. "If you keep indulging in vulgar language, I'll terminate this conversation, Carson."

"I said." I release an exasperated breath. "I enjoyed nothing of what happened last night."

"Your hard-on testified otherwise."

"That was a physical reaction."

"If you say so." A smirk tilts his mouth, and I want to stab it and watch his blood spill at my feet.

But I just smile back. "Just so you know. Yulian, that you

have the hots for, is crushing on someone else. So sad. For a prestigious professor, you sure don't have much luck."

My smile remains in place as I wait for the anger, the disturbance, but nothing rattles that look in his eyes.

The empty, dead look.

Hell, he showed more emotions taunting me than when I brought up Yulian.

It can't be. He must be masking his reaction somehow.

He *has* to care.

Last night, he was fucking enraged at the thought of me touching Yulian.

But, at any rate, since I know his identity now, that gives me a lot of options to trap him like he trapped me.

Humiliate him.

Shatter him on my edges.

"If you're done wasting my time and polluting my air with your revolting face." He clutches his briefcase and starts to walk past me.

I don't think about it as I grab him by the back of his collar. His smell overpowers my senses as I whisper in his ear, "Watch your back, Professor. You have no clue who the fuck you messed with."

5
KAYDEN

Someone is staring at me.

No.

Glaring.

The vicious eyes skim the back of my head like a breeze—
or more accurately, wind.

Turbulent, stormy wind.

I rip my gaze from the PowerPoint and face the class, then I
slip a hand into my pocket as I meet that glare.

It's a real effort not to let my lips fall into a smile.

An honest struggle.

Carson is sitting in the very last row, sliding his pen back
and forth without looking at his notebook. He seems to have

lost his grip on his usual calm façade, gradually disintegrating into my chaos.

See, he's truly a mastermind at masking his true emotions. I've seen how he exudes a collected demeanor with friends, looking the ideal part of a harmless kitten when, in fact, he's harboring a demon.

Hell, during that night I first saw him, he wore a poker face even after I shot him. And I thought he was putting up a front, but I'm starting to believe that's just his default—looking so terribly disinterested at the whole world.

This week, however, in our second class together, he seems to have lost the ability to tuck away his obvious hatred.

It makes it hard not to dismiss the entire class and back him into a corner, trap him in the palms of my hands, or squash him beneath my feet.

Break him to pieces once and for all.

My eyes lock with his for a brief second, and I admit that green looks far better in his irises than the fake brown. His eyes are electric, a charged mixture of impulsive loathing and patient retribution, each flicker a promise of something darker.

It doesn't fit with the rest of his poised appearance, though.

He's tall and muscled, his frame draped in quiet luxury clothes that could easily pay for a student's tuition. He has blond hair that falls in organized chaos on his forehead in a floppy hairstyle, a clean-shaven, sharp jawline, and high, chiseled cheekbones that lend him an almost otherworldly, medieval prince-like aura, as if he belongs to a world where power is absolute, and everyone around him is simply waiting for his command.

This particular prince, however, is broken. There's no charm or goodness within him, at least none that's not manufactured.

He seems so harmless and approachable, but then again, so were the most notorious serial killers.

Gareth Carson has the looks of a prince and the personality of a devil.

A man who'll paint the world in bright colors for his victims and then splash it all in red.

Which is why he's my red now. I'm the devil who'll bring another devil to his fucking knees.

Literally.

Figuratively.

A rush of anticipation slithers down my spine, and I force myself to stop fantasizing in class about fucking up my student.

Everything happens in the correct time frame.

Pulling my eyes from his, I stand behind the desk, my gaze sweeping over the students. "In the upcoming weeks, we will engage in a mock trial. This exercise will help you understand the delicate balance of evidence, the weight of reasonable doubt, and the very real lives that will be affected by our decisions. And because I don't mince any details, we will tackle a case that is as difficult as it is sensitive: a rape case."

The weight of my words settles in the room like a whip.

Carson's movements stop, and I expect him to break the pen like he did last week, but that doesn't happen.

Hmm. I haven't pushed him that far yet.

Continuing on...

"Now, on to the case." I click on the remote button, showing a summary on the screen. "The accused is James Rutherford, a wealthy businessman, charged with the drugging and rape of a young woman named Rebecca Blake. The victim is a twenty-three-year-old woman who was found unconscious by a staff member in a hotel room after a night out with friends. The police believe she was drugged and sexually assaulted."

Everyone is focused on the slides.

Everyone but Carson.

Because his entire creepy, intense attention is on me.

If eyes were lasers, he would've burned me on the spot.

I repress a smile as my composed voice carries on. "There is substantial evidence—witnesses, DNA, and the victim's medical report—suggesting the crime took place, but there is no clear memory from the victim, as she was in and out of consciousness, and there are conflicting statements from other witnesses. The defense is challenging the sufficiency of the evidence, claiming that there is reasonable doubt about whether the victim was truly assaulted or if it was a planned interaction."

Carson's scribbling picks up in intensity, but there's still no broken pen.

Pity.

"I'll email you all the case material, but now, I'll randomly assign roles. If I call your name, please stand." I go through the not-so-random list I have. "Meyers, Jones, and Omar, you'll be the prosecution team. You'll focus on building a strong narrative of the crime, utilizing the victim's testimony, the DNA evidence, and witness accounts. The prosecution needs to prove that the defendant intentionally assaulted the victim and should be held accountable for his actions."

All three students stand up with a gleam in their eyes. They're the smartest kids in this class and have a true talent for law. Carson is smart, too. On *paper*.

But his motives are wrong.

Not that I should judge. I never pursued law for philanthropic reasons.

"Carson." With an icy tone, I pretend to read his name from my monitor, and he slowly stands up, still clutching the pen. "You will act as the defense attorney for James Rutherford. Your role is to prove that there is no clear evidence that your client is guilty beyond a reasonable doubt."

This time, the pen breaks in his hand, and I let my lips twitch in a smile as I call other students' names on autopilot, assigning them as junior members of the defense team—all the idiot ones—and the smarter ones as jurors and witnesses.

"Your job is to scrutinize every piece of evidence, every testimony, and to come to your own verdict, just as you would in an actual courtroom. You'll have a week for pretrial preparation. We'll start with the opening statement next week." I turn off the screen. "Class dismissed."

I gather my belongings and exit the classroom before the students. Many of them fall into step on either side of me, particularly the prosecution team, asking follow-up questions about the assignment. The others are only using the assignment as an excuse to vie for my attention.

They're barking up the wrong tree. One, I prefer women my age. Two, I'd never fuck a student.

Except for the one I catch a glimpse of in my peripheral vision who's standing at the front of the class and watching me instead of listening to those surrounding him.

Though I don't particularly *want* to fuck him.

I'm actually straight and have never found men attractive.

So how come the thought of filling Carson's pretty face with tears as he chokes on my cock makes my dick twitch in its confinement?

Power.

Control.

Breaking someone into their subhuman form.

Those elements are clearly more important than actual sex or attraction to me.

Though I've never had an erection for a man I wanted to break. Hmm. What is it about Carson that's...so alluringly titillating?

The tears streaming down his face when he was choking on my cock? The way he sucked me roughly, giving me much of the pain I was giving him?

I am into fucking mouths, that's for sure, but most women

are delicate, and I've always been careful not to take it too far, so I've never really fucked a throat that hard.

Never had vicious, violent lips trying to suck my cum dry.

And I, honest to God, didn't give a fuck that it was a man's lips. Maybe because it doesn't matter whose lips?

No, that's wrong. I was consciously aware of his male scent, his sharp jaw, and his ruthless big hands.

I knew he was different from the usual softness I'm used to, and I...*didn't* hate it.

Some might say I enjoyed it way too much, to the point that my cock is twitching at the memories.

But I digress.

After I get rid of the clingy students, I finish my other classes for the day and head out.

I've opted for a full European life. No car or other means of transportation.

Brighton Island is small anyway, and I prefer to walk around in the UK's depressing windy and rainy weather instead.

As if.

I'm mostly observing.

Just like the little pest who's been tailing me.

Correction: a little monster.

Carson's words about watching my back are actually a job he took upon himself. Literally.

For a week now, he's been following me everywhere.

All the time.

Like a freak.

He's even skipping some classes. I know because one of the other fool professors that he has in the palm of his hand has expressed *concern* about his absence.

"He's such a bright student. It's not like him to skip. I'm worried about him."

You should be worried about your brain that he'd eat for break-fast if given the chance.

I walk into an organic food shop and skim through the freshly roasted coffee beans.

Carson does, in fact, make a decent stalker. He always keeps a safe distance, uses different cars, and even wears hats and sunglasses to cover his hair and face. He has a knack for making himself invisible when needed, and sometimes, it takes me a while to notice him.

Would give him four out of five stars. Knocking one star off for the unoriginal content.

"Hello there." A teenager with orange hair and chipped black nail polish says in a singsong voice. "Need my help with anything at all?"

I'd hope not. I don't expect someone like her to help me with my particular taste for coffee.

"Just looking around, thank you," I say, browsing the bags and offering no smile. I don't give a fuck how people perceive me.

I lost the ability to care about that a long time ago.

"That one is our bestseller." She motions at a bag with a huge red tag that says 'bestseller' on top. Young people these days share one brain cell, I swear.

"Can I smell samples?"

"Of course you can." She fumbles around to get the tray set up. Her anxious energy bounces off my skin like a ping-pong ball on a loosening thread.

If it were anyone else, they'd feel some form of sympathy or try to alleviate the situation, but I just stand there, letting her flounder in her own mental blood.

It's fascinating how her cheeks turn red as she fumbles over her word diarrhea that I effectively filter out. Even Carson seems annoyed in the discreet reflection of the glass, judging by the way he keeps bringing his finger to his mouth and then letting it fall back down.

Three times now.

Five if we count the two times he did it in class this morning.

His bad habits are pouring out like a damn fucking water-fall. It's euphoric.

And I find myself riveted, fully absorbed in what else I can squeeze out of that perturbed mind of his.

I buy the strongest-smelling bag of coffee beans, and as I pay, Carson inches away. He's methodical and could apply for a position as a professional stalker if he weren't already a rich kid with his entire blood-filled future set at birth.

To make his session worthwhile, I take a tour around the town center. And because small talk and typical human interactions seem to suck the soul out of him, I indulge in lengthy conversations about fuck knows what.

I want to see a pen snapping again, metaphorically, in his head.

Snub as many neurons as possible. Even if the whole ordeal bores *me* to tears.

By the end of the day, I feel like I've drained him enough. Like a kid, he'll retreat to his bed, probably fantasizing about killing me in the most painful way possible.

I smile as I walk to the large building where I'm renting an apartment.

Gareth stops near the oak tree across the street like he always does, and I pull out my phone while walking into the building.

JETHRO

This is child's play.

ME

I know.

And you're enjoying this?

> Surprisingly, yes. What do you think he'll do next?

Hire someone to kill you or do the honors himself.

> Don't get my hopes up.

This is fucking crazy, man.

> I prefer entertaining.

This entire thing is a waste of time. Just get back to the States.

> Not yet.

I'm still staring at my exchange with Jethro when my phone rings.

Grant, my brother, is calling. Three times today.

He's annoyingly clingy and staggeringly persistent. I'll give him that.

I click Ignore and walk into the apartment.

The space is huge but sparse, deliberately so, with clean lines and a minimalist design that leaves no room for profiling. The floors are dark hardwood, polished to a mirror sheen, reflecting the cold, clinical light from the overhead fixtures. The walls are painted in muted grays and blacks, devoid of decoration, save for a few abstract pieces of art that came with the house.

A single leather sofa sits in the center of the living area, its sharp angles matching the rest of the decor, too perfect to be comfortable.

The only trace of warmth is the scent of lavender. It presses on my chest like a fucking weight and I inhale it into my lungs before spitting it back out.

Turning on my vinyl record player, I wait until Bruckner's Symphony No. 7's mellow notes fill the space before I head to the kitchen.

I methodically grind the beans and then take my time brewing the coffee. The strong fragrance overpowers the lavender, smothering it, and I just stand there.

Watching the coffee dripping into the cup in synch with the music.

Drip.

Drip.

Drip.

Like blood.

It's soothing—or disturbing, depending on your school of thought.

After a sip of the over-roasted coffee, I empty it down the drain and throw away the full bag of beans. I pour myself a glass of whiskey on ice instead and then stare out the window.

Carson is gone.

He's so anticlimactic.

I've been waiting for him to act on his promise, but he seems content to watch from the shadows.

Though *content* isn't the right word. I believe he likes to know all the information before he takes action, but it's getting tedious.

Dull, too.

Might have to take things into my own hands after all.

Situations just don't work as well without my interference.

In my thirty-three years of life, I've never met anyone as efficient as I am.

What a nuisance.

I down my drink, take a shower, reply to some work emails, then turn off the music and lie down on the bed.

The smell of lavender fills my nostrils and I close my eyes, drifting off to sleep.

Clank.

Clank.

Clank.

The noise keeps repeating on a loop and I open my eyes. The faint sound of weeping protrudes through the walls like a spirit.

"No..." Mom wails, her screams bouncing off my skin. "Please, no. Nooo—"

But her voice is drowned by a shot.

Shadows crawl across the ceiling, twisting and contorting into grotesque shapes. Their hollow eyes gleam with a twisted hunger, and their mouths crack open, releasing a low, grating screech that claws at my eardrums, sinking deep into my skull.

They fall toward me, their cold, suffocating weight pressing down on my chest like a thousand unseen hands. The air thickens with their presence, a crushing force that makes it harder to breathe or move. Their dark forms press into me, the cold creeping deeper, dragging me under as if the darkness itself is trying to swallow me whole.

Die already.

Die.

Just *die.*

The weight on my chest is choking, a crushing force that pins me to the bed. I gasp, but it's as if the very air has been stolen. My body is frozen, unable to move, every breath shallow and labored.

The shadows in the corners of the room twist and loom, dark shapes that distort into her face.

Her blood-soaked face.

I gasp awake, staring at the white ceiling devoid of the sticky shadows.

Or the bloody face.

But the weight over me isn't gone, because I'm staring at a different face.

In the darkness, Carson's pretty features loom over me like a fucking demon. He's straddling my waist and holding a syringe as his lips tilt in a creepy smirk.

"Hello there, Professor. It's time to pay for your fucking sins."

And then he jams the syringe into my neck.

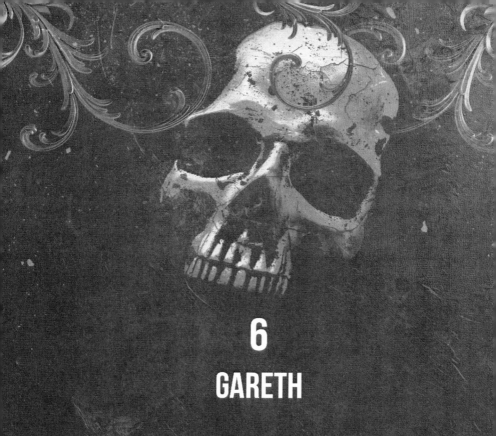

6
GARETH

I've been patient.

Extremely so.

Even when the impulse to inflict pain mounted and multiplied, reaching heights I hadn't experienced since *that* time six years ago, I repressed it all.

Leaving no room for mistakes.

This needed to be perfected. To a fault.

There's no way I'd be caught off guard like that night I was literally brought to my knees.

So I watched him—my criminal professor who's teaching criminal law.

I learned his habits to a tee and gathered some basic info about him through a private investigator. I had to hire someone who came recommended through dark web research myself, opting not to use the mafia's resources. If I went that route, the news would get back to Jeremy or, worse, my parents.

The private investigator Nadine, a serious-looking American woman who's ex-military, is reliable and already came through with some info.

Kayden Lockwood is boringly typical. He comes from a middle-class upbringing in Boston to a lawyer dad and a college professor mom.

He practiced law until a couple of years ago when he decided to take up teaching. He still helps with his father's medium-sized law firm, Lockwood & Associates, and owns a large portion of their shares.

He has a dull, meticulous life where he repeats the same events every day at the same time, like a fucking clock.

His morning starts at six when he goes for a swim in his building's pool then works out in the communal gym. Then, for breakfast, he only drinks coffee that he personally brews while reading physical newspapers like a grandpa. He walks to campus—for fucking forty-five minutes like a psycho.

He does his lectures. Talks to professors and students, then walks again to the town center. Shops for coffee beans every day—again, like a psycho. Spends most of the afternoon in a chess club. Then he goes home to listen to loud classical music as he brews the coffee he bought, usually throwing away the full bag right after.

Then he has a drink. Showers. Spends time at his laptop, and finally goes to sleep just to repeat the mechanical cycle again.

And again.

I swear, if I watched the monotonous events one more day, I'd stab my own eyes.

The only reason I kept coming back was because he knew I was there.

He even smiled when he engaged in soul-crushing small talk, as if he'd figured out it annoyed the fuck out of me.

I'm not sure when he found out I was following him around, but he did, and he was completely at ease with it. As if he expected me to.

As if I were *predictable*.

Well, he couldn't have predicted this scene.

Because since I knew he knew, I hid my cards.

And because he didn't seem to care that I was shadowing him like a grim reaper, he was careless enough to let me see the code he puts in the elevator to reach his apartment.

I didn't even have to figure out a way to hack into security systems or befriend the concierge and, instead, kind of just walked in here—after I made him believe I'd left for the day.

In fact, I've been on the side of the building, patiently waiting until the lights in his apartment went off.

Then waited some more until he was fast asleep.

And it was worth it.

Because now I'm on top of him, my knees on either side of his waist over the sheet, and my syringe is in his neck.

The black snake on his naked chest peeks out from beneath the sheet that's fallen down to his abs as if it's real and will jump up and bite me at any second.

But I'm the only venomous snake here.

As I slowly push the plunger, taking my time in enjoying this, his sleepy eyes, which were confused a second ago, slowly sober up. There's little light coming from the street-lamp outside, so I can't see him clearly, but I can make out his eyes.

Always those damn revolting eyes.

"Really, Carson? Drugs again?" His rough, slightly husky voice echoes in the air with apparent disapproval.

"Shh." I watch as the liquid slowly spills into his veins. "This one is better. It'll make you crawl at my feet with desire,

Professor, and I'll squash that limp cock of yours beneath my feet."

His hands slide to my waist, beneath my shirt, skimming over the skin before he digs his fingers into the flesh.

My spine jerks and I pause.

The fuck is this asshole doing?

"You don't have to resort to rape drugs. If you were that desperate to suck my cock again, all you had to do was beg and I'd let you choke on it."

I raise my hand and slap him.

Not a punch—even though that idea is growing by the second—but a humiliating slap.

He laughs, the sound sinister and low in the darkness. I feel his abs tightening and vibrating beneath me, and I don't like to think how my cock is reacting, getting heavy for no reason.

"Does wanting me so much piss you off?" His rough whisper lingers in the air between us.

"I don't want you."

"Breaking and entering while in possession of rape drugs with the intention of using them negates your claim. But I suggest you abandon any fantasies you have about fucking me."

"I don't *want* to fuck you."

"You won't. I'll be the one bending you over and teaching you some manners you desperately need."

"Like fuck you will."

"What did I say about vulgar language?" he whispers in a low, gruff tone, his fingers gliding across my skin, back and forth, back and forth. "You're surprisingly lean but nicely toned."

"Stop touching me. You're disgusting."

"Look at that. We're birds of a feather."

I grab his hand and start to shove it away.

I realize I've made a mistake too late.

In the split second of distraction, Kayden's grip tightens on my waist, and before I can react, he flips me over, pinning me beneath him. I try to inject the rest of the drug, but his hand comes down hard, slapping my wrist and forcing me to remove the needle as he knocks the syringe from my grasp. It falls to the pillow, just out of reach. I strain, trying to wriggle free, fighting to push him off, but it's like trying to move a mountain.

Then, in an instant, a large, strong hand wraps around my throat.

I can't breathe.

The pressure tightens with terrifying speed, and my airway is cut off in a fraction of a second. Kayden looms over me, his massive body a solid, overpowering wall. The snake tattoo on his skin seems to shift, the cold ink twisting into something more real—more deadly—like the predator it's meant to be, ready to strike. I can feel its fangs at my throat, and I know with brutal clarity that if he wanted to, he would strangle me to death.

While having that impassive look in his eyes.

And for a brief moment, I can see myself.

Dead eyes. Empty insides.

I gasp for breath that doesn't exist, clawing at his fingers and kicking my legs, but he's sitting on them, and I can't move much.

Through my blurry vision, I watch as he easily grabs the syringe and lifts it, the needle glinting in the dark.

"Let's see how good this stuff is."

He lowers his hand from my neck, and as I choke on air, he jams the needle into my skin.

I flail and punch him in the chest, but he injects what remains in the syringe into my veins.

Our harsh breathing echoes in the darkness, turning the silence more oppressive. Apocalyptic, even.

Fuck.

Fuck!

He injected me with the stuff he was supposed to have, and because I wanted to ruin him so thoroughly, I doubled the dose when I got it from my dealer. In his words, "It'll make you forget about reality and beg for more."

I was supposed to see Kayden on his knees. Not get a taste of my own medicine.

Fucking *again.*

I barely think about how I had a needle that was inside someone else in me. My slightly germophobic side is overpowered by a stronger side. The one that absolutely *loathes* losing control.

His weight disappears from on top of me, and I watch in complete and utter bewilderment as he stands up and turns on the light.

Fully fucking naked.

He was covered by the sheet earlier, so I didn't know he was actually sleeping naked.

Soft yellow light bathes the room as he looms over the bed where I'm lying. The muscles in his chest contract, making the snake appear monstrous.

I've seen countless men naked—in the gym and after football practice in high school. All the time. And I never looked at them twice.

Or with curiosity.

Hell, I truly despise it when Niko walks naked around the mansion because he "has a beautiful body and doesn't like to hide it."

And yet, right now, I can't stop staring.

Objectively, I can admit he has a body that demands attention. It's the kind of physique that's the result of taking workouts and physical discipline seriously. Chiseled muscles that carve through his skin, an eight-pack that seems almost too perfect to be real, and veiny-toned arms that speak of raw power beneath the surface.

My throat dries—due to the stupid drugs, no doubt.

This is no typical professor's body, not by a long shot.

I watch, unable to look away, as his veiny hand drags slowly down his abs, each movement deliberate, hypnotic. His fingers pause at his V-line, the muscles flexing under his touch as they linger there.

But he doesn't have to go on for me to see his cock standing at attention.

Maybe it's because his muscular thighs are naked, but it seems revoltingly bigger than the last time.

"Look what you've done." He rubs his stubbled jaw, his eyes looking as dark and empty as the night outside. "Your fight really turns me on, little monster."

Sick motherfucker.

I sit up in bed, my movements already a bit lethargic.

But I have to get the fuck out of here before the drug kicks in. There's no way in hell I'll be in this asshole's space when that happens.

I need to go back to the drawing board and come up with a better plan to ruin this bastard once and for all—

"Where do you think you're going?"

He stands in front of me, his hand shooting to my face before I can dodge. No, my reflexes are dulled.

I *couldn't* dodge.

...right?

Cruel long fingers dig into my cheeks. "You didn't possibly think you could be a little cocktease, then fuck off, did you?"

7

GARETH

The skin where he touches me burns worse than hellfire.

I latch on to his hand and try to pull it off, but I might as well be pushing a slab of steel. I'm not weak by any means. I work out and take great pride in my ability to squash people beneath my prim-and-proper looks.

But this asshole is different.

He uses violence as a method to exert power.

It doesn't add up with the rest of his fucking boring life.

"Let me go," I grind out from between clenched teeth.

He tilts his head to the side, his lips curling. "Say please."

"Please go fuck yourself, Professor."

"Why would I do that when I have you to fuck?"

I swallow and he can feel it, because those dead eyes spark. I noticed they only do that when he's messing with me.

When he has me under his thumb.

"You obviously want to be fucked, too, or you wouldn't have come here."

"I don't want to be fucked and will never allow it."

"Never is a reach."

"A definitive."

"Nothing is definitive, Carson. You study law. You should know better."

"You teach law. You should know better than to breach it so blatantly."

"But that's the whole point of learning law—it's easier to get around the loopholes and violate it. But you already know that."

There's an undertone to his words I can't quite decipher. His eyes stare deeper into me, attempting to penetrate the fabric of my soul and seep into a part not meant for the public.

A part even I stopped venturing into.

A buzz ignites my skin, and I hate it. I hate the feel of his fucking hand on me. It's supposed to feel disgusting, not create this low hum that trickles down my spine.

"Stop touching me," I say in a clear voice, as clear as I can manage. "I'm not into men."

"I'm not into men either." He rotates my head to the side. "But something about this pretty face makes me want to decorate it with my cum."

I clench my teeth because now I'm remembering his cock pulsing in my mouth as he looks down on me.

The image of him coming down my throat makes me murderous.

But I flinch every time his skin rubs mine, gliding over the heated flesh like an ancient potent curse. Sweat trickles down my back, and my hoodie sticks to it.

Heat builds beneath my flesh, a slow burn that spreads through my chest, making it impossibly hard to breathe. My skin starts to prickle, the warmth intensifying with every second, and every inch of space is charged with something I can't control.

Fuck.

I hate not being in control. Loathe it.

Despise it.

I need to leave.

Now.

"Not into men?" I smile, changing tactics. "You're so gay, you've been fantasizing about me since you saw me, Professor. Not to mention that you were so jealous about the whole Yulian thing. You'd have a better chance with him than me. I can help if you let me go."

I won't. If anything, I'll only use the Yulian angle to hurt him further, but I'll make him believe that just so he'll give up.

"Oh, you *will* help." He shoves me on the bed and then he's on top of me, his hard thighs pressing on either side of my waist, and he straddles my legs, pinning me to the mattress.

"Not like this." I push at his chest.

"Then like what?"

"With Yulian, idiot."

"Why would I wait for that when I have you under my thumb, wiggling powerlessly like a helpless fucking worm?"

I raise my fist and punch him. Maybe it's the drug that's making me lose my inhibitions, or maybe I've just wanted to break his jaw for a while now.

Because I bark out a laugh and say in my most condescending tone, "You truly disgust me like I've never been disgusted before. The idea of you touching me makes my skin fucking crawl."

Something flashes in his gaze before it quickly fades away. "Seems I have to test just how much I disgust you, then."

He reaches into his side drawer and pulls out black ropes. I'm wondering why the fuck he has ropes in his damn nightstand, but those thoughts vanish when he yanks both my wrists up and secures them to the metal headboard.

The motion is so quick and effortless, I can't stop it no matter how much I wiggle. When he's done, I can barely move my hands. He's tied them so tight, the rope digs into my skin.

And now, he's sitting on my thighs, his weight not allowing me to budge as he lifts my hoodie. I shiver as his knuckles brush against my abs.

"Let's get these out of the way." He retrieves a knife from his drawer of nightmares, and holds it close to my stomach, hovering it over the skin.

It's another of his intimidation techniques—it doesn't work, and I'm not scared.

I'm apprehensive, though, because I can feel the drug working its way through my veins.

The drugs I bought to humiliate him might be my downfall now, and once again, I have no way out.

The desperation is new, and I only feel it around this motherfucker. For that, I want to gouge his eyes out and slurp them the fuck out of their sockets.

His knife game stops as he starts to cut my hoodie right down the middle. Leisurely. Taking his damn sweet time. "See, this is what I like about you, Carson. You're not easily ruffled, and you have an impressive door-slam technique. You can patiently wait until the discomfort is over and you also don't rush plotting revenge. It's why you only broke into my house after observing me properly. But that repulsive rapist habit of yours can't go unpunished."

"You're the fucking rapist—"

The words die in my throat when he lays the knife flat on my lips.

"Quiet. I told you, didn't I? Your voice is off-putting." He runs his knuckles over my throat, then down my chest, and I stiffen. "Besides, you're the one who keeps using all these rapey drugs. I'm only indulging in your little fucked-up fetish by overturning the power you love so much. Doesn't feel too good when you're the one being toyed with, does it?"

I think I hear an edge to his rough, deep voice, but I can't look at him straight. Not when my skin catches fire. Every inch he touches burns, a sick feeling rushing to my groin.

Fuck. No.

Not again.

Absolutely *not*.

He slides the tip of his finger across my nipple and I jerk, a zap settling at the base of my stomach.

"Getting sensitive?" He glides his finger over my nipple again and again, and to my dismay, it bunches up, getting harder. His finger sends another tingle down my spine and all the way to my balls.

And I hate that I find it pleasurable.

That his touch, something I despise to my very core, is causing a sensation I've never felt before.

A groan rips out of me, but it's muffled beneath the blade.

"No skin crawling yet. If anything, you love this a bit too much. Hmm. You're just a natural slut." There's a mocking edge to his tone as he pinches my nipple between his thumb and forefinger until it hurts.

But that pain does something unexpected.

Like when he squashed my dick beneath his shoe.

Jesus fuck.

Just when I'm hoping he doesn't notice, Kayden removes the blade from my mouth and trails it down to my jeans and the tent forming there. "You *do* love this. What a seasoned whore."

"Fuck you."

"Is that your way of asking for my help?"

"Don't touch me," I say, but my voice is hoarse and it sounds like a moan, because he's still playing with my nipples, alternating, pinching, and rubbing

My head grows dizzy as I practically leak into my boxers.

What the fuck—

"Your mouth and body sing a different tune, little monster." He cuts through the waistband of my jeans, then puts the knife on the nightstand and lowers my pants and boxers enough to release my hardening cock.

It jerks and pulses in his hand—like a fucking hormonal freak. Even with the drugs, I shouldn't have this much of a visceral reaction to another man touching me.

And not just any man, but my professor who definitely enjoys overpowering and dominating me.

He squeezes me at the base and we both watch, me in horror, him in fascination, as it lengthens in his grip. "Mmm. You have a pretty cock. Huge, too. Not that I'm a cock connoisseur per se, but this is beautiful."

My breath hitches, my head growing dizzy as all my blood rushes to my groin.

"Let me go. Now," I growl, not really meaning it.

No, I do.

I don't?

He jerks my cock from base to tip, circling the crown with his thumb. Sticky precum slides over the sensitive skin, down my length, on his hand.

Everywhere.

"Fuck." A moan echoes in the air and I realize it's mine.

"You're weeping already. Want to come for me, baby?"

"I'm not your fucking baby—" I grunt as he pinches my nipple at the same time as he squeezes my cock. It hurts and I like it.

Why the fuck do I *like* it?

No one has ever touched me this way before, and I would

never give anyone this type of power over me. But this mother-fucker just snatched it away, regardless of what I think.

And I *like* it?

Someone needs to electroshock me.

"Mmm. You're getting so hard, *baby*." He smiles after stressing the word. "You're making a goddamn mess."

I am. My precum is all over the place and I hate it. I hate that he's the one dragging out this part of me. I'm not even supposed to get hard when I don't want to, let alone be...like this.

"You know why you're making a mess?"

"S-shut up."

"You like how I touch you. When I hurt you."

He leans down and bites my nipple, and I grunt as his teeth sink into the skin so deep, I think he'll draw blood. But then his tongue darts out, leaving a sticky trail on the assaulted skin as a dark chuckle leaves him.

"You *do* like it." He bites the sensitive tip again as he looks at me, his eyes darkening when I groan.

He hums, the sound sending bolts of electricity through my nipple. "I have a fucking masochist on my hands. Interesting."

"It's the fucking drugs." I let out a grunt.

"I don't think the drugs can make you enjoy something you're not into." He jerks me again, rougher this time.

His fingers squeeze my length, and I shake. Uncontrollably.

His movements are controlled but firm. Painful, even. He times twisting the crown of my cock with biting and pulling my nipple between his teeth.

It's driving me insane.

Pulling at strings I didn't know I had.

The power behind his every touch leaves me breathless, gasping like a slut. I'm tugging on the ropes so hard, I'm surprised they don't cut my skin.

"Enough," I let out in a moan even as I buck my hips. "I hate this..."

"Correction." His stubble scratches my areola as he flicks his tongue on my aching, sore nipple. "You want to hate it."

I do.

I want to hate it and I *can't*.

Because I'm falling into the rhythm as he jerks me up and down in long, powerful movements, like no one has ever done, not even me.

It's the drugs, I think as my balls tighten.

There's no way in hell I'm into men or *this* particular man.

He's a disturbing motherfucker. I would have never looked in his direction under different circumstances.

The drugs.

It *has* to be the drugs.

My back arches off the bed as I buck in his hand, needing that last bit of friction.

"You want to come, baby?"

"Stop calling me that, asshole...fuck..."

"You need to ask nicer. Preferably beg." He twirls his thumb along my crown and stars form behind my lids. "You look your best when broken, my little monster."

"Shut...up..."

"Beg me to let you come."

"Fuck you."

I groan, my eyes closing as I give in to the most intense buildup of my life.

But it doesn't *come*.

Pun fucking intended.

The friction disappears. Just like that.

I blink my eyes open, feeling disoriented. "Why..."

Kayden's sitting back, no longer sucking and biting my chest like it's a fucking dessert. And more importantly, my hard dick is up in the air, curving toward my stomach. Precum drips into my navel, forming a small pool, but there's no actual cum.

I glare at his equally hard cock that's resting on my thigh, then at him.

"Why did you stop?" I let the frustration translate into my biting tone.

His lips curve in a slow grin. "Didn't you ask me to?"

"You fucking—" I buck, but I only manage to thrust in the air with no real friction. "Are you enjoying this?"

He wraps his veiny hand around his cock, giving it a rough jerk that makes my mouth water. "*Very.*"

"Fuck...just..."

"Just?" He jerks himself, not as powerfully as he did to me, but the view only adds to my agony.

I pull at the ropes, groaning in frustration. "You know what."

"Why don't you enlighten me?"

"Let me come," I whisper between clenched teeth.

"Louder." He taps his crown against mine, and it's as if being touched by electricity.

"Let me come," I say in a clearer voice, the last word ending with a moan.

"Now, beg me to make this beautiful cock weep." He slides his dick against mine and glides his length up and down. We're almost the same length, but he's bigger in girth with larger angry veins lining his dick.

My mouth waters at the memory of him inside it, against my tongue and slamming into the back of my throat.

And he's still rubbing us together, firmly, with a rhythmic friction that drives me insane.

No, it's the drugs, actually.

That's what's making me writhe against the pillow, thrusting up and down against another fucking *cock*.

Then it stops—the rubbing, and the mind-blowing pleasure—because he wraps both his hands around our cocks, bringing the friction to a halt.

"This motherfucking..." I glare at him.

He only smiles, the motion never reaching his empty eyes. Though they're not so empty anymore. An unfamiliar dark and entirely vicious emotion shines through the lustful haze.

"I said. Beg."

My breaths leave in long, fractured spurts. I'd do anything to come right now. I'm de facto debasing myself to the subhuman hormonal fools I look down upon.

"Please," I let the word fall in a whisper.

"Please what?"

"Fuck...just—" I swallow, breathing deeply. "Please let me come."

"Say it again." He jerks us up and down roughly, adding painful friction, and a renewed jolt rushes through me.

It feels so good.

Why does it feel good?

Kayden rubbing our cocks together in that firm rhythm shouldn't feel like it's the best erotic touch I've ever had.

I don't even like jerking off, like it's really hard for me to reach orgasm with handjobs, or oral in general, which is why I rarely masturbate.

And yet, right now, his large, rough hand and throbbing veiny cock are sliding me to an unfamiliar edge.

My senses are full of him, the woodsy smell, the striking eyes, the menacing snake. Our scents mixing into a hazy erotic fog.

All male.

Completely fucking male.

No flowery perfume, no soft touch, and no tits.

Just hard muscles and powerful, painful, and entirely controlled touches.

That should turn me off, but I'm grinding into him, groaning as he uses our precum to lube us up.

"I said." He slows his pace. "Say it again."

"Please." My voice is so hoarse, I barely recognize it, but I don't care. If he stops again, I might die of frustration.

My mind is in a blissful blur as I thrust into his hand.

He rubs us together harder, faster, and my eyes roll to the back of my head.

"Mmm...your cock feels so good. You're leaking all over me."

"Fuck...fuck...I'm...I'm..."

"That's it. Fall into it. *Feel* what you do to me, baby."

"Fuck...oh God...please...I'm close...please..."

"So impatient. So fucking beautiful." He groans, his voice dripping with lust as he squeezes us with that sinfully good roughness. "Come with me, baby."

I don't know if it's his words or the way he touches me, or all the above, but I can't hold it in.

I wish I could.

If I weren't on the drugs, I would've held out better and convinced myself I was disgusted, appalled, and downright creeped out.

I would've put up a fight.

That's what I tell myself as I come the hardest I ever have. Against his dick. Spurts of my cum shoot all over the place, and he joins with a guttural groan.

Our cum mixes, covering his hands, and splashing my abs and his thighs.

I blink hard, but my head is complete mush.

But I still search my memories for a better orgasm. I do, thinking it's imperative to find that and my sanity, but I come up empty.

I'm deeply disturbed and fascinated that this is the best orgasm I've had in my almost twenty-two years of life.

"What a mess. Always a fucking mess, little monster," he muses, his voice rougher, deeper, and, if I were into men— which I'm *not*—attractive.

And for some reason, some fucked reason also called *drugs*, I can't stop coming, staring at him as he continues jerking up, using the cum as lube.

It's gross.

I tell myself that over and over, but then he does something.

The motherfucker leans down and wraps his mouth around my crown, sucking me dry of cum. The feel of his hot, wet mouth makes me moan out loud. "Fuuuuck...goddamn it... fucking hell..."

I come more in his mouth, unable to stop myself, because why the fuck does it feel good?

I never think about mouths when I'm being blown. So why...?

My question remains hanging in the air as he lifts his head and sucks cum off his hand, making a show of licking and letting me watch.

Our cum.

His and mine.

I swear to fucking God, I'm castrating my cock because even spent, the motherfucker twitches to life at the view.

My sore nipples and bitten chest hurt when he crawls over my body, but I don't have the capacity to focus on that when he slides one cum-filled hand into my hair, then grabs my jaw with the other one.

Maybe because I'm spent and can't resist him or because he squeezes my cheeks hard, I have no choice but for my lips to part.

Kayden leans down and spits cum right inside my mouth.

He spits my own cum—and his—in my mouth.

His eyes darken until they're almost black. They *have* black flecks, I realize, as his face hovers so close to mine.

Amidst the gray, there are tiny, curious black patches that match his thick brows and hair.

And those flecks are overtaking the gray in a vicious invasion as he watches our cum pooling on my tongue, his grip not allowing me to swallow.

Then he thrusts two fingers in and pounds them to the back of my throat. "Swallow every last drop. I want to watch that throat stuffed full of cum."

As I do, I accidentally swallow around his fingers. His groan drops on my skin like a fucked-up caress.

The taste is different from when it was only his cum the last time. It feels more fucked up, too.

Sick.

As someone who hates other people's touch and fluids, I can't seem to conjure a sense of disgust at his taste as I gobble everything he gives me the fuck up.

I can't stop licking and swallowing.

The damn fucking drugs. It *has* to be.

Then all of a sudden, he pulls his fingers from my mouth and stands up.

I keep staring at him through a weird haze, my mouth dry and my body a hot, sweaty, and cum-covered mess as he frees my wrists.

They fall on either side of me, lifeless, with no power whatsoever.

Kayden's long fingers tap my cheek. "You were a good boy today."

A strange sensation happens.

It starts low, deep inside, and like wildfire, the smoldering spreads, quickly flooding my chest, my limbs, until I can barely breathe.

I blink as he walks into the bathroom with measured steps.

What the fuck was that feeling...?

My every nerve sparks with heat, my skin tight and flushed with warmth, and my mind is overblown with confusion.

We had the same drug and yet it feels like I'm the only laughingstock around here.

I pull my heavy body up, shaking my head when I stand and the room starts spinning.

Doesn't matter if I die in a freak accident. I'm simply not staying here to find out what the fuck he's planning to do next.

This man is more dangerous than his profiling suggests. Not because of his actions per se—though they're unpredictable and disturbing—but what truly worries me is *my* reaction to those actions.

Pulling my jeans and boxers up in one hand, I stumble to the door, grabbing a jacket from the hanger on the way out and putting it on.

Forget about revenge.

I need to stay the fuck away before I get sucked into that disturbing man's orbit.

8
KAYDEN

Gareth stopped the part-time stalking job after he escaped from my apartment that night.

And he did *escape*.

I watched the security footage, and the little monster crashed into countless walls, nearly fell, and had to hold on to the elevator to remain upright.

He looked freshly fucked, his face red and streaks of cum in his messed-up hair. My jacket barely covered his hoodie's scraps and the marks I decorated his chest with.

I might have saved a few videos for...future reference.

Sure, I should probably feel some form of confusion that I want to fuck a man and dick him down to the mattress while he writhed in both pleasure and pain.

It's not normal, right?

For someone like me, teetering on mid-thirties to find a guy's cum more delicious than five-star meals. Or that the memory of him shooting that cum into my mouth while wearing that lustful and surprised look makes my dick throb.

Straight men don't fantasize about other men's dicks or cum.

Or do they?

Honestly, who gives a fuck?

I don't believe sexuality should be boxed in like some fools in my entourage. I still find women attractive and don't really care for other men.

Except for my little monster who left me hanging that night. He didn't even let me clean him up.

And I don't usually care for that, cleaning up my sex partners, I mean. So maybe I just wanted to toy with him a bit more.

But he ran away before I could do so.

Pity.

That was four days ago.

I still have a couple more days until I see him in class, so I haven't been able to monitor him properly.

A situation I attempted to rectify last night when I texted him.

ME

Did you happen to see a brown wool jacket on your escape route?

CARSON

How do you have my number?

You believe you are the only one with sufficient access to resources? Typical brain-dead rich kid.

> I don't know why you love insulting me every chance you get, but I'm telling you to leave me alone. I'm done with your games.

I glared at the text.

He *can't* be done.

That's not how this works.

Besides, I'm the puppet master, *not* him.

The only one who gets to put an end to anything is me.

> You didn't even last a week. What a coward.

> You might want to stop the provocation tactic. I see right through it and it doesn't work on me.

> No provocation is in sight. I'm only pointing out that you ran away with your tail between your legs. Can't admit you love what I do to you, baby?

> I'm not your fucking baby.

> But you love what I do to you?

> I was drugged. It means nothing and I'm not gay.

> Hmm. Is that what you told yourself when you wouldn't stop coming against my cock and in my mouth? Bet you recite those words like a mantra when you jerk off to the memory. Do you also play with those perky little nipples like I did?

He blocked me.

I still laugh as I stare at my phone now.

Because I know, I just know I'm getting under his skin.

Affecting his usual course of action.

Twisting him inside out.

Carson is not the type who retreats from a challenge. It's why he doubled down on the drugs and even picked up stalking.

It's why he looks murderous whenever I insult his looks or intelligence. He takes pride in those and everything about his person—which is why I constantly target them.

He might play the social game to perfection, might have people eating out of the palm of his hand, and even calling him well-mannered and a gentleman, but he irrevocably sees himself as superior to everyone else.

His strongest suit is his ability to mask his true nature. It's hard for normal people to see who he *actually* is—the depravity, lack of empathy, and streak of narcissism. Honestly, he could get an Oscar for acting the way he has for years.

Probably his entire adult life.

Gareth Carson is a criminal profiler's wet dream. He never makes mistakes and maintains a pretty normal, albeit privileged life.

He might not be officially diagnosed, but he has clear signs of antisocial personality disorder and possible narcissistic tendencies.

His moral compass doesn't exist, hence the way he was ready to rape Yulian and me, and if I hadn't turned the tables, he would've gotten off on that type of fucked-up power, too.

What does exist, however, is his careful, meticulous maintenance of his public persona—he spent a lot of effort to diverge from his brother's image.

The younger Carson is a proud diagnosed psychopath. The older Carson is a closeted one, so to speak.

And while I don't know why the golden-boy image is so important to him, I'll find out. And I'll break that purpose.

I'll break him to fucking pieces until he's a lifeless little toy.

And toys don't get a say in what happens to them.

Therefore, they can't decide they'll stop functioning.

I dial the number I need and put the phone to my ear as I stare out my window at the oak tree where Carson used to linger.

"Professor," Yulian's slightly husky voice filters from the other side.

"I'm not your professor if you don't attend class."

He chuckles. "I suppose that's true. To what do I owe the call?"

"You owe me your life after that night, but I digress."

"I repay my saviors pretty well, but you kind of left me on a cliffhanger by not giving me the identity of the motherfucker who roofied my drink. Is this a call to rectify that oversight?"

"I clearly said that won't be happening." Previously, I would've loved to see Yulian maim Carson into tiny pieces.

And Yulian would've. Killed Carson, I mean. No matter how many wars that would provoke. Hell, he'd do it just to start those wars.

But that was before I touched the little monster and saw a part of him I want to toy with further.

There's no place for Yulian in my games. At least, not this particular game concerning Carson.

Yulian trusts me and gave me access to the mansion, not because I'm his professor, but due to certain beneficial relationships I formed with his father back in the States.

His dad tells me to keep an eye on him, but I'm not his guardian, and Yulian is a lost cause who will eventually get himself killed.

It's just a matter of when, not if.

"Just checking." Yulian whistles as some rustling comes from his side. "If that is all, I have an important event to dress for."

"Event?" I play dumb.

"I'm paying our neighbors a little visit." I can hear the manic smile in his voice. "In disguise, naturally."

"Is this by any chance the Heathens' initiation?"

"Uh-huh. I want to see what the fuss is all about and confirm something about that night."

I stand taller. "I told you it's not one of them."

"I know, but someone was in my room after you left, and something tells me it's one of our Heathen friends. I'm getting all excited thinking about it."

If whoever that person was arrived after I left, then it's not Carson. In that case, Yulian can do whatever the fuck he wants.

"Were you sent an invitation?" I ask.

"How did you know?"

"A hunch." I smile to myself. Carson still didn't completely let go after all.

He seems to be under this misconception that I want to fuck Yulian—disturbing, to say the least—and he's often displayed a desire to hurt me through that.

Inviting Yulian to the initiation, to his domain, is a clear indication that he still hasn't given up. His destructive brain wouldn't allow him to.

Though I should be there to witness it. Otherwise, the plan won't work.

So how come he didn't send me an invitation?

Hmm.

"Yulian."

"Hmm?"

"Forward me the invitation text."

"Why?"

"Scientific interest."

He laughs. "I don't know what the fuck you even gain from all of this, but I like your way of doing things."

"Everyone does."

He laughs again. "Will send shortly. Laters."

As soon as I have the text that includes the admission QR code, I forward it to Jethro.

ME

Need access.

JETHRO

The fuck? Some kids' hunt?

A hunt is a hunt. Can you arrange it?

Do you need a replica access code?

No. I'm not lining up with students who can recognize me. Arrange background access. Staff or guard. They'll have masks on, right? It should be easier to infiltrate.

Russian mafia security is NOT easy to infiltrate. Their parents placed a rock-fucking-solid security system in place.

Surely not that rock fucking solid for you.

I'll be invoicing you for the extra hassle.

Invoice away. Prepare to control the cameras and cover my tracks while you're at it.

Did I tell you I fucking hate you sometimes?

I'll take that as an agreement.

Kayden.

Don't start nagging.

I'm reminding you that you can't escape your brother forever. He's doubling down on his threats.

He'll live. Besides, he knows I'm working in Europe now. Julian has been taking care of my side of the business back home, so that should keep Grant occupied for the time being.

How about Declan, then? If he finds out you're hiding this from him, he'll flip the fuck out.

He won't. Stop acting like an annoying in-law and get me access.

Hope you get impaled on a cactus and suffer excruciating pain 😜

With a sigh, I pocket my phone and head to my closet. Now, I understand why Yulian was whistling.

This is actually thrilling.

Nothing compares to the morbid excitement at the knowledge that I'll play with my new favorite toy.

———

THIS IS THE MOST LUDICROUS THING EVER DONE.

And that's coming from someone who considers most students absurd beyond redemption.

I caught a glimpse of them lining up, being all giddy about getting chased through the woods by some other kids who get off on violence.

"Two o'clock," Jethro speaks through the earpiece.

My steps are silent as I glide behind a tree. Jethro got me access as a staff member, and ever since then, I've had him in my ear, directing me through the forest.

I'm dressed in a black suit and a bunny mask, which all guards and staff are wearing tonight.

My hand rests on my tie before I loosen it. Preferably, I would've thrown it off, but I don't want to stand out.

A couple of students run by as a guy wearing a red-stitch neon mask chases them with a bat.

It's the less interesting Carson.

Jethro gave me all their identities since he saw them when they put on their masks.

But he didn't have to tell me my prey was the one wearing the green mask. I knew it as soon as I saw the five of them standing on the second-floor balcony.

The little monster has the most erect posture out of the five, and it's due to the bow slung across his shoulder.

He's an archer.

A *hunter*.

Probably the only thing that doesn't contradict with the rest of his image.

But I lost sight of him soon after the initiation started since everyone was running around like headless chickens in a zombie B-movie.

"Where is he?" I ask in the earpiece.

"Five o'clock," Jethro says. "He has company."

"Yulian?"

"No. A girl."

Hmm.

I walk in that direction, stopping when Jethro points at approaching danger.

The sharp, earthy scent of pine needles and damp soil fills my lungs, and I crane my neck on either side. Why the fuck is this tie so tight?

The ground shifts beneath my shoes, uneven, each step sinking slightly into the mossy earth. The trees' branches creak in the wind, their low whisper interrupted by the distant screams of students.

Sunset is settling in, its colors throttled to death by the thick clouds. The light is dim, the fading sun filtering through the tangled branches, casting long shadows that stretch and twist.

The cold creeps in, biting at my skin, but it's not the chill I'm focused on—it's the faintest hint of something familiar in the air.

Something that flexes my muscles and sends a rush of endorphins all the way to my cock.

Finally, I arrive at an open patch of land surrounded by tall trees and bushes. A small twitch lifts my lips.

Here we go.

I remain behind a big bush as I watch a tall man dressed all in black save for his neon green mask standing by a large tree, holding an arch with an arrow at his side. He's right across from me. Only a few feet away.

"Keep clear," Jethro says. "Don't get close, Kayden. I mean it. He can have you ambushed in a fraction of a second. They have a button that calls security to their exact GPS coordinates."

He keeps talking, but his voice filters in the background because I'm watching my toy talking to someone else.

A leggy blonde in tight shorts and a strapless top. She's holding her mask in her hand, and it has '#1' engraved on top. Her face is as attractive as his. They're both blond and the definition of a dream Disney prince and princess.

That is, until she speaks in this grating high-pitched voice. "You're amazing, Gaz. Thanks for protecting me."

"Anytime." He sounds bored and staggeringly uninterested.

She doesn't hear it, though, as she flattens her tits against his chest, and I see the movement of her fingers on his belt as she licks her lips. "Let me repay the favor."

He doesn't stop her as she unbuttons his jeans. Doesn't stop her as she kisses his neck or when she rubs herself all over him.

He makes no move to help her either, his posture remaining upright, and he's not responding to her touch.

No moaning, no muffled groans, and certainly no begging in a throaty, strangled voice.

But the fact remains—he's still *not* stopping her.

"You smell *so* good." She moans against his neck, darting her tongue to suck on his earlobe.

He does smell good, like a subtle hint of bergamot and

cedarwood mixed with his skin. It's a known fact that she doesn't need to point out.

"You taste amazing, too." More licking and sucking and fucking *touching*. "You're so hot, Gaz."

I lift a hand and yank my tie free, letting it hang loose around my neck.

Carson jerks his head in my direction, slightly lifting his bow and arrow in the process.

He has picture-perfect reflexes and is really super aware of his surroundings, including the slightest rustle.

For some reason, that makes me smile.

I'd intended to see how far he'd go with the blonde, but I've changed my mind now.

Scratch that. I changed my mind after she got her claws on him. If she doesn't remove them, I'll rip her neck off.

I pause.

The fuck was that thought about?

I don't even know this girl and I'm thinking about her *decapitation*?

But then again, maybe she shouldn't have touched *my* toy.

I slip out of the bushes in Carson's direct view.

"Kayden, you fucking—" Jethro's voice is cut off when I remove the earpiece and tuck it in my pocket, leaving my hand there.

The blonde doesn't notice a third participant has joined as she keeps kissing and licking, and I try not to look at her so that I won't act on my murderous thoughts.

But *he* notices and instantly lifts his hand that's holding the bow high.

Once again, I'm entranced by the view.

What a beautiful posture, wasted on a monster.

Every part of his body falls into sharp, distinguished angles, like chiseled stone, each line perfectly defined. His form is sculpted to precise detail—the edges of his shoulders, hips, and long legs all converging to create a painting of epic proportions, a masterpiece forged in strength and precision.

And he's aware of it. *Hyperaware*, actually. Because he somehow learned to hide his darkness behind the cold elegance of his body.

I wonder why he learned that or if it came naturally to him. But then again, I'm not supposed to *wonder* about toys. That would make him human, and he's anything but.

Carson pulls on the bow string, then pauses, his arm tight with tension.

Recognition, even.

So he can recognize me, but he *can't* keep his body to himself.

As if hearing my thoughts, he steps back, forcing Blondie to release him, her claws falling unceremoniously from around him.

When he speaks, his voice is deeper for some reason. "You should go, Cherry. Others might find us."

Cherry.

Of course her name is fucking *Cherry*.

"All right." She grins and puts her mask on again. "Which way are we going?"

"You go ahead first so I don't draw attention." He points to his right, speaking in a revolting soft, mellowed-out tone. "That way is safe. I'll stop anyone from following."

"Gosh. You're so awesome." She runs her red nails down his chest, but he's not paying attention as he steals a glance in my direction.

If he thinks I'll hide so his bimbo doesn't see me, that won't be happening.

In fact, I wish she'd do that so I could eliminate her.

Unfortunately, she blows him a kiss and hurries in the direction of where he pointed.

As she disappears behind the bushes, I remove my mask and let it fall on the ground.

I can't see his expression behind his mask, but I make out the twitching of his gloved hand around the bow. The way his entire body vibrates, humming to life.

"How the fuck did you manage to get in here?" he asks with a bite to his words and no hint of the softness he faked so well not a minute ago.

That's it.

The tension. The crumbling.

The way he's unable to control his reaction.

I want it *all*.

And more.

I want to shatter him so thoroughly, no one will be able to pick up the pieces.

Not Cherry.

Not *anyone* else.

"I'm disappointed, little monster." I walk toward him, adopting a bored tone. "Why is your type the female version of you?"

He lifts his bow and points it at me. "Don't come any closer."

"Why? Scared I'll touch you?" I let my lips pull in a smile. "Correction. You're scared of how much you'll like how I touch you, aren't you, baby?"

"I'm not your goddamn baby!"

"I disagree."

"Stay away. I won't repeat myself a third time."

"I'm only trying to have a civil conversation—"

The bastard shoots me. The arrow's rubber head slams against my shoulder, sending it backward. Pain erupts in my muscle and I suppress a groan.

"*That* scared?" I keep walking and he shoots at me again, this time to my thigh, and I hit the ground on one knee.

Motherfucker.

A shadow looms over me, his next arrow pointed down at me as his voice roughens, his eyes sparkling behind the mask. "You know, I was willing to let your insolence go, but you just wouldn't fuck off. You're always buzzing around my head like an annoying fucking fly, *Professor*. Buzzing and buzzing, and fucking *buzzing*. Maybe I should silence you for good."

He reaches into the quiver on his shoulder and retrieves a real arrow with a sharp head, then taps it under the moonlight slipping from beneath the clouds. "I use this for boars, huge fucking beasts like you. One shot to your heart and it's over."

I laugh, the sound loud and perhaps a bit deranged.

Like this piece of work.

His shoulders tense up as he stands straight. "You think I'm joking? You believe I can't kill you?"

"No, I'm sure you will, and you'll do it with flying colors. Hell, you'll make sure no one will find my corpse. You'll melt me with acid, maybe. Or attach me to heavy sandbags and throw me in the ocean to feed the sharks. If anyone can get away with murder, it's you." I grin at him. "You're a natural, baby."

"Stop calling me that." He points the arrow at my chest.

"What? Baby? Do you hate the actual nickname or that it reminds you of how good I can make you feel?"

"You seem to be tired of living, asshole."

"Go ahead. Shoot." I push my chest against his arrow. "Escalate from rapist to murderer. Prove me right."

He goes still, but I hear his panting raw breaths behind that mask. I can't see his eyes well, but they're either glaring or caught in a lost state.

Maybe both.

"Prove you right?" His voice is deeper, a bit on edge, but I can't place the emotion. I can, however, feel the tip of the arrow digging into my chest, cutting through the jacket and shirt and nicking my skin, right above my heart.

Fucking lunatic would kill me in a heartbeat.

And that doesn't stir any fear. If anything, a jolt of excitement vibrates through my veins and my dick.

Because, yes, his violent side turns me on.

Or maybe it's the idea of shoving this menace to his knees.

To control the uncontrollable.

To ride a wild horse.

"Yes, Carson. Prove to me that you can't ascend above your basic urges. That you can't shake off the constant voices that tell you to harm, kill, and watch life leave your victims' eyes. You're a natural at inflicting. It's your default setting. I thought you had better control over yourself, which is why you built and honed your public persona, but perhaps I was wrong about you. Truth is, you *can't* fight your nature. Like all animals, you easily succumb to your subhuman instinct."

It's subtle, but I feel the arrow shifting on my skin, grazing it. I'm definitely bleeding, and he did it on purpose.

To *watch* me bleed.

Because that's where his eyes are. On the arrow and the dark patch on the jacket he probably can't see so well.

But there was another shift. A tensing in his grip when I said a particular sentence.

Perhaps I was wrong about you.

He doesn't like that. If I were reaching, I'd say he cares about my approval.

Now that I think about it, he gets really offended when I insult him, but I believe that'd be his reaction to anyone insulting his looks or intelligence.

Carson doesn't have the ability to doubt himself. If he thinks he's better than anyone else, that's that. So it can't be that he thinks my words are correct, but maybe it's that he doesn't like *me* to say them?

Why?

His cool voice mixes with the breeze. "I thought you were a law professor, not a psychology professor."

"I don't need a degree." I stare up at him. "That fire. That need to hurt and maim? I had it, too. But I rose above it."

Dirt crunches beneath his feet as he shifts, caught off guard, maybe.

And my dick twitches.

Fuck. Why do I love being the reason he stumbles?

I'm starting to get addicted.

I want more of these unmasked reactions and his raw body language.

More.

Fucking *more.*

"That's right, little monster." I let my lips pull into a smile. "We're the same, you and I. Whatever humans are made of, you and I share that form."

"I share nothing with you." His voice is quieter, but he steps away, removing the arrow that drips with my blood. "Just get the fuck out of my life."

Then he turns around, probably to keep playing hunt or, worse, to protect *Cherry.*

His first mistake was turning his back on me.

The second was making me watch that scene from earlier.

I get up and run after him, the adrenaline suppressing the pain caused by the rubber arrows and the graze on my chest.

To his credit, Carson starts to turn around and lifts his bow, but it's too late.

I grab the back of his neck and slam him against the tree, and then whisper in his ear, "You really should've killed me when you had the chance, *baby.*"

And then I bite the lobe that blonde was sucking on. *Hard.*

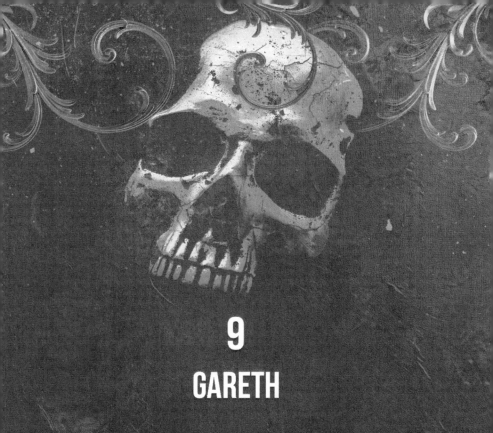

9

GARETH

Kayden is right. I should've *killed* him.

Why didn't I do that, again?

Because I can't prove him right. I can't allow him to confirm any of the theories he has about me.

Not *him*, of all fucking people.

But that ended up with me against a tree. Trapped under him again.

Being *touched* by him again.

Completely surrounded by him.

Fucking *again*.

And he knocked my bow and quiver away, so I have nothing to stab him with.

My mask squashes against the tree, and the smell of pine floods my nostrils, but it pales in comparison to *his* smell.

The tones of wood and amber provoke dark, fucked-up images that visit me in my dreams.

No, *nightmares.*

Images of him biting and marking my flesh, making me come against his cock. Spitting cum in my mouth and forcing me to swallow.

I've thought of killing him every time I've seen the dark purple hickeys all over my chest. I even considered just hiring an outsider to do it and then sending me the footage.

But for some reason, that didn't sound satisfying. Not as much as the fantasy of watching his blood spill on the ground.

Between my fingers.

Beneath my feet.

And I'd stand there, watching those silver eyes turn truly lifeless.

If someone is going to kill Kayden Lockwood, it *has* to be me.

And yet I didn't just now.

Not that I *couldn't*, because I could've in a heartbeat. But I made a conscious decision not to stoop that low.

However, now, I find myself under his thumb again, and I hate it, I hate that it's this easy for him to trap *me.*

But what I hate more is that he has the ability to dissolve every fucking ounce of control I have.

That he can provoke reactions I didn't know I was capable of.

After the last time, I wanted to blame the drugs, and I did, but the drugs don't fucking explain why he keeps appearing in my damn dreams.

Or the hard-ons I wake up with on the regular after said dreams.

It's why I decided to stay as far away as possible.

But he's here now, right behind me. His large body pushing mine, his rock-hard chest pressing against my tense back. His fingers digging into my nape, squeezing until it hurts.

However, that's not what's tilting my head upside fucking down. It's the way he's biting the lobe of my ear. His teeth sinking so deep, I think he'll rip the flesh off.

A ripple of pleasure starts where his lips are, coils in my spine and lands like a ball of fire in my groin.

"Stop," I grunt, but my voice is muffled by the mask. "That hurts. Fuck."

"Does it?" He licks the thin skin.

A jolt of electricity rushes through me, tenting my jeans against the tree trunk.

Fuck. *No.*

"You prefer to be licked here?" His rough voice shoots straight inside my ear and sets my skin on edge.

An uncomfortable yet thrilling edge.

It's an edge I keep escaping but continue being pushed into anyway.

An edge that messes with my fucking head.

"You wanted my tongue all over your ear, like when Cherry did it?" He flicks his tongue on the shell.

"W-what?"

"You like this, don't you?" He licks my lobe, nibbling slightly, then thrusts his tongue in my ear.

Sparks of electricity burst down my spine in blinding succession, and I have to bite my lip so I don't release obscene noises.

The fuck is he doing with his tongue and teeth?

Is it even possible to be so wound up just because of my ear?

And his body pressing into mine.

And him pinning me against the tree.

And his rough voice speaking directly in my ear.

No one has ever brought out this type of intense pleasure from me.

Hell, when Cherry was rubbing herself all over my body, the only thing I felt was a sense of boredom. I waited for any sexual stimulation to take me over as she enthusiastically licked and sucked my skin, but it never came.

And while I'd never admit it, I got a twitch in my fucking pants only after I saw this asshole standing across from me like goddamn impending doom.

But right now, as he sucks and bites and fucks my ear with his tongue, it's torture. My cock is so heavy, leaking precum into my boxers, I think I'll burst.

Why do I seem to get instantly hard around him?

That doesn't make *any* sense.

"S-stop." I bite my lip because what the *fuck* was that stutter about?

"You sure about that?" He slides his hand that's been on my nape up, pulls away my hood, then grabs a fistful of my hair, tugging my head back against his shoulder blade. "You're trembling, baby."

"With rage." I glare up at him. "And don't call me that."

"I think you're trembling for more." He slips his finger under my mask and pushes it off, letting it clatter on the ground. "There you are, my little monster."

His lips pull in a wide smile. One I've never seen before.

I thought he was disgusted at my face, so why is he smiling in this unusual way upon seeing it?

How does he even know *how* to smile that way? I was pretty sure he's a robot.

Sure, he smiles and grins, but I feel like it's learned, like mine. Usually, he's pretty grumpy and strict. He never smiles in class, and he has a domineering aura, so students swoon when he praises their answers, despite his disinterested tone.

He's never praised me, though.

Not that I *want* to be praised by the asshole.

"Let me go," I say in a composed voice.

"You keep saying that, but then you look at me with these eyes."

"What eyes?"

"Expectant eyes."

"Creeped out, more like."

"If you were creeped out, you wouldn't be itching for more." His mouth hovers dangerously close to mine.

I tell myself to seal it shut. To not allow him the opportunity to fucking kiss me—or, knowing him, he's more likely to spit in my mouth.

But then he darts out his tongue and licks my jaw, a rough long lick that sets my skin on fire.

Both my hands are on the tree trunk, fingers digging into the solid bark, arms tensing up so I don't hump my dick against the surface.

I don't find pleasure in this.

Not at all—

A groan rips from my lips as he slides his tongue down my skin. Then his teeth sink into my throat, the bite sharp, sending a jolt of pleasure to my leaking cock.

"Mmm. You do taste good. But only I get to taste you." He bites again.

And again.

His bites alternate—painful one moment, like he's marking me, and then gentle, teasing nibbles the next, pulling a soft gasp from me.

"Only I get to put my mouth here." His tongue flicks against the raw spot, a delicate lick that leaves me breathless.

A suck.

A bite.

"And here." His lips move to my jaw, my cheek. "Only *me*."

He rams his hips into my ass whenever I grunt, his hardening cock nudging, probing, rubbing.

It's driving me insane because I'm not supposed to find this hot.

I don't find men attractive, so a man dry humping me should be disturbing at the least and disgusting at worst.

And yet my spine jerks with every slide of his clothed cock against my ass. My arms hurt from how much I'm stopping my cock from seeking some pleasure against the damn tree.

He bites my throat again, then his hot lips wrap around the skin and he sucks hard, as if aiming to exorcise my soul.

"Fuck...stop that." I buck against him, and it's a big mistake, because his cock grows in size, bigger than I remember, and it turns me delirious.

"Why?" He looks down at me, his eyes all sorts of blown up, like a damn beast. "You let Cherry put her lips all over you while she called you *hot* and *amazing*. I'm only erasing her disgusting taste. Put up with it."

He bites again. Harder.

And I let out a groan, because the pain isn't serving as a turn-off like it would with most people.

Each bite, each touch, each flick of his tongue hardens my cock until it's throbbing, and I can hardly breathe through the intensity.

I'm drowning, consumed by the desperate, addictive need for more pain from his teeth, the heat of his breath, and every ounce of suffocating pleasure.

I slam my eyes shut so he doesn't see what he's doing to me.

"Look at me." His order lands on my skin at the same time as his hot breath. "Open those eyes and show me how much I own you."

"Fuck you," I mutter as I open my eyes, making sure to glare at him. "You don't *own* me."

"We'll see about that. God. I love your glares. You feel how hard you make me?"

"That's because you're gay and won't admit it."

"In that case, so are you. Look at that, more things we have in common, baby."

"I'm not your baby... The fuck you think you're doing?"

I tense up when he reaches in front of me and unbuttons my jeans. I'm horrified as my cock hardens at his touch.

At his hand on my abdomen.

How the fuck is something that normally disgusts me now turning me on?

Just *how*?

Maybe I am broken. I have to be.

The drugs never left my system, and now, I'm trapped with arbitrary feelings and this asshole.

I expect him to fist my cock, but he just lowers my jeans and boxer briefs all the way to my knees.

Cold air bites my skin, but it does nothing to deflate my cock. It's so heavy and aching, precum is trickling down its length.

And I refuse to act like a fucking teen and hump the tree. That just *won't* be happening.

I wait for him to grab my cock and relieve the pent-up pressure he's caused. That's the whole point of this, right?

Trapping me, then forcing me to feel pleasure for his sick entertainment. Then it'll be over, and I'll go back to shooting arrows while telling myself it means nothing.

But his fingers dig into my ass cheek, pulling it aside. I stare up at him with wide eyes as he looks down at where his fingers are. "I must say. You have a nice ass."

"Don't you fucking dare!" I say in a guttural tone and slam my gloved hand on his thigh.

Slap!

I go completely still, my mouth hanging open as a tremble courses through me with startling intensity.

Did this asshole just spank me? *Me?*

"You fucking—" I try to turn around, but he slaps me again and again. Three times. Each stronger than the last.

I go into momentary shock.

Pain burns in my ass cheek, and it hurts. Like fucking hell. And I wish there was only the pain mixed with rage.

I wish my cock wouldn't leak so much.

"Shh. Stop struggling. You can't push me away." He slides a finger against my back hole.

My muscles tense up so badly, I think I'll shatter like goddamn glass. "Kayden, I'm warning you."

"Say that again."

"I'm warning you."

"No." His hot breaths skim my skin. "My name. It's the first time you've said it. I like it."

"Fuck you, Kayden."

He chuckles, his lips rubbing against my jaw softly. Affectionately, even, and it makes me confused as fuck. "Love it when you talk dirty, baby."

"Don't fucking touch me there."

"Why? Afraid you'll like it, too? Mmm. No lube. This is a problem."

"Wait—" He shoves my head against the tree, but his hand disappears from my ass.

The relief is short-lived, though, because I hear the unbuckling of a belt behind me, and then something harder and bigger is gliding up and down my ass crack.

Apprehension builds behind my rib cage, trickling down my spine in a flood of unease. Painful, fucked up, but also expectant.

I should fight. I *can* fight. Hell, I can reach into my pocket and call for a horde of guards that will kill him on the spot.

But then again, I'm the only one who can kill him.

And I *will* kill him.

But there's this petulant side of me that kind of loves it when I say no and he goes for it anyway.

Because I get off on this, apparently, and he *knows* it.

He feeds on it, too.

Because neither of us is normal.

"Your hole feels so good, baby." He makes shallow thrusts against my back hole. "I think I'll love this."

"Wait." I breathe harshly against the tree. "Just wait. Why the fuck do you have to force everything?"

"Because you wouldn't admit to liking this otherwise." He grabs my ass cheek as he slides his cock up and down, touching that hot, dry hole as he whispers in my ear, "If it allows you to enjoy this better, think of me as forcing you, taking your will and fight and allowing you no way out just because I love to see you squirm. You can make me your villain, baby."

It doesn't entirely work, because a sick part of me I wish I could smother to death is enjoying this.

I hate that part and him, but I close my eyes and murmur, "Don't fuck me. You do that, and I swear I *will* kill you."

"Still apprehensive, I see." His cock grows thicker as his movements turn more frantic, hotter, wilder. "I won't fuck you dry. I'm not that much of a monster."

"You won't fuck me at *all*."

"*Yet*."

Slap.

I jerk at the sudden hit, and then his groan follows.

"I love how your ass turns red so fast." He kneads the skin. "You wear my handprints so nicely. Seeing my marks on you makes me hard. The way you submit to the pain I dish out makes me fucking leak, baby."

"Stop doing that."

"Mmm. Keep fighting. I'm close."

Sick motherfucker.

And yet I can't stay still. The way he's rubbing his erection all over me is making me so hard, it's painful. I want to reach down and touch it. Just once.

Something sticky slides over my hole and I think he's coming, but then he stops, so it must be just a lot of precum. I hear him spit a few times before he wedges his hand between my ass cheeks, the cool fluids nudging against my back hole.

"Should be good enough." He circles the rim with his middle finger. "Relax for me. You have to take my fingers before I can stuff you with my cock."

"Don't—"

Slap. Slap. Slap.

I grow still, my muscles turning lax against my better judgement.

"There. Pain helps, right?" It almost sounds as if he thinks he's doing me a favor.

He starts thrusting his finger inside, and all sorts of weird sensations overtake me. Pain. Discomfort. Disgust, even. But it's for myself because I'm letting him put his fucking finger inside me.

Inside my ass.

"Does it hurt?" he asks.

"Mmm."

"I love how you hurt for me. How you take all the pain I give you."

"Fuck..."

"Relax."

"I c-can't."

"You can. Breathe."

I do, slowly.

"Relax more. Is that all you got?"

The challenge makes me tense up but only for a bit before I bite my lower lip and focus on my inhales and exhales.

"That's it. You're taking my finger well."

"Mff..." God. Why is his praise making me so...horny?

"Fuck, baby. Your hole is so tight. Or should I call it pussy so it doesn't feel so gay? My pussy is so tight and warm."

"S-shut the fuck up."

"You hate it when I call this hungry ass a pussy?"

I bite my lower lip and say nothing.

"Should I call it my fuckhole instead? My fucktoy? Or will you submit to me and let me call your ass whatever I fucking please?"

A strangled noise leaves me. I probably should hate that he calls my ass pussy, as if I'm a woman or something, but I feel a weird sense of submission when he does it. And I kind of... like it.

Am I supposed to *like* it?

"Tell me you dislike pussy and I won't say it again."

I bite my tongue, mostly because I'm scared about the noise that will come out.

"Answer me."

"Do whatever you fucking want... Ahh."

My words end on a moan when he sucks on my earlobe as he thrusts his finger slowly, leisurely, and it's painful. But it's also pleasurable. Hell, I think they're one and the same at this point.

"No one's touched you here, have they? Not fucking Cherry, and certainly no other man, because you're *straight* as fuck. Even if you weren't, you would never allow anyone to have this type of power over you. It disturbs you how much you love this."

"You damn bastard...fuck you..."

"Talk dirty to me." He thrusts another finger, and for some reason, this feels easier than the first one. "That's it. Look at your hole stretching and accommodating me. My pussy is virgin, isn't it, baby? You saved it for me so I can ram my thick cock inside and stuff you full with my cum."

My ears heat.

My ears *never* heat.

But his words are affecting me in ways I hate. Ways that make me hotter than I've ever been, and the worst part is that... I don't hate it.

His fingers there.

In that part no one has touched.

Fuck, I'm falling for it, actually. No longer uncomfortable and more wound up.

"Mmmfuck, it's so hot inside you. My pussy knows it's mine. I love how it's clenching around me."

"Stop talking to me like that." I grunt as he pounds his fingers faster.

"Like what?" he speaks against my ear, his words rough and less refined than usual. "Like you're my new favorite hole?"

"Shut up—"

My words get caught in my throat when he curls his fingers inside, hitting a spot that sends my cock to full fucking attention.

A zap of pleasure rushes through me, like lightning and thunder. A fucking natural disaster that makes my entire body tighten up. I'm leaking like crazy, a whole bunch of precum dripping down onto the ground.

"There it is." I feel his lips curving against my ear. "My pussy's G-spot."

I'm about to curse him, but I can't, because he hits that place a few more times and then I'm coming all over the tree, my abs.

Everywhere.

He didn't even fucking *touch* my cock, and I refused to touch myself or hump the tree.

So the cum that spurts out of me in thick waves is all because of his fingers.

In my ass.

Forget about killing him. I might actually kill myself now.

Thanks for witnessing this fuckup.

"That's it, ride my fingers as you come for me, baby."

That's when I realize with goddamn bewilderment that I've been rocking back and forth. Back and forth.

Riding him.

And apparently, I don't give a fuck, because I don't stop. I keep going as my balls are dried of every ounce of cum with my cheek against the tree and his tongue in my ear.

The orgasm is so strong, my legs shake, and I'm surprised I'm still standing.

Kayden removes his fingers, and to my horror, my ass clenches around them, strangling the long digits.

I wait for his crude comment about that, but he only parts my ass cheeks again.

My brows pull in a frown, but then I feel large round skin at my back hole.

"No, don't—"

"Shh." He wraps his hand around my neck from behind, lifting my jaw with his thumb and forefinger. "You can't just come on your own."

"Wait...wait..." I gulp. "*Please*, don't."

I don't care if I have to beg. I'm not going to let him fuck me. Because he was right, I'd never give anyone that power over me.

It'd make me his bitch. I'm no one's fucking *bitch*.

"Fuck, baby. I love it when you beg in that hoarse little voice." He thrusts his crown against my back hole. "I love how my pussy is puckering up and inviting me inside."

"P-please...don't fuck me, Kayde..."

I pause.

He pauses, too. "Jesus fucking Christ, you have a nickname for me already, baby?"

No, I meant to say his full name, but the N got struck in my throat.

"You're driving me fucking crazy." He peppers gentle bites along my jaw, my throat, moving his fingers so he can have access. "How can you not let me fuck my hole? Can't you feel how ravenous I am for you?"

His words strike deep within a fucked-up part in my chest. His voice is rough but his choice of words is softer, almost as if he's trying to persuade me.

Like it matters for him that I let this happen.

He didn't seem to care about the rest, but he wants me to let him fuck me.

And that does something to me. Namely, my slowly hardening cock.

The fuck?

Why would I care about the words of a monster?

A literal damn rapist who seems to enjoy debasing me.

He keeps thrusting against my hole again and again, and my cock twitches as he rams me against the tree.

"I'm dying to be inside you, baby. I've never been this goddamn crazy about being inside anyone."

My throat dries, but I whisper, "No."

"Baby, please?"

"No, come on me, but d-don't fuck me. I'll never forgive you if you fuck me."

He grunts, pushing farther, and I think he'll just do it.

He'll fuck me against a tree in a forest.

But then he releases a shattered breath. "All right, I won't."

My stomach falls and I refuse to honor the feeling with a description. "Really?"

"Really. Instead, tell me you loved being fucked with my fingers, and call me Kayde."

"No way in hell..."

"So you want to be fucked? I'm game, baby—"

"I loved your fingers," I blurt.

"Say it properly."

"Fuck, I loved...being fucked by your fingers."

"You did, huh?" His breathing deepens, sharpening, becoming more guttural as he bites my cheek, his inhales peppering close to my parted lips. "You love how I make you come?"

"We didn't agree on that."

"Say it, baby. Say you love it."

"I...love when you make me come." I wish my voice were mechanical. I really do. But it sounded thick and low.

"Fucking hell, baby. I love your voice."

He does?

"I thought it was off-putting," I murmur.

"It's not when you talk dirty to me or say my nickname."

I grab onto his arm, turning my head slightly to face him, and he lets me, even though his hand stays wrapped around my throat.

His eyes are dark, so dark, I think I see my reflection in them. A muscle moves in his jaw and I watch it.

Then I find myself looking at his lips. His glistening parted lips.

Why the fuck am I looking at a man's lips?

"Come already. Fucking please, Kayde—"

His mouth devours mine.

And it is *devouring*.

Our teeth clash, the sharpness igniting something wild, and our tongues collide, a chaotic, desperate mess of heat and need.

There's no control, just raw frenzy and urgent hunger that twists between us in a fevered dance of dominance and surrender.

It's messy, unrestrained, like a twisted fucking storm that neither of us wants to end.

He bites me and I bite back.

He tugs on my lip and I feast on his.

It's a war. It means nothing, and I'm only giving him twice as much as what he gives me.

Until I taste something metallic. I don't know whether it's his blood or mine, but it makes my cock harden.

And he comes.

Against my back hole, grunting in my mouth.

He comes so much, hot liquid trickles down my thighs, and I feel some of it slipping inside me, and I clench, again, like a fucking whore.

I don't even have the energy to feel shame as he pulls his lips from mine.

His forehead starts to lower to mine and I headbutt him. "Get the fuck off me and don't kiss me again."

He chuckles, the sound vibrating against my throat. "You're right. This is so *gay* and we're definitely *straight*."

"I'm straight. I have serious doubts about you."

He laughs again, reaching for my mouth, and I expect him to spit in it, and honestly, I prefer his dirty side over what he does. Because he just wipes something from my lip. "Loving the hot and cold, baby. Adorable."

I'm about to headbutt him again, but he steps back, tucks himself in, and kneels behind me. I go to turn around, but he's already grabbed my hip in one hand, then retrieves the tie that's been dangling around his neck.

"I can do it on my own. Don't touch me."

"Quiet." He slides the fabric between my ass cheeks, and his handprints burn whenever his fingers brush against them.

"Stop."

"Don't push it." His voice darkens, and even though he's on

his knees, I can feel the domineering energy in waves. "I'm doing something nice for you, so shut up and take it."

I glare down at him. "You're anything but nice."

I expect him to laugh it off and mock me like he always does, but he just stares up at me.

Or *glares*?

The expression disappears before I can decipher it. "Believe me. I am being nice right now."

The humiliating feeling of being cleaned up by him dissipates at the cryptic look in his eyes.

It vanishes as he finishes the task and stands up.

A distant scream pierces my ears, and I stare ahead, dumbfounded.

The fuck.

I completely forgot that we were in the mansion's forest, during the initiation, where it's buzzing with over a hundred people.

Jesus fucking Christ. How could I *forget*?

Though the risk is minimal, someone could've passed by and seen me come all over my professor's fingers.

Fuck.

I face the tree and pull my jeans up.

"Lose the girl." Hot breaths skim my skin, and my fingers pause on the buttons. "Lose *all* girls."

I don't look at him as I release an annoyed breath. "Why the fuck would I do that?"

"I don't like seeing any of their claws on you."

"Jealous or something?"

"Territorial." He wraps his arms around me from behind, sliding his large hands up and down my chest, then tightens his arms around me in a possessive grip. "They're sullying my beautiful toy with their rancid breaths and cheap presence."

Give it to this fucker to call someone beautiful and a toy in the same sentence. Why the hell am I even *bothered* by that?

Still refusing to look at him, I grunt, "Why would I listen to you?"

"If you don't, I'll fuck you in front of them, so they know who owns you."

"No one owns me, least of all you."

"It's only a matter of when, not if." He releases me. "If you don't want me to pay you a visit every day, unblock me."

"What do you want from me, asshole?" I ask with frustration as I button up.

"Your *everything*." His voice sounds more distant now.

I turn around and my own goddamn devil is gone.

10
GARETH

I'm having a sexuality crisis.

    It's messing with my head.

    My fucking sanity.

I've shot more arrows than I can count since last night.

Hell, I barely recall what happened after my goddamn professor disappeared after he fucked my ass with his fingers and I liked it.

After he spanked me.

Then came *all* over me.

I could barely walk, but I made it to the security room where all accepted participants, those who made it without being eliminated, gathered.

No one did except for Cherry, because I paved the path for

her. Niko also brought someone. I kid you not, it was Landon King's twin brother, as in the leader of the Elites, the club at the neighboring posh British students' university.

Naturally, Jeremy didn't agree with his admission, and Brandon—Landon's twin—didn't seem interested anyway.

He was dead set on leaving more than anything, and he felt downright spooked and stunned when Nikolai had him on his lap.

I got kind of uncomfortable watching him squirming. It somehow brought up memories from my own fuckery.

But maybe Brandon was more ill at ease because his sister passed by. He had a mask on so she couldn't have recognized him.

She joined the initiation as Kill's new toy. We were only missing Landon to have fucking chaos on our hands.

Cherry, of course, didn't miss a chance to rub herself all over Kill, and that started a little drama that I watched with detachment before I escorted Glyn out.

Maybe because I pity her for piquing my brother's interest. I honestly don't know.

That entire night was such a clusterfuck of epic proportions. I saw Jeremy cornering a girl in the forest, which I found odd, because he's so stoic, he doesn't really *corner* girls. They come to him of their own volition.

But the most interesting scene is the one I witnessed on my way back as I could barely walk.

Vaughn had a certain serpent slammed against a tree with his chain around his throat.

Yulian just laughed like a maniac as he was being choked. "Love it when you get rough, Mishka."

Now, I don't really know Russian that much, but I'm pretty sure *Mishka* is a pet name.

I was thinking of inviting Yulian, but I actually didn't,

because I wanted nothing to do with that fucker Kayden and I chose not to antagonize V for no reason.

No clue how he got in or why Vaughn was dragging him with his chain across the ground, but it was none of my business.

Pretty sure Vaughn didn't even spend the night and left as soon as the initiation was over, though.

Me? I spent hours reviewing security footage. For some reason, Kill and Jeremy were doing the same, and I was on edge thinking they'd see me being finger-fucked by an asshole.

It was your asshole that was being fucked, though.

Very funny, demons.

But suspiciously, there was no trace of the motherfucker. I watched from all the angles, especially near that location, but it was as if it had been erased.

Maybe a hacker? It'd have to be a damn good one to be able to infiltrate our systems and get in without a QR code. Because I've seen footage of the people who lined up in front of our mansion, just in case, even if I didn't think he'd mingle with students.

I was right.

He's smarter than that and more resourceful than I thought. Because why the fuck would a normal college professor have such a high-rate hacker under his thumb?

Even his dad's law firm is small and has little to no influence. Maybe a previous client?

It doesn't really matter how he did it.

I run my hand through my hair as I lean against my desk chair and pull out my phone.

Supposedly, I need to study for the stupid assignment. I don't usually put much effort into school, but this time, because it's him, I want to make the best fucking opening statement in history.

I want him to be in awe and stop belittling me.

Though he didn't do that last night.

I wonder why.

This whole thing is confusing. I *hate* confusing.

With a groan, I pull out my text exchange with my PI.

ME

> I need you to dig deeper into Kayden Lockwood.

NADINE

> How deep are we talking?

> As deep as you can get. No detail is too small. His childhood, his favorite toy, food, color, movies, sports. Everything that makes him tick. I want to see his high school yearbook, any extracurriculars he was involved in, and a comprehensive list of all past relationships. Leave no stone unturned. I want to know every last one of his secrets. If there's anything buried in his past, I need to see it. Also, dig into his connections. Find out if he has any ties to underground organizations. The deeper you go, the better.

Was that too much? Probably.

Still searching for the fucks I have to give, though.

He lost all rights to his privacy the moment he touched me.

> That will cost you a lot.

> I don't care. Get me what I want.

> Noted. I will have to stay in the States for a while to accomplish this, so meetings might not be as frequent.

> That's fine. Update me via text or email.

I lean back in my chair, rolling my phone in my hand and still feeling lost.

Lost and I don't exist in the same universe, and yet I can't help but think that gathering info about him won't quite solve the big mystery.

The way *I* react to him.

So let's take this logically.

I've been straight my entire almost twenty-two years of life. My first actual crush and loss was a girl.

I've never, and I mean *never*, looked at a guy and been like 'Sick body, bro,' 'That's a hot dick,' or 'I wonder what your cum tastes like.' I barely notice shit about girls, let alone guys.

Closing my eyes, I picture tits, like Cherry's or Morgan's. Let's go with Morgan—hers are bigger. Hmm. Is that hot? I guess?

I swear it used to do something to me. Round, full tits, soft and pliant in my hands, the perky nipples engorging beneath my touch...

Images of my own nipples being squeezed and bitten and pinched rush in. Instead of tits, it's large, hard muscles with a snake tattoo—

My eyes snap open and I groan as my dick twitches. *You better not, bitch. I'm warning you.*

This isn't working. I seem to have lost my attraction to girls. I mean, not completely, but I'd still need to force myself into the mood to fuck—which is what I've been doing my whole life, really.

And I'm not attracted to men.

I need an experiment.

Unlocking my phone, I open a browser and type 'gay porn.'

It's beyond ridiculous, but I want to confirm I'm not having some sexuality crisis.

*You totally are *giggles**

Shut up, demon.

After putting my earbuds in, I click one of the most viewed videos and watch.

First thought: the fake, corny sounds grate on my very last nerve.

So I click on something else. The fake noises make me want to reach into the screen and shake the fuck out of them.

I type 'amateur' and go from there. These are better, at least they're not too fake and the noises aren't grating, but they still do nothing for me. If anything, I'm angling my head and watching them with pure objectivity as if it's an assignment.

If I were gay, I'd find this hot, right?

But I don't. Actually, I'm bored.

That means I'm not gay.

End of the story.

In your face, demon.

Though straight porn does nothing for me either, but that's not for here or now.

I'm about to close the browser when one of the guys on the screen starts fingering the other dude's ass and I swallow. Not because of what's on the screen, but because I'm seeing the image of that damn bastard behind me.

I close my eyes as my dick twitches back to life, throbbing as the sensations from last night play in my mind.

Motherfucker.

The porn video's sound pauses, and I startle when a text pops up at the top of the screen. And it's from none other than the asshole himself.

I close the porn screen as if he's watching me or something and remove the earbuds.

DEVIL

So you did unblock me. You want to talk to me that much, huh?

ME

I only did that so you wouldn't show me your creepy face.

I know you miss me.

Don't make me block you again.

Aw, so now you want to see me?

Not even in hell.

You say that as if it can't be arranged. Tell you what. You know where my place is, so if you miss me that much, you can drop by whenever you want.

No, thanks.

You say that a lot. It's starting to lose effect.

And you ignore it a lot. It's like talking to a fucking wall.

Language.

You're not my dad.

How is your relationship with him? Your dad?

If you're looking for some daddy issues, I have none. Dad and I are actually pretty close. Better luck next time.

Does he know who you truly are, my little monster?

I drop my hand from the corner of my mouth because I was about to eat the fucking skin around my thumb. Like a goddamn kid.

When I don't reply, he sends another text.

> He doesn't, does he? You wouldn't be so close if he did. Let me guess, he didn't know how to deal with your brother when he was diagnosed, and there was probably some form of wedge between them, and you didn't want that. You don't want to be discarded by your father, which means you respect him a lot, or you wouldn't have cared. Maybe that's why you wear different personas in public and private. You don't allow anyone, your closest friends and family included, to see what truly lurks beneath the Disney prince image. Are you scared they'll find you unsightly? Disturbing? You don't care about acceptance, so what is the true reason, my little monster? I can keep a secret.

I scoff at my phone, even if I find *his* words disturbing. It's unsettling that he can read me so openly like a damn book. Not all that is true, but much of it is.

> Here's a little idea for you, Professor. Instead of psychoanalyzing me, how about you commit yourself to a mental institution? I'm sure they'd have a field day with you.

> Only if you join me, baby.

> Why on earth do you keep calling me that? I hate you and we're not in any form of a relationship.

> Why do you hate me?

> Let's see. You raped me. Three times. Keep threatening me and won't leave me alone. Take your pick.

> You shouldn't throw stones when your house is made of glass. You started the rape thing first. I only let you get a taste of being on the receiving end instead.

> And last night? I wasn't going to do anything to anyone. What's your excuse?

You looked beautiful.

> wtf

What does that mean? I don't do acronyms.

> It's what the fuck, dick. What are you, from the Stone Age? That's been around forever.

Language.

> Well, you just admitted to forcing yourself on me because I was beautiful. Excuse me if I don't have the capacity to care about language. You won't even try to find an excuse?

You're the one who needs excuses, not me.

> Me?

Here are your excuses, Carson. Last night, you could've fought, but you didn't. You had the ability to call an army of guards to either restrain or kill me but didn't. You wanted that as much as I did. But that's just my two cents. Here's your homework to think about tonight. Since you're so straight, why would you come from prostate fucking?

I'm about to curse him, but I hear heavy footsteps running down the hall and flip my phone upside down, then pretend to be focused on my homework. Even if my insides are ripping with rage.

A few seconds later, my door is shoved open and rattles against the wall. I look up, feigning surprise at the sight of Niko.

He's wearing only jeans, putting his huge, extravagantly tattooed chest on display.

Before I went up to my room earlier, he was about to indulge in his insufferable acts of exhibitionism, so I speak in my usual calm voice. "Gee, thanks for the death scare. Please don't tell me you'll start stripping...?"

My cousin narrows his eyes as he walks toward me. The motherfucker has mood swings worse than politicians, and I don't want to see him naked.

"Don't you dare, Niko, or I swear I'll tell Aunt Rai about your annoying habits—"

"Have you ever been attracted to men?"

I pause.

Did he see something last night?

No, that's not possible. He's not subtle, so if he did, he would've advertised it in *The New York Times*.

I let my pen fall on the notebook and exaggerate an exhale. "What are you talking about?"

"You've always fucked women, but have you done that because you feel you have to due to peer pressure and what's defined by society as normal or because you want to?"

The fuck is he getting at? Did that motherfucker Kayden talk to him or something?

I wouldn't put it past him. He does seem like he loves to mess with his victims.

Is that what I am? A fucking *victim*? Me, Gareth Carson?

He also called me a toy.

Me. A *toy*.

"What is this about?" I stand up, tension crowding my shoulders. "What did you hear?"

"What should I have heard?"

Fuck. I can't believe I let that slip.

Even Niko, who's usually oblivious to cues, immediately picks up on it. He steps so close to me that he almost touches me, and even though he's my cousin and we grew up together like brothers, I still don't like to be touched.

Didn't seem like you hated it last night.

The prick demon is begging to be killed.

"So?" Niko peers down on me. "What? Tell me. Tell me! What should I have heard?"

I shove him away. "Stop doing that shit."

"Not until you answer my question."

I palm my face. "I love women. Happy?"

"What about men?"

"I...don't know. Could be." I can't believe I'm admitting this out loud. I don't even believe it myself, but I want to talk to someone about it—even cryptically.

Niko came out as bi over four years ago and he's the happiest goddamn queer I know.

I don't care about others' sexuality, and, really, Niko has the most adventures among us.

But me? Gay? No way in hell. It's not actually about being gay. I'm open to that idea, but I'll *never* be fucked.

Not in this lifetime.

Could I do the fucking, though?

I think that's okay, right?

I clear my throat, chasing away the cloud of confusion. "Why are you probing?"

His eyes spark in a rare thoughtful gleam. "I'm testing something. When did you discover you like men?"

"I don't like men. Jesus." I hurry to the door, knowing Kill could be listening, and then close it.

Niko is poor at connecting patterns; my brother isn't. He'd definitely get involved if he knew about Kayden, and they would clash.

Maybe kill each other.

And this isn't any of my brother's business.

I need to learn more about Kayden and then destroy him. Maybe after that, I'll let Kill take care of the scraps.

Facing Niko, I lean against the door, my arms and ankles

crossed. "I'm not sure. I don't know. I love fucking women, but..." *A certain man always makes me come like I never have before.*

"But what?" He stalks toward me, then tilts his head to the side as he looks at me with those wide manic eyes. "What changed your mind?"

"I didn't change my mind and, seriously, stop looking so intense. It's creepy."

"Blah fucking blah, just tell me what made your straight ass sway on the line. Figuratively, of course. Or is it literally?"

"Fuck you, asshole," I mutter, then close my eyes.

Maybe it's because the last couple of weeks have been weighing on me or because I can't just keep it all to myself, but I say, "If you tell anyone about this, especially Kill, I'll murder you."

"I won't if you just fess up. What made you change lanes?"

"I'm not sure I did—or *would*, for that matter. It's just...one person. That's it."

Fuck me.

Is that even a thing? Finding one man attractive?

There must be others.

There *has* to be others.

Because there's no way in *hell* the one man is Kayden motherfucking Lockwood.

Niko ruffles my hair. "Aw, welcome to the club. You top or bottom? Verse?"

"Just shut it, Niko."

"You give bottom vibes."

"Why the fuck would you think that?" I'm genuinely offended. Why is he so sure I bottom? Me? Being fucked.

Impossible.

"Because you don't take a lot of initiative, cousin, and you're such a prince. Though maybe you could be verse? Dunno. It depends. Experiment a lot and you'll find out which position works best for you. Though I knew from the get-go that I love fucking, not the other way around. But people are different. Some know straight away—or gay away, *see what I did there?*—while others use trial and error."

I'm deeply uncomfortable with this talk, but I still ask, "What does trial and error even mean?"

"A number of things. Like bottoming and hating it. Or topping and being ill at ease. Some people like switching it up, which means topping and bottoming. Some people hate those terms altogether. It depends on the person. You're usually the top if you like fucking and being in control, though there are power bottoms who take control but don't do the fucking. If you love being pounded or come by prostate fucking without dick stimulation, you're usually a bottom."

My ears heat. No way in fuck. "Who the fuck came up with these rules?"

"No one really. And there are no rules. Everyone is different. I'm speaking generally and in terms some might agree with yet others wouldn't. Anyway, I'll give you a free course on butt stuff. Lesson one, always have lube on you, like *always*. And prep yourself. Start with small butt plugs, then scale up. You'll thank me later—"

"Okay, I've heard enough. Get the fuck out." I push him out, then slam the door shut.

I bite on my thumb as I let out a long groan. There's no way in fuck I'm gay, let alone the one being fucked.

I do the fucking. Next time I see Kayden, I'm taking the upper hand.

Not that I look forward to that.

Absolutely *not*.

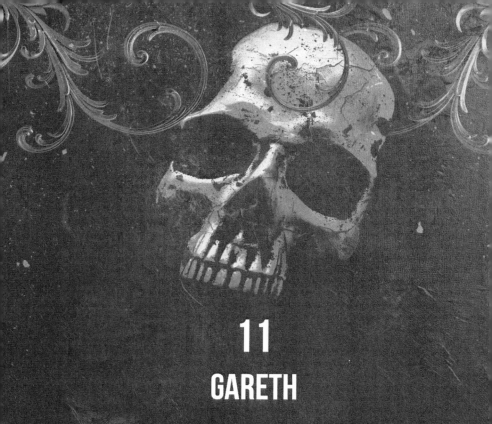

11

GARETH

Two days later, I'm early for criminal law class.

Not because I want to test Niko's theory about trial and error, but it's more because I'm actually a good student. And I'm not allowing some immoral professor to tarnish my track record.

My eyes zero in on him as he walks into class. Everyone grows silent, almost reverent.

Professor Lockwood has built an impenetrable reputation in the couple of weeks he's been teaching at TKU. Sort of a cult, really.

Girls visibly fan themselves when they see or pass him by—they love how he's so mysterious and strict and just *so hot*—and even the guys respect him.

He's annoying competition.

Though they're right about the mystery factor. I've been thinking, and I believe maybe the reason he's messing with my head—and, subsequently, my body—is because I can't figure him out.

His actions don't match his profile, so maybe when they do, I'll lose interest. I *always* do.

His gaze flits in my direction as if he knows I've been thinking about him, and a small smile grazes his lips before it disappears.

Asshole loves getting on my last fucking nerve.

He also definitely knows he's attractive and carries it well. Not attractive to *me*, but in *general*. From the *girls'* point of view.

He always wears his black hair styled to perfection, a sleek, controlled look that highlights the strength of his forehead and draws attention to his thick, dark brows, framing his gray almond-shaped eyes with a predatory intensity.

The dark stubble along his jaw only serves to make it appear even sharper, adding an edge to his already striking features.

Navy slacks cling to his long, muscular legs, each step emphasizing their strength, while the light-blue shirt stretches across his chest and arms, taut over the solid muscle beneath in a perfect blend of elegance and raw power.

But I guess the most attractive thing about him, aside from his physique and face, is the confident way he carries himself.

The way he also hides his true nature.

No one would look at him and think he loves to fuck his students.

Wait.

Is he doing this to *others*?

That thought is disturbing, but I don't focus on it as he

addresses the class and says we'll start with the opening statement for the trial case.

We shift into position, my classmates taking their notes and
reading them one final time.

I carry my empty notebook just for show, then decide
against it. I'm not going to hold back today at all.

Throughout the entire preparation, Kayden sits on the edge
of his desk, his arms crossed. He has his sleeves rolled to his
elbows now, exposing his muscular, veiny forearms, and I catch
a glimpse of the girls filming him discreetly.

What an attention whore.

Seriously, is he trying to seduce the others?

Zara steps up on behalf of the prosecution. She's black, tall,
and possibly the best public speaker in class. Her posture is
upright as she looks at her notes and speaks in a loud, clear
voice. "Ladies and gentlemen of the jury, today you will hear
the harrowing story of Rebecca Blake, a young woman whose
life was violently interrupted by the actions of James Rutherford. On the night in question, Rebecca Blake was alone in a
hotel room, far from the safety of her home, where she was
drugged, sexually assaulted, and left in a state of unconscious-
ness. The defendant, James Rutherford, entered her room with
the clear intent to harm, and that's *exactly* what he did.

"You will hear from the attending doctor, who will confirm
that Rebecca Blake's injuries are consistent with sexual assault.
Her body bore the physical evidence of violence, and the toxi-
cology report will show that she was drugged, unable to defend
herself or consent to any actions that night. Witnesses who were
at the hotel that evening will testify to seeing Rutherford near
Rebecca's room, and we will present DNA evidence that links him
directly to the crime. The victim's confusion and memory gaps
are not a defense for the accused's actions, nor does it absolve
him of responsibility for what he did to Rebecca that night. We

will prove, beyond a reasonable doubt, that James Rutherford is guilty of the assault on Rebecca Blake. The evidence is clear. The crime is undeniable. And we ask that you find him guilty."

The other two prosecutors high-five each other under the table.

"Solid statement and perfect delivery, Jones. No notes," Kayden says with a look of pride. Why the fuck is he giving Zara that look?

Is she one of the students he's also messing with?

I'll fucking ruin him if that's the case.

I'll ruin him either way, but if he truly sees me as a toy of many toys, I'll end him in the goriest way ever.

You know, to rid society of predators.

Just kidding. It's only for pure personal gain.

"Thank you, Professor." Zara smiles with utter arrogance as she resumes her place.

"Defense," Kayden says without even looking at me, seeming busy checking his laptop. "It'd be hard to beat that, but the floor is yours."

He's belittling me again. *The motherfucker.*

I bottle down those emotions as I stand right before the jury, speaking in a tone lower than Zara's but more confident. Unlike her, I have no notes, and I'm making eye contact with all of them. "Ladies and gentlemen of the jury, you've heard the prosecution's version of events, but what they won't tell you is the *other* side of the story—the part they conveniently left out to make their case seem cut and dried. Yes, something happened to Rebecca Blake that night, but that doesn't mean that what the prosecution is trying to force you to believe is accurate. They'll tell you that she was assaulted, that she was drugged and unable to consent. But what they won't tell you is that Rebecca Blake went with him to that hotel room *willingly*. She wasn't dragged there, she wasn't coerced—she *chose* to go.

And there are witnesses who will testify to this fact, people who saw them together before they entered the hotel."

I let my eyes stay on the ones who are held captive by my words.

"The evidence will show that the two of them were flirting with each other before even stepping into that room. They left the bar together, and Rebecca Blake didn't appear to be under duress. She was laughing, she was engaged, and she was in control of her actions. There was no indication of force, no signs of a woman desperately trying to escape an attacker. Now, the prosecution wants to focus on the aftermath, the fact that Rebecca couldn't remember all the details and that she felt unwell the next morning. But I ask you to consider this. When someone drinks alcohol, their memories can become foggy, they can become clouded, and that's what happened here. Rebecca's inability to recall everything from that night doesn't mean that consent wasn't given. According to witnesses, she never seemed out of control or intoxicated. The fact that she changed her mind or regretted her actions later does not negate the consent she previously gave.

"We're not here to deny what happened to Rebecca—what we're here to prove is that the sexual encounter between her and Mr. Rutherford was consensual. She went to that room willingly, she was an active participant, not a victim. She didn't say 'no,' she didn't resist, and that's why this case hinges on one simple question: did the prosecution provide sufficient evidence to prove that what happened was anything other than a consensual encounter? We will show you that the answer is no. There is reasonable doubt, and we will prove that Mr. Rutherford is not guilty."

I don't pay attention to the rest of my team, who are celebrating in the corner. Or the members of the jury who are already in my pocket.

Instead, I let myself wear a smug smile as I turn to face Kayden.

How is that for perfect statement and delivery, dick—

My smile falters the moment our gazes lock. His eyes are dark, several shades darker than gray, filled with a dangerous, threatening edge. His fingers tighten on the desk, and I think that if he were to touch me right now, he might strangle me to death or something.

What the fuck?

The threatening edge disappears as he stands to his full height and says in a monotone voice, "Too theatrical. Could be shorter. We'll resume next week. Moving on to today's lesson."

Everyone shuffles back to their seat, and I do, too, but that expression is etched deep in my mind.

Kayden doesn't acknowledge me for the rest of the class. No taunting smirks. No backhanded insults.

Nothing.

And all I can think about is that he looked like he wanted to kill me.

12
KAYDEN

Cold.

Somehow not cold enough.

Somehow *too* cold to breathe properly.

The ice surrounding my body is biting, an assault that numbs every inch of my bare skin.

The sharp, merciless water clings to me, the ice cubes scraping against my legs like jagged stones.

My breaths rush out in shallow, controlled gasps, the cold seeping into my bones, sinking deeper with every passing second.

The icy grip on my muscles makes the black-and-white bathroom fade into an indistinct blur.

My hands tremble slightly, but I force them still as I bring the cigarette to my lips. The acrid taste of tobacco fills my lungs, a sharp contrast to the icy burn.

I quit smoking a long time ago, when I thought I had everything I ever wanted.

Until I didn't.

Until the life I'd made for myself crumbled to fucking pieces.

I didn't relapse then.

But I am now. After today.

After I was punched in the gut by the reality and the fucking reminder that I let myself get too close.

Too *personal*.

I'm not supposed to *enjoy* this.

Which is why I'm indulging in this punishment. My father's favorite way to discipline me and my brother was throwing us in an ice bath—a room, actually—and not letting us leave until we were about to die of hypothermia. He had doctors on board to make sure we were pushed to our absolute physical limits.

So it's two punishments. Letting the cold numb whatever the fuck I was on and recalling dear old Dad.

My numb fingers struggle to hold the cigarette steady, but I take a drag, let it coat my throat, then exhale slowly. The smoke curls in the air, thick and heavy, before dissipating in the chill.

I inhale the scent of lavender, close my eyes, and feel every icy sting. My body is just a vessel of discomfort, floating in frozen silence. I let the cold wash over me, let it burn, let it pull at the edges of my thoughts, numbing the desire to get consumed by anything irrelevant.

And he *is* irrelevant.

And yet the shadow that appears behind my lids has deep light-green eyes and messy blond hair. He's wearing a little grin, taunting dimples creasing his cheeks, and I want to stab them.

To drink his fucking blood vampire style.

But I also want to grab that lean waist and sit him on my

cock. I want to feel him squirm and blush, to feast on his red ears and pinch his nipples.

I want to kill him as I fuck him.

That's how much I hate to want the motherfucker.

A damn *kid*. Not technically, but he's still over eleven years younger than me.

And I've never even looked at anyone who isn't my age. *Never.*

I've also never looked at a man with the intention to own him, but here we are. There's just something about my new toy that's making me a horny fucking prick at all times. The more I see him, the more I crave to do unspeakable things to him.

I want to break him as I own him.

To claim him.

Swallow him whole.

My cock twitches. In the middle of the goddamn ice.

The whole point of this punishment is to put that part under lock and key.

And yet here we are.

Full of thoughts of him instead of lavender.

What's even the point of that smell anymore?

I should get up and call my brother so he doesn't come after me. Should review what Jethro emailed me about a potential breach. Should keep up with the teaching curriculum.

But I stay still.

It's not enough.

There's room to get more numb.

"Is this some sort of kink?"

For a second, I think I'm imagining his voice. I'm obsessing over him so much, it's starting to mess with my brain.

But when I slowly open my eyes, he's standing by the side of the tub, dressed in his stalking attire—black jeans that hang low on his hips and an oversized hoodie that betrays his muscular frame.

Blond strands peek from beneath the hoodie, and his eyes appear darker under the dim lights. With high cheekbones, a straight nose, defined lips, and a sharp jawline, he looks like a true Adonis. A god that's right beneath my shoe.

And I don't want to squash him.

Yet.

I lift the cigarette to my mouth as I watch him, letting my eyes linger on his lips. Lips I have the urge to kiss again.

Lips I shouldn't have tasted in the first place, because one taste was enough to convert me.

My little monster is one of those obscure niche religions that revolve around pain.

And dominance.

And goddamn forbidden desires.

He clears his throat, clearly uncomfortable with my staring, and that makes me smile.

I truly find pleasure in seeing him squirm.

I release a cloud of smoke and wait until it ripples in the air. "Your unlawful conduct is spiraling out of control. Breaking and entering again?"

"I didn't break anything. I just put in your code and got in. You should've changed it if you didn't want me to have access. Besides, you're the one who said I could drop by since I already know where your place is."

He talks a lot when he's out of his element. I suppose it's because he's not used to having someone mess with him. Though I don't think he enjoys messing with others either since he disregards them too much to waste his time on them.

But he is giving me his time.

His attention.

He's here because he can't *not* mess with me.

When I continue watching him in silence, he narrows his eyes. "Aren't you cold? Your lips are blue."

"You've been looking at my lips?" I let my mouth curve in a grin. I can't help it.

This little fucker merely exists in my vicinity, and no amount of ice can numb me.

"Observing your sorry state," he says with that natural condescension, and the arrogance he hides so well in public rushes through in warm waves against my freezing skin.

"And you do that by watching my lips? If you want a kiss, all you have to do is beg."

"Get over your fucking irrelevant self."

"Language. And if I were irrelevant, you wouldn't be standing in my bathroom like a lost puppy looking for his master."

His lips lift in a snarl, and I wait for him to attack me so that I can yank him into the depths of the bath. My fingers twitch around the cigarette, and any trace of fucking numbness disappears.

It must be the look in my eyes that gives me away, because his widen a little, and he presses his lips in a line. The dimples appear in his cheeks, but they're not deep, not like when he smiles.

And he does that a lot on campus. With his fake friends and fake acquaintances. He smiles like it's a sport.

He never smiles around me, though.

I wonder why.

I know exactly why, but it doesn't make me despise the others any less.

"Just come out. I'll wait outside. If you faint, I'll let you die."

"Ever thought of writing a *How-to Tough Love* book?"

"No, but I'm thinking of writing a *How to Murder Your Professor for Dummies*, though you might not get to read it."

I laugh, and he pauses, a curious look lightening his bright greens, but then he seems to shake off his thoughts as he stalks out the door.

I tilt my head, watching the way he walks. He's confident, but it's not that. It's the posture.

The upright, perfect posture. I want to break that fucking spine so he never lifts his head again.

But maybe I should have a picture of that posture first.

I kill the cigarette in the ice, then get up and go into the shower, turning the water on full blast. My muscles protest and the lavender scent is barely there, now overshadowed by sandalwood and bergamot. The smell is so male and *him*, I drive my fist into the wall as I stand under the hot shower.

The pain does nothing to expel the foul energy rippling my abdominal muscles and twitching my cock.

Because he's outside.

And I *can't* stop thinking that he's outside. In my space.

Around me.

Because he also couldn't stay away.

I close my eyes and summon every ounce of control I have, but that only lets me stand in the shower for a couple more minutes.

"Fuck this." With a mutter, I step out of the shower and dry myself.

After putting on a pair of silk pajama pants, I cast a glance around my bedroom and then focus on the nightstand's drawer. I wouldn't have noticed it if I weren't anal about fucking details, but there are fingertip traces. Not mine, because I haven't touched that drawer. Not since the night he was first here.

Someone was snooping around.

Trying to figure me out.

Good luck with that.

I walk into the living area and pause. Carson is in the bar-style kitchen, sitting on the stool with a bowl of strawberries in front of him.

He tilts his head in my direction as he wraps his lips around a large strawberry, the red flesh parting under his teeth as he bites down. My gaze zeros in on his mouth as the juice stains his lips, his tongue flicking out to catch the remnants.

And my cock is noticing it, too, getting all fucking excited as if he's that strawberry.

A rush of awareness flickers in Carson's gaze, and he licks his lips as he pulls off the cap. "Stop looking at me with those eyes."

"What eyes?"

"You know exactly what eyes."

"If you don't want these eyes, maybe you shouldn't seduce me."

"I was just eating strawberries."

"That's subject to interpretation." I walk toward him and sit on the stool beside him.

He recoils a bit. It's barely noticeable, but I put him on edge. *Good.*

Can't have him getting comfortable. He'll be miserable for the rest of his short life.

"Were you rummaging through my fridge, Carson? That's inappropriate behavior."

"We have that in common. Inappropriate behavior, I mean."

My mouth twitches in a smile. "You like strawberries?"

"What made you think that? I could've picked them randomly."

"They were tucked away at the very back of the fridge, hidden among all kinds of fruit, which means you were deliberately searching for them."

He purses his lips. He really doesn't like it when I read him.

I should do it more.

"Why strawberries?"

"Because. Why does your house smell of lavender?"

"Because."

He narrows his eyes and picks up another strawberry but doesn't eat it. "Don't own any shirts?"

"Now, you're looking at my chest, baby?"

"It's disturbing."

"The snake?"

"Your nakedness." He cocks his head to the side. "What does it mean? The snake?"

"Should it mean something? Can't I have a tattoo because I think it looks good?"

"I find it hard to believe you'd do something without purpose."

Now, *he* is the one reading *me*. I like this game.

Mostly because I have more cards up my sleeves than he'll ever have.

"I'll disclose the meaning if you tell me the story behind your tattoo."

"How do you know I have one?"

Well, damn. It's on his upper arm and I haven't seen that yet. And of course he remembers that I haven't seen it.

I keep my expression neutral. "Don't all kids your age?"

"I'm not a kid. I'm almost twenty-two."

"Almost?"

"Yeah, my birthday is in four months."

"Is it important to you that I see you as older than you are?"

"What?"

"I'm thirty-three."

"And?"

"Does an eleven-year age difference really feel any less significant than twelve? Trying to narrow the gap, are we?"

His lips part and he soon presses them in a line. "I don't care."

"But you do. You didn't like it when I called you a kid."

"That's because I'm not." He pops a strawberry into his mouth, and I fight to keep my attention from lingering on the red tinting his lips. "And I'm not falling for your changing-the-subject tactic, by the way. Why do you seem to know a lot of things about me? Like my brother being diagnosed? My relationship with my dad? Are you stalking me?"

"Wouldn't you love that?" I drag my gaze from his mouth to his eyes. "It didn't take much effort to piece it together. Your brother is an attention whore, and plenty of professors are aware of his diagnosis. A quick dive into both his and your social media gave me all the pieces I needed. In case it's not obvious, I have a knack for spotting patterns."

"So you *are* stalking me." Another strawberry. And another. He stuffs his mouth with three at the same time, and I watch his Adam's apple bob as he swallows them down. "You have IG?"

"Show some respect for your field of study and articulate your words fully. Don't lower yourself to the brainless habits of your peers."

"IG is Instagram, you dinosaur. You know, this app on which you can upload photos and videos so people can swoon and drool at your fake life?"

"I know what Instagram is, and I don't use social media."

"Hmm. Sus af."

"Carson."

"What?"

"Full words."

"Suspicious as fuck, Professor."

"Language."

"You're the one who wanted full words." He lifts his shoulder in a small shrug and eats more strawberries, one after the other, like a ravenous kid.

His mind is so sharp and criminally cunning that I often forget he's only twenty-two.

Twenty-one.

"So tell me, little monster, why are you here? Don't tell me you made the trip just to steal my strawberries." My voice lowers. "Unless you had another thing in mind to wrap those lips around?"

Carson shoots me a glare, pushing the bowl with only three strawberries left across the counter as he stands up, sliding between me and the stool.

He wants to tower over me. And I let him. Because I love how the lines in his face harden, and I want to see what the little menace is up to.

"Speaking of lips, how many other students have wrapped theirs around your cock, Professor?"

"How many do you think?"

His hand shoots to my neck before I can stop it, and he squeezes the flesh. It's strong enough that my breathing is cut off, but I allow him to choke me.

Who would've known his psychotic side was this adorable?

And a turn-on.

Because my cock is lengthening by the second.

But then again, I happen to be in this state whenever he's around.

This is turning into a serious problem.

"You seem to think I can't kill you just because I didn't last time." He lowers his face, speaking so close to my mouth, I can taste the strawberry off his lips. "You're right, I do repress that part of me, but it's such a hassle whenever I see your fucking face."

"Language," I strain through a smile.

"You—" He exhales sharply. "Did Zara suck your cock? Is that why you were singing her praises?"

"If that were the case, shouldn't I have been singing your praises as well?"

His lips part, and he narrows his eyes, clearly contemplating the meaning behind my words. "Why...didn't you?"

"Is that important?"

"My opening statement wasn't bad. It was clearly better than hers."

"That's debatable."

"No, it's not! You were just playing favorites." His pupils dilate and a manic look slips into his eyes, darkening them faster than an eclipse. "Is Zara that good at sucking cock?"

"I wouldn't know, considering she probably prefers women. She's got a thing for that girl who's always clinging to you and begging for your attention like a low-rent whore. Maybe you'd notice the way Jones looks at you with pure envy if you weren't so pathologically self-absorbed."

His grip loosens a bit and that calculating look rushes to his eyes, making them a darker green.

Rainy forest green.

Dead green.

He probably comes to the same conclusion as he connects patterns. Jones is so obvious that anyone with little analytical skills could tell. It's a pity she's crushing over a dumb girl, but smart people are usually stupid as fuck in these types of situations.

"Finished with the jealousy fit, baby?" I ask with a grin.

Carson's fingers tighten again, so hard, I cough, my airways closing and my lungs burning.

"I told you to stop calling me that. I'm not your baby!"

"Whatever...you...want...baby..." I battle to speak every word.

"This fucking..." He rolls the stool and shoves my head against the counter, the sharp sting reverberating in my skull, but I'm smiling up at him.

At his harsh breaths, his rising and falling chest as he leans close with that manic look in his eyes.

I love it.

The loss of control.

The confusion.

The chaotic fucking mania.

Honestly, he could kill me—maybe even by accident—but none of it matters when his strawberry-laced breath fans across my face, brushing against my lips like a forbidden whisper.

"Who else sucks your limp dick, Kayden?"

My vision blurs at the edges, but I reach out a hand and grab his face. He tries to pull away, his mouth falling open, but I tug him close and feast on those lips.

I shouldn't.

Kissing him is a boundary I'm not supposed to cross.

But fuck if I care.

I thrust my tongue inside his mouth before he can clamp his teeth shut, then slurp the remnants of strawberry off his tongue. I've never cared that much about the fruit, but now, mixed with him, it's an aphrodisiac that shoots straight to my balls.

He shakes, my little monster. He's losing all fucking control, shuddering like a goddamn leaf as a small noise escapes him.

And I use that noise to fucking devour him.

Nipping on his tongue, lips, eating his goddamn beautiful face until it's etched inside me.

He tastes like forbidden fruit—something I shouldn't even be near, let alone touch. And yet here I am, licking his skin, devouring and consuming him whole.

"Mmmf..." Carson tries to stop me, his fingers tightening, but it only lasts a second, one measly second of fight, before he bites my tongue.

Hard.

A metallic taste explodes in our mouths.

The menace sure loves to draw blood. I do, too, because my cock is thrusting against the thin fabric of my pants.

And I bite him back. He grunts, his hold loosening, and his taste exploding in my mouth.

Fucking beautiful. I can swallow him whole, both literally and figuratively.

He acts so disinterested until I touch him, and then he's putty in my hands.

A toy to play with however I goddamn please.

I wrap my arm around his lean waist and slam him down on top of me. We groan in unison as his bulge rubs against mine, because he's also hard, my little monster.

The line of his cock glides over mine, eliciting a shudder from him.

"Love it when you're hard for me, baby," I whisper against his lips, then sink my teeth into the pillowy surface of the bottom one and bite.

He grunts, the sound vibrating against my chest and rushing to my cock.

"Shut...the fuck up."

I bite harder until the skin breaks, then I lick on the small droplets of blood, wiping it clean. "Language."

"Fuck." His bulge grows hot and heavy, rubbing unconsciously, chaotically, like he can't control his hips.

"I said." I lower my hand from his waist and spank his ass over his jeans. "Language."

That makes him shake, his breaths coming in quick, fractured puffs. He truly loves the pain. It makes him lose inhibition and become such an adorable little slut.

He blinks, struggling to regain control of his thoughts. "Stop doing that."

"This?" I slap him again and he jolts, his neck growing red. "But you crave it far too much."

His lips tremble, but he chokes me again, shoving my head back on the island. "Don't touch me with hands you've had on other students."

"You're my one and only, baby."

I don't know why I say it. In reality, I shouldn't give a fuck what he thinks, and I certainly shouldn't be exclusive to the asshole, but I'm glad I said it, because something mesmerizing happens.

Red creeps up his neck, forming a hue over his fair complexion and tinting his ears red. The reddest I've ever seen.

And he all but loses strength in his hand. It's still around my neck, but it's unsteady and weak, so I lift my face again, darting my tongue and licking those ears.

The lobe, the shell, even thrusting my tongue inside, and he shivers. He's so hot and hard, it's driving me absolutely insane.

Because I can't get enough of his muffled noises.

His little twitches.

The way his green eyes brighten up until they're as clear as the Caribbean Sea.

The way his hand rests on my chest, tentatively, like he doesn't want to touch me, but he can't not do it.

Look at that. We really have so much in common.

"S-stop," he stutters and then puffs out a long, fractured breath against my face.

"Say it again and mean it, baby," I whisper right into his ear, and he jolts, muffling a noise. "You can't. Want to know why? Because you're desperate to see what I'll do next. You've been rubbing yourself against my cock, making it nice and hard so I can fuck you."

"You'll *never* fuck me." He headbutts me weakly, out of breath.

"Care to place a bet?" I wrap my hand around his throat and flip us over so fast, he blinks up in confusion as he half lies on the stool, his back to the island and I'm half lying on top of him, my knee jammed between his legs, right against his cock.

"There. Much better." I stroke his clean-shaven jaw, not really choking him. "You look stunning pinned beneath me."

Gareth's wide eyes lock with mine, a sharp flash of what

seems like panic darting across his face. The air thickens with charged tension as he whispers, "Let me go."

"You know the exact answer to that."

His breaths quicken, turning shallow, and I can feel the pulse racing in his throat like he's on the edge of something he can't control. It's the power, the idea that he has to give it to me —and he does *have* to give it to me—pushes him to the edge.

I expect him to try to hit me like he usually does when he's pushed, but he doesn't—he's trapped in the storm of his own confusion, exposed in a way I haven't seen before.

The shift in his energy pulls at something inside me, something cold and calculating, but also unsettling.

And I find my voice softening—as much softening as I can manage. "There's no need to fight the inevitable. I'll make sure you love every second of it."

"I don't want this."

"You're rock fucking hard. Stop lying."

"I..."

"What is it this time, Carson? Another one of your back-and-forth tactics?"

"No, it's..."

"It's what? Use your words and articulate clearly."

He gulps at the command, his eyes widening a bit and then says, "Let me do it, then."

"Let you do what?"

"Let me be the one who fucks you." His voice is so low, it's not like him.

He's just grasping at straws at this point.

It's obvious that Gareth isn't proactive but enjoys being devoured. The fact that he still can't see it—or more accurately, *admit* it to himself—after so many encounters is a bit concerning, but I must deal with this carefully so he doesn't balk.

"Do you even *want* that?" I ask, stroking his jaw again.

He gets distracted, his nostrils flaring and his eyes drooping a little as he speaks in the same quiet tone. "Yeah."

"Do you truly want it or are you just saying that so you don't have to surrender control and let me fuck you?"

"I won't be fucked," he snaps.

I see. So *that's* the problem.

"All right. You can fuck me."

His eyes widen, his body losing the tension, but that unsure edge still lingers on his pretty face. "Really?"

"Really. If you manage to flip us over so you're on top, I'll let you do it."

Most people would have a moment of hesitation, a few seconds where they think of the meaning or derive the best strategy.

Carson, however, doesn't waste time.

He bucks his entire body and grabs my arm to flip us. Unfortunately for him, I've already tightened my grip on his throat, my hand on his waist as I shove my knee further into his cock until he groans.

But he doesn't give up. Not when his face turns red or when his cock pulses against my knee, enjoying the wrestling a bit too much.

"We both get off on violence," I whisper against his ear. "You're just playing with fire now."

"Fuck you."

I bite down on the lobe. "Language, baby."

"Ugh—" He flails and even tries to knee me, but the position doesn't allow him to.

It doesn't matter that he works out and has a vigorous archery practicing schedule. I'm a trained killing machine he'll never win against.

That's why I made the offer—to make sure he loses, gives up, and sees there's no other way.

"You done?" I lick his lower lip, and it twitches, the wound oozing blood again. "Ready for my cock now?"

A shock goes through me.

Literally.

The next thing I know, I'm holding on to the island, then he kicks me and I'm on the ground.

Bolts of electricity surge through me, and I look up to see him holding a Taser, his chest heaving, hoodie pushed up to reveal a sliver of his waist.

"I should've electrocuted you in that tub, but then again, I don't want you to die yet." He pants, a little grin spreading across his face as those deep dimples make their first genuine appearance.

Deep. Mischievous. Malicious.

"It's time I play with you, Kayde." Then he grabs my arms and starts dragging me across the floor.

13
GARETH

This wasn't really part of the plan.

Not that I know what the plan was exactly except that I needed to confirm he wasn't fucking another student.

It's not that *I* care, but it's pride.

Something related to my demon's ego.

Okay, so maybe I've kind of got gory thoughts fit for snuff movies about the students who could've sucked his cock.

And about *him*.

Which is why I bought the Taser.

Listen, I meant to use it to torture him for answers, but then he said I was his one and only and that kind of confused the shit out of me. Because I liked it. So much so, I think I was speechless.

Something that I'd never experienced before.

So goddamn random.

I'm not supposed to like *anything* coming out of this man's mouth.

And yet here I am, dragging him to his bedroom, where he has all the ropes and lube and weird devices. I know because I snooped into his drawer of nightmares, hoping to find something, but, instead, ended up with visual assault.

Anyway, his skin is hot and a bit tingly due to the electrocution. Thanks to one of Niko's guards, I got one of those strong black-market ones. The dude specifically said it can't be used on anyone weighing less than a hundred eighty pounds or with any health issues. And that it can black out certain people, even if they're over the weight limit and have no health concerns.

My dear professor is slabs of muscle, so he's over two hundred pounds and he looks as healthy as Satan to me, so we're good on that front.

Unfortunately, he didn't black out, though, and keeps shaking his head.

I'm disappointed he didn't scream or even grunt when he took the hit. He would've looked hot.

Not that I think he's *hot*.

I mean he *is*, but that's beyond the point.

Once we're close to the bed, I try to lift him up and his entire weight falls on my shoulder, nearly knocking me over.

Jesus fuck.

The man is a truck. Or like this goddamn steel wall that's always hell-bent on crushing me.

"You'll be punished for this, you little fucker." His speech is a bit slurred.

"Language, Professor." I grin as I throw him on the bed.

He falls on his back at the edge, his cock forming a tent in his silky pants, apparently not fazed by the electricity. I have to adjust mine, because why the fuck is that view so tantalizing?

Starting to think asking these questions is a total waste of time because my dick has a mind of his own now. Guess I should stop overthinking these awkward boners around Kayden.

They happen. End of story.

Maybe tonight will be the end of it, once and for all.

I peel off my jeans and hoodie on autopilot, down to just my boxer briefs. When I look up, his dark stare is locked on me—rage or arousal, hard to tell.

With him, they're pretty much the same thing anyway.

I have a great body and even better posture, I know I do. Years of disciplined workouts and relentless archery training have made sure of that. Enough muscle to show off abs and look defined without being bulky.

I yank the knife from the holster strapped to my calf and leap onto him, straddling his waist. My gaze flickers to his chest, broader than mine, shoulders sculpted, and, seriously, eight abs? The snake tattoo coils across his torso, making him look like a dragon.

And that dragon is now at my mercy.

I spot a tiny lily tucked under the serpent's scales on his side, oddly out of place with the rest of the ink. Asking about it would scream interest, and I'm not about to go there. So I shift my focus to his face.

He stays perfectly still, his breaths shallow yet deep, breathing like he's wrestling with some invisible force. Electricity? Sure, let's go with that.

"Don't give me that look." I let the tip of my knife flirt with his chest, skimming close but never breaking skin. "You're the genius who said I could fuck you if I got on top. Didn't say I couldn't cheat, so I did. I kind of have to with assholes like you. Survival of the smartest, right?"

His cock presses against my ass, just the thin barrier of my boxer briefs and his pants between us, but I stay stubbornly upright, refusing to give him the satisfaction of even a millimeter of friction. Sure, I said I wanted to fuck him, but let's be real—I wouldn't know where to start. And if I'm being brutally honest, screwing a guy isn't exactly on my bucket list.

But being his bitch? Yeah, that's not in the cards either. The very idea makes my teeth itch.

Still, keeping my ass from giving in and grinding against him is becoming a full-time job, and my cock is not helping, stretching and aching like it's about to file an official complaint.

The frustration boils over, and I want to punch him for it— so I do. My fist flies up and slams into his ridiculously gorgeous face.

His head jerks to the side, and I grip his jaw, yanking him back to face me. "If you weren't in my life, none of this damn confusion would've happened!" *Punch.* "I could've gone on living just fine, no issues, no complications." *Punch.* "But tonight? Cherry was naked and all over me, begging me to fuck her, and I couldn't get it up." *Punch.* "Yet now, I look at you, and I'm about to lose it."

I'm panting, my knife hovering dangerously close to his heart. I should kill him. No, skin him alive and see what's hiding under all that flesh.

Maybe then I'll find the witch blood he's clearly cursed me with.

"I told you to get rid of her, didn't I?" His voice sounds a bit clearer, almost biting.

"What?"

"Cherry. I told you to get rid of her. In fact, I distinctly remember saying to get rid of *all* girls."

"That's none of your—"

His hand snaps to my throat, so fast it's almost supernatural for someone who was just fried by electricity.

Wait. Was he really paralyzed or just faking it?

I lash out blindly, my hand swinging and catching him in the abs —and I mean it *actually* catches him. It's not a deep cut, but it grazes him. Blood wells up in a neat line before trickling down, and for a second, I'm too fixated on the scene to hold on to the damn knife.

He knocks it out of my hand, the clatter sharp against the floor. I lunge to punch him, but he's faster, trapping both my arms in an iron grip and getting on top of me.

A frustrated growl rips out of me as I thrash, but it's useless. He's already reaching into the drawer and pulling out the ropes with terrifying calm.

"Wait..." I squirm and twist, desperation creeping into my voice. "Let's talk, okay? I'll negotiate. Just don't tie me up."

A feeling of helplessness washes over me at the thought. It was one thing when I was drugged, but now? Now, it feels like I'll be served to him on a silver platter.

"There's no negotiation, Carson." He tilts his head, all focus and quiet menace as he yanks my hands above my head and ties them to the headboard. The bindings feel tighter this time. I can't even budge. "You've tested my patience enough tonight. I might've let the cheap Taser stunt and even the punching slide, but I made it clear—no girls. I don't share my toys."

"I'm not a *toy*!" The sharpness in my tone surprises even me, and I hate the reasons clawing at my mind. Maybe it's my growing apprehension.

Or maybe it's because I hate being just a toy to him.

"Not *a* toy. *My* fucking toy." He tweaks my nipple, pulling a grunt from me as he moves, removing his pants, and then he sits on the pillow, his thighs caging my head. Blood drips from his wound onto my forehead, but he doesn't even flinch, like it's the least of his concerns. "You'll be punished for disobeying simple orders, Carson."

"Fuck you—"

He forces his cock all the way to the back of my throat. I choke, my eyes wide, my heart pounding with pure, desperate instinct.

I pull at the ropes, trying to shove him off, but they only bite deeper into my wrists.

"The next time you think about being naked with someone else, I want you to remember the punishment waiting for you." He holds his cock there at the back of my throat until I think he'll choke me to death. "I don't share what's mine, and you *are* mine. I can play with you, hurt you, even let you hurt me, but you belong to me and no one else, you hear me?"

I'm thrashing, survival instinct surging through my veins. My vision blurs, and then I realize it's tears. They're streaming down both sides of my face, soaking my temples.

He groans.

The motherfucker *groans*.

His fingers slide across my cheek, wiping them. "I have no qualms about hurting you. I will fuck your face until you cry every time you act like a slut for someone else, Carson. You can only be *my* slut. Am I clear?"

"Mmmff..."

Just when I think I'll black out, he pulls his dick out just the slightest bit to allow me some breaths, and then he's slamming in again. Saliva and precum flood my mouth and trickle out.

It hurts. My jaw, the back of my throat. Everything hurts.

And it's making my cock hard.

It's not even funny anymore. I'm being humiliated in the worst way possible and I'm hard?

Why?

Just why does the pain he inflicts make me so horny?

I rub my legs together, trying to get friction, something, *anything*.

"Your mouth was made to take cock." *Thrust.* Hold. "*My* cock. You look pretty when being stuffed full with *my* cock."

"Mmf," I mumble around his girth, and I don't know what I'm trying to say, or why my chest squeezed when he called me pretty.

"Your fuckhole will also take my cock so deep, you'll lose your goddamn mind. It's only a matter of time." *Thrust.* "You despise the idea of submitting because it shatters the grandiose image you have of yourself, but I *will* have you beneath me, whether you like it or not. You'll take my cock in my pussy and thank me for it."

I struggle to breathe, my ears ringing as he forces his cock all the way down my throat. I swallow around it, my airways constricting, and the discomfort sending a rush to my balls.

"You had the chance to fuck me, and you still played with your knife like the little deranged psycho you are. You know why?" He grabs a fistful of my hair, pulling at the roots. "Because you love being dominated, and you sure as hell don't like putting in the work. Bet it bored you to death with the girls."

I try to shake my head, to hit, to do anything, but I can't. I'm trapped by both his touch and his words.

It's breaking me down, stripping away the things I thought I knew about myself.

Because it's true. I really, *really* hated putting in the effort.

My least favorite thing about sex, actually.

Still thrusting into my mouth, Kayden reaches behind him and lowers my boxers just enough to grab my cock, stroking it in that delicious rough way.

Precum trickles onto his fingers and he uses it to jerk me painfully, just the way I like it.

The way he *knows* I like it.

I grunt around him, huffing a breath that makes him groan, the humming sound spreading in my chest.

God, I'm close.

I'm so stimulated and wound up, I'll come in no time.

"See? You're getting so hard by being used like a little slut." He thrusts deeper, brutally, making me feel his wrath, his punishment. "No one's ever seen you like this, and no one ever will."

I breathe through my nose, gasping around his large cock, the veins pulsing against my tongue, the walls of my mouth, and I'm feeling every agonizing inch.

Every aggression he promised.

He's big, like *really* huge in both length and girth, close to nine inches, if not more, so it actually hurts to be throat-fucked by his cock.

The fact that he doesn't hold back somehow makes me twitch and shudder in his hand.

It makes me so horny, too, because I'm apparently into pain.

So much so, my balls are close to explosion.

Just when I'm about to come, he fists the gland hard and presses on my cock's opening.

"Mffuck..." I groan and protest, but he just keeps thrusting and thrusting, and *thrusting*, while his hand on my cock remains motionless.

"This is a punishment, not a reward. You don't get to come." His pace grows rougher and more frantic, and I'm in agony. Because he won't let me come.

I've never felt this edged before—except when he did it the other time. He always toys with me and I'm helpless, completely at his nonexistent mercy.

What seems like forever passes, before he jerks me again.

I thrust my cock in his hand, shamelessly chasing the unhinged intensity I've never felt before.

The deeper he goes in my throat, the harder I thrust up, swallowing around him, wanting him to come, too.

"I said." He squeezes my cock again, stopping right before I shoot cum in his hand. "This isn't about your pleasure."

Fuck.

Fuck.

I'm turning delirious. Completely and utterly mindless, I think I'll kill someone just to come.

My skin tingles, tears streaming down my face and sweat covering me from head to toe as he pounds and pounds and pounds me with his cock. It's so far back, I think I'll swallow him.

He jerks me again, sending delicious waves through my wound-up abs, and then stops at the brink, right when I'm about to finally let go.

A small whimper leaves me, but I'm so numb, so light-headed, my lids grow heavy.

"Eyes on me. I'm not done." He pulls at my hair, startling me awake. "Your mouth is only mine, isn't it? I'm the only one who can choke it and stuff it full of my cum, right?"

I stare, dazed, really going out of it, actually. It's like I'm swimming in the middle of nowhere and I don't feel on edge.

My mind is blank, empty of all the thoughts and plans and lies. It's just a white room in the middle of nowhere, and it's only him and me here.

In that white room in my usually busy brain.

"Nod your head. Tell me I'm the only one you'll allow to touch you. Fuck you whichever way I please."

I nod without thought.

"Good boy. I love it when you're obedient."

Something lights up in my chest, and I blink at him as his blood trickles down my forehead and cheek, then mixes with his cock in my mouth.

I swallow around it, gulping the metallic taste and the precum.

"Fuuuck." He grunts, seemingly loving the view as much as I like the taste. "You're made for me, my little monster, aren't you?"

I nod again.

"Fucking Christ. I love how you take me. You feel so good, you know that?"

My stomach is full of these rampant little bats that are slaughtering each other, and I can't stop looking at him as I lick him and swallow around his crown just the way he likes it.

Because apparently, I love his praise.

It's sending me to the edge.

"I'm close. Mmm, you're doing so well, baby."

That spark comes again, and I swear the bats are multiplying by the second. I like that he's close and that I'm the reason, but mostly, I like that he's not calling me by my last name.

"Fuck," he grunts. "You going to drink my cum?"

I nod again, mesmerized as his abs tighten. The blood is still trickling down, making a mess, and I swallow anything that comes into my mouth, taken by his expression.

There's deep euphoria on his handsome face, an erotic bliss that shakes his large body, as he shudders and comes down my throat.

Somehow, I find myself licking around his cock as he pulls it out. Our eyes meet as cum cascades down either side of my mouth, mixing with the blood.

"What a mess," he mutters, his voice less harsh as his thumb grazes the corner of my lips.

And I have this urge to lick him. The cum and the blood.

The second shouldn't be a surprise since I'm kind of sick, but the first? What the fuck?

Since when did I become addicted to his cum?

My jaw aches, but it's nothing compared to how my cock stands painfully hard. So much so that I can't think past the constant throbbing.

"A *whole* fucking mess." His deep, raspy voice carries in the room like a whip as he glides down my abdomen and then over my cock, smudging it with blood.

I grunt, but he doesn't offer any friction as he kneels between my legs and removes my boxers, tossing them aside.

"Want a reward?" he asks with a small smirk. He really, really loves messing with me.

"Mmm." The sound is so low, I can barely hear it. It's hoarse, too. Damn, I think I'm losing my voice.

"Do you think you earned one?"

"Mmm."

"Use your words. Speak louder."

"Yeah." I try not to glare at him but probably do.

"Since you were obedient, you did earn this reward, baby."

My chest does that tightening thing again and my breathing deepens.

"Now, be a good boy and say please."

"P-please." I thrust up and he presses my hips back down.

"Patience."

I groan but say nothing, not wanting to provoke him, not when I'm practically dying. I have no doubt this asshole would leave me like this the whole night just to teach me a lesson.

His gray eyes flicker, like he's waiting for me to rebel, and then a soft light glimmers in them.

A hint of pride?

Why would he feel that for me?

And why does it feel like a gentle caress on my face?

"Mmm. Since you're behaving yourself, I'll let you experience completely submitting to me and liking it."

I start to tense up, thinking he'll fuck me, but he pulls my legs apart and lifts my ass so that I'm on my upper back and shoulders, and then his mouth is on my ass cheeks, peppering kisses and nibbling.

At first, I'm confused, but then it hits me when he darts his tongue out and licks my back hole.

A jolt rushes through me and my ears feel like they're going to explode.

"W-wait...what are you..."

He lets out a hum against my hole, the sound reverberating somewhere inside me as he licks and slurps around the rim until I think I'll either detonate or die of shame.

"Take what I give you, baby." He speaks against me, his hoarse voice vibrating through me before he thrusts his tongue inside.

My whole body convulses and a strange noise rips out of my throat. I try to thrash, but his big hands are digging into my thighs, preventing me from moving.

I pull at the ropes, moaning. "Mmfuck..."

I can't help but watch through the awkward position as he thrusts his tongue in and out, in and out, the rhythm making my cock leak down my abs, the stickiness trailing to my chest.

I'm so damn close, I cry out.

His eyes meet mine, shining, challenging, and I look back even as I grunt, biting my lip.

Fuck.

Motherfucker.

"K-Kayde...fuck..."

"That's it, baby." He looks at me. "Come for me. Show me how much my pussy loves it when I eat it."

He nibbles on my balls, then slides his tongue back to my hole.

That does it.

I groan loudly as my dick shoots cum everywhere, my abs, my face, the bed. It's the strongest orgasm I've ever had, and that's saying something since all the orgasms this man has given me have been mind-blowing.

But this one? This one pulls on the last string of my sanity.

It's like being transported to a different headspace. That white room again. All mine.

And *his.*

A nibble on my ass cheek brings me to the present before

he lets my legs down. They fall lifeless, and cool cum trickles down my belly and onto the mattress.

It's a messy clusterfuck, but I can't seem to focus on that as I watch him from beneath lowered eyelids.

He hovers on top of me and strokes my hair from my forehead, his touch gentle, and it creeps me the fuck out. Because I kind of like it.

And I *shouldn't* like it.

"That's why you'll take my cock, baby. Not because you're forced into it, but because you're not that proactive but enjoy being ravaged and can come with ass play alone."

"I don't. You're the goddamn gay one," I say with a weak voice.

He chuckles, the sound low. "Don't use that as an insult. It's beneath you, and you're better than that. If I can accept wanting you and eating your ass, you can accept being attracted to me, too."

I want to say no, I'm not, but my lids are heavy, so I let them fall.

I think I feel him untying the ropes and cleaning the cum—and blood—off me, but I can't be bothered to get up.

Just a sec. I just need a power nap and then I'm fucking him up.

In the middle of the haze, I think I feel his fingers stroking my hair as he says, "You should be thanking your lucky stars that I want you, little monster."

14

GARETH

"**J**oin us!"

I sidestep Niko's hand as he tries to drag me into the pool.

"What a killjoy." He narrows his eyes as he floats on his back, kicking Jeremy, who's chilling in the water by the edge, hyperfocused on his phone. He doesn't even pay attention to Niko's attempts to start a fight.

Jeremy's been more wound up than usual, which I would've paid better attention to if I weren't stuck in my own head.

I walk to Glyn's side and offer her a glass of her favorite pink grapefruit soda that my brother stocks in the mansion for her.

She beams up at me, her features softening.

Glyn is Killian's new obsession. His only obsession, really.

I've never seen anyone have such a deep effect on him—until her.

She's pretty, I guess. Delicate, round face, long chestnut hair with blonde strands, and those inquisitive eyes.

But that's not special, not for Kill, anyway. He's had countless people, of all genders, throwing themselves at him, and he never gave a single one the time of day—especially Cherry.

But Glyn? She's like a spoiled British princess, minus the pretentiousness, and there's this innocence about her that someone like Killian would love to break.

I don't understand it. I prefer being with my match instead.

At the thought of that asshole, I scoff on the inside and sit down, trying not to think about what happened two weeks ago. The pleasurable punishment and mind-blowing sex.

The type of sex that I can't stop thinking about.

After which he disappeared.

For two weeks.

Sick leave, apparently.

Hope he dies.

"Thanks," Glyn says with a smile. "You're so kind."

"It's nothing." I check my watch. "Kill has a late shift, I believe. He might not be here for a while."

"I know. I just like talking to you." She grins. "I feel comfortable around you and kind of feel camaraderie because we both have to deal with Kill."

Right. So she's *that* naïve.

I guess I did paint the image that I was struggling to deal with Kill my entire life, but I also tried to kiss her about a week ago just to mess with him, and he nearly killed me.

In my defense, it was right after the initiation night, and I was suicidal.

"But you've been dealing with him for longer, so it must've been hard." She gives me a look of pure sympathy.

The girl who's kind of trapped in a relationship with my brother actually has the capacity to worry about me.

I guess that's...normal? This is how people who don't have the constant thoughts of inflicting violence or just chasing after more pain feel.

But I think Glyn's just that pure, in a way.

"Worry about yourself," I say with no maliciousness whatsoever, staring at Niko splashing water at Jeremy.

She takes a sip of her soda. "Guess I'm used to it."

"Used to it or used to the thrill?"

"Both?"

"The thrill eventually goes away, so search for another branch to hold on to."

She swallows, her throat working up and down. "You know Kill would never let me go."

"The real question is, are you willing to let *him* go?"

She falls silent, and I can see the unsettling realizations rushing to her wide eyes, darkening them, even making them glisten with unshed tears.

It's one of my superpowers, I think—making people face things they never would've considered otherwise. I don't waste it on anyone I don't care about, and I don't particularly want to hurt her.

She's probably the best thing that's ever happened to Kill. Since she entered his life, he's less consumed by chaos and even stopped pestering me.

And I'm thankful.

Despite my flawless act, pretending to be all about school and maintaining the perfect GPA, I'm on edge. No one notices, of course. But there's a fire building inside me, swelling, growing, threatening to burn everything down.

Like an inferno.

"Come here, Gaz! Let me drown you!" Niko splashes water our way, and I grit my teeth when some of it hits me.

But Kill rushes in, immediately shielding Glyn from the mess.

"Should've mentioned you were coming. Miss me already?" He grins down at her, still in his white coat. Wouldn't surprise me if he cut his internship short just to be here.

"Who says I'm here for you?" She glares up at him. "I actually came around to talk to Gareth."

Well, fuck me catching strays.

Kill tilts his head toward me, a murderous glint narrowing his eyes.

I lift my hands, smiling. "I plead not guilty. Not my fault I'm better company than you. Right, Glyn?"

"The fuck did you just say?" Kill growls.

"I'm just repeating Glyn's words," I tease. "She said I'm better company than you and that she's more comfortable around me."

It's that suicidal mode again—the need to provoke, to get my head rattled or something.

Anything, really.

Kill starts toward me, but Glyn grabs his arm, and to my surprise, he stops dead in his tracks. He looks down at her, like he's completely forgotten I exist—or that anyone else is around.

Then he drags her away.

To fuck, I suppose.

As I watch them disappear, my mind keeps circling back to that look in his eyes when she touched him. Manic...mixed with something else. Reason? No, calm?

She calms him? How the hell does she do that?

And why does he get that, while I'm left drowning in this raging volcano of emotions I can't even explain?

Kill is the one person who resembles me the most. In a twisted way, I consider him someone who belongs to me. The other day, he was attacked and I felt murderous because I don't like people touching what's mine.

But right now, I'm more...*envious.*

Of what? Him? His relationship? His goddamn luck?

Fuck this.

I pull out my phone and frown at the thousand notifications I got on some stupid Reddit thread I made with a throwaway account.

All so I wouldn't text that prick Kayden.

After the most intense sexual experience of my life, I woke up alone in his bed.

And he was gone.

Waiting for me on the kitchen counter, I found a strawberry smoothie, another bowl of strawberries, and a plate of breakfast food covered with plastic wrap.

The note said, "Eat so you'll have the strength to handle me."

I crumpled it.

But I did eat because I was hungry. Surprisingly, I was all clean and smelled like him, as if he ran a cloth with his shower gel all over my body.

I was fuming at the humiliation of it all, at him being right— that I might enjoy submitting and taking whatever he dishes out.

I hated how much it upset me.

And was ready to headbutt and punch him again. But not right away, because, honestly, my ass and jaw hurt, and I thought if he tied me up and touched me again, he might as well fuck me and erase my last shred of dignity.

So I stayed away.

For, like, three days.

And then I was pissed off because he didn't get in touch at all.

I saw him on campus, so I knew he was teaching other

classes and doing just fine, but he didn't send any of his distasteful texts.

And I got more furious at myself for wanting his texts. It's not like we're in a damn relationship or anything, so why would he check in?

Anyway, even if he did text, I would've ignored him.

So I was looking forward to class to ignore him harder while I impressed him with my witness questioning skills.

But he called in sick on that day.

He wasn't on campus the whole week.

And he wasn't in his house. Yes, I went in again two times after he called in sick just to kick his face in and make him sicker.

Okay. *Three* times.

I don't know where the hell he's been, and I refuse to text him first. That's just *not* going to happen.

Because, in reality, I should be elated that he finally fucked off out of my life.

And I am.

That's all I wanted.

Right?

But somehow, the hole of emptiness I was born with has been burning at the edges like paper, slowly but steadily growing in size.

The PI, Nadine, wasn't of any help. She just sent me what I asked for.

His yearbook picture in which he looked hot—*kill me*.

His favorite color is gray. Boring fucker.

He doesn't have a favorite show or movie and doesn't actually watch them.

His favorite music is classical, which I kind of knew, and his favorite composers are Bruckner and Rachmaninoff for some reason. Something I need to look into further.

The most surprising fact I learned is that he played hockey up through college.

His parents separated when he was nine and he chose to live with his father.

I'm paying Nadine more to dig further, although I considered asking her to locate him right now.

But then I thought better of it and made this stupid thread on one of those NSFW advice forums.

An impulse in the moment just to see what normal people think about this. I kept it generic.

Title: *"I'm not gay, but I can't stop thinking about my superior —Help?!"*

Let me start by saying this: I'm not gay. I've never been into men or found them remotely attractive. But if I'm honest, I haven't exactly felt that way about women either. I've just gone through the motions because, well, society. I can get hard when needed and make sure the girls have a good time, but truthfully? It feels like a chore. I don't enjoy it—except for the climax and maybe a little of the power play.

Now, here comes the curveball: my superior. I won't go into details about how we met or where, but let's just say it wasn't under ideal circumstances. I hated him on sight. Yet, somehow, this guy has unleashed a side of me I didn't even know existed.

He's the only man I've ever found attractive, and it's driving me out of my mind. I can't stand him as a person, but every time he's near, I get this primal urge to push back, to defy him. And, of course, he loves the cat-and-mouse game. The whole dynamic is infuriating.

I'll admit it—the oral sex was next level. He has this way of blending pain with pleasure, and as much as I hate to confess it, I liked it. It gave me some of the most intense orgasms of my life. But here's where it all gets messy: I hate the thought of another man fucking me. It's just something I can't wrap my head around.

And yet when the tables turned and I had the chance to fuck him, I froze. Couldn't do it. He says I like to be dominated, and that cut deep because I thought I was the one calling the shots.

Now, he's ghosted me. Part of me is relieved, but the other part? Seething. Frustrated. He claimed he wasn't into men either, but I don't know if I buy that—especially since he always seems ready to...well, you get the picture.

So what's happening here? Is this just some weird one-time thing, or am I heading for the mother of all sexuality crises?

It was flooded in the span of a day. I scroll through the comments, my frown deepening by the second.

Looks like y'all are having a bi-awakening at the same time. Go ride that dick, my man.

My bro is having both gay and masochist awakening. Pray for his ass.

WHY THE FUCK DOES THAT LOOK LIKE SOMETHING NIKO WOULD write?

I read through more trolls.

Bro, you're describing a romance novel but with less love and more frustration. Maybe you've just found your 'enemy-to-lovers' kink.

I'm not saying you're gay, but the fact that you can't stop thinking about the guy who 'ghosted' you after giving you the best orgasms of your life kinda says otherwise. Just saying.

You're not gay, but you're definitely confused, my dude.

Someone hand this man a mirror so he can check if he's 'straight' or just really into mind games and power dynamics.

Plot twist: you're just really into mindfucks.

I pause at that one but continue reading the most awarded comments with more serious answers.

It sounds like you're in a confusing place. Attraction and sexuality are complicated, and it's normal to feel conflicted. Your feelings toward this guy might not even be about sexuality but could stem from power dynamics or unresolved emotions. Take some time to reflect on your feelings and relationships.

You seem torn between what's familiar and something entirely new. Don't shame yourself for your feelings, even if they're confusing. If you're unsure about your sexuality, explore it without pressure or labels. There's no need to force yourself into a box—just feel and figure it out as you go.

You're not necessarily gay, but it sounds like there's a deeper emotional tension at play. Stepping back to examine your relationship with power, control, and submission might help. These dynamics can sometimes blur with sexual attraction, especially when they challenge your understanding of desire.

I exit the thread and turn off notifications when everyone starts asking about any updates and putting forth personal questions. One of them said, 'Big dick?' and I wanted to reach out and punch them and say, 'So is mine. Your point?'

It's not about dick size. Bunch of morons.

This was a shit idea in the first place.

Also, why is everyone talking about emotions and stupid shit I don't even relate to?

Useless. Every last one of them.

A few people message me, and I ignore them, too, but one catches my interest.

QUIETRAGE

Hey, man, I'm actually going through the exact same thing right now. I've never been attracted to a guy before, but this one guy is flipping my world upside down, and suddenly, I'm feeling all kinds of things I didn't expect. It's confusing af, like my brain can't keep up with it all and it's kinda affecting my day-to-day life. So, yeah, just wanted to let you know you're not the only one dealing with this.

TOOPRETTYFORTHISMESS (WHAT? I AM.)

Thank fuck. It's kind of driving me insane ngl.

Bcz u want it or don't want it?

Idk, I don't think I mind oral anymore, but even that is hard to admit out loud.

Ever thought of trying with other guys?

Why? U offering?

Nah, idk where to start with that tbh lol but heard from a friend of a friend that porn helps 😏

Can't watch that. I don't find it hot like at all. I find all porn cringe somehow.

Man, you might be on the asexual spectrum.

The ones who don't like/don't have sex? Because I do.

Nah, ace is actually a whole spectrum. Like you might not like sex at all or you may only like masturbation. You can also love your partner but don't want to engage in physical action, or you might be demi where you only become sexually attracted to the person you develop feelings for. Or gray which is like experiencing limited sexual attraction. TMI lol I've been reading too much about it lately. Take a look around. You might find it enlightening.

I'm still rereading the guy's text when my phone slips from my hand, clattering to the ground as I'm yanked suddenly.

By Nikolai.

Before I can react, he's dragging me toward the pool. "Got you!"

I'm soaked in a second as he holds my head underwater and his laugh echoes in the air. "Told you to join. Should've listened!"

Instead of flailing around, I just float still, thinking about what the dude said on Reddit.

Should I just try another guy. Is that it? Taste someone else's cum and touch someone else's abs? And suck someone else's dick?

Why does the mere idea disgust me?

"You're gonna fucking kill him, Niko!" Jeremy's voice reaches me first before he pulls me from the water.

I suck in a breath, gasping, only then noticing the fire in my lungs.

"Pfft, it doesn't take that little to kill my Gaz." Niko head-locks me, jamming his fist against my head. "Right?"

I grab him by the head and shove him down, holding him underwater as he tries to overpower me. Motherfucker interrupted my train of thought.

See, I can beat someone bigger than me.

You just choose not to with Kayden, you little slut.

Fuck off, demon.

"Gareth?" Jeremy looks at me as if I've been possessed and is considering whether or not to call the local priest.

I loosen my grip, allowing Niko to resurface again, but before he comes for the attack, I lift myself out of the pool.

"Boo!" Niko yells. "Come back here and fight me, you boring bitch."

"Not in the mood for your antics." I remove my shirt and shorts, remaining in my boxers, then dry myself.

I run a towel through my hair as I grab my phone and head upstairs. My steps falter in the middle of the stairs, a rush of electricity bolting through me when I see a text.

DEVIL

I'm hurt. Are you seriously not going to check to see if I'm dead?

ME

I was hoping you were.

Ouch. Direct hit to the heart.

Surprised you have one tbh.

Full. Words.

TO. BE. HONEST.

Why are you yelling?

Because I want to punch you.

You always let the violence take over, baby. I'm starting to enjoy it.

A shiver goes through me and I doubt it's because of the cold.

The fire that's been consuming me is so strong now, I feel like exploding.

> Don't call me that if you're just going to disappear.

> But I was sick.

> With pathological lying, because you weren't home.

> My, upping the stalking game?

> Don't deflect.

> I was seriously ill. Had to be treated at a private clinic in Switzerland.

> You want me to believe that?

> It's your choice whether or not you believe me, but I did miss you, baby.

My heart thumps so loudly, I'm actually alarmed. Note to self: find a heart specialist to fix this malfunction.

> Your goddamn hoarse voice when you come haunts my dreams. I can still feel how the walls of your pussy strangled my mouth and it's been driving me insane.

Instant boner.

"Seriously?" I mutter at myself, then frown because now, I'm turning into Niko, who loves talking to his dick as if it's a person.

> I wanted to test you, see how long it'd take before you messaged me first. I'd rather deal with your hot and cold than go through this again. Just thinking of you makes me so hard.

My throat closes when he sends a picture.

Of him fisting his cock through his PJ bottoms. Even though he's not naked, the thin material leaves nothing to the imagination. The lines of his cock are clear in the picture and when I zoom in, I can see those veins—

I release it as if I've been burned when another text appears.

> I want you to choke on my cock and let me come down that throat. Better yet, I want to stuff my cock in my tiny little cunt, baby. Let me fuck you. I'll make sure you like it.

> No.

> What if I say please?

> Nope.

> You're playing with fire, baby. Just say yes while I'm asking nicely.

> You're not going to fuck me, Kayde.

> Yet.

> Ever.

> Stop flirting with me.

> When did I?

> The idea of forcing you turns me on, baby. You're well aware of that fact, and yet you still pull these stunts. I think you're doing it on purpose.

He sends another picture, and in this one, his abs are on full display, his PJs pulled down enough to show his groin.

Cock-fucking-tease.

I hurry up to my room so no one sees me battling with a goddamn boner.

As I linger behind the door, staring at the picture he sent and winding myself up, something catches my eye.

Something that shouldn't be there.

A red-patterned silk scarf lying by the foot of his bed.

It's feminine, delicate—not his style at all. I've never seen him wear a silk scarf, and I know for a fact he doesn't own any.

Yes, I checked his wardrobe.

My eyes narrow.

Who does that belong to, and why is it in his bedroom?

Not that I care.

———

An hour later, I punch in the code to his apartment.

Snooping around here is pointless—I've done it before. No matter how hard I look, everything is annoyingly in order. Just a typical professor's place.

He doesn't even have a TV, the weirdo. Just a record player and some vinyl records.

The scent of something delicious cooking hits me as soon as I step inside, flooding my senses.

Then, the cold press of a gun clicks against my shoulder.

I freeze, my hands lifting slowly as a petite woman with East Asian features, shoulder-length hair, and piercing dark-brown eyes steps into view.

"Who the fuck are you?" she asks in a no-nonsense tone.

I narrow my eyes on her. This is the owner of the scarf? So his type is middle-aged Asian women? What the *fuck*?

If I can reach into my calf holster and get my knife—

"Jina!" a slender woman with shiny blonde hair calls in a soft voice. She walks into the living area, the red scarf wrapped around her neck, supporting Kayden.

He's leaning on her, his face pale and complexion different.

So he *is* sick?

And who the hell are these women?

His gaze locks onto mine, emotions flickering through his gray eyes, shifting between light and dark. His jaw tics, but his face quickly smooths out as he detaches from the blonde and strides toward us.

"Honey, be careful," she calls after him, extending her arms like she expects him to collapse, as if she could catch someone twice her size.

Wait a damn minute. Did she just call him *honey*?

"It's fine, Mom," he says with a gentle smile, placing a hand on Jina's arm.

Mom?

I'm getting whiplash. Since when is he this soft? And wait—does that mean he's half Asian?

"He's an intruder who just walked in," Jina says, not lowering the gun.

"Put the gun down, sweetie. What the hell?" Blondie says, throwing Kayden a distracted glance before gently pulling Jina's shoulder.

"He might hurt Kayden, Rachel. You never know."

"He's just my student, Mom. You can let go," Kayden says, calm but firm, removing the gun from Jina's hand and clicking the safety back on with practiced ease.

That was smooth. Does he shoot targets or something? Most people aren't that comfortable around guns.

The more I learn about him, the less, I realize, I know.

"Why doesn't your student ring the bell like a normal human being?" Jina narrows her eyes at me like a stern teacher. "Where are your manners, boy?"

"Sweetie," Rachel scolds.

"Ma Jina is right, Mom." Kayden's eyes stay on me, though he's speaking to them. "He has no manners."

I glance between the three of them. Two moms. Married, judging by their matching wedding bands that I didn't see in my red haze earlier.

Rachel must be his biological mother—he's got a faint resemblance to her. She must've married Jina after separating from Kayden's dad.

Well, this is interesting. Finally, someone—two someones— who might shed some light on him.

"You can leave now," he says in his usual firm tone, brooking no argument.

Too bad for him, I have other plans. I flash my most charming, golden-boy smile and address his moms.

"I'm so sorry for barging in. I was just really worried about Professor Lockwood. He's kind of a star on campus, and his absence has been felt."

His eyes narrow, but I ignore him.

"Oh my," Rachel says. "Don't worry about it... I didn't catch your name."

"Gareth," I say, sidestepping Kayden and shaking her hand. "Old-fashioned, I know. I was named after my grandfather because my mom missed him so much."

"That's so sweet. I wish I had a story like that. I'm Rachel, and this is my wife, Jina. She can be overprotective over Kay, so don't take it personally."

Kayden's mom calls him "Kay." Hmm.

"I understand completely. My apologies again, ma'am." I offer my hand to Jina, who shakes it with more force than necessary.

"Don't do that again, or you might actually get shot," she warns.

"Jina!" Rachel says, exasperated, while Kayden smirks smugly.

"Promise." I keep smiling and nod toward the oven. "I think something's burning."

Jina mutters what sounds like curses—Korean, maybe, judging by the dramas my cousin Maya forces us to watch— and runs off.

"What a shame." Rachel sighs. "I was hoping to invite Gareth to dinner."

"There's no need, Mom," Kayden says firmly.

"Nonsense. No one comes here and doesn't eat. Give the kid a break, Kay."

I smile at her. "I'm no chef, but I'm an excellent sous-chef— according to my mom, though that might not be the best endorsement."

"Aw, bless you. But you really don't have to."

"It's the least I can do after intruding." I step toward the kitchen, but Kayden blocks my path, his pale face taut, jaw ticking.

"What are you doing, Carson?" he whispers, low and close enough that I can feel his minty breath on my lips.

"Figuring you out." I jab a finger at his chest. "Brace yourself to see me in my full glory tonight, Kayde."

15

KAYDEN

The last thing I wanted was for my moms to meet Carson.

That was literally the last thing I'd ever wish for.

But then again, I never thought he'd actually show up, especially after playing hard to get. But he thrives on the push-and-pull nonsense, so I should've seen it coming.

My second miscalculation was not changing the code as soon as my moms showed up. They're not supposed to know where I live right now, but, of course, the bastard Jethro gave them the address.

"What? They were worried sick, and Jina threatened to kill me," was all he said in his defense.

So now, I have three dangerous variables in my house. My

moms aren't dangerous, not by a long shot, but the real danger lies in their encounter with Carson.

"You sure you don't want to lie down, hon?" Mom rubs the back of my hand as we sit together at the table.

Although she's been through a lot, she's still beautiful in a delicate way. Her face is small, her movements soft, and she always wears her hair in this elegant bun with a couple of strands escaping.

But as she looks at me, a deep frown forms on her forehead, and her eyes are slightly red. As soon as they arrived, she hugged me and cried for what felt like an hour. Mom Jina tried to hold it together, but then she was hugging us, too, tears streaming down her face.

I can't stand seeing them cry. I'll be the first to admit that I have little to no capacity for interpersonal emotions, but I've always seen my moms in a different light.

Maybe it's because of the protective streak I've developed after everything I've witnessed. Maybe because they've already suffered more than anyone should, and I hate to see them in pain again.

That's why I keep them completely out of my business.

My gaze shifts to Mom Jina, who's scolding her amateur sous-chef. Carson just grins and apologizes, letting her sharp words slide right off him. I can't help but watch the dimples that crease his cheeks, making him look so young and charming, almost...normal.

Almost.

If I didn't know him, I'd probably think he was the most well-mannered kid. But then again, I really don't like thinking of him as a kid.

That's just disturbing, to say the least.

"Hon, are you listening?" Mom squeezes my hand.

"Yes?"

She smiles knowingly.

"What?"

"Oh, nothing," she speaks with cryptic glee. "I was just asking if you need more rest, but you seem energized."

Pissed off, more like. I want Carson gone, but I doubt I'd manage that now that he wormed his way into what would've been a quiet evening otherwise. Mom seems halfway in his pocket already.

He does have the knack to mess with my system to no end.

I face her and lower my voice. "No personal information revealed tonight, Mom. Promise me."

"Why?" she whispers back. "Is he *that* important?"

"It's because he's *not* important that he doesn't need to know anything. I'm serious, Mom. Nothing. He's an outsider."

"If you say so." She laughs along, seeming too giddy for someone who said they'd die if something happened to me not half an hour ago.

"What are you laughing about?" Carson is carrying two dishes, smiling like the ray of fucking sunshine he's not. "Can I join?"

"Oh, certainly." Mom gets busy as they both set the table.

When I try to help Mom Jina, she just scolds me in Korean and basically tells me to sit the fuck down and not aggravate my injury.

Well, they think it's an injury. In fact, I've been helping the motherfucker I grew up with, Julian, do his stupid medical experimentation in exchange for him helping to cover my tracks with my brother, Grant.

I still have to meet Grant once in a while, but at least he won't show up and sabotage what I have here. Using my body as collateral means nothing. My physical form is only a weapon I wield to get where needed and another device of power.

Considering my upbringing, physical pain never fazed me and never will.

My moms think I got into an accident, thanks to Jethro, who at least kept his mouth shut for once.

Soon enough, we're all sitting around the table staring at enough food to feed an army. Mom made Korean-style roast chicken and fusion salads incorporating kimchi, then added dozens of her side dishes that she brought over and stocked my fridge with—while shaking her head at my 'bad eating habits.'

Apparently that's because I don't cook, and she hates that. Mom Jina thinks any food that's not homemade is unhealthy and shouldn't be consumed.

"Eat a lot." She stuffs my bowl of rice full of chicken and kimchi, then does the same to Mom. "You, too."

"Thank you for the food, sweetie." Mom rubs her hand on the table.

I'm glad they both seem happy. Took them a long time to come this far.

Mom Jina was there since before I was born. In fact, she was there as her best friend when Mom nearly died from domestic abuse. They grew up together but separated around college. That's when Mom had an arranged marriage with dear old Dad as his second wife.

My moms reunited around then, and Mom Jina fought for Mom's freedom. They both did. Against Dad, and the people controlling my dad, and even that motherfucker Grant.

Even though Mom is his stepmom, she treated him well after his own mom took a rope to her throat because she couldn't handle being with Dad anymore.

Honestly, if Mom hadn't met Mom Jina again, she would've had the same fate as Grant's mom.

She went through almost ten years of emotional and physical abuse, but she eventually managed to escape.

Which is why I'll never drag them into the mess again.

"The food is amazing," Carson says, and his voice sends both apprehension and appreciation through me.

I like how it's deep but not too low, and now that he's speaking cordially and being on his best behavior, he sounds smooth and hot.

No idea why I find him hot, but I do. His voice, his face, his body. It's all so perfectly proportionate and tantalizing that I want to own every inch of him.

Lock him in a cage so only I can look at him.

My cock twitches and I lift another spoon of rice to ignore it. We're literally in my parents' presence, but all I keep thinking about is burying my dick in Carson.

Of all people, and even all men, it's fucking *Carson*.

"I love kimchi." He grins. "I first tried Korean food a couple of years ago at my cousin's insistence, and I've been a fan ever since."

"That shows good taste," Mom Jina says with a note of approval.

I give her a look. Seriously, I expect her not to fall for his grandiose charms.

She clears her throat. "So, Gareth, how are you doing in school?"

"Top of my class, ma'am. 4.7 GPA."

"That's amazing," Mom marvels. "You're like a genius."

"Not bad," my other mom says. She has a weakness for studious people, and something tells me she likes the asshole now.

Fuck me sideways.

"Not amazing enough since I'm still not Professor Lockwood's favorite." He flashes them a small pout, acting like the most pitiful little monster on earth.

I scoop a spoonful of rice with chicken, my eyes on his pale green ones. "You'll have to work harder for that, Carson."

He narrows those eyes but only for a second before he takes a piece of cucumber and munches on it. Hard.

I know he's trying to make me think he'll bite my dick or

something equally obnoxious, but it's only managing to stimulate my cock into a state of arousal.

What a flirt.

"Oh, he *must* be your favorite," Mom says. "He's so well-mannered and loveable."

"It's okay. I think he just needs time," Carson replies with a boyish smile.

Letting my lips curve with a grin, I say, "I think you're the one who's been stalling for time."

He purses his lips and my grin widens. Why does messing with him bring me so much joy? I love his reactions around me and how he can't really control them.

"Or maybe you already have another favorite," Carson shoots back. "You can share with the table, *Professor*."

I'd say Jones, but then I'd be putting a target on her back. I joke about it, but Carson is a little psycho—a young one, at that—so he gets impulsive, and I don't want to be the reason behind the murder of a top student.

My gaze remains on him as I take a sip of wine. "I'm just waiting for you to do better and be my favorite."

"Challenge accepted." Fire ignites in the depths of his eyes, and it's almost a crime how bright they are.

"You guys seem so close," Mom says with the same knowing look from earlier.

"He's just a student," I say.

"We're not," Carson says at the same time, then smiles at Mom. "He's kind of a dictator, actually. It's hard to imagine how he never got your guys' cool temper."

"That's because we didn't really raise him." Mom's fingers tremble around her spoon. "Well, not all the time, anyway. He was brought up by his dad."

Her expression sours, and Mom Jina strokes her hand gently.

"I'm sorry for bringing up something that upsets you," Carson says. "He's still lucky to have you."

"We're lucky to have him." Mom side-hugs me. "Don't worry us again. I know accidents happen, but be careful."

"I will."

"It was an accident?" Carson narrows his eyes. "I thought you were sick."

"Oh, it was this bad accident. Thank God the car took the hit and he only suffered from bruises and stuff, but it was scary as hell and we rushed here immediately." Mom, the resident oversharer, ladies and gentlemen. And this is after I practically *begged* her not to say anything.

"That must've been a shock." He shows my mom his most sympathetic look, but then he glares at me for a fraction of a second. "We were also *so* worried."

If I went by his tone alone, I would believe him, but then again, why would I want to believe him?

"I didn't know Professor Lockwood drives," he veers the conversation again. "He usually walks to campus."

"Just because you don't see me drive doesn't mean I don't sometimes," I say before my moms share any unnecessary details.

Like I've been in the States, not in Switzerland like I told him. Partly to be Julian's lab rat and to take care of the Grant problem, even temporarily.

Carson gives me a mysterious look, but then he tactfully changes the subject. He talks about his family and his mom and how close he is to his dad and grandfather. He puts all his qualities at the forefront, shamelessly using his golden boy persona to charm his audience.

I'm immune to that, but I can't help listening to him talk. His cool voice and delivery are top notch, and he'd make an excellent attorney—but he won't hear that from me.

Mom is definitely under his spell while Mom Jina tries and

fails not to like him. She even starts putting food in his bowl, which is a clear indicator of her feelings.

If she feeds you, she cares about you.

Once Carson senses they've warmed up to him, he switches tactics and starts asking about me.

"I've been curious, actually." He takes a sip of water. "When did Professor Lockwood's love for law start?"

"College years, wasn't it?" Mom says.

Carson tops off her glass of wine. "I can picture him being the best in his class."

"Of course he was," Mom Jina says proudly. "No one could beat my boy."

"That's impressive. Maybe the reason he chose teaching law instead of practicing it is because he wants to help others achieve that," he says with a smile.

"Practicing?" Mom asks.

"Yeah, Mom. I don't do that much anymore, remember?" I keep my cool, because I should've seen the little prick's tricks from a mile away. He's been asking seemingly harmless questions but digging deeper every time.

I really underestimated his ability to charm people.

So I expertly change the subject, but he somehow returns to his line of questioning. It's a seemingly endless tug-of-war until the end of dinner.

He jumps to help Mom, making her smile wide when he compliments her red scarf.

"That boy of yours better watch it and stop flirting with my wife," Mom Jina mutters under her breath in Korean as she takes a sip of wine.

"He's not a boy of mine, Mom," I say in the same language, which makes Carson gawk at me before he focuses back on something Mom says.

"You want me to think he's just a student?" She gives me a

look that says, *I was in the room when you were born, boy, don't be trying to be a smart-ass.*

"What else could he be?"

"A little boyfriend."

"I'm not gay. You know that."

"Gay or straight or bi, who cares? Feelings have no sexuality."

I drop my glass on the table and try not to appear pissed off. "I absolutely have no feelings for him. The fuck, Mom? Aside from being a guy, he's a kid. Like, over-eleven-years-younger-than-me *kid*."

"He's old enough, and feelings have no age limit."

"I said. There are *no* feelings."

"I'm not so sure about that. I haven't seen you this carefree in a long time, and you look at him differently. Even more fondly than you used to look at—"

"Don't finish that sentence, Mom. Just don't."

"Are you scared of the sentence itself or what it means?" When I say nothing, she sighs, stands up, and hugs my head to her chest. "I don't know what you're doing or what you're hoping to achieve, but maybe it's time to let go, my boy."

I *can't*.

Not now when I'm close to the finish line.

My eyes meet Carson's, and he stares for a second, seeming mesmerized by the scene.

I already have everything going to plan, so why on earth does the idea of not having him at that finish line squeeze the fuck out of my chest?

16
GARETH

The low hum of conversation scatters around me as I stare at my phone.

I can't help the small smile that tugs on my lips, and one of my friends—the fake ones—says to stop scrolling.

I'm not, but they can't tell with the privacy screen.

They want to do some late afternoon group study in a local coffee shop, and I usually join them just to incapacitate them and make them feel like they can never be at my level. Without even saying anything. They still like my company, though, which isn't a surprise—I'm the most interesting person I know.

Well, I don't show all my interesting parts, but they're still mesmerized by the image I project, which is a superpower in and of itself.

I reply to a few texts from Rachel—yes, the one who's Kayden's mom. I went to say goodbye at the airport two days ago and got her number before she left despite Kayden's attempts to stop it. So Jina demanded to have my number, too, which I gladly gave.

We've been texting regularly in this group chat I made for the three of us. Mostly Rachel texts back, though. But Jina reads. Everything. Unless I talk about archery or shooting targets, then it's Jina who's chatty, while Rachel just sends GIFs that imply she's bored.

I prefer Kayden's moms over him, but I also get why he doesn't like that I've been trying to milk them for information ever since that dinner a week ago.

I mean, I am, but he didn't need to figure it out so fast.

Or try to throw in hidden meanings while his parents were there.

Anyway, he went back to campus a couple of days ago, and he's been texting me since his moms left. Texts that I ignored but am reading through right now.

> You finished playing hard to get, little monster?

> If you are, I would love to pick up right where we left off.

> By deflowering my pussy, I mean.

> Don't ignore me, baby. You make me so hard, it's not even funny.

> I've been dreaming about you begging me to fuck you in that hoarse little voice of yours and woke up with a massive erection.

> Want to know how I resolved that problem?

Glad you asked. I closed my eyes and summoned the feel of how my cunt tightened around my tongue. Came straight away. Mmm. Just thinking about it makes my dick throb.

Why don't you stop avoiding the inevitable and come to my place while I'm still asking nicely?

But then again, you're not a fan of anything nice, are you? You get so hot and bothered at the idea of pain and being forced.

Have it your way. Let's see how long you can run away.

The last two texts pissed me off, but the rest are *acceptable*.

Good to see him on the edge.

Dreaming of me, wanting me, going crazy about me, and not having me. He's no different from all the other professors who've wanted to fuck me.

He should get in line.

My friends are talking about all sorts of stuff when my phone lights up with a text.

DAD

How was your day?

ME

Awesome. Got an A+ on a test.

You keep amazing me. I'm so proud of you, son.

Thanks, Dad.

I'm grinning wide. I love being his source of pride—something Killian definitely isn't.

Something I wouldn't be if he knew Kill and I have more in common than he thinks.

> I miss hunting with you, Dad.

> You shouldn't have moved away, then. You can always come back and finish school here. Drag your brother, too. Your mom hates having her boys away, and I'm the one suffering.

> How about we visit instead?

> Small compromise.

> Limited offer. T&Cs apply.

> I see you're pushing your luck. Kill's influence, I presume.

> Speaking of Kill, how is he doing?

> Can't ask him yourself?

> You know he barely replies to me. And I don't want to push him.

Because Dad said Kill was defective at a young age and my brother heard it.

He came to talk to me about it. I was eleven at the time.

"GARY," HE CALLS ME BY THE NICKNAME I HATE MOST, JUST BECAUSE *he knows I hate it.*

I'm in the garden practicing archery when he strolls over and flops onto the grass in front of me.

"What?" I snap, annoyed at the interruption.

"Why am I defective and you're not?"

"Because you're stupid," I say, drawing my bowstring and releasing an arrow that lands just shy of the bullseye.

"I think Dad hates me." His dead eyes fix on mine—those empty, hollow eyes he's always had. I noticed them long before Dad did, because I saw them in myself.

"Because he called you defective?"

"Yeah. He said he and Mom should've only had you. Mom scolded him, but she gave me a weird look when I showed them the dead mice."

"Then maybe don't do that."

"But I wanted to see inside them."

"You shouldn't let Mom or Dad see inside you." I notch another arrow and fire. Bullseye.

"Why can't they just be proud of me?"

"Because you were born different, and they can't handle that kind of different."

"How different?"

I pull another arrow and aim it at his throat, and he doesn't even flinch. "How do you feel when I do this?"

"I want to hurt you for wanting to hurt me."

"That's different. Most people would feel scared, frozen, or nervous—that's how their brain works." I raise the arrow and fire again. Bullseye. "If you want Mom to stop looking at you like that, watch how your friends act and mimic them as best you can. It'll get easier with time."

He jumps up, a grin breaking through his usual blank expression. "Will Dad stop hating me, too?"

"Maybe stay away from Dad. I don't think he's ever going to accept you."

So I might have unknowingly contributed to the rift between Dad and Kill. I think Kill wanted to try when we were young, but it faded out.

Dad tried more than Kill, though. He came up with all sorts of activities for all three of us, including hunting, but I believe Kill didn't really like seeing Dad and me getting along, so he stopped coming.

They grew further and further apart the older Kill got, and

it turned into a cold war of sorts.

One I wasn't changing, because I don't like the idea of Kill getting close to Dad. I barely tolerate his attachment to Mom, but with Dad or even Grandpa, that's a red line. He has the rest of the world to charm.

I assure Dad that Killian's doing well, and he insists that we should come visit.

In the end, I'll drop by alone since Kill wouldn't want to go anyway.

I slide my phone back into my pocket and focus on something one of the guys is talking about, jumping in with the most basic replies.

We step into a local coffee shop, the familiar hum of conversation and the sharp scent of espresso filling the air. It's one of those quiet places, tucked away from the town center's chaos, with mismatched furniture and a cozy, lived-in feel.

The soft clink of spoons and the low murmur of the barista at the counter blend into the background as my eyes lock onto none other than my professor.

Kayden's sitting at a small corner table, effortlessly commanding attention. His dark hair is styled just enough to look casual but still sharp, framing his defined cheekbones, defined jawline, and his slight stubble adds to the maturity of his look.

His pressed white shirt strains against his muscles, the sleeves rolled up just enough to reveal strong forearms, and is paired with well-tailored black pants. His gaze is intense and piercing, with natural magnetism as he directs it at a woman.

Because, yes, there's a fucking woman sitting across from him.

And he's talking to *her*.

She's older, maybe in her mid-thirties, with long auburn hair that cascades over her shoulders and her tight black dress. She has a sultry look and a flirtatious smile that's all too confident for my fucking taste. Her eyes linger on him, warm and inviting, as she leans in to say something, her laugh low and rich.

"Oh my God, is that Prof Lockwood?" one of the girls squeals as we sit at the biggest table in the middle of the room.

I choose a seat that's right across from him.

But he doesn't notice me.

Not when his entire attention is on the woman with red lipstick.

"Is he on a date?" Myers asks with glee.

"Get it, Prof. She's hot as fuck," another one of the dumb-ass guys says.

"I think she's a prof at the business school."

"I'm gonna cry." Morgan pouts beside me. "If I can't have him, no woman should."

"They could be doing one of those things professors do," Zara says, stroking her arm.

"Yeah, right. She looks ready to unzip his pants and give us a show. Why is life so unfair?"

"He's never shown interest in you or anyone in class, actually. I think he prefers people his age. Don't take it personally, Morgan."

"It still sucks."

They chatter and buzz and talk and talk and talk, and I'm on the verge of banging each of their heads on the table and cracking their skulls open.

But I don't do that.

I'm the good boy Gareth. I don't fantasize about murder in public.

Okay, I do, but not to the point where it's hard to control the urge.

And the main reason is because Kayden still hasn't noticed me.

Me.

There's been a sudden irrational burn in my chest since I walked in, and I can't look away. I watch as the motherfucker—who was so sick his moms nursed him back to health like a goddamn baby—leans forward, his expression calm, collected. It's like he's not even noticing how the woman is practically hanging on to his every word.

If she doesn't stop looking at him like *that*, we'll have a serious fucking problem. Like an unidentifiable dead body.

Fuck. Why do I even care who he meets and how they look at him? Or how he speaks so low, I can't hear anything.

I throw open my notebook and slide my pen back and forth so I don't start biting my goddamn fingers.

Because he hasn't looked away from her.

Not even once.

I pull out my phone and click on the conversation with him.

ME

What's the meaning of this?

He picks up his phone from the table, glances at it, without a change in expression, then puts it back down—on its face.

That motherfucker—

I release a long breath. It doesn't matter. *He* doesn't matter, and the woman *definitely* doesn't matter.

Why am I getting worked up about this?

My fingers fly over the phone as Morgan grabs onto my arm, saying shit about being the only one for her, but I'm barely listening.

If you don't lose her in the next five minutes…

I delete the text and turn off my screen. I'm sounding desperate. Almost as if I'm…

Fuck.

I lift my head and see it. In Zara's eyes as Morgan kisses my jaw, my cheek, biting and flirting and getting her fucking germs all over me. Just a small distraction, and she's turning horny for no reason.

But it's not her that matters. It's Zara and how she glares at me, then lowers her head and clears her throat, after being caught being jealous in full HD.

Is that what I look like?

Fuck no. I don't care enough about that motherfucker to be jealous.

I push Morgan off me—a reminder to get sanitized—and smile. "Sorry to cut this short, but I'm getting a bit of a headache. I'm leaving."

On my way out, I throw one last glimpse at Kayden, and he's smiling at something she said.

He never shows me that soft smile. It's always malicious or mocking.

As I walk toward my car, I type.

> You have half an hour. If you don't show up at your place, I'll hunt you the fuck down.

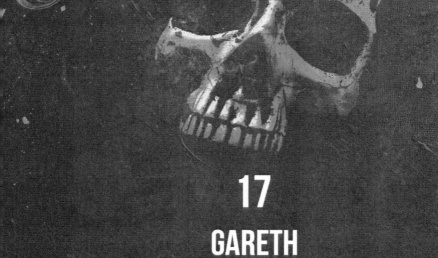

17

GARETH

Fifteen minutes later, I've driven to his place.

Maybe I should've told him not to show up with her.

I punch in the code, narrowing my eyes. If he has the audacity to bring her, he can't blame me for whatever fuckery my brain cooks up in retaliation.

With a large sigh, I head to the kitchen for a drink and pause at the fridge. There are three packs of organic strawberries, and a large bowl of the cut fruit sits in the middle, neatly covered.

He did this?

Why the fuck would he?

Whatever. I pull it out and nearly demolish the whole thing

while obsessing over the clock.

Five minutes left.

Unless he's still with her. Or, worse, went to her place.

My jaw tightens, and I push the bowl away, my fingers brushing the Taser in my jacket. It's a new one since the asshole confiscated my last one. And my knife.

He's ten fucking minutes late.

I'm pacing now, my mind racing with options.

If he went to her place, I might have to use the guards to try and locate her. But that'll definitely get back to Jeremy, and he's already been giving me suspicious looks. But at least Kill is so preoccupied with Glyn, he barely pays any attention to me.

I'll deal with him later. First, I have to find that bastard before he screws something up.

It's *totally* about protecting the woman from his ruthless way of having sex. She should *thank* me for being a goddamn Good Samaritan.

The door lock clicks, and I freeze, every nerve on edge.

Then I move, sliding behind the door, my back to the wall, knife in hand.

Relief hits me like a punch to the gut. It's twisted and unnerving, mixing with this bubbling anticipation.

My breaths come in and out in deep, quick succession, and while my hand around the knife is steady, my palm is clammy.

It's contagious—these mixed feelings whirling through me.

A sense of excitement.

A touch of malice.

The door opens painfully slowly, and he steps inside, all deliberate movements and irritating calmness.

There he is, the bastard.

Clad in a trench coat and a cashmere scarf, hair ruffled by the wind, cheeks flushed red.

As soon as he turns around to close the door, I pounce.

I slam him against the door, gripping his nape and pressing

the knife to his pulse point. The impact rattles the frame, but he doesn't even flinch.

The scent of wood and amber hits me like a fucking drug, and I can't help *sniffing* him.

Why does he smell so good?

Heat radiates from him, the warmth of his hard back muscles pressing into my chest as I lean in closer. Every ridge of his defined physique is a sharp outline, and I feel each one against me as if his body is a map I can't stop tracing.

Exploring.

Dismantling to pieces.

His firmness, his strength, his steady breathing is all I can focus on as it drowns me deeper.

I'm underwater now as I lean closer, pressing further, inhaling him into my lungs instead of air. The sensation of his muscles flexing under my fingertips and the feel of his power pulling me to newer depths.

The low, rough rumble of his voice vibrates through me. "Jumping my bones the second I walk in? Didn't know you missed me that much, baby."

"You're ten minutes late, *Professor*," I growl in his ear.

"And that's enough to bring out the psycho in you?"

"I don't like people who aren't punctual."

"Hmm. I don't believe that's the real issue."

He grabs my hand holding the knife, dragging it down his coat, slicing through the expensive fabric like it's nothing.

I let him. His fingers tighten around my wrist, guiding the blade lower...and lower...

"You want to know what your real issue is?" He stops right above his groin, and just when I think the crazy asshole will make me cut him, he twists my wrist, forcing the knife to fall and clatter on the ground.

"I think you just couldn't stand the thought of me being with someone else." He slams my palm on the bulge in his pants, and it grows beneath my touch, hardening at an alarming speed. "Your adorable jealousy drives me crazy, baby."

I swallow, but don't try to remove my hand. I love how his erection keeps lengthening and pressing against his pants and my hand. I love it so much, actually, I have to push my hips back so he doesn't feel the evidence.

"I don't know what you're talking about," I say in a quiet voice.

"Focus. We're discussing your jealousy."

"I don't do that." I squeeze him hard, a form of punishment so he'll shut his trap.

His rough groan hums against me. "That's it, make me hard so I can stuff my cock in your ass. I'm dying to fuck my pussy."

I apply pressure to his bulge, my fingers digging in and tightening. "I told you that's not going to happen."

It happens so fast, I'm slightly disoriented.

Kayden shoves my hand away and turns to face me so easily, it almost feels like I wasn't cornering him.

Was he pretending I was cornering him?

I step away, mostly because of how dark his eyes seem, so far from gray and close to black.

He folds both arms over his chest, staring me down, using every inch of his height to make me feel small.

I *hate* it when he does that.

"If that's not going to happen, what are you doing here?" His voice is monotone and closed off, like the way he is in class. Completely detached and distant.

I narrow my eyes. "To put you in your place."

"You know, I can tolerate your push-and-pull game for only so long before I snap." His hand shoots in my direction and I step back, but he clutches my jaw and spins me around, then slams me against the door.

The rattle reverberates through my bones as I lift my hands, trying to remove his arm, but he jams his knees between mine, against my hardening cock.

He speaks so close to my mouth, his lips touch mine with every word. "You don't get to act murderous over my date, drag me here with threats, and then play hard to get, Carson. That's not how this game is played."

My hand shoots up to his throat and I squeeze. "You were on a fucking *date*?"

A smirk tilts his lips. "Her name is Jessica. Hot, right? She's one call away, and she definitely would let me fuck her whenever I please."

"More like force her like the sick fuck you are."

"I don't do that with women. Or anyone, for that matter. I only reserve the uncivil treatment for little monsters like you." He darts his tongue out and licks my jaw, my cheek, over and over as if he's erasing something, leaving a trail of saliva that tingles. "I should punish you for letting that girl suck your face."

He nibbles on my jaw and cheek and then sinks his teeth into my lower lip and pulls. "Teach you a lesson so you know who the fuck you belong to."

"I don't belong to you," I speak in a low voice, one hand barely pushing at his stomach while the other is loose around his throat.

"In that case..." He presses his knee against my cock and I grunt. "I should invite someone who does before I actually take your ass by force. Jessica, for instance."

Then he releases me.

Without so much as a glance, he strides to his bedroom, shrugging off his coat. "Don't let the door hit you on the way out."

I stand there for a second, seething. My body's too warm, too hard, too fucking frustrated, and it's unraveling everything I thought I knew.

Confusion claws at me. The pang in my chest, the murderous thoughts swirling in my head—toward him, toward myself. I even consider electrocuting one of us just to stop this madness.

To keep him from leaving. To make sure he doesn't have the energy to call her.

That thought propels me forward, and I march to his bedroom.

But my steps falter at the entrance.

He's removing his pants, leaving him in nothing but boxer briefs, standing there like he knows exactly what kind of chaos he's erupting in my stomach.

My chest.

My mind.

Every inch of him is sculpted to perfection. Broad shoulders, a chest carved from stone, muscles sharp and defined like they're designed to taunt me.

My gaze locks on the snake tattoo coiling across his chest and abs in stunning 3D detail. Every scale, every curve pops in the dim light, making the ink feel alive, slithering over his skin with dark, hypnotic intent.

It shouldn't make my throat dry.

But it does.

The way the tattoo moves with the power in his physique freezes me in place, and the Taser plan evaporates from my mind.

"Want to stay around and watch?" His lowly spoken question snaps me out of my reverie.

"What?

"You want to stay around and watch me fuck Jessica?"

I lunge toward him, pulling out the Taser. "I'm going to fucking kill you."

He slaps it away, letting it fall on the ground, then clutches my wrist. "We both know you won't do that."

"Call her and see what I will do. I fucking *dare* you." I'm breathing harshly against him, trying and failing not to be affected by his warmth.

He's too warm for a cold-blooded asshole.

"Then you stayed for option two?" He grabs my waist and presses me against him. "Where I said I'd force you?"

My throat dries, but I say nothing.

"I know you want me, Carson. I see it in your eyes, and feel it in your rage about Jessica."

"Stop saying her fucking name."

"You can stop me."

"How...?"

"If you agree to be mine alone, I won't touch anyone else, baby. Jessica included."

"You'll be only mine, too," I say, my blood rushing hot in my ears. "My fucking property, Kayde."

A smirk curves his lips. "Want to possess me, baby?"

"I'm not joking. If anyone comes close to you, I will break their legs and then yours."

"Violent. I love it."

"Do we have an agreement?"

"Mmm, whatever you wish." He nibbles on my ear. "Will you let me fuck you now?"

"No."

He lifts his head, and I can see the lines of frustration etching deep in his forehead. "Is this another game?"

"Not really."

"Then what?"

"It's just..."

"Just?"

"I won't let you do it willingly." I swallow, my fingers twitching. "I *can't*."

"Then what do you want?"

"Tie me up," I speak quietly, not believing what the hell is coming out of my mouth. "Make me feel as if you're forcing me and I have no option but to take it. I'll enjoy it better that way."

"Fuck." His cock grows, nudging against my thigh. "I knew you were my favorite."

My heart jolts and my own erection hardens until it's painful.

We're so sick.

And toxic.

And that puts a smile on my face.

Because I think this is exactly what I always wanted.

Kayden pulls away, a malicious grin curving his gorgeous lips. "Now, fight me, baby. Show me how much you want me to force you."

18

GARETH

The fight drags on for a long time.

Too long, actually, because now, I'm panting, and my Taser's been kicked under the bed.

What? I wanted to see him shake with electricity.

Didn't happen. Instead, I'm down a jacket because he grabbed it, and I had to shrug it off to escape his grip.

But here I am, shoved against the bed, on my stomach. I lift myself onto my hands and knees, but he's already behind me, kneeling, his legs trapping mine.

My muscles tense as he reaches into the drawer and pulls out the ropes.

Sex ropes. I googled them. It's why they don't bruise for long no matter how much I pull against them.

I know I told him to tie me, but the idea of giving up all control sends a jolt through me. I try to elbow him, but it's like hitting a damn wall. The guy's all muscle, solid as stone.

"Get the fuck off me," I let out in a grunt.

A low, dark chuckle rips out of him as he catches my elbow and then throws my arm away. "The more you fight, the harder I get, baby. There's nothing hotter than your little struggle."

He thrusts his pelvis against me, his huge bulge nudging against my ass cheek. It feels so hot that I get distracted, and he uses my lack of fight to start removing my shirt.

His long fingers graze my heated skin, sending a shudder through me as he drags the fabric over my head and tosses it aside.

My lips part when his large hands follow, gliding down my spine, vertebra by vertebra by vertebra. Then lower, tracing my waist, my stomach, my chest.

It's like he's memorizing me. Every ridge, every line, every inch of skin.

And somehow, it makes me feel *worshiped*.

That thought churns my stomach, transforming it into that war zone all over again.

How the hell can a malicious, stoic, practically robotic man find my body so damn fascinating?

Both his index fingers rub my nipples, sending a zap through me. "I love how your little nipples perk up when I touch them. Or pinch them."

He does that, pinching them so hard that I recoil, a strangled noise escaping me.

"I also love that you enjoy the pain I unleash on you," he whispers against my ear, then nibbles on the shell. "You look fucking adorable when you fight it. But we'll work on that."

"Shut your mouth." I try to elbow him, but he shoves me forward.

I land on the mattress with a slight bounce, and he looms over me, his weight pressing into my back.

I strain my neck to the side, catching a glimpse of him. Even though I'm tall and muscular, he's broader and bigger, and in this position, he radiates pure dominance.

Effortlessly, he grabs my wrists, yanking them forward and securing them to the bedposts like it's second nature. The thought of how many women he's done this to twists something ugly in my chest, coiling tight.

But those thoughts evaporate when his lips trail down my spine, soft and deliberate. He kisses, sucks, then nibbles, each touch sending shockwaves through me.

I bury my face in the navy silk pillow that reeks of him, desperate to smother any embarrassing sounds threatening to escape.

"Stop kissing me like that," I grit out from between clenched teeth.

"Mmm. But I love your taste, baby." He continues kissing, licking, sucking the skin that's not supposed to be sensitive but apparently is, because my cock is growing heavy against the sheets.

Still kissing, he unbuckles my belt and removes my jeans and boxers, throwing them somewhere I can't see.

"Stop fucking doing that," I snap as he sucks somewhere on my lower back. "I'm not a girl."

"Never been with a girl this muscular before, but I'm not complaining." He drops a kiss on my ass cheek, then bites hard, so hard, my eyes roll back and my dick drips precum on the bed. "Never bitten a girl's ass before, and I'm fully aware you're a man. That doesn't stop me from wanting to mark your fuck-hole, baby. I want to claim every inch of you."

"Fuck." I grunt when he does it again, this time slapping the other cheek.

Hard.

I jolt against the sheet and my cock is full like I've never experienced before.

Fuck. Jesus.

Kayden alternates between biting and slapping, slapping and biting, keeping me on edge with anticipation for what he'll do next.

"Mmm. Red does look good on you." He kneads the skin, and I think I'll just come from the torture alone.

He shifts behind me, and I turn to the side to see him grabbing a bottle of lube from the drawer.

My hands pull at the ropes. I'm still fucking apprehensive about this. Part of me doesn't want it and is getting really freaked out at the idea of being fucked.

I don't like it.

The loss of control.

The idea of being under someone else.

Of being hurt when I should be the one inflicting pain.

I've always been in control, so this entire thing kicks my survival instinct into overdrive.

And I twist beneath him, wanting to fight this for real. To stop it—not that he'd let me.

The other part, the part that can't help coming back for more, likes that he *won't* let me.

Jeez. I knew I was fucked up, but I didn't think I was *this* fucked up.

Kayden shoves my back down when I fight and slaps my ass, then lifts it in the air. "Stay still so I can lube my pussy up."

A groan rips out of me when his fingers lather cold gel all over my back hole, and I bury my head so he doesn't see my face. I don't even want to imagine the type of expression I'm making.

"My virgin cunt is dripping wet. Mmm." He thrusts two fingers in and I tense up, but it only lasts a second as he thrusts in me in a firm, soothing rhythm. "Look at you taking my fingers so well. The view is driving me insane, baby."

His cock, hard and absolutely heavy, glides up and down my ass cheek. When did he even remove his boxers?

My question remains hanging as he adds another finger. I strain and tense up. "That's..."

"Shh. You'll have to take my fingers to be able to fit my cock, baby."

"God...fuck..."

"You're doing well, little monster. Stop overthinking and just take what I give you."

"Fuck..."

He leans over my back and bites my nape, then does that wicked sucking of my ear. "I know you're used to being the one in control, and this terrifies you. I know you despise the idea of being fucked by a man. I know all of that. But, baby, you're also making me lose control. I never thought about fucking another man, but the idea of not taking you is driving me out of my goddamn mind. So be a good boy and take me."

Something throbs in my chest. Not my dick. My *chest.*

I mumble a throaty noise against the pillow as his fingers tap that spot inside me, but only for a few seconds, before he pulls out.

"I'm fucking desperate to be inside you." He lifts my hips, his fingers digging into the sides before he releases me, and I strain my neck to look at him.

My throat dries at the view of him kneeling behind me, squirting lube over his cock, and lathering himself from top to bottom.

I think I downplayed his size before to avoid praising him even in my head, but the guy is criminally huge. How the fuck will that fit inside me?

Apprehension slithers to my tight stomach, but it soon vanishes when my eyes drag to his stormy ones.

There's an intensity in the way he watches me, like he's memorizing every inch of me, every breath I take. It's not just a stare; it's a raw, unspoken claim, as if he knows exactly how much power he holds over me and takes sick pleasure in making me feel it.

But there's something else there, too, something magnetic. His gaze softens, just a fraction, before he exhales a long, deliberate breath that makes my chest tighten.

"Fuck, baby. I love that look on your face."

What look?

I want to ask, but I don't get the chance when he latches on to my hip and holds his cock at my back hole.

And then he thrusts in. His crown presses against the tight ring of muscles and the round tip breaks through.

He's in my ass.

A man's dick is in *my* ass.

I drop my head on the pillow, my lips trembling.

Fuck.

Fuck.

Fuck.

Slap.

The spank on my ass wrenches me out of my head and brings me back to the present in full-blown colors.

"Relax, don't allow your body to fight me." He kneads the skin he just slapped in firm movements. "I want you to enjoy it when I claim my pussy, baby."

He thrusts his hips again, this time pushing so far in, I strangle on a cry, pulling on the ropes so hard, I think I'll dislocate my shoulders. He's so big, I'm being stretched out, completely and utterly impaled by him.

It hurts.

Fuck, it *hurts.*

Why am I doing this? Why didn't I just let the asshole go—

Slap.

This time, his fingers dig into my hair. It's not short, but it's not that long either, and he manages to lift my head, then leans down so his lips hover near my cheek. "Don't go there. Stay with me."

"It hurts..." I mumble, feeling weirdly vulnerable.

"I know." He stays still for a while as he slides his tongue from the corner of my mouth over my cheek and to my eye. "You love the pain, so use that and fall into it, don't fight it."

"I feel every inch of you, prick." I pant. "I even f-feel your veins pulsing inside me."

"That's because I'm holding on to my last goddamn smidge of control not to bottom out."

"Y-you're not fully in?"

"A little over halfway through."

"No way...fuck..."

"I'll take that as a compliment." He chuckles, the sound low and dark, but his voice catches, proving just how much he's losing that control.

Because of me.

Because I'm also *owning* him.

Because I'm the *only* man he's ever wanted to fuck.

This time, when he moves, I relax my body as much as possible, my breathing getting so chaotic and heavy until my lungs burn.

Kayden releases my hair, letting my head fall back down, but I look back at him.

His muscles bulge, the veins in his neck, arms, and the back of his hands protruding from how much he's straining not to fuck me like an animal.

Because I'm the only man who drives him crazy.

Just me.

"You with me, baby?" He grabs a handful of my ass cheek, digging his fingers into the bruises he left there.

"Mmm." I choke on a moan.

"You're really making me work for this ass, you know."

"As...you should."

He chuckles, but it's strained as a drop of sweat trickles down his temple.

And as I watch that, I grow a bit conscious since, well, I really hate putting in the effort. My biggest fucking pet peeve about sex, actually. So what if he's also...

I dart out my tongue, licking my suddenly dry lips. "You hate it? Working for it, I mean."

"No, I'm loving it. Best challenge of my fucking life."

My chest shudders as I pant. So when he nudges again, I control my breathing, relaxing even more, *allowing* him access inside me.

I drop my head on the pillow and fall into the pain as he drives in farther and farther, stuffing me full of his cock.

My body adapts, molding to him, accommodating him, letting him reshape me.

Literally and figuratively.

"That's it. You're taking my cock so well. Mmm. Your walls are strangling me so good."

Slap.

A muffled grunt slips out of me and my cock thickens, precum forming a wet pool on the bed.

"You're making a fucking mess."

"Can't...stop it."

"I know, baby, I know."

"M-more..." I whisper.

"What was that?"

"Go all the way in. Slap me in the meantime. I can take it."

"Goddamn... God fucking damn it. You were made for me."

A rush of heat floods my chest, melting something deep inside me.

It's not supposed to. Not over words. I don't trust words—

not since I was twelve. That was the moment I stopped believing anything people say.

But now, as he calls me baby and tells me I'm doing well, I believe him.

Maybe it's because his voice wavers and his breaths strain when he says those words.

Or maybe it's because I'm not just hearing the words. I'm *feeling* them.

He gives a hard shove, burying himself all the way in my ass, hitting that sensitive spot in the meantime. "Fuck, baby. This is the best feeling in the world."

"Mmmfuck..."

It doesn't hurt.

Or maybe the pain is crushed by the euphoric throb that pulses through me.

And I'm leaking so much precum, it's like I'm coming in increments.

He's positioned my ass so far up in the air, I can't have any friction from the mattress, and I look down to see my precum still dripping and soaking the sheet.

Fuck. Who would've thought I would be so turned on by being dominated?

Being so delirious due to ass penetration?

And the pain.

And *him*.

"My cunt is so warm and wet. You're so tight, baby."

"That's because you're b-big."

"Mmm. Love how you keep complementing me, baby. You're taking this big cock so well." He's moving now, his hips jerking back and forth, not viciously, but the rhythm picks up by the second.

God. I can feel every ridge of his cock, every vein, every bit of friction. It's driving me insane.

He slaps my ass again, then kneads it, and I think I come a

little.

"I wish you knew what it feels like to be in your virgin pussy. Your hole is swallowing me so well. I can't stop."

"Kayde...fuck..."

"Love how you call me in that husky little tone, baby."

"K-Kayde...y-you're tearing through me."

"That's right. I'm tearing through my tight little cunt."

"There...that's, yes...fuck!"

He pounds harder, his hips smacking my ass with every thrust. I'm delirious, so close, on the edge myself, but instead of focusing on that, I focus on him, on his labored breaths.

Something wraps around my throat, my belt, as he lifts me up slightly, my arms stretching to the bedposts. His hard chest presses against my back. Both of us are so slick with sweat, we're rubbing against each other in a cradle of warmth.

"You're so fucking beautiful. Let me see your face."

My chest does that annoying throb again. "I thought I d-disgusted you."

"I lied." He nibbles on my throat, my jaw. "You're the most beautiful man on the goddamn earth, baby."

Fuck.

Why is he saying shit like this?

And why is my heart beating so loudly, I think it'll burst through my chest? What is this motherfucker doing to me?

"I love your hoarse little voice when you moan my name." He sucks on my bottom lip, fucking me deeper, harder, the slaps of flesh against flesh and my shameless moans echoing in the air. "I love all the noises you release when overwhelmed by pleasure, how your throat bobs up and down, how your ears flush. But most of all, I love how your body accommodates me, how you let me fuck my virgin cunt when you wouldn't let anyone else have this power over you."

"S-shut up."

"You smell so good, baby." He inhales sharply by my ear, his breaths breaking and stuttering. "Why the fuck do you smell so good? Feel so good? Fucking hell."

He sounds mad, I don't know whether at me or himself, but I can't focus, because he's hitting that spot.

Once.

Twice...

"Yes...right there...fuck me!"

"This tight hole was made for my cock. It's only mine." His lips suck my parted ones, and he kisses me.

Deep and raw.

I let him suck my tongue, my lips, and I bite, but it lacks strength because he's fucking me so good.

A man is pounding the living fuck out of me and I'm delirious.

He merely chuckles in my mouth as he devours me.

Kayden kisses me as he fucks me, his tongue matching his dick's rhythm, nearly pressing into my goddamn throat.

He releases the belt and wraps his hand around my jaw. "You like how I'm owning you, baby? How your body submits to mine?"

Low groans and moans echo in the air and it takes me a second to realize they're mine. I'm releasing all these embarrassing noises as he fucks so hard, I can barely breathe.

I don't want to fucking breathe.

Every time he bottoms out, shoving against my pleasurable spot, I come a little, groaning and crying out.

"Tell me you like it," he insists, biting on my ear. "Say you like being fucked by me."

"Fuck..." is my only reply because I'll probably die if I admit that out loud.

"You don't have to say it, I feel it. I see it in your eyes." He peers at me, his eyes so dark but alive, and not empty. Far from it. He actually looks a little unhinged. "These eyes never lie."

A droplet of sweat drips from his hair on my forehead, then

mixes with my own and slides down my nose and onto my cheek.

"Your ass is glorious, baby. I don't want to leave it. Ever. But I need to come balls deep inside you." He goes deeper, and deeper, I think I feel him in my stomach.

Am I supposed to *feel* him in my stomach?

"Ask me to fill you up with my cum, baby."

"I'm not saying that..."

He goes harder. "But I want to claim my pussy."

"Then...do it."

"Say the words. I want to hear it, baby." He hits that spot inside me as he wraps a hand around my cock. "Now."

The command sends a tingle through my quivering insides, and I lick my lips.

"Come...inside me, please, Kayde... Ahhh—"

My words end with a moan because I'm coming in long waves. I'm coming and coming, I think I'll never stop. He didn't even jerk me up, not even once.

I came by being fucked.

Jesus Christ.

"Fuck, baby, fuck. I'm going to fill my pussy with my cum."

His rhythm turns more frantic and then he groans deep as he swells and throbs inside me with his lips against my neck.

The fact that he's coming with me somehow coils and deepens until I release a long sob of relentless desire.

The pleasure haze swirls and swirls until I think I'll faint. Hot liquid fills up my insides as he jerks his hips, his pelvis slapping in pulses against my ass.

His hot breaths fan my neck and I close my eyes for a second to calm my fucking heart after the most intense pleasure I've ever experienced.

Our heavy inhales and exhales mingle and fill the air as he also pauses, probably needing to slow the hell down.

Because what the fuck was *that*?

Since when is sex supposed to feel like an out-of-body experience?

His arms wrap around my chest and waist as his whole body presses down onto mine from behind and he buries his head in my nape. We're so glued together, it should make me apprehensive, try to run away, even, but I don't want to move.

I don't want to lose this peace.

It's that white room again. The empty comforting space that someone like me shouldn't need, or like.

But as he breathes into my neck, harsh and heavy, I think I'll fall asleep.

In that room.

With no demons screeching out from the void.

Peace.

Quiet.

When was the last time I had this?

"Fuck." His voice is so low, and I think I feel him tense up before he lifts himself off, letting me fall on the mattress.

Cold air raises goosebumps on my naked skin, and I'm mad at myself for not telling him to get off me before he did.

He pulls out and that's when I realize he's been buried inside me the whole time. As in, I fell asleep not minding that he was inside me.

My face heats as liquid pours out of me and onto the sheets.

The realization dawns on my hazy brain.

I've been really fucked by Kayden.

I search for the part of me that should regret this, but there's nothing. I can't even pretend I hated it, not even slightly. If anything, it feels like a pivotal moment in my life.

He walks into the bathroom and comes back with a warm wet towel, then starts to wipe his cum off my ass.

"Don't touch me," I snap, wiggling against the ropes. "Untie me and I'll do it myself."

"That's the second time you've said that, and I'm telling you to drop it. Learn to let me take care of you." He slaps my ass cheek, and I jolt, my spent dick twitching.

"I don't want you to take care of me. I'm a grown fucking adult."

"Language."

"Just don't do it. It makes me feel weird."

"Because you're not used to it, but you will. With time."

"No, I won't."

"We're not having a conversation. I'm telling you that's what will happen and that's that." His voice drips with quiet authority. "Got it?"

I glare at him.

He ignores me and continues his task. Kayden is surprisingly gentle when he wipes me up, almost too gentle. It's giving me the creeps.

I let my head drop onto the pillow, screwing my eyes shut. I tell myself it's so I don't look at him treating me like that.

Like no one has ever done before.

And, actually, I don't...I don't hate it per se.

I'm soon floating to sleep, feeling so sedated and goddamn tired.

"Sleepyhead," I hear him mutter as he unties my wrists and rubs them softly for a while.

He really is treating me so gently for someone who has no qualms about hurting me. But I guess I hurt him, too, with the drugs and tasering and knifing.

Besides, he thinks I'm sleeping so I don't have to put up a front.

After finishing with my wrists, I feel something being pulled from beneath me. The messed-up sheets, probably, and the pillow I wet with my saliva is also replaced, and then he disappears for a while, and when he comes back, his fingers rub something cool on my ass.

A soft whine slips out of my lips as the marks burn, but he

taps the skin, carefully lathering it with what I assume is ointment.

The gentle rhythm lulls me into a deeper sleep, and I barely make out a warm duvet being placed on top of me.

As I float and float into that white room, I hear his voice laced with a touch of darkness. "What the fuck am I going to do with you now?"

19

KAYDEN

I've spent the past however many hours smoking.

Whole packs.

I'm almost out of cigarettes, but the nicotine rush did nothing to expel the agitation gnawing at my goddamn sanity.

The cold air bites into my skin as I stand on the balcony in nothing but pajama bottoms. But it's not cold enough, not uncomfortable enough. Nothing is enough to make me loathe what I did a few hours ago.

Maybe I should ask Julian to inject me with his drug again.

Not that it worked the last time.

Nothing is working.

I crush the cigarette in the ashtray and, like a hopeless

addict, step back into the room. The night air clings to my skin as I close the door behind me.

The reason for my sleeplessness—and pending life crisis—is sprawled across the bed.

My bed.

Gareth is on his stomach, hugging a pillow, the duvet slipped down to reveal the smooth curve of his back and the purple hickeys I left all over his skin.

My marks.

My touch.

Mine.

His blond hair spills across the pillow, messy and disheveled from how I yanked and pulled at those golden strands while I owned him.

Claimed him.

Made him all *mine.*

The thought that I'm the only one who can fuck him, touch him like that, sends a rush of blinding possessiveness through me.

I sit on the edge of the bed, unable to stop watching him.

There's something ethereal about him, like he's not quite real. Like if I reached out to trace the contours of his body, he'd vanish beneath my fingers, fading into nothing.

I've seen plenty of beautiful people, but I've never given it a second thought. His beauty, though, is the kind that hurts to look at. And now, asleep, with all his maliciousness gone, he looks so vulnerable and soft, I could strangle him.

I should've done that the first time I touched him and liked it.

I *should* have shot him.

But I wanted another taste.

And another.

And another.

I thought the urge would fade once I fucked him and staked a claim, but it's only gotten worse.

One taste isn't enough. Hell, two won't be either.

Not even a dozen.

Because right now, I want to shield him from the entire world so he's only mine.

Just replaying the way he moaned, the noises he made, the way this proud, goddamn major pain in the ass of a little monster submitted to me—

It makes me delirious.

My cock is filling up just watching him, and that's not ideal.

It's disastrous, to be honest, because he's not supposed to have this effect on me.

And yet I can't look away, even as the ache in my chest deepens.

I reach out and trace my knuckles over his face—the curve of his jaw, the slope of his cheek, the pout of his pillowy lips. My fingers pause at the tiny freckles dotting his straight nose. Up close, they look like stardust, otherworldly.

The desire building inside me feels suffocating, a weight lodged in my throat, because I know I shouldn't touch him.

Want him.

Feel this...*obsessed* with him.

But he nuzzles into my hand, and it's like a jolt of electricity shoots through me. My heart pounds so loudly, I hear it in my ears as I yank my arm away.

What the fuck was *that* about?

I shift and lie back on the bed, staring at the ceiling, refusing to look at him. But it's harder than I thought.

A literal struggle.

The urge to fuck him again, to do something, *anything*, to relieve this mounting aggression is unbearable.

Maybe I should go for a swim—

My thoughts scatter when a warm body presses against my side, his forehead nuzzling the crook of my neck.

He throws an arm over my chest, right where the snake's fangs are inked. I don't like that—illogical, I know—and I clutch his wrist, absently rubbing the faint rope marks, then slide his arm up to rest near my shoulder.

His soft breaths land like a curse against my throat.

I close my eyes, letting the pull of sleep take over. But just as I'm drifting, I realize his wrist is still in my hand.

For some reason, I don't let go.

———

"Have you forgotten me?"

Those words dragged me out of a nightmare.

Her words.

Her shriek as she shot Gareth in the face.

I can still feel the warmth of his blood on my skin—my face, my chest, everywhere.

I swam until my muscles screamed, but I can still feel the fucking blood.

It's around six in the morning when I step back into the apartment. I head straight to the safe hidden behind an obscure French artist's painting and toss in the knife and Taser I picked up earlier.

They join the others I've confiscated before. He keeps finding new ones, so it's not making much of a difference, but I'm trying to stop him from rushing headfirst into violence every time something doesn't go his way.

In some ways, he's grounded and shows impressive self-control, but when he indulges his impulses, they're destructive.

I need to train him to manage those instincts before he lands himself in a situation he can't get out of.

Not that I should *care* what happens to him.

I slam the safe shut and return the painting to its rightful place.

When I step into the bedroom, I expect to see him asleep. He's a deep sleeper and barely moves, even when I'm up pacing or leaving early in the morning. He always looks peaceful, his Adonis-like face completely at ease.

I suppose that's what it's like to have no empathy—sleeping like an actual baby.

My steps falter at the doorway.

He's not there.

The images from my nightmare seize me, wrapping tight around my throat. I claw at my collar, trying to loosen its suffocating grip.

Jethro's and Simone's warnings replay in my mind on an endless loop: *They will find him. It's only a matter of time.*

I used to be one of the "they" Jethro and Simone—the closest people to me—talked about. Hell, I was at the top of the list.

But now, every fiber of my being rebels against that thought.

My pulse steadies slightly when I hear the sound of the shower running.

The fact that my ears were ringing so loudly I missed it should set off alarms, but I don't care. I need to see him—to confirm that the little menace is breathing and intact. That he's not the disfigured version from my nightmare.

I step into the bathroom and stop dead.

Gareth stands behind the glass door, and I have a perfect side view of his lethal body.

The sound of water hitting the tiles fills the room as steam swirls in the air, curling around the edges of his glistening chest. Rivulets of water trace the lines of his muscles, accentuating skin I've started to memorize.

His body looks to be carved from marble, the curve of his spine the most perfect fucking thing I've ever seen.

My cock throbs at the sight of the purple and red marks on his back—most of them on his ass. Traces of my teeth, handprints, fingers.

And I want to add more.

I want to mark him so completely that no one will dare come near him again.

Not Morgan, not Cherry.

Not *anyone*.

He tips his head back slightly, droplets catching in his shimmering blond hair as he reaches two fingers to his ass. His eyes close, a faint frown appearing between his thick brows as he bites his lower lip.

Fuck *this*.

All remnants of my control snap.

I make quick work of pulling off my shirt, sweatpants, and boxers before striding toward the shower.

Gareth is so focused, he doesn't even notice me opening the glass door.

I step in behind him, the water soaking me instantly as I press my chest against his back and wrap my hand around his wrist. "You're struggling to get my cum out, baby? Let me help."

He jerks his head in my direction, and his eyes are so green, so bright, it's almost blinding to look at him.

"G-get out!" he snaps, but he also stutters. He's always been a pool of contradictions, my little monster.

"I said I'll help with my pussy." I tug his hand free and then push him against the glass door.

We're right across from the mirror, so I can see his cock bulging against the glass, the ridges of his muscles pressing against the fogged-up surface.

He wasn't this hard when I was watching him earlier, so his cock is performing a standing ovation for me.

I like that.

"Mmm." I jam my knees between his thighs and thrust my index and middle fingers inside him.

He grunts, the sound like music to my ears.

"My cunt is so full of cum, we need to remove that nice and slow."

"Just shut up. Why does everything need a commentary, asshole?"

"Because it makes you shudder beneath me." I nibble on his ear and slide my cock up and down his ass cheek as I curl my fingers inside. "It turns your face red and I love that color on you."

"You damn—" His words end with a moan when I scrape his sweet little spot with my fingers. "What are you doing... fuck..."

"Removing the cum."

"You're not...stop messing with me, Kayde."

"I can't."

And I mean that shit. I'm physically unable to stay the fuck away from him. I see him and I'm bursting with the need to fuck and hurt and claim and bite and mark him everywhere.

Is it an obsession?

A damnation?

A fucking curse?

I bite his lower lip hard and he groans, then pulls away and drops his forehead on the glass, both his hands holding on to the surface, curling with every thrust.

"Does it feel good?" I ask, thrusting my tongue in his ear.

He shudders beneath me, the water sliding down his hair, his neck and back, and I bite his nape. Like a goddamn animal marking his territory.

"Yeah..." He sucks in a harsh breath, his voice wavering. "That feels good..."

"How good?"

"Good..."

"Better than when you fuck?"

He tenses, his fingers curling against the glass.

"Answer me." I stop, pulling out slightly, caging him until he's shivering.

"Maybe..."

"Maybe isn't an answer. Tell me how you truly feel."

"It's better," he whimpers, grinding against my fingers.

"So much better?"

"Mmm." He grunts, his cock so hard now. "I want to come..."

"Already?" I chuckle against his earlobe. "But I'm only helping you, baby."

He whips his head in my direction and grabs me by the throat, his fingers tightening. "Just..."

"Just?"

Red creeps up his cheeks and my cock throbs, lighting the fuck up at his aggression, and I'm sure he feels it against his ass. Maybe that's why he swallows, his Adam's apple working up and down as droplets of water cascade down his lashes.

A piece of fucking art.

"Just do it."

"Do what?" I pause the thrusts, and he rubs his ass against my cock.

I'm sure he doesn't even know he's doing it, and that makes all the blood rush to my groin. He's such a menace, it's adorable to see him be a bit clueless and lost, slowly leaning into his sexuality and quitting the denial game.

We'll get to the point where he's more comfortable admitting what he wants without me pushing.

Little by little.

It should be frightening that I'm accepting *my* sexuality so easily, but it's not.

Wanting Gareth was the most natural fucking thing that's happened to me.

He squeezes his fingers around my throat, nearly cutting off my air supply, then whispers, the slightest noise, "F-fuck me."

My chest expands in a harsh breath as a primal feeling grips my balls, but I manage to sound normal when I say, "Want to feel my cock inside you again, baby?"

"I'm just horny. Hurry up." He releases me and looks away again.

I chuckle as I pull out my fingers. "If you're just horny, you could've asked for a handjob. But no, you can't get enough of my cock, can you?"

He freezes, his gulp audible in the midst of the water. "That's not..."

"Shh, it's okay, baby. I can't get enough of my cunt either." I reach for a black tube I kept here especially for this. I've filled my house the fuck up with lube since that time he broke in. Water- or silicone-based in the bedroom and living room. Oil-based in the shower.

Maybe I wanted to fuck him long before I finally admitted it to myself.

He looks back at me with blown-up pupils and parted lips. "Why do you even have that here?"

"Because I plan to fuck you everywhere."

"What a massive pervert," he lets out in a huff, but dimples crease his cheeks as he fights a smile.

I nibble and kiss his ear as I knee his legs farther, part his ass cheeks, and squeeze the lube around his hole.

I was never really an ass man, but this? This is the best fucking hole I've ever been in, and that should disturb me. Considering *her.*

Gareth grunts, probably because I'm gripping his bruised

skin tightly, and even though his cock hardens, I make a mental note to give him more ointment later. I suspect he'll let me apply it to him like when he was asleep last night.

I'll eventually make him get used to that, too, but baby steps.

He leans more into his animal instincts when cornered or uncomfortable, so I can't spook him.

I circle my finger around his rim over and over until he whines, planting his hands and forehead on the glass. "Just do it."

"Can't wait to have my cock inside you, baby?"

"Stop talking and fuck me already."

My balls tighten and I'm honestly concerned I'll come the moment I feel his walls clench around me again. "Give me your hand."

"Why?"

"Don't question me. Give it."

He looks back at me as he hesitantly stretches out his right hand. I take it in mine, then squeeze lube onto it and wrap it around my cock. "Make me nice and wet so I can fuck you."

I expect him to resist or throw a distasteful comment a la Gareth, but he simply jerks me up and down.

The position is awkward, but he strains to look at how his hand struggles to close around me, his lips parting, seeming utterly fascinated. His pace is slow at first, but then it turns rougher as he squeezes, going from base to top, flicking his thumb over the crown.

It takes all my goddamn control not to come, my cock leaking precum all over his fingers.

"I love your hand. I love how you're working me up so good."

"You do?"

"Mmm. Can't you feel how I'm becoming rock hard?"

"Yeah. You're sort of...pulsing in my hand. Your veins...uh... your cock does do that a lot. Pulsing, I mean."

Fuck, he looks so flustered and turned on, it's a sight to behold. He's so goddamn adorable for a little psycho.

"Baby, much as I love your hand, I need to blow my load inside you."

He stops and releases me, seeming unsure as he bites the corner of his lip. So I lick that lip as I position myself behind him and give a shove of my hips.

My muscles wind up when his walls clench around me and he cries out against my lips.

God damn.

God fucking damn.

I fucked him for the first time last night and it already feels as if I've been here my entire life.

Like this is the only place I belong.

He relaxes even as his ragged breaths fill the shower, and just like last night, he forces his body not to fight, *allowing* me in.

And I know he's allowing it, because Gareth is deadly when he wants.

But right now, as he slightly sinks his teeth in my lip, letting me go all the way in, I can feel his muscles loosening, his breaths stuttering.

"You feel so fucking good, baby," I speak close to his lips, licking the water off him. "My cunt is swallowing my cock like goddamn crazy."

He gulps, his throat working up and down, water clinging to his Adam's apple, but my view is constricted when he turns away, dropping his head on the glass as he grabs onto it.

Jerking my hips, I slam into him, bottoming out, and he cries out, the hoarse voice echoing with the sound of the splashing water. "Fuck."

"That's it. Take me. *All* of me."

I wrap my arm around his groin and squeeze his weeping cock. His back vibrates against my chest as I fuck him harder and harder.

"I've been thinking about being inside your ass nonstop, baby."

"We just...did it yesterday." His words are spoken in a moan.

"Doesn't matter. I can live here, just watching my cock slipping in and out of my pussy, knowing how much you love it."

His noises go up and up in volume until they fill my ears. Until they're all I can hear.

My eyes focus on him in the mirror, where we're visible up to his cock. He's smaller than me and I look like a fucking animal behind him.

It's the look in my eyes. I'm unhinged, out of control, filled with a primal need to claim him.

But he has his head down, looking at the floor or his cock in my hand, I don't know.

"Don't hide." I grab his jaw from behind and lift it up so he's looking at the mirror. "Look at who owns you."

Despite the steam, his eyes meet mine, and his are droopy, his lips parted. He doesn't look away as I fuck him deeper, so deep, he can't shut up.

He's grunting and moaning and clenching and being my fucking undoing.

All the while looking at us.

"The scene is making you harder, baby." Thrust. Bottom out. "You love looking at me fucking you, don't you?"

"Mmmfff..."

"I love looking at me fucking you, too. You're a goddamn masterpiece, baby."

"Kayde..."

"Baby?"

"I..."

"Talk to me."

"T-tell me I'm beautiful," he whispers with an edge of uncertainty, and it's so fucking cute.

He's so damn adorable today, I can't take it.

I turn his head so he's looking at me, and murmur against his mouth, "You're the most beautiful person I've ever seen."

And I mean that.

Fuck. I *mean* that?

My bewilderment is short-lived as he wraps his hand around my neck, wet fingers digging into my nape, and presses his lips to mine.

His kiss is urgent and almost frantic, as if he never kissed with such fire before. It's a sharp contrast to the way he usually reacts to me. Right now, he kisses me with raw, hungry heat as he comes in my hand.

While I fuck him.

He groans and grunts, but his lips never leave mine, like he wants to possess me, to kill me with his lips.

To suck my soul through my mouth.

I fall into the taste of him, the desperation in his kiss, my pace as frantic and urgent as his.

"Come..." he mumbles against my lips. "Come with me... Kayde...please."

The fact that he's like this—wanting me, needing me, losing all his goddam control for me—shoves me over the edge.

I come in long spurts, so deep inside his ass, we'll need some time to get that out.

But he doesn't stop kissing me, or me him, sucking my face, keeping me absolutely tethered to him with invisible strings.

There's no biting or breaking skin or blood.

Just raw, hungry, and entirely passionate kissing.

I don't think I've ever kissed anyone the way I kiss Gareth.

And fuck, since when did I start to call him by his first name in my head?

As we stand there, under the water, while he kisses me, I'm hit with an uncomfortable realization.

I might be the one who fucks Gareth, but he's the one who's owning me inch by agonizing inch.

Because I like kissing him more than I've liked kissing anyone.

My wife included.

20
GARETH

"You made this?"

I stroll out of the bedroom, rolling the cuff of my denim jacket.

So, yeah, I shouldn't be here. In hindsight, stepping into Kayden's house the first time was mistake number one. Pretty sure he had a witch cast a spell on me, because ever since, I keep coming back.

It's a valid theory for this disaster of a situation. Because, seriously, what the fuck was I doing just now?

Let's say yesterday was about being stuck and pretending I had no way out—literally—thanks to those damn ropes. But there were no ropes in the shower, and I still practically begged him to fuck me.

I came because he called me the most beautiful person he'd ever seen.

And I *kissed* him.

I *claimed* him.

I couldn't stop.

Pretty sure I only snapped out of it when he tried to help with, well, the cum in my ass, and I managed to kick him out. I think he caught the wide-eyed "holy fuck, I'm so fucking screwed" look before he left, though.

He also left me ointment on the bed, next to my folded clothes.

And I took some time to get dressed. One, because my ass is sore. Two, I needed time to think. To sort through this cluster-fuck and reach a logical conclusion.

If my so-called genius brain could deliver one, that'd be great. He sure is useless lately.

For now, I considered running away, and I needed a change of clothes before school anyway. Then I walked in on *this* scene, and, well, now I'm frozen.

Again.

There's that weird tight feeling in my chest.

Again.

Kayden's at the table, setting down plates of eggs, the smell of fresh coffee mingling with the sweet tang of strawberries. The red fruit glistens, perfectly sliced, ripeness on point.

He's changed into navy blue slacks, tailored so well, they practically worship his legs. The sleeves of his white shirt are rolled up, snug around his forearms, and showing off veins and muscle.

"I only cut the strawberries and brewed the coffee," he says, glancing at me with a small smirk. "The rest is from a nearby restaurant."

I glare, and he laughs—a rich, distracting sound.

The soft morning light catches in his styled hair, giving it a faint blue sheen. I'm watching every flick of his long fingers on the dish towel, the stretch of his shirt across his chest as he sits down.

The chest that pressed me against the mattress, the glass as he fucked and pounded and rearranged my fucking insides.

I have to stop myself from thinking of those images so that I don't get hard. Again.

This isn't normal.

Why am I hyperaware of him?

"Don't just stand there gawking," he says, motioning to the chair opposite him. "Sit down."

"I'm not gawking."

"Drooling, then?"

"Ugh. Get over yourself."

He grabs me by the waist and yanks me down, and I hiss when my bruised ass lands on his thighs.

His minty breath ghosts over my jaw as he murmurs, "Don't be a brat, or I'll bend you over my knee and give you a good spanking."

I purse my lips because, why the fuck would I find that... interesting?

"Like fuck you will," I whisper.

"Language." His grip tightens, and his scent floods my senses and I discreetly sniff him.

"You don't mind the language when you're—" I cut myself off.

"When I'm fucking your brains out? It's fine then. I love seeing you lose control because you love my cock so much."

"I do not," I snap, shoving off his lap and stalking to the chair. My cheeks burn like hellfire, and the bastard *knows* it.

He smiles as I sit. My ass throbs, and I make a mental note to cover every hickey and mark he left on my neck and collarbone. Might have to wear turtlenecks or something. What a hassle.

I clear my throat. "Why do you always brew coffee?"

"It's calming and I like the smell."

"But you always throw away the full bag of beans after."

"I'm particular about my coffee. It needs to be roasted just right."

"You're particular about a lot of things. Your coffee, your whiskey, your music. Even how things are organized around your house."

"My. The stalkerish habits are showing."

"I'm just observant." I swallow a piece of strawberry. "Do you ever cook?"

He sips his coffee, that infuriating smirk back. "Why? Want me to cook for you?"

"I never said that."

The smirk widens. "I don't cook. No passion for it."

"Me neither."

"See?" He lifts his cup in a mock toast. "We have so much in common, baby."

I stab a strawberry with my fork. "Would you stop calling me that?"

"Baby? But you loved it last night. Your cock got hard every time I said it."

I nearly choke but manage to swallow. "That's different."

"Different how?"

"It feels gay, okay? Stop it."

"So me coming deep inside you isn't gay, but 'baby' is?"

"That's...a physical reaction. It means nothing."

He sets his cup down, calm but with tension crowding his shoulders.

"I would've found your attempts to find excuses adorable under different circumstances, but you need to stop that line of thinking. Is being gay the end of the world? Do you have something against people like my moms?"

"Of course not. I don't care what others do. More power to them."

"Then why is it the end of *your* world?"

"I don't know. It feels weird."

"Weird how?"

I shrug, munching another strawberry. "I'm not used to the idea of being fucked. You're not the one giving up control, so it might have been easier for you to accept the sudden shift in your sexuality, but..."

His gaze softens slightly. "Being fucked is vulnerable, and you're still uncomfortable with that."

I lift a shoulder, avoiding his eyes. "Would *you* identify as gay?"

"For security reasons, I wouldn't do it publicly. But personally? Sure. I still find women attractive, though, so I'm probably bisexual."

"Women like Jessica?"

He sighs. "Yes, women like Jessica."

I stand up and grab the knife, but he slams my hand down. "Sit the fuck down, Carson. Enough."

"I'm going to fucking stab you."

"I said. *Enough.* Cut it out and stop with the impulsive actions." He presses on my hand as his authoritative voice penetrates my skin. "Let go."

I glare but release the knife, and he removes his hand as I sit back down. I stuff another strawberry in my mouth to keep from exploding.

Because what the fuck? Since when am I this quick to jump to action?

More importantly, why does the mention of someone else turn me murderous?

"Count to ten," he says in that same austere tone. "Or, better yet, try having a civil conversation instead of stabbing. I will not stand for these types of tantrums again. Got it?"

Something about his tone and the quiet command does something to me. But I tuck that away. "Are you meeting Jessica again?"

"No. We established exclusivity last night, remember? Or is that too *gay* for you?"

"But you still find *Jessica* attractive?"

"Don't you find other people attractive?"

No.

I pause with the fork near my mouth.

Fuck.

I *don't*.

Even before him, I picked girls based on vibes, not attraction. I got off, but not like this. Not like now, where I can't stop staring at his lips.

I shrug, feigning indifference.

"Who do you find attractive, hmm?" His voice darkens. "Morgan? Cherry?"

"You were the one drooling over Jessica. Stop with the mixed signals."

"I said that to piss you off."

"Well, I let Morgan touch me to piss *you* off."

He narrows his eyes, and I narrow mine back.

"Lose the attitude, Carson."

"I'm just mirroring yours, Professor."

"Carson..."

"Yes, *Professor*?" I grin, and he exhales sharply, clearly torn between anger and amusement.

We eat in silence for a while, until he stands and rummages around in the living room.

When he returns wearing thick-framed black glasses, my brain kind of short-circuits.

He looks hotter. How is that even *possible*?

Are people supposed to look even more attractive with glasses or am I just tripping?

Soon, though, he starts reading *The Financial Times*—gag—hiding his face and the glasses.

"Next time," I say in an attempt to get his attention, "order strawberry cheesecake."

"Noted."

"And granola."

"Sure."

"And strawberry protein bars."

"Will do."

"You should also consider getting a TV. You know, like normal people."

He lowers the paper, his glasses amplifying the sharpness in his eyes. "Anything else?"

"I'll make a list."

"You've been a spoiled brat your whole life, haven't you?"

"Oh, please, you're spoiled by your moms, too." And because I can't stop staring, I say, "Why haven't I seen you wear glasses at school? Are they just reading glasses?"

"Yes." He pulls out a cigarette.

Before he can light it, I snatch it away.

"Now what?" he grumbles.

"I hate the smell. It's also rude to smoke indoors."

"Didn't think you cared about what's considered rude."

"I do sometimes."

Not really. I also don't care about the smell, but I noticed he doesn't smoke much. I've only seen him do it once in his bath and never on campus, so it's better he quits.

He folds the newspaper and, unfortunately, removes the glasses. "Anything else you hate? Let's hear it."

"You, for instance."

"I'm well aware. Next?"

"Dogs."

"Why?"

"I was attacked once. Rabid."

"Did it scare you?"

"No, it disgusted me."

"Anything else?"

"French."

"French?"

"Learned it as a kid, but I hate it now."

"Fair. It's overrated."

"You speak it?"

"Yes."

"Wow. Korean and French. What other languages do you speak?" I know—German and Chinese, but talking to him is different than reading the cold information Nadine sends.

"Some German and Mandarin Chinese."

"Why did you learn those languages?"

"German and Chinese for business. Korean for Mom Jina, because she prefers speaking it instead of English, and French because my moms live in Lausanne, which is on the French-speaking side of Switzerland."

"Have you lived there?"

"Not for long."

"Because you chose to live with your dad?"

"How do you know that?"

Fuck. Shit.

I got that from Nadine. He shouldn't know I hired a PI to stalk him for me.

"Rachel mentioned it," I say with a shrug. "Why did you choose your dad over your moms?"

He stills, his gaze getting lost in the distance. "Sometimes the choice is made for you."

"In what sense?"

"Like when I gave you no way out. You don't have a choice in being with me, baby."

"I can still choose to stab you. Don't test me."

He chuckles. "Always a little menace, Carson."

"Why do you call me that?" My eyes widen. "Do you even *know* my first name?"

"Of course I do."

"Then say it."

He remains quiet and I narrow my eyes. "You really don't!"

"Gareth Carson, son of Asher and Reina Carson. The older brother of Killian Carson. Grandson of Alexander Carson. Is that enough for you?"

"You didn't have to go full stalker mode."

He strokes the rim of his glasses, his long fingers sliding up and down, and it's so distracting, I barely hear him. "Do you like being a Carson?"

"I guess. I like being born into my family."

"Of course you do." He scoffs, the sound so unlike him, it makes me frown.

But I can't read him, because he slowly stands, takes his newspaper and the glasses, then retrieves his briefcase.

"You're leaving for school this early?" I ask.

"Unlike some students with supercars, I'm walking."

"You can just get a car. Surely you can afford it." I swallow the last bit of strawberry and stand up. "I can drive you if you ask nicely."

"I prefer to walk."

"Whatever, not that I was dying to drive you."

"Suits us both then. Great."

"Awesome."

He puts on his coat and scarf, and then he's out the door before I can call him names.

Hope he breaks his legs on his walk.

Why was I trying to do something nice for him anyway? As if I wanted to take care of him or something equally ridiculous.

Fuck *him*.

21
GARETH

Turns out, he ended up being the one fucking me.

Ten times since that first night.

It's been over two weeks now.

My hopes for this entire illogical and dangerous infatuation to go away have significantly diminished.

Because I keep showing up at his place. I tried keeping a distance, but then I'll start obsessing about him bringing home other people—namely fucking Jessica—and I'll go over there in the middle of the night, armed with a new Taser and knife.

Kayden keeps confiscating them, and I keep getting new ones.

Truth is, he's never given me a reason to believe he's with

Jessica or anyone else but me. That still hasn't put my mind at ease, though.

My obsessive mind that I barely recognize anymore is spiraling.

"Never get obsessed again, son. Don't get caught."

Those words that have been my mantra for six years are dissolving with every touch, every encounter, and every mind-blowing orgasm.

I know I should take a step back, because, holy fuck, this is new.

I didn't know I could be this hyperfixated on a person, so caught in a lethal halo of hateful limerence until it becomes a noose that's getting tighter around my throat with each passing day.

Because I know I shouldn't have him, and, in retrospect, I won't be able to keep him.

This physical thing, as gratifying as it feels, is only surface level. I mean, not really, because this type of sexual connection feels like it transcends my body sometimes.

But it's still a phase, and all phases come to an end.

And then *what*?

That's all I keep thinking about. The *after*.

Not so much the now, but the after.

And I don't like that, because it's making this feel deeper than it should.

I've had sex before, plenty of it, but it's never felt like this. Intense and mind-stimulating and capable of putting me in a loop I can't leave.

The type of sex during and after which I just exist in that peaceful quiet of that white room.

It's addictive but also dangerous.

Because, despite his warnings and authoritative orders, I can't stop the impulsive thoughts.

Seeing girls and some professors flirting with him on

campus is driving me insane. The fact that I can't go there and pull him toward me by the throat and announce ownership is making me even more irritable.

I'm the one who refuses to come out, but even if I did, this is still a forbidden relationship. A professor isn't supposed to fuck his student, and if this is found out, he could be fired, so we can only be a secret. I know that, I do, and yet I hate *anyone*'s claws on him. Not that he indulges, but he still needs to stop being so fucking polite about it.

Three days ago, I saw him talking to Yulian on campus and smiling casually as that slimy fucker put his hands on him.

I haven't answered his texts or gone to his place since.

No matter how much he's threatened to punish me or put me over his knees to teach me some discipline.

And now, I'm going through withdrawals. The whole putting-some-distance-between-us thing backfired, and I've been a moody prick.

Am I that addicted to the asshole? It's been only three days. It's not that serious.

But the thing is, I felt the same when I went home the other day, and I kind of ditched Grandpa and came back within two days.

So three days is too much according to my body, because I can't sleep properly now and woke up with a headache.

Honestly, I'm the best sleeper I know. It's blasphemous that I'm struggling now.

Come to think of it, the only other time I couldn't sleep was after I first met the prick.

And to make things worse, last night, I dreamt of him holding me until I fell asleep.

Cuddling?

Seriously, kill me.

I mean, he's disturbingly soft after sex, and I kind of like the contrast. It was weird in the beginning, but I don't fight when he wipes me down or puts ointment on my ass, or even when he steps in the shower with me and lathers me with soap—that usually ends with another fuck, though.

But while he slides in bed with me, he never holds me, and he's always not there when I wake up. Either swimming or working out or brewing his fucking coffee while listening to classical music.

And it's not like I want him to hold me.

Right?

I never have in relationships, and I'm *not* needy.

Anyway, that dream was a hoax, and he can choke.

"Hear me out." Niko jumps up while we're having dinner, pulling me from my macabre thoughts. "We go to the Serpents' mansion tonight and play with those motherfuckers."

"Not unless you want them to play with us." I swirl my fork in the spaghetti, not bothering to bring anything to my mouth.

"Gaz, I'm telling you this for the final time." Niko glares at me. "Stop being a killjoy."

He's half naked, as usual, all his weird tattoos, mostly gotten on a whim, on full display. His long dark hair is pulled into a messy bun.

Jeremy looks up from his phone after he's been half smiling at it like a goddamn idiot. "He's right. They tightened their security after last week, Niko."

"Worst sidekicks ever," he grumbles and throws his massive body on the chair, and it rattles under his weight. "Satan's heir?"

"After last week, I'm not in the mood." Kill is speaking without looking up, busy texting with Glyn, if the permanent smirk is any indication.

"Last week was a necessity for revenge and to single a rat out. This is different. I want to pummel Yulian to the ground. How about this? If any of you backs me up, I'll let them name my firstborn." He pauses, then his lips curl in an evil grin as he mumbles, "If I have one. Maybe I need to ask about kids on the next run. Too soon? Would that be a turn-off? Hmm."

"What are you talking to yourself about?" Jeremy asks, watching him closely. "You good there, man?"

"Never been better." Niko's grin widens, but then he frowns. "Focus, Jer. Yulian. I want a fight with that prick. He throws a good punch, like a fucking bear."

"Then fight him in the underground ring," Kill says, still focused on his phone. "He loves that place as much as you do."

"Nah, doesn't feel as euphoric as pummeling him in his own castle with all those little bitches screaming their heads off around him." He laughs, getting all excited at the idea of violence. "I'll need you all to join."

"Pass. I'd rather be with my Glyn," Kill says.

He and his girlfriend have been joined at the hip for a while now, but it's gotten more serious after he took her home with us over a week ago. To meet Mom and Dad.

The trip during which he had a heart-to-heart with Dad—or Dad did. He apologized to Kill, too, for everything. Dad has been calling him more than me lately, pushing me to the background so he can fix his relationship with his real golden child.

I knew this day would eventually come. That Kill would finally face Dad, and Dad would feel guilty and try to repair things. Or that I'd slip, and they'd find out, and I'd be worse off than Kill. Because he's at least unapologetically himself. I've been deceiving them all this time.

But it happened too soon.

And it's been fucking with my head. Add the whole thing about fucking my professor, and I'm twitchy.

Enough to spend hours practicing archery and bite my fingers unconsciously.

Niko scoffs at Kill. "What the actual fuck, Satan's heir? Glyn is more important than me?"

"Not sure why that's a question. Of course she is."

"This motherfucker—"

"I'm also busy, Niko," Jeremy says, peeking at his phone.

"With what?"

"Something."

"Well, un-busy yourself and join me. What are bros for?"

"Can't. You should stay away as well."

"Well, fuck me sideways, I'm left with pacifist Gaz." He narrows his eyes on me. "Don't bore me to tears with all the reasons why I shouldn't do this either."

"Ask Vaughn to join," I say.

"The most useless of all due to his constant absence. Why the fuck that little shit is still in New York is beyond me."

"I'll convince him."

"You fighting will be more possible than him flying here without an initiation."

I tap my fingers on the table, then grab my phone. "Let me try something."

So I also need Vaughn to show up and put a leash on that motherfucker Yulian. And no, Niko beating him up isn't a permanent solution.

Also no, this has nothing to do with how I saw Yulian laughing and hitting Kayden on the shoulder on campus.

ME

V, miss me?

V

Only if you missed me, G.

Of course I did.

Something tells me you're going to manipulate me now.

Aw, you have that little faith in me?

Sometimes. Let's hear it.

> I'm only texting to see how you're doing with your girlfriend.

Ex-girlfriend.

> Wow. She really cheated with Yulian? That sucks, man.

I had my revenge :)

> Do you believe the initiation night was enough?

For now.

> I think you could do better than that, V. Not sure it affected Yulian that much tbh. He's such a fuckboy who's always flirting around.

I attach a picture I took of when he was with Kayden, specifically picking one where Kayden's face is hidden as Yulian wraps an arm around his shoulder and laughs like a whore.

What? I only took pictures for an occasion like this. And it pays off because Vaughn immediately replies.

Who's the other man?

> A professor you don't need to worry about. Yulian does that with everyone.

Everyone?

> Uh-huh. Can't keep it in his pants and goes for anyone. Heard he's openly bi, like Niko, and equally adventurous.

Openly? Does the motherfucker know what type of mafia he's set to fucking inherit?

He's cursing. Good. Vaughn rarely curses, so this is a promising sign.

> Maybe he thinks it's okay because Niko is doing it.

Niko isn't the son of the leader. He can get away with it, but even he has to watch himself in front of older family members.

> Idk, really. Maybe it's just rumors floating around.

Of what sort?

> All sorts. I can collect info if you like.

I'll owe you one.

> You got it.

Niko wants you to come help him raid the Serpents' mansion and beat Yulian to a pulp.

I'll arrange something.

I take a screenshot and cut everything except for the last two texts. "Niko?"

He pauses bickering with Jer and Kill, calling them traitors and being an absolute drama king. As I show him the screenshot, he grins wide. "You're the motherfucking best, Gaz."

I know.

I lean back in my chair with a small smile. Yulian has been on my nerves since that first night.

And while Kayden said he's never been with another man besides me, I'm not going to give him any openings.

He said I didn't have a choice in being with him, but he's wrong.

He doesn't have a choice in being with me.

I'll slice his fucking dick off if he even entertains putting it in another person.

And that's only the beginning of the things I'd do to him if he considers betraying me.

I blame it on the chest disease he gave me.

He's the one who started this whole game, so he shouldn't reproach me for taking it too seriously.

Kill stands up and puts the phone to his ear. He smirks at me as he says, "Hi, Dad. I've been meaning to call you..."

My mood immediately darkens, and I throw the fork on the plate as my brother goes up the stairs as if he has some sort of secret with Dad.

He doesn't.

But it still sours my fucking mood.

I need my arrows and a goddamn target.

22
KAYDEN

I step out of the taxi, pulling the lapels of my coat over my neck as I open the umbrella.

Because of course it's raining, as per the UK's shit weather.

My phone vibrates and I stare at Jethro's name and consider not replying. Yes, he got me Gareth's location by hacking into his phone, which is why I'm by the archery range, but now, he should kindly fuck off.

With a sigh, I pick up, fleetingly noticing the pretentious matte-green sports car parked by the entrance. "What do you want?"

"Aside from you returning to US soil and abandoning all this nonsense?"

"Aside from that, yes. Make it quick."

"You're obsessing way too much over that kid. You need to reconsider this and see if you're doing it for the right reasons at this point."

"If that's all..."

"Management is struggling, and Grant is making everyone's life hell. You should come back, even temporarily—"

"No."

I don't even think about it, because I won't. That would undoubtedly make me lose Gareth. He's still trying to slip away at any chance possible, giving me the silent treatment and ignoring me in a heartbeat.

If I go away, he'll be rid of me, and that's just not on the menu.

"Just to pacify things," Jethro insists. "It's getting out of hand fast. Simone and I are straining to hold it together."

"I said. No."

"Is it because of the kid?" He pauses, and when I don't reply, he speaks low. "Jesus Christ. Who the hell are you and what have you done with the Kayden I know?"

I hang up so he'll stop blabbering in my ear.

But also because I have no answer to his last question. Jethro, of all people, would notice the change, but the truth remains, I have no clue what the fuck is happening to me.

Except that I lose any semblance of control at the sight of bright, expressive green eyes.

I've quit trying to explain it even to myself, stopped being all-consumed in my thoughts, and chose to just feel.

For the first time in a long time, I feel alive.

I'm here.

Breathing properly.

I'll think about everything else later.

The archery range reception has only one staff member. A middle-aged woman with gold-framed glasses eagerly lets me buy a one-day pass and keeps talking about their monthly and yearly memberships, which I cut short. Because I'm not here to talk to her.

After she gives a quick explanation about the facilities and shows me to the locker room, she finally leaves me alone.

I shrug off my coat at record speed and take one of the rental bow and arrows as if I have a clue about archery.

In reality, I shouldn't be here. I shouldn't have asked Jethro to track Gareth down either, but he was pushing it.

He's been ignoring me for three days, and while that amount was tolerable in the past, now it's no different than walking around with one lung. It's suffocating, and I can't breathe properly.

All the toxins are gathering in my one lung and causing pressure in my chest.

When I tried to text him, he was elusive.

ME

I'll be home by seven. How about you?

LITTLE MONSTER

Won't be coming.

Why?

Because.

Can you elaborate on the reason for this episode?

You should ask yourself.

What have I done?

Something annoying af.

Full words, Carson.

Something annoying AS FUCK.

> Language. And what is this annoying thing?

> I can't read your mind so if you don't tell me, I won't know.

> Carson. If you don't reply, there will be dire consequences. I will put you on my knee and punish you, are we clear?

He didn't reply to any of my last texts and he didn't come over either. He knows I can't just go knocking on the door of the mansion he shares with his friends. Or grab him by the arm on campus, bend him over on my desk, and fuck him.

Though I did fantasize about that countless times, but it's too risky. Being a popular professor in college is infuriating because my office is always full of students and other professors.

And while I don't give a damn about my position, Gareth is a genius student and I don't want to sabotage his studies.

Fucking ironic, really.

So I tried bribing him with pictures of ripe strawberries, telling him Mom sent them over for him—though, really, I asked her to.

Tonight, I sent him a picture of the package of strawberry-flavored hot chocolate I scoured the internet for since he loves everything with strawberries, but he didn't see it. And when I called his phone, he didn't reply. That's when I asked Jethro for help, and he sent me this location.

I walk into the indoor range, where two other men are practicing, but there's no trace of Gareth.

He couldn't have possibly been on the outside range in this fucking weather—

Sure enough, when I storm out, he's right there, standing under the pouring rain, pulling an arrow against the string. His muscles flex beneath his soaked T-shirt, and the faint outline of the crossed arrows tattooed on the underside of his arm peeks through.

He's drenched, water clinging to his hair and cascading in rivulets down his pale neck.

Like a piece of art, his body aligns in perfect, almost geometric precision as he pulls back and releases the arrow.

Bullseye.

I wouldn't expect anything less from him.

He doesn't stop. Another arrow, then another, each one hitting its mark with mechanical consistency. Rain streams down his face, dripping off his jaw, but he's completely unbothered.

I, however, am not.

Because he'll get fucking sick.

I stride toward him, rain soaking me to the bone. As I approach, he turns in my direction, an arrow nocked and aimed at me. His eyes narrow as recognition sets in.

There's something turbulent in his gaze, the color not quite right. And what does it say about me that I can read his mood in a single glance?

Too fucking far gone, probably.

Honestly, I wouldn't put it past him to shoot me like he did during the initiation.

But instead, he lowers the bow and focuses back on the target. "Picked up archery just to stalk me?"

"To see you."

He releases the arrow, but it lands slightly off-center. A frustrated breath tears out of him, and he lets the bow fall to his side as he faces me. "What if I don't want to see you?"

"I'd need a proper reason for that. You've got to communicate, even when you're mad. Otherwise, how am I supposed to know what's wrong?"

"Forget it." He pulls another arrow, rolling the tip between his fingers.

"Not if you're still mad about it."

He tilts his head, frowning a bit. "Why does that matter to you? Whether I'm mad or not."

"Why wouldn't it? I want to take care of you."

"I can take care of myself."

"I know you can, but I want to be there anyway. Like right now." I grab his arm, the chill of his skin jolting against my hand. "You're not taking care of yourself by standing in the rain shooting arrows. Your body is mine, so you don't get to be reckless with it. Are we clear?"

He swallows hard, his turbulent eyes wavering and flickering. They're so lost and disturbed it makes me want to kill whoever put that look there—even if it's me.

His lips are bluish, and I notice a small cut at the edge of his archery glove. I gently remove it, inspecting the wound. It's shallow, but the sight of it irritates me anyway.

"How did this happen?"

He shrugs, silent, as if his mind is miles away.

The fact that he isn't throwing out a snarky comment is more worrying than the wound.

After wrapping a tissue around his hand, I tug him toward the locker room. "We're going home."

He's got spare sets of sweatpants and shirts in his locker, and I grab the loosest fit for myself. As we change, I keep stealing glances at him.

He's acting...odd.

It's concerning.

Now, why I am concerned about a literal psycho is anyone's guess.

"Stop that," he mutters, his voice quieter than usual.

"Stop what?"

"Ogling me like a massive pervert."

"Why can't I look at what's mine?"

He turns away, but not before I catch the flush creeping up his neck.

At least, one thing hasn't changed.

He acts like a goddamn menace, but he blushes around me. It's endearing and adorable as fuck.

Once we're dressed, I make sure he stays under the umbrella as we walk to his car.

"Give me your keys. I'll drive if you're tired."

"No way. Do you even know how to drive this?"

"It's a car, not a spaceship."

He strokes the top of the car reverently. "It's a special car. My twentieth birthday gift from Grandpa. The only one of its kind with its matte black-green exterior and 1,200 horsepower on a quad-turbo W16 engine that pushes 1,500 Nm of torque. Don't get me started on the aerodynamic design that cuts through the air or the carbon body filter. You're so special, aren't you, Medusa?"

"You named your car Medusa?"

"Sure did. She's badass."

"That's ridiculous."

"Don't listen to him, baby girl," he murmurs, stroking the car like a lover.

Am I jealous of a goddamn car because he speaks to it so softly and calls it baby girl?

Yes. Yes, I fucking am.

Something scurries from under the car and both of us remain still as a rat climbs up Gareth's leg.

Wait. Not a rat.

A small drenched black cat meows its head off, its tiny claws grabbing on to Gareth's pants for dear life.

"Get it off me." Gareth tries to wiggle his leg, but the cat holds on tighter.

"So it's not just dogs. You're also afraid of cats?" I ask, amused.

"No, I just don't know how to deal with animals. They're unpredictable little fuckers like kids."

"It's probably just hungry." I hand him the umbrella and crouch down.

The cat lets out a pitiful meow, its tiny claws gripping Gareth's pants.

"Hey, little one. You're freaking out this big, tall muscular guy who loves stabbing things. Mind getting off?"

"I'm not freaking out. Just hurry up."

I chuckle and grab the cat, and it hisses, then meows in one long high-pitched sound. "Hard life this young?"

When I stand up again, holding the cat in the palm of my hand, Gareth pulls away a little, eyeing it as if it's a bomb. "Just put it down or something."

"It'll die in this rain."

"Then let's drop it off at a shelter."

"They're closed this late. We'll take it home and figure something out tomorrow."

He says nothing and slides into his precious car that I kind of dislike now. What? He treats it better than me.

The cat, a girl, is shivering in my lap as I slide into the passenger seat.

She burrows into the scarf I've wrapped around her as we drive to a nearby pet store. Gareth parks, grumbling under his breath while I head inside to grab the essentials. The shop-keeper gives me a crash course in kitten care and recommends a visit to a 24-hour vet just to be safe.

My moms have two dogs and I've never had a cat, or a pet, for that matter—Dad would've never allowed such nonsense, so this is new territory for me.

When I return, Gareth eyes the bag suspiciously but doesn't comment as we head to the vet. He stays near the door while I take care of everything, his posture stiff and defensive, like he's preparing for a fight.

When I come back with the kitten in a carrier, bundled in my scarf and fast asleep after her checkup, Gareth grimaces.

"Can't you leave her here?" he asks, already halfway to the car.

"It's a vet, not a shelter. And she's fine now—just starving and in need of a few routine treatments."

"Great." He casts a wary glance at the tiny creature as he starts the car.

"You never had pets?"

"Not exactly. Mom had this fat cat when I was a kid. Evil bastard scratched me and Kill every chance he got. Even Dad wasn't safe. He only liked Mom. The rest of us avoided him like the plague."

"Aw, traumatized?"

"No." He scowls. "That thing better not scratch me."

I laugh, unable to help myself. "So you *are* scared of cats."

"I'm not scared," he snaps, his tone sounding almost offended.

"Sure, whatever you say."

"Kayden!"

"What? I believe you."

"But you're laughing. Is this funny to you?"

"Very. Your weakness is harmless little animals."

"They're not harmless. Those buggers are unpredictable."

I laugh again and he gives me a murderous look, but, truly, I only see it as cute now.

At least he's not in a bad mood like when I found him at the range. I'll still need to learn everything about that, though. But for now, I'll just enjoy teasing the hell out of him.

23
KAYDEN

By the time we get to my place, he's opted to carry all the bags, leaving me to deal with the cat. As soon as I open the carrier, she darts out, heading straight for the sofa.

Gareth all but jumps behind me, dropping all the bags on the floor. "Motherfucking bitch!"

I throw my head back and laugh.

"It's not *that* funny," he grumbles, peeking out from behind me as the kitten hides under the sofa.

But, really, I love how he's holding on to my waist, even if it's to use me as a shield, he's touching me without trying to choke, knife, or tase me.

Baby steps, right?

"It's hilarious. Who knew the great Gareth Carson would be terrified of a tiny kitten?"

"She can do serious damage."

"Oh, I'm sure. A real threat to humanity."

"Stop laughing, Kayde! I mean it."

He says that and yet he's ogling me, as if he's mesmerized.

He has these instances where he just looks at me, his lips parted and ears flushing a bit. I don't think he's aware of it, and I don't want to draw attention to it or he'll stop doing it.

As the laugh dies out, I face him. "I'll give her some more food. Want to help?"

"No, thanks. I'll go change." He all but bolts in the direction of the bedroom.

Shaking my head, I set up a temporary litter box and put out food and water. The kitten, now a curious ball of energy, emerges from her hiding spot to eat before exploring her surroundings.

Meanwhile, I heat some milk and make Gareth a cup of his new strawberry hot chocolate.

A few moments later, Gareth comes out of the bedroom wearing black shorts and a white tee. He started leaving his stuff around after that time I first fucked him. He has a whole section in my closet now, and he keeps adding all his things to it.

Not that I mind.

He's been around regularly for about two weeks, and in the span of that time, he's been ordering all sorts of unnecessary stuff online that he uses once or twice, then loses interest.

It's in his innate nature to get easily bored. Nothing can hold his interest for too long. Not possessions. Not relationships.

Not people.

Once something becomes ordinary, he just drops it.

Which is why his disappearance the past few days started a niggling doubt. He can't possibly be bored of me.

He's too obsessed with me, possessive of me, and—he would never admit this—craves my approval and affection too much.

So I need to figure out the reason behind the change.

My gaze follows him, admiring his form while he searches around for the cat.

"She's behind the curtains," I say.

"I don't care." He flops onto the sofa and I place the cup in front of him as he opens Netflix.

He's been watching a lot of Korean dramas and shows lately, even while he scoffs at how ridiculous they are. But he still asks his cousin—Maya, I believe—for recs. I realized it's because he's trying to communicate with Ma Jina.

She said he sometimes sends her ridiculous Korean texts, and I don't know why that made me smile.

Gareth takes an absentminded sip from the hot chocolate as he clicks on the show he was watching here three days ago. I don't really watch TV and only got it and Netflix because he was complaining about the lack of both like a spoiled brat.

But seeing him so comfortable and natural in my space is worth it.

"Strawberry-flavored hot chocolate?" he asks, his eyes lighting up.

"How do you like it?"

"It's amazing. Where'd you even find this?"

"Just stumbled across it."

"Thanks—motherfucker!"

The kitten jumps onto his lap, startling him so badly, he nearly spills the drink.

"Ah, fuck, Kayde, get her off!"

I suppress a smile. "Relax and behave while I go change."

"No, seriously. I'll let you choke me with your cock if you just take her away."

My dick twitches at the offer, but I play it cool. "Tempting. I'll think about it."

"Kayde!"

Chuckling, I step away, pretending to leave. Behind me, Gareth mutters curses under his breath, clearly unsure how to handle the kitten.

Eventually, I hear him mumbling, "Asshole."

I'm by the corner, my dick seriously questioning why I'm sacrificing his well-being just to help Gareth work on his issues with animals.

He lacks some empathy toward them and that's not good. It's textbook criminal ASPD behavior, and I need him to be different from those monsters.

"Okay, little demon, what's your deal?"

A loud meow answers him, and he sighs begrudgingly.

"Oh, hell no. Also, Mom said milk isn't good for cats." He tries to push her away and she falls, but then she climbs back up on his T-shirt.

"I guess a bit won't hurt."

He pours a small amount of hot chocolate into his palm and lifts it toward her. She laps it up eagerly, her tiny pink tongue darting out.

For a moment, Gareth looks...soft. His shoulders relax, and he carefully strokes her head, as if testing the waters. "You won't scratch me, right?"

I smile and disappear into the bedroom, answer some texts, especially from my nephew—while I ignore my brother's—and then I change into PJ bottoms.

When I finally join him again, Gareth is lying on his back on the sofa with the kitten curled up on his chest, purring loudly.

He looks up and his lips part, then he swallows thickly, his

Adam's apple bobbing. It's because of the glasses he's gawking at me. Ever since I noticed he wouldn't stop staring at me when I wear them, I started putting them on more often.

The other day, I fucked him while wearing them, and he was extra noisy. Well, until they fogged up and I had to remove them.

"Be quiet. She's asleep," he mutters.

"What happened to not wanting her near you?"

"She's okay, I guess. Purrs like an engine for such a tiny thing."

"Should I keep her?"

His expression brightens briefly before he schools it into indifference. "I don't care."

"What should I name her, Mr. I Don't Care?"

"Moka," he says without hesitation.

"Mocha?"

"The European spelling, with a *K* instead of a *ch*. She's black with brown eyes. It fits."

"Moka it is, then."

I sit on the edge of the sofa beside him, sliding my hand over his chest as I lean in. "You did well tonight."

"It's not that serious," he mumbles, attempting to sound casual, but his chest hums beneath my touch. He does love my approval. It turns *him* into a docile kitten.

He also really hates it when I scold him.

Which is why I'm using those two edges to tame him better, balance his unhinged personality so he doesn't commit any impulsive actions.

This wasn't in the cards when I first got to know him, but now it's my mission. Someone like Gareth needs a more emotionally mature and strict person by his side to keep him in check, otherwise he'd eventually spiral.

He has this calm expression when he looks at me now, almost content.

"Does that mean no choking on my cock tonight?"

"Nah, missed your chance." His dimples flash, and I can't stop myself from grinning as I settle in beside him.

"There's not enough room. Just go sit on the chair," he grumbles as I move closer.

"Scoot over."

I push him slightly, sliding one arm beneath his nape and the other over his chest, throwing a leg over his in a sideways hug. He's so warm, and his scent—bergamot and something uniquely Gareth—wraps around me like a drug.

He releases a low grumble, tapping my arm. "It's hot."

"You're the one who's hot."

"Corny," he mutters, coughing slightly to hide his smile.

"It still worked." I study the sharp line of his jaw and the freckles scattered over his nose. My fingers find the hem of his shirt sleeve, lifting it just enough to trace the inked arrows on his arm.

"What do these mean? Is it about your love for archery?"

"Yes and no." He stares at the ceiling, his expression clouding. "Do you know what crossed arrows symbolize?"

"Balance between opposing forces? Maybe it's about how you balance your public and private personas?"

"Not quite. My personality bleeds into every part of my life anyway." He lets out a small exhale. "The arrows remind me that no matter how tightly I try to hold everything in place, chaos is always lurking beneath the surface. It's not about weakness or lack of discipline. It's the tension and the constant pull between staying in control and being drawn to the uncontrollable. Think of it as a paradox, a memento that I'm never as in charge as I want to be."

I stroke the pad of my thumb along the arrowhead, absorbing his words. I didn't think it had that deep of a meaning. "Am I one of the things you can't control but can't help being drawn to?"

"Stop being so full of yourself," he scoffs, though his gaze softens. He flicks a glance at my chest. "What about your tattoo?"

"It's about rebirth."

"Rebirth? Not danger?"

"No." I let my fingers skim the ink. "A snake shedding its skin represents survival and growth. Power through transformation. It's about staying fluid, adapting, and never getting too comfortable."

He falls silent, his hand drifting to the edge of the lily inked on my side. His touch is hesitant and it burns even though he's not touching the lily. He pulls away, returning to petting the purring kitten on his chest.

He's always like this—fine with being bent, tied, or dominated in every way, but hesitant about simple gestures of affection. It's as though touching me too freely will cost him something he's unwilling to give. The only reason he's still touching my arm that he tried to remove from his chest earlier is probably because he forgot it's there.

"What about the lily?" he asks, breaking the silence.

"I've always admired its strength and how it blooms under the harshest conditions."

He hums softly, neither agreeing nor disagreeing, his thoughts seemingly somewhere distant.

"Baby?"

"Yeah?" he murmurs absently. At least he doesn't bristle at the nickname anymore.

"Why were you in such a bad mood at the archery range?"

"I wasn't."

"Gareth, I know when you're not being yourself. You had that distant look in your eyes and didn't even notice it was raining. Hyperfixation is your tell."

He blinks, his eyes widening slightly. "You called me Gareth."

"Am I not supposed to?"

He shrugs, but his dimples appear. "I prefer my first name to my last."

"All right, but you're not changing the subject. What had you so upset?"

His humor fades, replaced by something guarded. "Dad and Kill are reconciling. Or in the process of it."

"And?"

"And I'm shoved into the background." He pauses, his jaw tightening. "Well, that sounded dramatic, but yeah. I don't like it. I'm supposed to be Dad's favorite."

Hmm, I suspected this before, despite his clear negation of the fact, but Gareth has some hidden daddy issues. Probably because he thinks his father will never accept him if he sees his true face.

Not that I know his dad, but if he doesn't? Gareth should walk away. Or walk all over him.

But then again, I don't have the best track record since I never liked my own dad.

"This changes that?" I soften my voice.

"I don't know."

"Does it matter if it does?"

"Of course it does." His voice hardens, jaw clenching tighter. "Without that, I'd have no purpose. I loathe the very idea of it."

"Then don't concern yourself. You'll always have a purpose."

He blinks at me, wary. "Which is?"

"Being mine, baby."

A laugh bursts out of him, the sound rich and unrestrained. His dimples deepen, making him look younger, boyish.

"Laugh all you want, but being mine is an important purpose."

"Yeah, right."

"I'm serious. Your presence is important to me."

He swallows hard, his throat working as his eyes meet mine. "How important?"

"Important enough that the last three days were hell without you. Are you going to tell me why you disappeared?"

"It's nothing," he says, his gaze drifting back to the ceiling.

"What did I say about communication?"

"Do I have to tell you everything?"

"Yes."

He remains silent, frowning slightly.

"I'm waiting, Gareth," I say firmly.

After a long pause, he mutters, "If you must know, I didn't like Yulian throwing himself all over you."

"Yulian?"

"Yes, *Yulian*," he snaps. "The one you went crazy over the first time we met. Did you have a crush on him or something?"

"No. And I didn't go crazy because of him."

"Then why?"

"Your actions. It didn't matter who was on the receiving end —I would've acted the same."

"Countering assault with assault? Seriously?"

"Not something I'm proud of, but we were both equally fucked up. We *are* both equally fucked up."

He's silent for a moment, his fingers absently stroking my arm.

"I'm not offering excuses for your actions, and it's not like I was that innocent anyway, but I liked that." He closes his eyes, his lashes fluttering on his cheeks. "From the start, I think I enjoyed how you dominated me and gave me no way out."

My chest tightens as he turns his head toward me, his forehead almost touching mine.

I think he's fallen asleep, but then he whispers, "I don't believe I would've ever discovered that part of myself if it weren't for those encounters, so a part of me is grateful. The other part would still stab you, though."

A laugh leaves me, but it's cut short when he opens those green eyes. They're dark, as if peering into my soul.

"I mean it, Kayde. You betray me or put your dick somewhere it shouldn't be, I'll rip your heart out and watch you bleed out. I'm that brand of crazy, so don't test me."

"I'm that brand of crazy, too. So let's not test each other. Deal?"

"Deal."

"And, Gareth?"

"Hmm."

"You'll communicate properly from here on out. I will not stand for these tantrums in the future. Are we clear?"

"Okay." He swallows thickly, his eyes softening. "What's your relationship with Yulian anyway?"

"He's my student."

"That's all?"

"I helped his dad in the States, and he asked me to look out for him."

"Do you *have* to look out for him?"

"Not really. Why are you asking? Jealous?"

"I don't like it when he throws his arm around your shoulders. I can't even do that in public, so he shouldn't either." He gulps. "You're the one who asked me to communicate, so I'm just doing that right now."

"Fine. I'll make sure to not allow him to do that again."

"Really?"

"Really. You communicated properly and asked nicely, so you deserve a reward."

He smiles, his cheeks creasing, and his lips remain frozen in a soft smile as his lids grow heavy and close again.

As I hold him until he falls asleep with some cheesy drama playing in the background, I think of all the ways my plans are fucked up beyond repair.

And I'm not even that sad about it.

Forget about what I came here to do.

I need to tuck Gareth safely away from those in my entourage.

I need Jethro to prepare me a gadget.

24
GARETH

QUIETRAGE

How is it going with your man?

TOOPRETTYFORTHISMESS

He's not MY man. I still dislike him sometimes, but apparently, that's when I'm sex deprived because it takes being fucked to exhaustion for me to fold.

BWAHAHA we've come a long way from 'I'd never get fucked' to 'I'm being fucked to exhaustion.'

Don't push it, man.

Hey, I'm just glad you're having fun, my dude.

> You're not? Having fun, I mean?

> I never will.

I stare at Vaughn's texts in class, smirking. So, yeah, QuietRage is V.

Speak of a small goddamn world.

I figured that out shortly after we took in Moka about a month ago—or Kayden did, minor details. The little demon only sleeps on top of me and likes me better than him anyway. He's just the spare human according to the internet.

Anyhow, V kind of gave himself away when he mentioned that he had a girlfriend for years and thought he was happy with her and even thought of marrying her one day, but then she cheated with this guy, and ever since then, he can't stop obsessing.

About the guy—not the girlfriend. He's even considering transferring to another university in a 'whole-ass other country' that, apparently, he avoided because of this guy—Yulian, *duh*— even though he had to separate from his friends in the process. Something about hating the fuck out of the guy's guts, but he's still being drawn to him anyway.

Same.

Ever since our first convo, we've been texting daily and checking on each other's clusterfuck of a gay awakening which sort of grew into a friendship. I like that we're both going through the same shit, and I prefer the cloak of anonymity to talk freely—which I'm sure he does, too.

I also speak to him in reality often as well, mostly to warn him. From the little research I've done on Yulian, he's sort of a basket case that should be locked up. But who am I to judge?

> U think you'll stay with him for long?

> Idk. I'll stab him if he tries to leave, though.

> You're falling for him, huh?

I stare at his text, my chest experiencing that shitty ache again.

> Nope. I don't do feelings.

> Bro, I'm telling u this bcz I care about u and feel a weird camaraderie, but u kind of do. Normal people don't think about stabbing their sex buddies if they think they'll leave. Unless they're a psychopathic narcissist, which is cool if u are. Not judging. But over these past few weeks, u said you're having fun even when fucking isn't involved, and your favorite thing is aftercare and when he gives you affection, right? So maybe u need to analyze the 'no feeling' statement further.

"Mr. Carson." The too familiar deep, calm voice pulls me out of my reverie. "I hope whatever you're reading on your phone is more important than your education. If you're done paying attention, feel free to leave. We wouldn't want to waste any more of your time."

His eyes are dark and stormy. Turbulent, even.

My fingers tighten on the phone as I glare back.

He's been a major asshole since I obviously won the trial earlier. He gave the jury one hell of a critique for their reasoning, and me? Well, he dismantled me.

"Mr. Carson, your defense was superficial at best, and you tremendously failed to grasp the gravity of the case. It wasn't just about your legal arguments, but about the human element and the empathy you should have shown for the victim. You came off as cold-blooded, indifferent, and menacing, particularly during cross-examination.

"You didn't approach the victim with precision or care and wielded a sledgehammer where a scalpel was needed. Your tactics were harsh, dismissive, and reeked of arrogance, as though the nuances of this case could be handled with aggression or by seducing members of the jury with your intellect and charm. But rape cases, especially ones with this level of complexity, aren't about flexing your power or stroking your ego. They're about understanding the victim's trauma, their fear, and the lasting impact on their lives. You missed that entirely.

"If you can't grasp something so fundamental, how do you expect to fight for the truth without crushing it under your own self-importance? I expected more from you, Carson. I'm not just disappointed—I'm unimpressed."

Needless to say, I've been fuming since. Which is why I picked up the phone in the first place—to forget about his asshole side.

And he *was* an asshole. Even Zara and the rest of the prosecution team told me I wasn't that bad. I *know* I wasn't bad at all, actually, and didn't deserve to be humiliated in front of the entire class.

I didn't deserve to be told, *"I'm not just disappointed—I'm unimpressed."*

So now, I pick up my notebook and stand.

Kayden's eyes follow my movements, remaining as still as a frozen lake. "Where do you think you're going?"

"Leaving, as you instructed."

"Quit the toddler tantrum and sit down."

"I'm good. The lecture isn't holding my interest anyway."

"Carson. I said. Sit down." His voice booms in the hall.

I glare at him and make a beeline to the door.

This is the first time in my life I've left in the middle of a class, but fuck him, really. He's been a pain in the ass since the start of this case. No matter what I've said or done, he's only criticized and disrespected me. Maybe I would've let that go before, but now that I truly hate his disapproval, it's causing a deeper pain in that fucking part of my chest.

"I expect you in my office after class, Carson," he says when I'm by the door.

I tilt my head in his direction. "No, thanks."

His eyes hold mine, strange tension whirling beneath the gray, muting it until it's almost dead, like a brewing storm. "Be there unless you wish to fail criminal law."

Me? Failing a fucking subject?

He wants to die. He clearly does.

The whole class goes into shock, because why the hell would the top student fail a core fucking subject?

My lips pull up and I clamp them back down, then storm out.

As I stalk to the library, I tell myself he can't actually fail me, not with my grades, and I can ask for a different grader if he does. I'll sabotage his fucking career with the dean if he even comes near my GPA. I'm the star student here, and the dean is Grandad's friend, who'd be livid if he heard about this episode.

And yet I can't remain calm.

I realize I'm biting the skin under my nails and curse beneath my breath as I drop my hand and hold my head in my palm, staring at the blurry lines of the random constitutional law book I picked up.

Rage is throwing a mist over my eyes, and even still, I can recognize the underlying feeling beneath. Pain?

Fuck, am I hurt by his treatment?

Hurt because he said he's *disappointed* in me?

Hurt because he threatened my spotless GPA just to make me feel small?

Hurt because I stayed up all night perfecting my closing statement just for him to stomp all over it.

My mind is full of stabby impulses, but, really, I noticed I only have those when he treats me like shit.

Or when I'm jealous.

Over the past month, ever since the first time he hugged me to sleep and called me by my first name, I thought things had changed.

We don't just get together so he can fuck my brains out anymore. He's been joining me at the archery range. I have my own personal range at the mansion but usually stick to the public one to avoid friends barging in uninvited. Lately, though, I've been spending more time at the club, and it's quickly become my favorite spot.

Mostly because I've been teaching Kayden. Turns out, he's pretty interested—and annoyingly good at it. A fast learner, actually.

The club is discreet enough that no one bats an eye at our existence. They'd just assume we're there by coincidence.

We've also started playing chess, and honestly, it's my favorite thing ever. We're both stubborn as hell, and he *never* lets me win. Not once. Which I'm determined to change.

I love how he challenges me, keeps me sharp, and quiets the demons in the void.

Of course, Moka keeps knocking over our pieces during matches. Kayden scolds her, and I immediately scoop her up and hide her away. What? She's a sweet, innocent baby. Okay, fine, maybe she *did* ruin the sofa, and sure, I spoil her a little—ordering her all kinds of stuff—but I digress.

Kayden even lets me talk to his moms when he FaceTimes them. They're not stupid; they know what's going on. Rachel said, "You're young and should think carefully before making any decisions, hon." Which was confusing, but whatever.

All in all, we've been having fun.

We've been watching hockey together. I've never been a hockey fan, but seeing it through his eyes, knowing he used to play—the violence, the sheer chaos—I'm starting to like it.

Kayden noticed, of course, and said he'll take me to a game someday.

I don't know when that day will be, but I'm getting too accustomed—and too addicted—to how much he notices everything about me.

And I mean *everything*.

Whether it's my bad moods, the stress of thinking that Dad doesn't care about me now that he has Kill, or when I need to purge.

In those moments, he ties me up and fucks me until I'm too wrung out to think.

I believe the reason I struggled so much in the beginning was because I thought I always needed to be in control, so actually submitting to someone else made me panic. I don't like feeling vulnerable, but with him? I love it.

I crave how he dominates me, that I can give up control to him and he'll set my world ablaze. He stops my brain from overthinking and makes me feel powerful in my submission.

In a way, I just like...letting go when I'm with him. I don't have to worry about anything, because he'll make everything right.

I'm accepting my sexuality better now and even get frustrated when we don't have sex for...two days.

That's my limit, don't judge.

I think my dick is having its revenge for all the lackluster fucks I put him through.

Kayden fixes that by edging me until I beg. He loves keeping me on the brink, and I love when he forces me on my hands and knees, leaving me no way out.

It's our dynamic. Not something average people would call healthy, but it works for us.

At least, in the bedroom. Or when it's just the two of us.

On campus, though? He's indifferent. I get that it's a necessity, but he doesn't have to be such an *asshole* about it. Like earlier.

Or like every single time we've worked on the trial case.

"Hey, handsome," a low voice whispers in my ear.

I glance up to find Morgan scooting her chair closer, her overwhelming floral perfume practically punching me in the gut.

Class isn't even over yet—I check my watch to confirm. I don't want to see *him*, but I also don't want to give the bastard a reason to act on his latest threat.

"You skipped?" I ask her.

"Overslept. Whoopsie." She giggles softly. "Figured it was better to stay out than risk Professor Lockwood scolding me. You know how big he is on punctuality."

"More like punctual pain in the ass," I mutter under my breath.

"What?"

"Nothing."

"What are you doing here anyway?" she asks, sliding her hand into mine and leaning closer to whisper, "Not that I'm complaining. I really missed you and your big dick."

"Don't." I pull my hand away from hers.

I could swear her touch used to do something to me once—don't ask me what, but it was there. Now? Every touch disgusts me.

With one glaring exception.

"But why?" She pouts, her big purple lips looking cartoon-ishly exaggerated.

"Not interested, Morgan."

"What if I bring a friend?"

I raise a brow. "Like who?"

"Who do you want?"

"Hmm. How about Zara?"

"Not her. She swings the other way."

"Oh? Who told you that?"

"I'm not as gullible as I look. She's dropped plenty of hints and even implied it once."

"So you're also aware she has a crush on you? And you still led her on?"

Her eyes widen, snapping to mine. "How do you— Doesn't matter. I didn't lead her on."

I grab her arm, tightening my grip just enough to make her freeze.

"But you did. Because you're a goddamn parasite. Zara is ten times smarter than you and way out of your league, really, but you like how she puts you on a pedestal. She covers for you, helps with your homework, and you repay her by throwing out mixed signals and *innocent* little kisses, keeping her hooked on you." My voice drops low as I shake her. "Either make it clear you're using her so she can move the fuck on, or I will. And trust me, Morgan, it won't be pretty if I do it."

I release her, ignoring the tears welling in her eyes, and stand up.

Fuck this.

Why am I so worked up on Zara's behalf? I have no clue.

Maybe because I *hate* the manipulations and the fucking lies.

Figures.

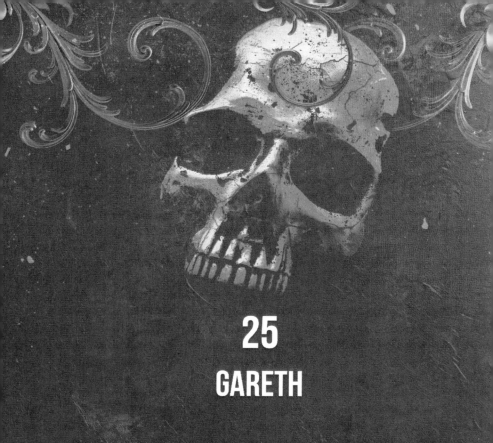

25
GARETH

I stand outside Kayden's office, the buzz of students and distant chatter from down the hall a dull hum beneath the pounding in my own head. That white silent room I love so much is smudged with swishes of gray, and I want them to come off.

My fingers twitch at my side, reluctant to knock. I can't shake the thought that I'm about to walk into something I won't be able to control.

That's what I've always liked and disliked about Kayden. The idea that he can strip my control and give me something is what I like.

But now, it's going to the side I dislike—where in this case, he might use the power he has over me to hurt me.

The hallway is full of movement, but it feels like I'm the only one here, stuck in this moment, torn between turning away or stepping forward into whatever mess this will become.

Finally, I knock.

"Come in." His voice, although muffled, is still deep and piercing, and my skin prickles.

When we first started this unorthodox relationship, I was hoping I'd stop being so attuned to him, but it's kind of getting worse, not better.

I slide the door open and walk inside, feigning nonchalance. "You wanted to see me, Professor?"

Kayden's office feels colder than it should, the stark, minimalist decor giving it a sharp, impersonal edge. His desk is neat —too neat—papers lined up just so, a sleek pen resting perfectly at the edge. The soft glow of the desk lamp casts long shadows on Kayden's face. He seems to fill the space with his presence, every inch of the room an extension of his control.

"Close the door," he says without looking up from a paper he's highlighting.

"You're not supposed to do that, Professor."

"Close the door and lock it, Carson."

I hate the fucking last name. He only calls me that when he's being a major prick.

"I'll be accusing you of sexual harassment," I say just to annoy him.

He lifts his brow, finally looking at me. "You think I give a fuck?"

Of course he doesn't. With a sigh, I click the door shut and press the lock, turning the outside noises into mumbles.

He stands up and taps his desk. "Come here."

"Why?"

"Quit the questions and come here."

I release an exasperated noise and walk to him. His scent is all I breathe, and he's so warm, but closed off. I can't read him.

"Now what?"

"Bend over the desk."

"You must be out of your mind. We're on campus."

"I said. Bend over, Carson."

My body kind of folds of its own volition when he orders me. But if he calls me Carson one more time...

"What happens now?" I scoff. "You're going to spank me or something?"

I hear unbuckling and look behind me, and sure enough, he's undoing his belt.

Ah, fuck me.

He tried that before and I couldn't sit properly for days. I came like crazy, too, so there's that.

The first slap comes and I jerk against the desk, holding on to the edges with white knuckles. Even though it's over my jeans, I feel it on my skin, and my dick is swelling. Fast.

No surprise there. I'm apparently a masochist, as V—the Reddit version—calls me.

"You need to watch that mouth." *Thwack.* "You can't run it however you please." *Thwack.* "Next time I tell you to sit down. You." *Thwack.* "Sit." *Thwack.* "The fuck." *Thwack.* "Down."

I'm groaning and grunting. The pain is so great, I think my cock will burst, the sense of pleasure is surging through me despite all my attempts to remain unaffected. My groin is pushing against the desk, trying to get any form of friction.

"Quiet." He shoves two fingers in my mouth, making me choke on them. "Unless you want them to come and see you being punished for being a fucking brat."

He slaps me again and I grunt, my teeth grazing his fingers as I deep-throat them.

"But then again, you're a little slut, so you might be into that." He drops the belt on the table and reaches beneath me, his hand brushing against my engorged cock before he unzips my jeans. "You're already hard with a little belting. What a fucking mess."

He lowers my jeans and boxers just enough and then slaps my ass over the burning welts. I gag on his fingers, my eyes blurry, and I realize moisture is gathering there.

"Even if you're into that, there will never be an audience." He kneads the skin, and I release a choked sound. "No one gets to see this. No one but me. You're only *mine*."

He removes his fingers from my mouth. "Say it."

I remain quiet, motionless, and he spins me around so that my back is on the desk. My ass burns when it meets the cool surface, but that's the least of my concerns, because his eyes widen upon seeing my face.

Apparently, I'm fucking crying. So, yeah, I do cry during his punishments sometimes because I enjoy the pleasure mixed with pain.

But there's something else this time.

And, of course, he notices it.

Fuck my life.

"What's wrong?" He reaches out a hand, and I look the other way at an ugly floor lamp.

He pulls my pants up, covering my still raging erection because my cock is refusing to read the room.

His large palm grips my nape, stroking the skin as he speaks in a low tone, "If you don't like me touching you on campus, I won't."

"It's not that." I'm still speaking to the lamp. "Idiot. Asshole. God, I fucking hate you."

"Stop saying that."

"Idiot. Asshole."

"The 'I hate you' part. Don't say it. I don't like it."

I stare at him through blurry vision. "I hate you, hate you, hate you—"

He grabs my jaw, leaning down, so that his face is a breath from mine. "I said. Stop it. Enough with the tantrum."

My lips wobble and I try to pull away, but he keeps me locked in place. His demeanor feels all-encompassing, like I couldn't escape him even if I tried.

"What on earth is your problem today, Carson?"

"What the hell is *your* problem?" I headbutt him for the first time in months. "And stop calling me by my last goddamn name."

He flinches a bit, touching his forehead. Good. Hope it cracked so he'll be in pain for a while.

"I wouldn't if you hadn't been a brat from the moment you walked into my class. Flirting with students in the jury, texting and smiling at God knows who, and challenging my authority."

"That's because you *humiliated* me." I grab him by the collar of his shirt. "You've been an asshole since the case started, when I know I'm doing a good job. It's not perfect, but I was trying my *best*, aiming for approval you never gave me! You're only using me, just like him! All of you are fucking bastards!"

His fingers tighten around my jaw. "Who is *him*, Gareth?"

My stomach falls.

Well, at least he's saying my name, even if his voice sounds the deepest I've ever heard.

"No one important." I try to stand, but he shoves me back down on the desk so that he's looming over me.

"Tell me and I'll decide whether or not it's important."

"Fuck. Can I sit down first?"

He lets me, then steps between my legs, his hand still on my jaw, not allowing me to look anywhere but at him.

"I'm waiting," he says when I don't speak, his eyes looking more intense than a fucking nuke. Jeez.

I let out a long sigh. "I had a teacher who came into our house, Mr. Laurent. He taught me and Killian French. I was around ten at the time and was already beginning to realize that my brother and I were different from other kids. But Kill still managed to make all the teachers like him, while I was always alone, feeling suffocated by humans. Laurent saw it differently. He always praised me in front of my parents and told me I was smart and brighter than Kill. It was the first time a teacher had done that, and I got intoxicated by the feeling."

Kayden's other hand falls to my waist, tightening slightly. "Did he...groom you?"

"Not really? I don't think so."

"Fuck, Gareth. Did he assault you?"

"No. But he *used* me." I snort out a laugh. "Apparently Mr. Laurent's sister was taken by the New York Russian mafia, so he'd pay his debt, and since I'm related to them on my mom's side, he took me to his house, saying it was for a lesson, and then locked me up in the basement. The fucking weakling was crying while he did it, saying he didn't want to, but it was my fault for being born into a rotten family."

"And then what happened?" His voice is soft, so soft, and he's holding my cheek in his palm now, and I'm leaning into it, because, apparently, I really love it when he shows me this side.

"It didn't last long, maybe a day. He called my aunt saying he'd release me if they let his sister go and erase his debt. My aunt kind of blew his house down." I chuckle. "She and her husband came with an army and shot him to death. She tried to shield me, but I saw his corpse. His head was blown up and his intestines were on the floor. But I was mostly fascinated by his dead eyes and wanted to see more of that. Dead people. Especially if they fucking lied to me or used me. I wanted them all dead.

"Ever since then, I don't trust teachers or people in general. It made my already existing trust issues so bad." I grip the desk tighter so I don't touch him. "Which is why I never stayed with anyone like I've stayed with you."

"Because you trust me?"

"Maybe. I don't know. But when you..."

"When I what? Talk to me."

I gulp the ball in my drying throat. I don't know why he always has the ability to ground me and wrench the words out of me.

"When you say things like I disappointed you over a meaningless case, it hurts. When you call me by my last name like we're strangers, it hurts. I didn't know I was capable of being hurt, but apparently, I am."

"I'm sorry, baby." He wipes beneath my eyes. "Won't happen again. I promise."

"I don't want you to treat me like I'm special, but don't say shit like being disappointed in me."

"Is it important to you? That I'm not disappointed in you?"

"Yeah. So, like, don't do it again."

"I won't."

"If you do, I'll stab you."

He chuckles. "My worst fear."

"Better be." I smile and he kisses the corners of my mouth.

The dimples, I realize.

And my chest squeezes again. Fuck, I don't think it's a disease anymore.

His hand slides down to my erection. "Do you want to continue with the punishment?"

"Mmm. Are you threatening me with a good time, Professor?"

He laughs as he seals his lips to mine, sucking the tears off of them, sort of kissing me through it as I shudder and moan.

Then he does punish me by making me come on his cock and using my cum as lube to jerk off—which is hot as fuck. Then he chokes me with his cock and comes down my throat.

I'm delirious as he puts me back together again. My clothes. My hair. My jeans. But he doesn't hide the hickeys he left on my collarbone, wanting the whole world to know I'm taken.

I leave some of my own, too, which will make all those crushing on him lose their minds trying to pin down Professor Lockwood's *wild* partner.

Lately, I've been wanting to shout, *That would be me, bitches!*

The other day, I posted a picture of myself on IG, pulling my collar to the side to reveal a few hickeys he left there, with the caption: *My favorite dirty little secret.*

The others gave me a hard time, thinking they're from some new girl I'm into, but I just smiled and brushed it off. It's not for them anyway. It's so for me—and him if he stalks my social media.

As Kayden drops a kiss to my forehead, all I can think about is the disease in my chest—or the lack thereof.

V was right.

A chilling epiphany settles over me: I might have deep, unsettling feelings for my professor.

26
KAYDEN

Where are you?

What are you doing?

Who are you with?

You haven't texted me back in two hours, Kayden. You better fucking do that before I stab you.

Pick up the phone.

Seriously, where are you?

Not on campus or at the archery range or in the chess club or shopping for coffee beans.

Not in the house either.

> I swear to fuck, if you don't answer, I'm going to slice your goddamn face open.

> Okay, not the face.

> Where the fuck are you?!!!

> KAYDE!!

> Okay, then. I'll go find better company 😒

The better company is apparently some girl from school. Not Morgan, but another one. Blonde and pretty—another version of Cherry, who I thought we got rid of.

I'm watching him from the corner of the coffee shop as he laughs along with something she says and allows her to put her arm around his shoulders.

Yes, they're with a group of friends, but she still has her arm around him.

And he's *not* removing it.

I slide a hand in my pocket to stop myself from barging in there and somehow breaking that arm.

As the others talk, he flips his phone over, his thick brows drawing into a line.

Probably staring at all the texts I left unanswered. It's not that I did it on purpose in the beginning. I was in a lengthy offshore meeting at an office in London and had my phone on silent, so I didn't get the chance to see them.

However, around halfway through, when he was starting to get anxiously obsessive, I left them on unread on purpose.

He needs to stop with the threats when things don't go his way.

I thought the emotional control training was going well lately. He gets rewarded when he behaves, and he gets put back in his place when he's being a brat.

However, ever since he told me about his French teacher three days ago, he's been acting...odd.

He's more obsessive, somewhat anxious about my absence. He tries to act unaffected when I'm around him, but then he keeps following me everywhere, and the moment I touch him, he releases this tiny sigh of relief.

As if he got a drug hit or something similarly obnoxious.

He's also sniffing me more than usual lately, even burying his face in my neck and falling asleep like that.

He's also more vocal during sex, asking me to bite him, to mark him, to leave hickeys all over him. And he loves when I praise him—he demands it now. He'll say things like, "Was I good? Tell me I was good." Or, "Tell me how you love being inside me." Or, "Say it, please, say I'm so beautiful you can't stop fucking me."

I love that.

I love that he's owning up to the submissive streak in him, that he's accepting his sexuality and leaning into his kinks. But while I like that he's attached to me, I don't appreciate the unhealthy behavior. Someone like Gareth will spiral if he keeps going down this path.

It's a matter of when, not if.

I should probably wait until we're at home to teach him a goddamn lesson, but then again, I won't leave him with Blondie.

ME

Come outside. Now.

I watch with curious amazement the way his lips pull in a smile and his eyes brighten as he lifts his head and sees me standing across the street.

Then he quickly hides the smile.

LITTLE MONSTER

Nah. I'm busy with that better company I told you about.

If you don't come outside now, forget about dropping by later.

Fire ignites in his eyes.

While I don't like threatening him, I also have to manage his uneven bursts of impulsiveness.

Then I won't. I only visit for Moka anyway.

If that's the only reason, you can take her and stop coming altogether.

I catch a glimpse of him standing up, and I turn around to leave.

Well, *not really.*

I know he'll follow.

Sure enough, soon after I slip into an alleyway, he rushes in, his shoulders bunched with tension and his eyes shooting lasers.

He grabs me by the collar and slams me against the wall.

It's amazing how he can look so beautiful even when he's enraged. Messy blond hair, slick, sharp features. Full pillowy lips.

I could stare at him for hours.

"What the fuck are you playing at, Kayde? You think you can ignore me the whole day and then start talking bullshit?"

"Language," I speak calmly. "Release me."

"Like fuck I will. Explain yourself."

"I said." I grab his hand and twist—hard—forcing him to let go. "Watch your language and let me go."

He winces and I drop his hand. I don't want to hurt him,

which might be ironic considering all the punishments, but he enjoys that.

Outside of sex, I truly don't like causing him pain. He's not delicate or anything, but to me, he's someone to be protected at all costs.

"Why didn't you answer my texts?" he asks in a low tone, then his eyes grow wide, his breathing frantic. "Were you with another woman? Someone like Jessica? I told you, didn't I? If you betray me, I will rip your heart out."

"Gareth, that's enough. Control your temper."

"I'm serious. You don't know what the fuck I'm capable of, Professor. If you ever leave me or replace me, I will kill you and chop you into tiny goddamn pieces, then stuff you in a box and feed you to the fucking sharks. I'd rather you die than be with someone else."

"You think I'd let you kill me?"

He reaches a hand to my throat, and I grab his wrist and twist it to the side. "You believe you have power in this relationship just because you're capable of killing? Your threats don't work on me, Gareth. You will never hurt me. You're too obsessed with me to ever do that. And even if you succumb to your impulses, I will tie you the fuck up and punish you. So cut it out and behave."

"But..."

He trails off when I level him with a look. This time, when I release his wrist, he doesn't attempt to choke me again.

"I understand you're hurt, which is why you're throwing this tantrum, but I'm telling you, Gareth. You bring someone else into this just to be a brat again, and I will forbid you from seeing me for a whole week. Are we clear?"

His eyes widen. "You wouldn't."

"Try me. Just try making me watch a display like that again and see the consequences for yourself."

"It's not that I want to do that. Just...don't disappear on me again."

"I will if needed. You're a grown adult who can survive a few hours without a text from me."

"It was a whole day, actually," he murmurs with a pout, and it's nearly impossible to keep up the stoic mode.

He looks so goddamn adorable, I want to eat him up.

My tone darkens. "And that was enough to find *better* company?"

He shrugs. "I thought that might get your attention."

"You will not do that nonsense again. There will be no girl's arms around you. Are we clear?"

He nods.

"Use your words."

"Yeah, whatever."

"Now..." I run my fingers over his T-shirt. "How would you like to be punished for your insolence?"

His lips part as he looks up at me, and whispers, "Here?"

"Shh. Don't talk."

"Kayde..."

I slam him against the opposite wall with my grip on his T-shirt. "Shut the fuck up."

His fingers clench in my shirt, digging into my waist as he shivers. I'm about to devour him when I feel a third presence.

"Gaz?" The guy watches us with narrowed eyes.

He's tall, about an inch shorter than me, though, and bulky. Chaotic full-sleeve tattoos peek from beneath his shirt and he has his long, dark hair tied in a messy ponytail.

Gareth stiffens as he looks up at him, his lashes fluttering and his heartbeat quickening beneath my fingers.

Now, I want to maim the intruder just because he's stressing my little monster.

The newcomer flexes and then tightens his fist as he glares

at me. "What's your name, motherfucker, and what's your favorite way to die?"

"Niko, it's not..." Gareth trails off, and I realize I'm tightening my grip, because why the fuck is he calling him by a nickname and sounding...apologetic?

"Step the fuck away from him." This *Niko* storms toward us. "*Now.*"

"Who the fuck are you?" I ask in a low growl, feeling so goddamn territorial.

"My cousin, Nikolai." Gareth pushes me, forcing me to release him as he gives me a pleading look. "Please leave, Sir."

Fuck. I love how he calls me that.

"Sir?" Nikolai, the cockblocker but at least a cousin, scoffs. "Why the fuck are you calling him sir?"

"He's my professor. Kayden Lockwood." Gareth casts a fleeting glance at me before he trudges to his cousin's side.

I give Nikolai a look of disdain for ruining my session and pin Gareth with a look. "We are not done, Carson. I expect you in my office tomorrow morning."

Instead of leaving, I remain by the corner, my arms crossed as I listen in. While I can't see them, I want to make sure Gareth is okay.

None of his family members know about his sexuality, and I know how freaked out he was about the gay thing. He's more comfortable now, but I'm not sure if he's comfortable enough to come out.

"Why the fuck would your professor corner you in an alley?" Nikolai asks the very obvious question.

Gareth, to his credit, answers in that mellow, pliable way he usually communicates in public. "We...had a slight disagreement."

"And he couldn't solve it in the classroom like all other professors?" *Another good question.*

"I...uh, I pulled something outside of law school and he was pissed."

"That still doesn't give him the right to attack you. Want me, Jer, and Kill to add him to the MIA list?"

"No, no. That's not necessary. I can take care of this situation."

"Didn't look like you were doing a very good job at it. Kill and I will maim the fucker."

"Niko, no. Don't...tell Kill. Don't tell *anyone* about what you just saw."

Hmm. He sounds distraught.

Honestly, I don't care whether or not he accepts his sexuality as long as he accepts me, but was his apprehension this bad?

"Why not...? Fuck me," Nikolai says. "Is this that man you told me about that time? The only one you're attracted to?"

My brows rise.

He talked to his cousin about me? He said I was the only one he's attracted to?

Am I supposed to feel a twist in my chest at that?

"N-no," Gareth says in such a cute little voice.

"You just stuttered. You never stutter."

"Just forget it. Since when are you this perceptive?"

"Since now. It's him, isn't it?"

"No," he says with more force than needed.

"In that case, I guess I can discuss this further with Kill and Jer and see if it's true or false."

"Nikolai!"

"Or you can just tell me."

"Fine! It's him."

My chest expands, and I'm grinning like an idiot in the streets.

"A much older professor, huh?" Nikolai says in a teasing

voice. "You're much more adventurous than I thought, cousin. I'm actually impressed."

"It's nothing serious, so don't tell anyone."

My smile falls.

Not serious? He was on the verge of committing murder just because I didn't reply to him, and it's *nothing serious*.

I know he's putting up a front, but it's getting tedious now.

I hear them move, and I walk away so as not to be discovered.

But all I can think about is the pain in my chest because the little monster who's been carving himself beneath my skin for months said we're not serious.

27
GARETH

Suspecting—or knowing—I have feelings for my grouchy asshole professor that I met under the worst circumstances has been an *experience*.

Not the best, according to Kayden, who's been bombarded by what he calls 'excessive indulgence.'

It's been about two weeks since I came to that realization and it kind of altered my brain chemistry.

So I've only had one genuine-ish relationship with Harper. Aside from her, my relationships have been fleeting and meaningless, and even Harper didn't stay for long. Yes, I took a girlfriend or two home, but they were the girls I fucked at that time.

I certainly have no damn clue how to have a relationship with a man.

An *older* man.

Like another generation, really. He's definitely more mature than anyone I've ever been with. More than me if I'm being brutally honest.

But his age has never really bothered me. Actually, I think I've been drawn to his domineering personality from the get-go. And while I'd never say this out loud, the way he orders me around does strange things to me.

The fact remains, he's entirely different from anything I've experienced. So I've been calling my parents and grandpa.

Dad said acts of service are his love language, which is true. He often does things for Mom before she even asks for them.

Mom said it's words of affirmation and touch, which is...a no, I guess.

I have no clue what to say to him, and I kind of feel awkward touching him of my own accord. If it's not sex, I don't know where I'm supposed to put my hands. And he's not a girl, so I'm not sure if I can wrap my arms around his waist all the time like I truly want.

It's odd that I often told girls what they wanted to hear without batting an eye. Praising their looks, their bodies, their smell. It came all too naturally to me, but with him...it's hard.

No, not hard.

Embarrassing? I don't know, maybe because he's the first person I've cared about this deeply, so I don't want to fuck it up.

And I'm not sure if you can praise a man's looks out loud, even if you're fucking. He knows I'm obsessed with his smell and doesn't mind when I bury my face in his neck, but I'm not sure if I can take it any further.

Anyway, Mom was a bit useless.

So I had a convo with my new bestie, V, the Reddit version.

TOOPRETTYFORTHISMESS

So, you were kind of right. It's not only sexual. I don't think it ever was tbh.

QUIETRAGE

I KNEW it haha you're in looove.

STFU I'm not in love. Anyway, I kind of want to take care of him. Is that a thing in gay relationships?

I don't see why it shouldn't be. But you're barking up the wrong tree. Never had a gay relationship.

I don't want to treat him like a girl. I think that would be offensive or something?

Not sure if it'd be offensive, bro. Just do what feels right.

Have you had dates with your guy yet?

He's not my goddamn guy and I don't want to see his fucking face.

Getting pissy, are we?

Just don't bring him up today, okay? I'm getting a headache.

Okay. What did you use to do with your girlfriend? My real serious one left way too soon and I was a teen.

She loved movies, so we did that.

We can't do anything in public. That's so unhelpful.

Then maybe you should come out in public. Have you talked about a relationship or something?

> We HAVE to talk about that?

Uh, kind of? Jeez you're like a fetus on the emotional side.

> But why? We're already together.

As fuck buddies. That's different from a relationship, my dude.

> But I already told you it's not only about the sex.

Telling me is cool and all, but you kind of have to tell HIM. Talk about it and all that jazz. Jesus. Get a grip, man. Even I have more emotional awareness than you. The bar is in hell.

That convo with V left me even more confused.

Next. Grandpa.

I had to be careful with him, because the moment I said I was brainstorming about how to make my recent crush happy, it went like this.

"Are you obsessing, Gareth?"

"Absolutely not." *Lie of the fucking century.*

"Good. As long as it's harmless."

"Cross my heart." Epic liar. *Hey, that's me.*

But if Grandpa thinks I am obsessing, he'll put an end to this whole thing.

Because he's seen me obsessed with Harper and he's seen the pool of blood and the dead eyes that followed.

Ever since then, I promised him that I'd never allow myself to get obsessed again.

Well, I'm more than obsessed with Kayden. These deranged feelings make my fixation on Harper seem like child's play.

But Grandpa doesn't need to know that.

He suggested I should dazzle her with my money, looks, and prestigious background. Any girl should be grateful I'm even giving her a chance.

Of course, there's no girl, and Kayden is far from impressed by my riches and prestigious background.

Like, the man truly hates it when I overspend and keeps giving me this frown as if he doesn't know how to fix it.

I bought him a car—a slick Aston Martin Vantage—because he doesn't have one. When I took him to his building's underground parking garage and dangled the keys in front of him with a *"Ta-da!"* he looked at me with that poker face, then raised an eyebrow. "You're replacing your *baby* Medusa?"

"Over my dead body."

"Because she's so *special*?"

"Yes, she is, and stop being jealous of a car."

"I will when you stop calling her *baby*."

"Wow. Petty."

He scowled and I laughed. "Anyway, this is for you."

"For me?"

"Uh-huh. What do you think?"

"You bought me a car?"

"Yeah."

"An Aston Martin?"

"Obviously."

"Why?"

"Because you have to walk too far in this shitty weather, and I can't drive you all the time."

"You bought me an expensive car because I walk in the rain?"

"Yeah, it's nothing." I grinned, trying—and failing—not to sound too eager. "I'm rich, so this didn't even scratch my trust fund."

"Clearly." He gave the keys a side-eye. "Return it, Gareth."

"But why? You don't want to commute to college comfortably?"

"This is flashy and will draw attention. No one would believe a college professor can afford this." He pinned me with an austere look. "And I don't need you to be my *sugar daddy*."

I swallowed, my chest falling at the rejection and his stoic tone. "I just wanted to do something nice for you."

He let out one of those soft sighs mixed with a smile and stroked my hair—the same hair I've been letting grow long because he likes yanking me up by it and running his fingers through it until I fall asleep.

"It's the thought that counts. Thank you, my little monster."

Then he gave me what he called an "appropriate gift." A custom-made gold bracelet with two crossed arrows that match my tattoo engraved on the top.

Best. Gift. Ever.

I've been wearing it nonstop since he clasped it around my wrist.

That said, he *still* wouldn't accept the Aston Martin. I left it in the building's garage anyway for when he needs something for non-work use, then got him a boring Range Rover. He frowned at that, too, but at least he's driving it most of the time. That's a win, I guess.

After that, I couldn't stop myself. I started buying him rare whiskey, imported coffee beans, high-end watches, only accessible because of my last name, custom-tailored suits, and a personalized leather briefcase.

I also bought a lot of decor items for the apartment and stuffed his wardrobe full of clothes. He frowns at every single gift, muttering about my "irresponsible spending habits," but honestly, this is the only way I know how to take care of him. So he can just deal with it.

It's weird, but I can't stop myself. I want to shower him with things he loves, and lately, I can't stop taking pictures of him, and sometimes, I force him into selfies that he doesn't seem to enjoy. However, he lets me do whatever I want.

On top of that, I've been bribing Jina to teach me how to cook his favorite foods—not that it's going smoothly. Half the time, he ends up joining me in the kitchen, trying to help, which leads to us making a complete mess.

Or he ends up fucking me on the counter.

Still, at least we're not ordering takeout every day or I'm not sneaking leftovers from the cook at the Heathens' mansion.

But tonight? No cooking. We're watching a hockey game, and I'm not in the mood to mess around with food.

I hum to myself as I stack the food containers the chef prepared in a bag.

My phone vibrates, and I grab it, assuming it's him. He hasn't texted since this morning, so it's about time.

My mood sours when I find my PI's name.

NADINE

Is there anything else you wish to know, Mr. Carson?

So this was her reply after she sent me the entire dossier on Kayden's ex-lovers. Isabelle Monroe, Lena Konstatinou, Hadil Kalif, and Sophia Li.

A partner in a big firm, a socialist, a company executive, and a pianist.

I've got stabby thoughts about every single one of them.

Didn't help that they're all drop-dead gorgeous. He clearly has a type: leggy, beautiful, and probably annoyingly perfect.

Sure, I could've just asked him about his exes, but that would mean listening to him talk about them, and I'd rather choke on glass.

What really grates is that he spent some time with all of them. Four serious exes? One is too many.

ME

You can go on hiatus, Nadine. Thank you for everything.

Noted. I'm always here if you need me, Mr. Carson.

I've been contemplating letting her go for a while now. Partly because I'm starting to feel guilty for spying on him, and partly because I know I'll start obsessing—more than I already am—and asking for more videos, more pictures of him with those women, and I don't want to go down that rabbit hole.

I have enough self-awareness to realize I'll spiral, and it'll be a worse bloodbath than the one with Harper.

And Grandpa will be like, "I told you so."

I categorically can't stand the thought of him with someone else, like it truly provokes my monster side. These emotions I have for him are kind of terrifying because I don't know how the fuck I'd act if he doesn't stay exactly where I want him.

Completely mine.

But then I remember that, in reality, I'm the one with him now.

So those four can choke.

With that cheerful thought, I pocket my phone and go back to packing dinner.

"Oh, you've definitely lost it." Killian strolls to the fridge, grabs a beer, and leans against the counter across from me, ankles crossed as he takes a sip.

My good mood starts to chip away, but I ignore him and continue adding chili flakes to the containers. Kayden likes his food spicy—definitely Jina's influence.

"Heard you're in love?"

I lift my head and narrow my eyes. "I'm not in love."

"That's not what Mom and Dad are saying." He takes another sip, his eyes gleaming with mischief. "They keep asking about this girl who apparently has all your attention."

"They're exaggerating."

"You wouldn't look so happy preparing some couple's meal if they were." He pauses, smirking. "I've never heard you hum before."

"You've never seen me do a lot of things. Your point doesn't hold."

"Hmm, true. You do run deeper than you show, big bro. But here's the thing." He moves to the other side of the island, planting his elbows on the surface. "I haven't seen any girl around you since Cherry was out of the picture. I thought it might be that clingy fool from school, but she's way too pliant for your tastes. You prefer fighters, no? So, tell me, who's this mystery girl?"

I let my lips curl into a smirk. "Wouldn't you like to know?"

Kill would never suspect it's a guy—or my professor, at that. He's convinced I'm straight. Hell, I thought I was, too, until recently.

Not that I know what I am. I'm not gay, I don't *think*. I'd have been drawn to Kayden even if he were a woman. And I still don't find men attractive. Maybe I'm somewhere on the ace spectrum as V suggested. Or something else entirely.

Doesn't matter. I don't like labels anyway.

Kill tilts his head. "Scared she'd like me better?"

My hand freezes mid-motion.

He...wouldn't. Right?

I mean, Kill is fluid—he's fucked men before. Always on top, though, since for him, sex is power.

But Kayden wouldn't let anyone fuck him, let alone be tempted by *Killian* of all people.

Right?

I'm better-looking, better company, and *everyone*—including Kill—knows it.

"In your dreams," I mutter.

My brother always pulled this shit about the girls I dated, claiming they'd prefer him over me. I never cared, because those girls didn't matter.

But I'd bash his head in if he so much as looked at Kayden.

"Ooh, you've got that unhinged look in your eyes, Gaz." Kill grins wide. "I'm officially intrigued."

"Keep your intrigue focused on your girlfriend."

"But I'm in the mood to play."

"Stay away from what's mine, Kill. Don't make me hurt you."

"You mean like the way you stayed away from Glyn?" He taps my cheek, his grin smug and infuriating. "Hide her while you can, big bro. Payback's a bitch."

I slap his hand away, and he laughs as he strolls out, looking far too pleased with himself.

Goddamn prick.

Maybe I need to have another chat with Niko, make sure he keeps his big mouth shut.

He's been unbearable since he found me corned by Kayden in the alley by the coffee shop the other day. Normally, he's oblivious, but this time, he pieced the patterns together and figured out Kayden is *the* guy I mentioned months ago.

"You're way more interesting now, cousin!" he'd shouted, barging into my room. "*Fun Dick Alliance*, let's go!"

I kicked him and made him swear to keep it to himself.

How long he can hold out before spilling to Jer or Kill is anyone's guess. Niko's not exactly known for his discretion.

That's why I prefer V. He's a vault I can trust.

But the Niko angle is worrying.

It's got me thinking I should stake a public claim.

Except there's one glaring problem: Kayden is my professor. Going public would spark chaos—and possibly ruin his career.

I don't want that.

At the same time, I hate this secrecy. I want him to touch me in public, kiss me in the street, and I want to blind everyone who dares look at him.

The thought of not being able to do that for three whole years sits like a brick at the bottom of my stomach.

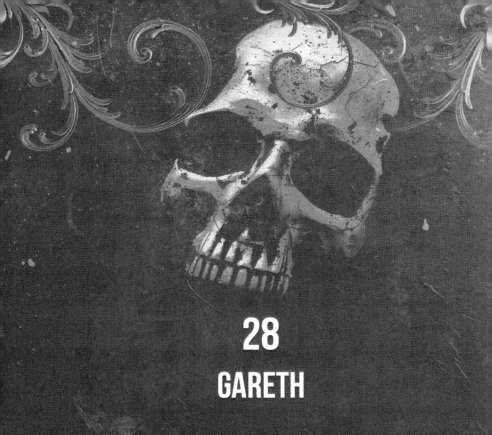

28

GARETH

"**I**'m here!" I announce as I step into the apartment. "I brought food so we don't have to worry about cooking."

The first thing that hits me is the silence.

It's oppressive.

Usually, he has some boring classical music playing.

The second thing is the relative darkness.

A ball of fur rubs against my leg, and I crouch to scoop Moka into my arms. She snuggles close, purring softly. "What's up, girl? Did Kayden not come home yet?"

It's weird to call this place home, but I guess it kind of is.

She meows, her eyes glowing faintly in the low light. "Aw, are you hungry?"

A long, dramatic meow confirms it.

I drop the bag on the kitchen counter, fill her empty bowl, and leave her to eat before heading to the bedroom.

He should be here by now since he only teaches in the morning today.

"Kayden?"

My feet halt the moment I step inside. Dim light casts eerie shadows across the room, and Kayden's restless form lies tangled in the bedcovers. At first, I think it's strange he's sleeping this early.

But then I notice the shivers racking his body, the furrowed brow, and the sweat plastering his jet-black hair to his forehead.

The sound of his labored breathing fills the silence, and my chest tightens as I move closer.

"Kayde?"

I touch his shoulder, and his entire body stiffens, heat radiating into my hand like a furnace. His skin burns feverishly, and his lips are discolored as he grunts and mumbles something unintelligible.

I lean down, listening. Most of the words are jumbled nonsense, but then I catch it.

"No...no...don't...touch..."

I've always seen him as invincible, indestructible. But right now? He looks vulnerable. Just human. And it makes something shift deep inside me.

A need to protect him from whatever nightmare has him trapped.

For the first time, I take his big hand in mine, stroking the veins on the back. "How did you even get so sick? Were you walking in the rain again? What's the point of having a car if you won't use it, idiot?"

Slowly, I brush the strands of damp hair away from his face. Sick people shouldn't look this hot. Just saying.

He was coughing the other day after coming back from a short trip to his dad's firm in the States. And, yeah, he's been using the glasses more—not that I'm complaining—but this is the first time I've seen him like this.

Well, aside from that one time when his moms were here.

"I'll go buy you some meds," I say, starting to get up, but his fingers tighten around mine.

"Don't...go..."

"I'm not going anywhere," I murmur, stroking his hand again. Weirdly, it feels natural, like I should be doing it more often. "You'll never get rid of me, Kayde. Remember?"

He doesn't reply, but his grip relaxes, and I peel his hand away, then I place a cool, wet rag on his forehead.

After telling Moka to hold down the fort, I drive to a night pharmacy and come back with a bag full of meds—and some English porridge.

When I return, Kayden's still burning up, and Moka's curled by his head, purring away.

"You feel bad for him, too?" I scratch under her chin before focusing on him.

He's so out of it, I have to sit him up and carefully pour the medicine into his mouth. Then, noticing the drenched sheets, I wrestle his ridiculously huge body to lay a clean blanket underneath and swap out the duvet.

I wipe him down to cool him off, which would be easier if his cock didn't thicken beneath my touch.

Seriously? Sick *and* a tease?

It takes all my self-control to cover him up and stop looking.

Finally, I lie beside him, keeping an eye on his fever throughout the night, with Moka offering her emotional support in the form of soothing purrs.

At some point, I must fall asleep, because I wake up to something hard pressing against my ass and heavy arms wrapped snugly around my waist.

My own cock swells against my shorts, and I groan when his

crown presses against the thin fabric and slips between the crack of my ass.

Let's just say I'm not wearing anything beneath the shorts—his influence. No shirt either. Again, thanks to him. He's always walking around half naked, so I might have picked up the habit.

His fingers find my nipple, pinching and rubbing as his face buries into my nape, his lips sucking and nibbling on the sensitive skin.

"I missed you, baby," he murmurs, his voice low and gravelly.

I'm so turned on and disoriented that all I manage is a strangled moan.

"I love how you're pushing back into my cock. Mmm." His teeth graze my nape, sending a shiver down my spine. "I want to mark you, to breed you."

My throat dries, and I strain to look at him, catching the glassy haze in his eyes. The clock reads four in the morning, and the heat radiating from him confirms he's still feverish.

"You're speaking nonsense," I mutter, trying to pull away despite the fire he's ignited inside me. "Just go to sleep."

"I've never been more serious. I want to own you, to chain you to me," he whispers, nibbling on my ear. "You can't leave me."

"I won't."

"Promise."

"I promise."

"You can't go back on that promise, Gareth."

"I won't."

I stroke his hair, pressing the back of my hand to his forehead. "I'll get you some more medicine."

But when I try to move, his grip on my stomach tightens, and he thrusts his cock against my hole, the fabric of my shorts doing little to shield me from the sensation.

"You're not going anywhere," he growls.

"Fuck...Kayde. You're feverish."

"Don't care." His lips trail over my neck, the lobe of my ear, my jaw—everywhere he can reach. "I need to stuff you full of my cum."

"You can barely breathe, Jesus—" I groan as his fingers pinch my nipple again, sending shock waves through me.

He's got me so worked up I can hardly think, let alone take his sickness into account.

"Let me hear your voice," he murmurs, his tone husky and demanding. "I love how you groan and moan whenever I touch you."

I push myself upright, sitting up and trying to create some distance, but my ass clenches, and my cock throbs so hard, it's difficult to catch my breath.

Kayden lies sprawled out on his back, the duvet discarded, his naked body fully exposed. My gaze drops to his cock—hard, thick, and veined purple, pointing right at me like it owns me.

He grabs my hips, dragging me onto him so that my legs straddle his waist.

"Ride me, baby," he breathes, his voice rough with need. "Show me how much you want me."

My first instinct is to shake my head. I'm not a girl, and while I love the subtle variation of feminization kink—yup, googled it, that's what it's called in D/s circles—because him calling my ass cunt or pussy turns me on, I sure as hell don't want him thinking I am an actual *girl*. The way he talks about my ass is the *only* aspect of feminization I like and I told him that. He also only uses the name calling in a power exchange way where he dominates me and I submit.

That's *all*.

While the idea of being on top of him like this sends a jolt of fire through my bones, I ask, "Do you like being ridden?"

"Not really. I actually prefer always being on top, but I

want to see you like this," he replies, his droopy eyes fixed on me as his hand palms my cock through my shorts and squeezes my balls. "My own little monster fucking himself on my cock."

A strangled whimper leaves me as his words light me the fuck up.

His cock nudges against my ass, and I release a choked noise as I lift myself, strip off my shorts, and reach for the lube in his drawer.

His big hands rest on my hips as he watches my every movement, his chest going up and down in a slightly perturbed rhythm.

My hand shakes a bit as I'm about to squirt the lube into it, but he shakes his head.

"What?"

"Spit on your hand first, baby."

I find myself doing just that, because I apparently fold when he orders me around. I love it, I just truly love the way he makes me stop thinking.

He says I'm more of a brat lately, but it's because I want to hear him order and dominate and force me to my knees.

I reach behind me and jerk him up and down with my spit and then add some lube and squeeze him roughly like we both like.

His grunts are reassuring, but not entirely.

I'm so used to him doing all the work, this is making me feel self-conscious. Sure, he usually makes me lube him, but he never makes me actually *put* him in me.

"Want me to do it?" he asks, reading me so openly, it should be disturbing.

I let out a stuttering breath and shake my head because he wants to see me do it. I read it loud and clear in those darkened eyes, and for some reason, I need to prove I do want him.

"Get my fuckhole nice and wet, baby."

My hand is a bit steadier as I finger my hole a bit, getting some lube inside me.

"Whose pussy are you touching, Gareth?"

"Y-yours."

"That's right. Mine. So make it wetter."

"Mff. I want your cock."

"Not yet. Go deeper, get more lube inside you."

I grunt, my cock twitching at the order as I add another finger and loosen myself up. "Please, Kayde."

"Please what?"

"Please let me put your cock in my dripping cunt."

"Jesus fuck. Sit on my cock. *Now*."

I don't have to be told twice. I remove my fingers, latch on to his slick cock, and align it with my back hole, then push down slightly.

Our groans mix together as his crown nudges inside me.

"Fuck, baby. You look like a god." He reaches a hand up and pinches my nipples, then rubs and presses, playing with them in ways that make me delirious.

So I relax further, taking more of him in, throwing my head back at the sensation. I love how his cock stretches me until it's painful. I love the pain because I know, soon, intense pleasure will follow.

Every time he's inside me, I can't help the low hum that rips out of my throat or how my cock pulses. It's resting close to his tattooed abs now, the snake glistening with sweat.

"Mmfuck!" I scream when he pulls me down all the way, his pelvis and balls slapping against my ass.

My cock leaks as it hits his abs and I grunt, placing both hands on his chest, for balance.

"Good boy," he says in a low growl. "Take my cock in my pussy."

I let out a strangled noise of desire, his words humming through me with raw power.

"I might call it pussy, but this feels better than anything I've been in before. No other pussy or ass can compare."

"Oh fuck...say that again, please..."

"Say what again, baby?"

"That I feel b-better than anyone else."

"You do. You're my favorite fuck."

"And the first man you fucked because you couldn't stay away?"

"Yes, baby. You make me lose control."

"And the only man you'll ever fuck?"

"You're my one and only."

My cock leaks all over him, my muscles relaxing, my mind going to that happy place. "Fucking hell. I'm *so*... turned on."

"I can feel it. You're making a mess on my stomach."

"Can't...stop myself." I'm breathing harshly, letting my body accommodate his size. It's a moment he always gives me, usually kissing and praising me.

"You with me, baby?"

"Yeah..."

"Does it hurt?"

"A bit, but I like that."

"Mmm. I know you do."

"Kayde..."

"Talk to me."

"You feel so good."

A small smile lifts his lips. "You like my cock inside you?"

"Mmmff." With my hands on his chest, I lift my hips and then come down.

My movements are awkward at first, but I soon work up a rhythm and Kayden lets me. He doesn't interfere, being patient as I fumble around. Then, soon, I'm going up and down, riding him with everything in me, letting his cock hit deeper and deeper.

"Is that all you got, baby?"

My body snaps into a rougher rhythm at the challenge, whimpering as he thrusts up once, and his eyes light up because he knows exactly what he's doing to me.

He kneads my ass. "Whose cunt is this?"

"Mmm. Y-yours."

"You're so goddamn beautiful, Gareth."

"Say...say that again." My rhythm is so fast, my cock bobs on his abs and his balls slap my ass.

"You're so beautiful, mesmerizing, unearthly. You're the most beautiful fucking thing in this universe, baby."

"Ah, fuck...Kayde...fuck...more...please..."

"My own pretty little monster looks like a sex god."

"Fuck...please...more..."

"If perfection exists, it's you, baby. You're made for me, aren't you?"

"Yes...yes..."

He thrusts from the bottom, making me bounce on his cock, hitting my prostate, and ramming inside me with a force not fit for someone who's sick.

"You're riding my cock like a very good boy."

"Holyfuckingshit... I'm gonna...come—"

"Not yet." With a grunt, he sits up and pushes me all the way back so I'm lying down, then he pulls his thighs from beneath me and pulls the crown of my fully erect cock into his mouth.

I grunt as he sucks the orgasm out of me while still ramming his cock inside me, against my sensitive spot over and over and over.

My grunts are inhuman as I reach for his hair, pulling. "I'm... Fuck, your mouth feels so good, fuuuuck!"

I rock my hips up, coming in spurts down his throat, and he swallows it all, as he swells and pulses inside me.

"Yes, yes, please...come in my ass, please, Kayde...fuck!!" I'm begging in mumbled, jagged breaths as he pumps into me so deep, I'm sure he's carving himself inside me.

He shoots off, filling me up as my cock pops out of his mouth. And I stare, in a fucking sex daze as he licks his lip while holding my eyes.

Making me watch him swallow my cum.

My spent dick twitches and I rock my hips, milking him, taking every last drop.

"You're a goddamn masterpiece, baby."

My heart soars and I reach out my hand, but before I can touch him, he pulls out and then he's shoving my legs up in the air and licking his cum clean.

"Kayde!" I moan as he thrusts his tongue inside me. "Jesus Christ. That's... Fuck!"

"We're not wasting any cum, baby," he groans, eating my ass until I'm delirious. "My pussy tastes so good."

"Kayde...that feels good...mmmfuckkk." I'm writhing, grunting, and moaning, as his hums vibrate against my back hole.

My body, head, and soul are so full of him, I feel like I'll burst.

Like one day, this will get to be too much, and I'll lock him the fuck up. In a basement. An ivory tower.

Anywhere where only *I* get to have him.

There will be no exes, no nothing. I'll purge them all out of his mind, body, and goddamn memories if needed.

Finally, he crawls on top of me, his slick body rubbing against mine as he brings us nose to nose.

I don't think about it as I open my mouth. I probably shouldn't since he's sick, but fuck if I care.

He spits inside it, then kisses me, hard, sucking my face, and I kiss him back with the same urgency, running my fingers through his hair.

My head is so dizzy, but I hold on to the now—the way his chest vibrates against mine, how tightly he holds me, and how, when he releases my lips, his breaths shake against my nape. It's like he's silently admitting I affect him as much as he affects me.

It's that white room again. Quiet. Peaceful.

He's the only person who's ever managed to tame my demons, shove them back into that void, and gag them the fuck up.

And I want this for my whole life.

I never want to leave his embrace.

Kayden flips us so that I'm lying on top of him. He always does this, probably to keep from crushing me. Not that I'm light, but I like this side of him.

His eyes flutter closed, his breaths evening out, and I lean on my arms on his chest. Slowly, I stroke his hair, his forehead, his face. It's the most I've ever touched him, even after sex.

He hums faintly in his throat.

I think he likes it.

And I like that he likes it.

Still, guilt nags at me. He's sick, and I had sex with him anyway. He seems more drained than usual.

Since when do I feel guilt?

Growing soft, are we?

Shut up, demon.

"Hey, Kayde?"

"Hmm?" His eyes stay closed, his voice soft and raspy.

"What do you think about moving back to the States?"

His eyes snap open, suddenly alert. "What?"

I swallow, unsure why I'm even bringing this up. We're not really in a relationship—not officially, as V loves to remind me.

"I mean, I was accepted into Yale, Harvard, and Princeton, so transferring is an option. I could pick Harvard, and you could teach at a nearby college. That way, we wouldn't be in the same place."

"Why?"

I hate it when he replies to my rambling with a single question. It forces me to talk more, which isn't my strong suit when it comes to him. God, it was so much easier when I hated him and constantly threatened to stab him.

With a sigh, I say, "So there aren't any stupid codes we're breaking if we're seen together in public."

He wraps an arm around my back, his hand rubbing soothing circles as he squeezes my legs between his.

And now I'm distracted again because I *love* how he showers me with affection.

"You want to come out?" His low voice demands my attention.

"I don't know about coming out. I've decided I don't like labels, so I'm not doing that. I've accepted I'm into you, and that's that. But I want to take you to meet my parents and grandpa. Maybe my cousin Niko, too—he keeps teasing me about it, so why not? Maya and Mia as well. Maya's the one who keeps recommending those soapy dramas. Oh, and my brother, but you better not fall for his bullshit, or I swear I will stab you."

I pant, having said the last bit in one breath.

Kayden stays silent, and my chest tightens more the longer the pause stretches.

"Say something. If you don't want to, tell me—"

"I do want to, and I'm extremely proud of you, baby."

The praise warms me, and I press closer to him, soaking it in.

I lift my head to look at him. "You're really proud of me?"

"Mmm. You've come a long way."

"Is it okay if I don't believe I'm gay? I think I'm just fluid or ace. I don't want to box myself in."

"Then don't. And don't ask if it's okay. People are different and don't usually share the same experience, especially for something as complex as sexuality. I like you the way you are and that's that."

"God," I breathe out, my voice catching. "How do you do it?"

"Do what?"

"Be so accepting? You don't even seem hung up on your own sexuality."

"Life is too short. All I need to know is that we're sexually compatible and that I wanted you from the first time I saw you."

I form a *V* at my chin with my thumb and forefinger. "Because I'm beautiful?"

"There's that, but I also wanted to explore that untapped rebellious submissive streak I saw in your eyes when I had my shoe on your cock and you trembled."

"Asshole," I mutter, stroking a line across his chest.

He laughs. "Wasn't I right?"

"Fine. I love the pain and submission, but only if you're the one dominating me and making me take it."

"And that's how it'll always be."

"Deal." I grin. "Back to my earlier suggestion. When will you come to meet my family?"

"Not now." I feel him stiffen.

"Why not?"

He strokes my hair. "Remember when I told you I couldn't come out for security reasons?"

"Yeah."

"I truly can't. My family wouldn't accept it."

"But Rachel and Jina..."

"Can't set foot in the States if they want to remain safe. I can only see them when I travel to Europe."

"Oh." My heart sinks. "Is your family one of those that's homophobic bigots?"

"Unfortunately, yes. Massive pain in the ass—no pun intended."

"Can't you just disown them?"

"It's not that simple."

I swallow hard, the weight of it hitting me. I thought the professor-student thing was our only hurdle, but this feels bigger, and more permanent.

"So there's no hope?" I whisper.

"There's always hope." He kisses my forehead, his lips lingering as if to reassure me. "Just give me time, baby, okay?"

I nod, grinning as he strokes my dimples. He's obsessed with them—probably why I've been smiling more than usual lately.

It's not because I actually feel like I'm bursting out of my skin with excitement whenever I see him or anything equally ridiculous.

I let my fingers skim over his collarbone, the strong lines there. "Sooo does this mean we're in a relationship now?"

"Weren't we always?"

"We were?"

"That's what being exclusive means."

"V said fuck buddies are different from relationships."

His hand fists in my hair, tightening his grip. "Who's V?"

"A friend."

"What type of friend?"

"We grew up together in the States. You done being jealous?"

"Depends on how close you are."

"We discuss dicks." I grin. "Is that close enough for you?"

"Gareth..."

I chuckle, my chest vibrating against his. God, I think I *like* seeing him jealous.

"Relax. We're just close because we're both new to the whole being-into-guys thing."

"I still don't like it."

I shrug. "Price you pay for being with a beauty like me. Everyone loves me."

"The ego is staggering."

"It suits your inflexible personality."

"Is that so?"

"Yeah. One of us has to be a people person. Honestly, you're lucky to have *the* Gareth Carson. Must've done so many good things in your past life."

"The elusive Gareth Carson no one can have is all mine?"

"Uh-huh. You've seriously hit the jackpot."

"I have?"

"*Duh.* You're welcome, Professor."

He laughs, the sound deep and warm, and then he brushes his lips against mine and he kisses me. Sort of...slowly, without urgency or the animalistic way that usually leads to sex.

He's kissing me like he's worshipping me, and I vibrate, my whole body melting into his, stroking him everywhere, touching his hair, his face, his jaw.

Because we're in a *relationship*.

Kayden and I are together—have been for a while, apparently, because V is an idiot.

He needs his own Reddit thread.

Anyway, if time could just stop right now, that'd be great. Thanks.

WHEN I WAKE UP, IT'S TEN IN THE MORNING, AND I CURSE MYSELF for it. Must be because I barely slept, keeping an eye on Kayden's fever.

He's left me breakfast and a text.

KAYDE

You looked so peaceful, I didn't want to wake you up. You can skip the morning classes, but I can't.

Thanks for last night, baby (the taking care of me and the mind-blowing fuck). See you tonight.

So, yeah, I kind of changed his name from *Devil* to *Kayde* a while ago.

I'm even contemplating *My Man,* but my demons might revolt from the cringe overdose.

After a shower, I sit on our bed, absentmindedly petting Moka while typing.

ME

Is your fever down?

Yes. Thanks to you.

I just didn't want the hassle of dealing with your corpse.

Your hot and cold moods are so fucking adorable.

Murderous, not adorable.

Adorable little monster. Is that better?

Hmm, undecided. I'll let you know when you come home tonight.

Will you ambush me just so I'll shove you down and make you choke on my cock?

Maybe I'll do it naked.

Behave. Don't make me hard when I'm on my way to class.

> Or what?

Or I'll bend you over my desk and punish you, baby.

> Don't threaten me with a good time, Professor.

Fucking Christ. I said behave.

> Mk ig.

Full words, Gareth.

> 😳 MMM OKAY I GUESS.

Don't yell.

> Don't be a dinosaur.

You'll be punished for that, brat.

> Me: Shaking in my boots *cat hiding GIF*

He left me on Read, probably because he's in class.

I'm bummed I didn't see him this morning, but I could always swing by his office on campus.

Since that day he punished me for the first time, it's become a thing, and honestly? I love the thrill of it.

Not that I *should* see him before tonight, but I already miss him. It's not even funny how much I want to be with him at all times.

There has to be a name for this disease. Maybe I'll ask Reddit and let them troll me again. I definitely need to tell V the good news about the relationship and call him out on his stupid advice.

He'll probably tell me this is *totally normal* and call me dramatic.

I'm starting to suspect V knows exactly who I am, but like me, he probably prefers it this way.

After I get dressed, I sit at the kitchen counter, eating breakfast and playing with Moka.

When my phone vibrates, I grin, popping a strawberry in my mouth and grabbing it. I *knew* Kayden couldn't stay away.

But my smile vanishes the second I see the text is from an unknown number.

> UNKNOWN
>
> Your PI is lying to you.
>
> Attached is a video.

My ears ring as I click on it.

A mist of red clouds my vision as I watch a happy couple walking down the aisle, laughing as confetti falls around them and cheers erupt from the crowd.

The cheers are so loud, they rattle my bones like I'm hearing them from underground.

But I can't tear my gaze away from the bride's and groom's glowing, blissful smiles.

I can't look away from the tall stunning brunette and the tiny lily tattoo on her wrist—the same tattoo I've seen countless times before.

I can't look away from Kayden and his wife.

29
KAYDEN

"Kayden Lucas Davenport."

I wince at Mom's voice as I tap my pen on the desk. She only uses my full name when she's mad. And she's almost never mad.

Leaning back in my campus office chair, I let my gaze wander to the neatly organized files in front of me. It's impossible not to think about the last time I bent my little monster over this desk—his moans, groans, and the way he called my name in that hoarse, aroused voice he reserves just for me.

Only me.

The thought of anyone else seeing him like that, hearing him like that, makes my vision haze red.

But then again, I've already decided—there will be no one after me.

Never.

"Is it true?" Mom's voice quivers, pulling me back. "Did you use my last name and go all the way to the UK for Cassandra?"

"It's not what it seems," I say, keeping my tone calm. "Is Mom Jina there?"

"I'm here, Kay," Mom Jina replies, her tone gentler. "But I won't interfere. Rachel wants the truth, and she deserves that. We both do."

"There's no truth, really," I reply absently, glancing at my watch—the one Gareth got me. It's the least expensive of the bunch, and I only wear it because he pouts when I don't.

And when I do? That wide smile of his stabs me in the chest faster than one of his arrows.

"No truth?" Mom's pacing. I can hear it in her voice. Fuck. That's not good. "You said you needed time away from the pressure back home. That you wanted to escape Grant, the company, and the organization. You said you wanted to clear your head and be closer to us."

"I did, Mom. I wanted to see you more, without Grant's interference."

"But that's not all!" Her breathing is harsh, uneven. "Grant said you still haven't let the Cassandra thing go. He said you're being impulsive, reckless, and that if we don't send you back, he has his methods to force you."

My pen pauses mid-tap. "Grant visited?"

"He called earlier today," Mom Jina interjects. "She's been like this ever since."

"Why would you even talk to him, Mom?" My voice rises slightly. "If you knew it was him, you should've hung up."

"How else would I know what you've been up to?" Mom's voice cracks. "You promised you'd let it go, Kay. You said it was over, that you wouldn't dig deeper or go on more murder sprees. You promised."

The familiar weight of my demons coils around me, their snakelike forms writhing in the shadows, yellow eyes flashing as their tongues graze my skin.

"I couldn't," I admit quietly. "I tried, but I just couldn't."

But now, I think it's because the thought of being aimless once it was all over terrifies me. Because really, when was the last time I thought of Cassandra?

"Kay," Mom Jina's voice softens, almost catching. "Why didn't you talk to us?"

"Because you'd worry. You'd try to stop me. But I can't stop. It's impossible."

"She's dead, Kayden!" Mom's scream cuts through the air. "She's been dead for over two years, and we almost lost you to bloodlust. I don't want to lose you, Kay. I already did when your father took you from my arms and made me live without you. Please stop this. I'm *begging* you."

Her sobs echo through the phone. At least she has Mom Jina to comfort her. She always has.

In truth, I don't know how to handle Mom's emotions. As much as we both hate Dad, I'm more like him, and when faced with raw emotion, I draw a blank.

It's like I'm made of steel, and feelings simply slam against me before falling to the ground.

"Who are you after in the UK?" Mom Jina asks, her tone steady. "Is there even anyone left on your list?"

"Just one," I whisper. "One final name before I get closure."

"And then you'll be done, right?" Mom's voice shakes again. "I'd rather you go back to Grant than continue this madness."

"It'll be over soon, Mom. I promise."

"She left the room," Mom Jina says softly. "Probably to cry alone. I need to go check on her."

"Mom...I'm sorry for lying."

"I know why you did it, but I don't agree." Her sigh is long, weary. "You were born into bad luck, my boy, and it hurts to see you like this. Being a Davenport, and the child of the second wife, no less, brought its own brand of demons. Especially since your mom had her own demons to fight and couldn't help you."

"You did, Mom. I'm grateful. Truly."

"And I'm grateful to have you, Kay. I don't care what biology says, you are *my son*, and I worry about you. You were ripped away from us so young, and I always wondered what you would've become if your father hadn't forced you to go with him."

"I chose to go with him, remember?"

"To protect us."

"Who told you that...?"

"I'm not an idiot, Kay. I know he must've threatened to kill us if you didn't go. You were only nine, but you still took all that burden on yourself." Her breath hitches. "I'm sorry we didn't try harder to get you back."

"You did everything you could. I don't blame you. Neither of you."

"But you won't stop? Not even now that Gareth is in your life?"

I tap my pen harder, but I stay silent.

"You can deny it all you want, but that young man is the best thing to ever happen to you. He calms you, makes you happy, and brings out your best traits. He doesn't deserve this half-truth version of you, Kay." Her voice lowers. "Rachel's becoming more uncomfortable the more she likes him, and she hates hiding things from him. If you don't tell him the truth, we will."

After she hangs up, I stare at the phone in silence.

I've been considering telling Gareth for a while now, but after last night—after he said he wanted me to meet his family —it's become inevitable.

But first, I have to deal with my own family. Grant would lock me up if he found out about Gareth. Hell, he'd probably torture me to death before letting me tarnish the Davenport name.

Worse, he might target Gareth just to eliminate the "threat."

Fuck. He absolutely *would*.

I unbutton my shirt, feeling the collar choke me.

This wasn't part of the plan. Gareth *wasn't* part of the goddamn plan, and yet the mere thought of him is muddying my whole thinking process.

Because I'm only considering options where I can keep him off Grant's radar, away from the organization's reach.

But like Mom Jina said, Gareth deserves the truth.

While I love having him to myself, love watching trash TV with him, playing chess, or cooking disastrous meals, I've been feeling like a fraud lately.

Especially when he tells me about his family, friends, and past. Or when he buys me all those gifts as if I can't afford them, as if my family isn't actually much richer than his.

In the beginning, I didn't care about his mental perception of me, but now I do. I don't like that he has no idea about who I truly am.

But how will I broach the subject?

Gareth doesn't exactly have the easiest personality to deal with, and while he's been smiling more around me and he's behaving himself—even trying to pamper me with gifts—he'll go fucking ballistic at this.

If he wants to stab me, so be it.

And I mean it. If he wants to rip my heart out like he promised, I'll just stand there and let him take it.

The phone vibrates in my hand and a jolt zaps from my arm straight to my chest when I see his name flashing on the screen.

Little Monster.

The cloud of suffocation eases, and the demons retreat to

the shadows, one by one, their ugly forms immediately disappearing at his presence.

I've always felt a form of disturbing comfort with him, usually after I fuck the life out of him.

Last night, when he nursed me back to health when I got sick due to the side effects of Julian's meds, I felt the same warmth I'm feeling as I look at his name.

Maybe I should ditch afternoon classes, call in sick or something. Because I'll feel like I'm suffocating as soon as he hangs up.

It's alarming at this point. I never felt so attuned to someone to the extent I wanted to chain them to me.

Not even with Sandra.

I pick up with, "Miss me already?"

There's silence on the other side, harsh breaths, almost panting filling my ears.

"Gareth?"

No answer. More pants. Fractured breaths.

I stand up so fast that the rolling chair slams into the cabinet behind me. "Gareth? Say something. Is everything all right?"

"Did you lie to me?" His voice is so quiet, I can barely hear it.

"What?"

Surely Mom Jina wouldn't have talked to him already. She said she'd give me time.

"Are you married?"

Fuck.

How did he know? My moms wouldn't have said anything, right...?

Summoning my calmest tone, I say, "It's not—"

"Yes or no," he cuts me off, his voice turning deeper, more guttural.

"Yes."

"Am I a side hole? Are you cheating on her with me?"

"No, fuck. She's dead. She died two years ago." I run a hand through my hair. "How did you know about the marriage?"

Who the fuck gave him this information? It's surely not the PI.

"What was her name?" He completely ignores my question. His voice is calm, unperturbed, and it's creeping me the fuck out.

Gareth is violent when he's upset. If he's this deadly calm, then it's worse than being upset.

"Let's meet and talk about this." I grab my briefcase. "I'm coming home now."

There's a long slashing sound echoing from his side. "I asked for her name."

"Cassandra," I speak low as I rush through the students and professors, ignoring the blur of greetings. "What are you doing, Gareth? What's the sound on your end?"

"Cassandra." The slashing stops as he repeats the name in a gruff, almost choked voice. "Did she go by Cass? Cassie?"

"Sandra." I hop into the car and put him on speaker, not wanting to leave him alone.

I'm actually scared he'll do something. I don't give a fuck if he hurts others, but himself...

My heart thunders in my chest so loudly, I don't hear the car's engine kicking into gear.

"Sandra," he repeats it, his voice so monotone now, it's lifeless, like that first time I met him. When he looked like a monster. "What did you call her during sex?"

"Jesus Christ, why is that important?"

"Was it baby?"

"No."

"Then what?"

"I don't think you need to know that."

"I do. Tell me."

"Just her name, okay. Sandy or something."

"Did you tell her she was beautiful, too?"

"Fuck, Gareth. You're spiraling." I pull out of the parking lot. "I'm on my way."

"Did you?" The slashing starts again, louder, more unhinged.

"No, I didn't."

"How do I know you're not lying?"

"I don't know how to answer that if you're refusing to believe me."

"Hmm. True. You're a liar."

"Listen, Gareth. I need you to tell me who passed on the info."

"I had a PI on you. For months," he confesses. "But she's been lying to me, too. She told me about Isabelle, Lena, Hadil, and Sophia, but not Cassandra. The most important one. The woman you married and looked happy with while you were doing it. While holding her hand and walking down the aisle and kissing her. You were smiling the whole time."

A video?

How the fuck did he get a video?

Grant? Fuck. If he knows Gareth exists, wouldn't he come for him?

I drive at supersonic speed, sliding between traffic. Gareth is reacting to this unlike a normal person. Because he's *not* normal. Other people wouldn't care that much about a dead wife, but he's obsessing.

He's letting his nature take over as if she's a real person standing right in front of him.

"How long were you married to her?" he asks in that same detached voice.

"Two years."

"How long were you with her?"

"Two and a half in total."

"Kids?"

"No."

"Why not?"

"She didn't want them."

"And you listened?"

"Yeah. I don't particularly want them either."

"Wow. You listened. You must've really loved her. You looked good together. Perfect match. Made in heaven, as they say. I bet everyone was jealous."

"Gareth. You're driving yourself in a loop. Ground yourself and stop spiraling out of control. Do breathing exercises. Count to ten. Go practice archery. Just stop with the illogical thoughts. I'll be there shortly, okay, baby?"

"Don't call me that!" he yells, his gruff voice filling the car. "I'm not your fucking baby!"

He hangs up and I curse under my breath, then dial him again, but he doesn't reply.

Fuck!

I'm inhaling and exhaling so loudly, I think I spit my lungs out.

If he's reacting this badly to Cassandra, he might actually hurt himself if the other stuff comes out.

Jesus fucking Christ.

I need to somehow redirect that energy like I've been doing these past few months. Whether with sex or chess or showering him with the affection he craves.

Those calm him, more than archery. He doesn't carry a Taser anymore, but he always has a knife strapped to his calf or in his car. *Always.* He stopped wielding it at me, but it's there.

A constant reminder of his own demons.

My phone vibrates and I perk up before I see the name of the head of my security, Simone.

I'd ignore her if not for the goddamn fuckup that just happened.

"Simone, why on earth did Gareth receive a damn video of my wedding?"

"I don't know, Sir. He texted me to find out why I lied to him and I'm reporting back to you. What should I reply?"

All this time, Simone has been Nadine—Gareth's PI. I knew he'd be digging into me, so I needed to have control over what he could and couldn't know, so Simone cosplayed as a PI.

As an ex-Navy SEAL and a top-notch security leader, she's absolutely hated that mission.

She didn't say it out loud to me, but she's been constantly complaining to Jethro, my second in command, who, in turn, wouldn't stop nagging me.

Like my moms, Simone grew uncomfortable lying to Gareth, but I'm her boss, so she's doing what I ask, including only giving him information I approve of.

"Don't reply," I say. "Tell Jethro to hack into his phone and trace who sent him the video."

"Will do." She pauses. "Also, Boss, you need to return as soon as possible. I received info that Grant will be sending men over. I'll arrange pickup."

"Not yet. I'll call back in a bit."

The last thing I need is my goddamn brother.

I jerk the car to a halt in front of the building and hurry to the apartment, cursing the elevator for taking too long.

When I arrive at my apartment, I pause at the entrance, a metallic scent hitting my nostrils.

Blood.

It's everywhere.

Dark, sticky droplets dot the floor, trailing toward the hallway. My heart pounds, each step making the sight more real. I follow the trail, the crimson stain smeared across the wood, pooling in the center of the room, a red mess that stands out against the cold, clean space.

My stomach drops when I see Gareth's bloody knife lying on the floor.

Moka steps in the blood, her paws leaving prints wherever she goes. She meows softly, bumping against me, but I'm shaking.

He *hurt* himself.

Was that slashing the sound of his knife in his own fucking skin?

I've never seen him do that, and I studied his body—all of it. There was no sign of self-harm. I know he bit his finger until it bled a couple of times, but I didn't think any more of it.

I should have. I really should've considered he could be self-destructive.

That's a lot of blood.

On the counter, the stool, the floor.

Fucking fuck!

I rush to the bedroom, but I know he's not there even before I search.

Sure enough, there's no trace of him. I call him, but his phone is turned off.

Pushing my hand in my hair, I curse out loud. God fucking damn it.

Why would he leave if he was bleeding that much?

My phone vibrates, and my muscles wind up at the view of Declan's name. I consider ignoring him, but I have an extremely bad feeling about this.

"Davenport," I reply in my usual detached tone.

"My dearest brother-in-law." His cheerful, slightly high-pitched tone grates on my frayed nerves. He has an Irish accent and a prominent position in Chicago's Irish mafia.

"We stopped being related a long time ago, Declan."

"That hurts, ye know. I thought we were having fun these last couple of years, avenging Caysie and shit."

I keep looking at the blood—Gareth's blood—and a

headache forms at the back of my skull, snapping to the front with dizzying speed.

Declan is right, we were.

Truth is, Declan really cared about his sister, and he was there when we hunted each of the motherfuckers who raped and killed my wife.

Every single one who was present in that house.

All except for *one*.

"If there's a point behind your call, you should reach it now, Declan." I put him on speaker and shoot Jethro a text.

ME

Track Gareth.

JETHRO

First, take a look at this. We have a problem. A big problem.

He's still typing as Declan speaks. "Heard you found our last name, Davenport, but you somehow hid him from me? I'm so wounded, I could cry."

"Don't you dare—"

"Alexander Carson's grandson isn't yours to keep." His voice darkens. "His blood is fucking mine."

My whole body snaps upright, my throat closing with rage. "Don't you touch a hair on his head or I will—"

"You'll what? Kill me? Find me first. Caysie would be rolling in her grave that yer protecting the grandson of her rapist."

"Gareth is not Alexander."

"No, he's not, but he's the one person Alexander loves the most, even more than his own son. He loves him so much, he's been depressed since he left the States for school. Ye must've noticed that, too, which is why ye pulled this. It's pointless to kill Alexander when we could torture the old man first. I wonder if he'll have a heart attack if I send him his grandson's fingers one by one before I ship him the corpse in a box."

"I will kill you, Declan. You touch him, and I will fucking kill you." I'm breathing so loud, I'm panting.

"And I will kill *you* if you interfere."

The line goes dead.

An emotion I've never felt before courses through my veins. It's so strong and overwhelming, my entire body tightens.

Fear, I realize.

I'm scared I'll never see Gareth again.

I'm *terrified* he'll be hurt because of me.

I'm shaking at the thought that his peaceful face this morning might have been the last time I saw him, or that the kiss I pressed to his forehead as he sighed in his sleep was the last time I touched him.My eyes fly over the texts Jethro sent. Screenshots of further texts Gareth received after the wedding video.

From Declan, no doubt.

> They look happy, right? That's because they were. Kayden and Cassandra Davenport. The envy-worthy couple.

> That's his real last name, by the way. Kayden Davenport. And he's no college professor. Yeah, he studied law, but he never practiced. He's actually one of the two heirs of Davenport Corp., the largest imports and exports corporation in the States.

> Caysie and Kayden had a happy marriage until the senator they were dealing with wanted her. Senator Baltimore, have you heard of him? Anyway, he really tried his best to fuck her, and Caysie indulged his flirting, thinking she could keep a leash on him until the company signed the governmental contract. Then she dropped him after they had no use for him. He got mad, like all men with small dicks. Guess what happened next?

He invited her to a vacation house to discuss an upcoming project. He drugged and gang-raped her with his friends. They passed her around as if she was a fuck doll until she died. And then they dumped her in the river.

We wouldn't have found her decomposed body if a maid hadn't felt guilty and called Kayden two weeks later.

There was no evidence, so the justice system was useless. Kayden took it into his own hands to get her that justice.

Now, guess where you fit in this little tale, Gareth Carson?

For more information, let's meet.

30
GARETH

The person who was texting me all that information about Kayden and his wife is a bulky bald man with a blond beard and bulging blue eyes.

An ugly dagger and roses tattoo slither from beneath the collar of his black shirt, up his neck and his bald head.

We're in the location he gave me over the phone—near the beach, in front of a warehouse with a rusty roof and a door off its hinges.

The sea's cold air seeps into my bones as I lean against Medusa, my blood slowly dripping onto the concrete. I wrapped my wounds in a bandage earlier, when I decided I'm not dying yet. Not until I hear the entire story.

But I still messed up Medusa's interior with all my blood.

She seems to take the hit whenever I fuck myself up because of a certain fucking—

No.

I need to stay calm.

I can't go through this if I'm not calm.

"Name's Declan O'Connor," he says in an Irish accent, toying with a toothpick between his teeth.

"Don't give a fuck about your name." My monotone voice sounds far away, as if I'm separated from my physical form and can only hear my words from underground.

"You probably should. I'm Caysie's brother. Different mammies, though."

Figures. He's ugly as fuck compared to her.

Cassandra Davenport. Kayden's wife.

He had a wife.

A *wife*.

A dead wife, but a *wife*.

And apparently, he's richer than me. *Way* richer.

Even I have heard the Davenport name. He's one of them— the people who own the imports and exports sector on a national and international scale.

And he has a wife.

Had.

Their wedding video still plays in my head on a loop. The smiles. The happiness. The goddamn *soft* look in his eyes.

I scratched the screen with my fingers over and over again as if I could erase her, but I couldn't.

And I *can't*.

Because she's already dead, but she still lives inside him. No matter how much I scratched, I couldn't remove her from his side.

So I wanted to remove *him* from my blood, which is why I cut the length of my forearm again.

And again.

And fucking *again*.

But he's still there, beneath my skin, while she's beneath his.

Because he's made up a whole new life for her, and I'm here to hear where I fit into this fucking circus.

"While I'm sure your family story is to die for, I'm more interested in what you brought me here for." I stare at Declan. "What do I have to do with the revenge?"

"Ye always this disrespectful, boy?"

"I'm being respectful now, believe me."

"Ye bring a man to fucking England, of all places, ye have to be thankful I'm even talking to ye."

"I'm so thankful, I'll cry," I say with a poker face. "But if you're going to waste my time..."

I turn toward my car, my eyes blurring. The ground shifts beneath my feet as my vision crosses. I'm lightheaded.

Must be all the blood loss.

"Your grandfather was there."

I let go of the handle and slowly face him. "Grandpa?"

"Alexander Carson, yes. He was present in Senator Baltimore's house the night Caysie was raped and killed."

I shake my head once. "He would've never done something like that."

"Cause he's so gentle and loving toward you?"

Because he thinks people like that are subhuman. He wouldn't indulge in what he calls 'barbaric' acts, not after Harper.

"Well, he did, or he was there and covered for it, which is the same according to me and Davenport. We had a list of all the people who were there that night, and we slowly but surely took them out. Boat accidents, strokes, suspicious deaths on foreign soil. You name it. We tortured some of them, too. I thought we were done about a year ago, but apparently, Kayden has been digging deeper, and he confirmed that there was one more man who was wiped from the cameras, but a maid verified that she saw him. Yer dear granddaddy."

He throws away the toothpick. "He must've covered his tracks as soon as the senator died. He's smart and discreet, but Kayden is just that in love with Caysie, and he wasn't satisfied with all the people we killed. He just needed more and more. He became obsessed and lifeless; only revenge kept him afloat. I like that about him, ye know. The undying love and unbreakable loyalty. I still hate that he hid Alexander—and you—from me."

My hand twitches and I stare at him.

It all clicks into place.

Kayden's reaction to when he thought I wanted to rape Yulian—he thought I was the same as what he thinks Grandpa did.

The way he belittled me during the mock trial for defending the accused.

How he used to say he was giving me a taste of my own medicine.

Did he adopt a new identity and come all the way here to... destroy Grandpa through me?

"Ye figured it out, yeah?" Declan smirks. "Kayden wanted to break you, then kill you. Would hurt yer granddaddy worse than his actual death, since ye're the apple of his eye."

"He made me attached to him for revenge as well?" I ask, not recognizing my choked voice.

"Why else? Kayden only ever loved Caysie, ya wee fool."

Only ever loved Caysie.

Sandra. That's what he called her.

The woman he loved so much that he went crazy to avenge her death.

The woman he loved so much, he injected himself beneath my skin just so he could get her justice.

I scratch at my wounds, peeling the bandage off and ripping the flesh open, then digging my fingers inside.

I want the blood out.

All of it.

I want *him* out of my veins.

My skin.

My insides.

I want to throw him up.

Spit him out.

Send him back to his Sandra.

But no matter how much I dig, he's still there, somewhere I can't reach.

Beneath the outer layer of my heart, maybe in the beats themselves.

Maybe I need to dig my knife there, see if I can make it stop.

The thumps and the pain.

I just want it to *stop*.

It's so loud in my head, the demons screeching so noisily, it's deafening.

My quiet white room is now splashed with blood from the void and I want the red gone.

Stop.

Someone make it *stop*.

My vision blurs and I stagger, falling against my car, still digging and probing and scratching at the skin, over and over.

And fucking over again.

Why can't I get him the fuck out?

"What a weird little cunt."

Declan's voice is close now—behind me, I think—but I don't give a fuck.

I want the blood gone.

I want the pain to stop—

"Right, boy." Something pricks the back of my neck. "You're coming with us."

I think I hear other heavy footsteps and voices, and my eyes are closing, my fingers still twitching in my arm, in the blood.

The blood that I can't remove him from.

Because I'm drifting.

Into the pitch-black void.

———

I wake up in water.

No. Water was thrown over my face, reeling me from sleep. Drug-induced sleep.

Because the inside of my mouth is dry and tastes funny, like sandpaper and detergent.

I'm in a metal chair, my hands bound behind my back and my legs strapped to the chair's legs. My arm wounds are messily bandaged, probably so I don't bleed out.

A mixture of humidity and the rancid body odor of the two buff men standing in front of me fills my nostrils but fails to disgust me.

I think I'm losing my sense of feeling. Maybe it left my veins with all the blood.

It's better this way. I need my ability to shut down now.

The room looks like a basement, with stone walls, low lights, and a metal door.

Typical torture chamber shit, I suppose. I've never been in one because my grandfather made sure I wasn't caught. Maybe I should have been.

If I had been, I wouldn't feel so...insignificant.

Like a goddamn speck of dust.

A toy that you throw away and it bounces back just to be kicked and used, then thrown away again.

And *again.*

I'm being punched now. I don't feel it.

Sure, my body is rattling against the chair, my hair is pulled until I feel it ripping, and my stomach and chest are kicked. The chair topples over, and I fall on the floor, hitting my head.

Yes, it hurts physically. It does. My pain receptors are working overtime, my nerves shocked from the assault.

But inside? It doesn't hurt.

I'm still in that white room with all the blood splashed on the walls, and I'm trying to wipe it away, to get back my peaceful white room where I can just close my eyes and breathe.

Just for a while.

But they're talking now—the men who were hitting me— saying things about how I creep them out and how I don't scream no matter how hard they hit me.

They need to stop talking, because their voices are polluting my white room. The one in my head that I escape to when my mind gets too loud.

The one Kayden turned so white before he splashed it in blood.

My blood from that useless organ behind my rib cage that won't stop beating.

Being alive.

And for what?

A shoe presses against my stomach, and I ignore Declan, who's peering down at me, his face uglier in the dim light.

"Ye wanna die, don't ya?" He smirks. "Ye think it'd be that easy?"

I don't reply, because I have nothing to say to him. Maybe it's better if he kills me, because that white room is dripping in crimson no matter how much I wipe the fuck out of the walls.

"Torture doesn't hurt freaks like ye," he says while sliding a toothpick in his mouth.

"That's true. It'd save you time and manpower to kill me,

actually." My voice is husky, my jaw bursting with pain when I speak.

"No shit, ye weaselly cunt." He grabs me by the hair and then lifts my head up. "Heard ye a goddamn fag who's been sucking Kayden's cock. Ye do have eyes similar to Caysie's. He must've thought of her while deep-throating ye—"

I headbutt him. Hard.

So hard, I reel from it and blood explodes on his forehead and mine, because my vision is red—literally—rivulets sliding down my nose and into my mouth.

Declan curses, then bursts out laughing. "So ye're a little quiet psycho until he's mentioned? Ye don't like the thought of being Caysie's replacement?

"I'm no one's fucking replacement!" I glare up at him, thinking about how to strangle him. Watch the life bleed out of those repugnant eyes.

"Maybe I have a better way to torture ya." He grins and calls his men, who once again inject me with something.

And then my world turns black again.

31

GARETH

I wake to the sound of soft, mocking laughter, like a distant echo bouncing off the sterile white walls.

My head is heavy, my limbs bound in the tight grip of a straitjacket. I sit up on the white tiles, the cold digging into my bones. The room smells of suffocating antiseptic, the walls blurring in and out of focus as I try to figure out if I'm in my head.

No.

I'm here. In the real world.

Sitting on the floor. My pants are white, too, like the straitjacket.

The same straitjacket Grandpa tried everything to save me from—even hiding the truth from Dad.

I smile and my jaw hurts.

Ah, fuck. Looks like I'm not keeping my promise to him after all.

I'm sorry, Grandpa.

The laughter draws my attention, and I stare at the flicker of light. Projected images dance across the wall, crude and distorted at first, but then clearer.

That's when I see them.

Kayden and *her*. Cassandra.

It's a loop of videos. The first one is homemade, where she's laughing, her voice soft as she films Kayden asleep, his face relaxed.

"Darling, wake up." The camera zooms in on his lips as he stirs, and he smiles at her, a lazy, affectionate grin that's all for her.

Only *her*.

My breath catches and I stand up, ignoring the throbbing pain in my chest, stomach, and face as my feet carry me closer to the wall as if I'm floating on air.

I can't breathe.

My inhales are small wheezes, like I'm choking on the air.

But I keep watching. Video upon video of him hugging her at an event, her kissing him in public, both of them swaying to music.

Things I never had.

Will *never* have.

The videos go on and on and on, and I lift my hand to scratch her, but the straitjacket restricts me.

Binding me.

Forcing me to watch without acting.

Each image stabs me worse than a knife, tearing me apart.

And I can't look away.

Or breathe.

I'm drowning in the rawness of their intimacy, the connection he never had with me.

Cassandra is the normal woman that fits him, and it's something I'll never be.

Normal. Or a woman.

Or a fit for him.

Because he loves her, and I'm only a vessel for revenge.

The laughter echoes again—this time, it's not coming from the video, but from me.

I can't stop the hollow sound as I hit my head against her. Cassandra. And the wall.

The louder she laughs, the harder I hit.

Again.

And *again*.

Until my vision is red, blood dripping down my lashes, over my nose, and into my mouth, but she won't stop laughing.

And calling him *darling*.

And laughing.

And kissing.

And hugging.

And dancing.

Even as my blood drips on the ground at my feet, he's still there.

Inside me.

In my head.

In that beating heart that wouldn't purge him out.

And I can't get him away from her, because she's inside him and will *always* be inside him, and I can't do anything about it.

Not like I did with Mr. Laurent or Harper.

I have this tendency to get too attached to people I like, too often, and in different ways. It's not romantic or anything, I don't think.

It's my brain's way of prioritizing people in my life.

Like Dad. He's my role model, the person I've always

wanted to be like. I studied law because he's a lawyer. I dress like him and even adapted his manner of speech. He truly fascinates me. He's the normal version of me that I strive to be, so when he started dividing his attention between me and Kill, I wanted to remove the hazard—Killian. But I didn't, because that would make Dad sad.

Besides, at the time, I had Kayden, who muted my destructive thoughts and even reminded me that he's both my and Killian's dad, so sharing wouldn't kill me.

That was okay, I guess. Maybe because I'm older now, so I have more self-control. Besides, Kill is also one of my things, so it's not like I would hurt him consciously.

Mr. Laurent was also one of those people I thought belonged to me. I was attached to him and I liked him. He was smart and well-read and had a beautiful French accent. I liked listening to him talk and being in his company.

Not in a romantic way, but like with Dad, I respected him. A lot.

But when I found out he'd used me, I wanted to get rid of what took away what was mine—him. As Aunt Rai hugged me after I saw his dead eyes, I pushed her away. She thought I was in shock and wanted Mom, but, truly, I was a little mad that she was the one who got rid of what was mine.

I wanted to do it myself. Carve his eyes out with my own hands.

Those thoughts were ten times worse with Harper.

She was my one serious girlfriend. We started going out at fifteen. She had a crush on me for a while, so I agreed to go out with her because of her eyes.

I don't know how to describe it, but she had these very sad eyes, almost lifeless, and I wanted to know the story behind them. Harper was super popular in our high school, but no one seemed to see beyond that image.

She had a façade like me and I saw through it. I saw how

she flinched around men who had loud voices. How she secretly went to the bathroom to throw up her lunch.

But for some reason, she always said she liked my voice, because it was mellow and made her feel safe.

Me? Making someone feel safe?

Me, who pictured shooting people with my arrows whenever I went hunting with Dad?

She was clearly a bad judge of character, poor Harper. But I liked her personality, mostly because it was so different from mine. Where I feigned happiness, she was always smiling and laughing, making everyone feel safe and welcome. She volunteered at charities and stood up to bullies and was genuinely a good person.

Too good, actually. I suspected she cried herself to sleep, and she did.

Because Harper's life that looked perfect on paper was, in reality, a living hell.

After a three-year battle, her mom died of cancer when Harper was ten, and after that, she was brought up by her dad, David—a local Pilates coach who everyone adored.

Once Harper had a panic attack when she was kissing me in the locker room after a football game. She was hyperventilating badly and kind of threw up on me.

I helped her clean up and she burst out everything in a heap of tears. Her dad had been sexually assaulting her for years, since her mother's death, and told her she was her mother's replacement and that it was her duty to satisfy him. In fact, he started in the final months of her mom's life, when she was too out of it to notice anything, let alone protect her.

Harper said she tried to talk to one of her neighbors, but they said that was impossible. They said David was such a good guy, and Harper was just a troubled teenager who wanted attention.

Harper was ugly crying and choking as she talked. She kept

hugging me but also looking like she was about to be sick again. She wanted affection. Craved it, even. But the male touch disturbed her, and she hated that she couldn't have sex with me because it would only remind her of David.

So I promised to talk to my mom and dad and get her help

She smiled and told me I was the best thing that had happened in her life. I asked her to come spend the night with me, no pressure, and said I definitely wouldn't fuck her. She could stay with my mom if she wanted.

I simply didn't want her in David's vicinity anymore.

But she shook her head and kissed me, this time without hyperventilating. Then she hugged me close, telling me how much she loved me.

The next day, Harper was found dead in the bathtub after cutting her wrists open.

She killed herself.

Because of her father.

I watched with a tilted head as David cried at her funeral. He looked so sad and pitiful, as if he wasn't the razor that had slashed Harper's wrists.

Everyone showered him with sympathy, hugging him and calling him a saint for surviving both his wife's and daughter's deaths.

He touched Harper's cheek in the casket, patting her cold skin, and I had to stop myself from cutting his hand off.

But it was at that moment that I decided he'd die.

Because he took Harper away from me.

Because he should've been in that casket, not her.

I spent a few weeks planning his death, taking my time to learn his habits.

Like with hunting, you have to be patient with your prey and wait until all the circumstances are aligned.

Then, one night, I slipped into his house unnoticed. I

planned to spike his wine that he drank every Tuesday and Thursday with his bath.

The undetectable sleeping powder would make him fall asleep and drown.

A freak accident.

It wasn't violent enough for my taste, but it was more methodical.

But then I heard his obscene groaning sounds.

So I grabbed a kitchen knife and went upstairs.

I stood in the darkness as I watched David fucking the sheets on Harper's bed and moaning her name as he thrust his hips between the pillows.

I snapped, I think, because the next moment, I was behind him and I'd slit his throat. Then he turned around and I stabbed him in the chest and his dick.

My palm held his face on the bed as I stabbed and stabbed until he was lifeless, unmoving, just a pile of blood and shocked, lifeless eyes. Then I cut off his dick and stuffed it in his mouth.

I looked at him and felt nothing.

But I wanted to see Harper and tell her it was over now. She could rest in peace.

If there's a Heaven, she better get access.

I cursed myself for not killing him earlier, actually. When Harper was ten.

Killing a man in cold blood made me feel nothing, but I was still left with a bloody crime scene. So I called Grandpa.

I needed a lawyer, and I didn't want to wake Dad up.

Grandpa came straight away and found me sitting in the corner staring at the blood on the knife. He immediately understood the situation. He didn't scold or even blame me. He just made a few calls and said he'd bury the whole thing.

Even before I told him Harper's story.

He took me home, to his house, made me shower, and gave me a bowl of strawberries that I finished in record time.

I was hungry, or maybe empty, ravenous, gluttonous.

Since then, strawberries have become my comfort food, what I eat instead of fantasizing about blood. I told Grandpa about Harper and what David had done and that I didn't regret it.

Not one bit.

My only regret was not doing it sooner.

I don't even feel guilty that I'm the reason a man was erased from the face of the earth.

Grandpa just sat across from me and listened, his eyes flashing with both understanding and faint sadness.

"Why didn't you turn me in, Grandpa?" I asked.

"Because you're my grandson."

"That's all?"

"I don't need another reason."

"Will you tell Dad?"

"No, he's not as fluid as me. He'll have you diagnosed like Kill, and we all know what a shitshow that'll be."

"Oh. You already knew?"

"That both my grandsons are special?" He smiled and nodded.

"Is it good to be special?"

He ruffled my hair. "Of course. You're strong and unlike any of these fools roaming the earth. My daughter was like you and I lost her. So I'm not losing any of you again. I'll protect you from a world that doesn't understand you."

"Even if I kill people and feel nothing?"

"If they deserve to die, I don't see why not." He stood up and clutched my shoulders. "But you need to rein it in, son. Don't get attached to the point of obsessing and then fixate about killing. I think that's your trigger, so avoid getting too attached at all costs. You can never get caught, Gareth. None of them will understand."

"Why not?"

"Because people like you are treated like animals. They're abused and poked with needles. They're probed and violated and eventually put on death row. Promise me you'll never get caught, son."

"I promise."

Obviously, I failed my grandpa.

Not only did I become attached and obsess worse than all the other times, but I also got caught.

I let Kayden flow in my bloodstream, and I can't remove all the blood. No matter how much I hit my head.

And Cassandra won't stop laughing.

Mocking me.

And my inability to remove the obstacle.

Maybe because this time, the obstacle is me.

32
KAYDEN

I was born with a silver spoon hanging from my mouth.

Somehow, that spoon transformed into a blade, scraping, stabbing, and rotting my tongue.

You know, rich people's problems.

My half-brother, Grant, never liked me. He was fourteen when I was born, and we grew up in different worlds. Jealousy was the undercurrent of his disdain, mainly because our father didn't punish me as harshly as he did him.

Don't get me wrong—I got my fair share of "discipline." Being kept in a well with snakes for three days, watching execution-style murders since I was seven, and undergoing poison and pain training weren't exactly vacations.

But honestly, it was probably better than what Grant endured.

Courtesy of dear old Dad.

Harrod Davenport was the personification of a totalitarian monarch.

As the head of the prestigious Davenport family, he ruled with an iron fist.

Most people know us as pioneers in imports and exports. They think we're just one of the four founding families of Graystone Ridge, an affluent town in the Northeast US.

But we run much, much deeper.

Like secret society deep.

The name's Vencor—not that anyone outside the inner circle or conspiracy theorists would know.

The founding families—Davenport, Callahan, Armstrong, and Osborn—are Vencor's Founder members. We don't just manipulate power; we redefine it. Maximizing profit, planting politicians, reshaping society's fabric—we've been doing it for generations.

From a young age, I was primed for my role within Vencor. Harrod made sure of that, subjecting me to every initiation and trial to prove my worth. Physical and psychological pain were just part of the curriculum.

If I died, well, that was that.

In our families, weakness is a death sentence. Offspring either prove their worth or get discarded like trash.

But I didn't die.

I had plans.

Lots of them.

And, truth be told, I had an easier ride than Grant.

Harrod held him to a higher standard, and failure wasn't tolerated. I watched as he broke both of Grant's legs for planning to elope with his college sweetheart.

Then Harrod killed the girl.

One shot. Point-blank. Her brains splattered onto a kneeling Grant.

I was seven. And I had to watch.

To learn.

To never become a failure like my brother.

Something inside Grant died that day. His soul, maybe. His humanity. I don't know what exactly, but it turned him into something unrecognizable.

He'd already been through hell—finding his mother hanging from the ceiling at thirteen—and now the love of his life was taken from him in the cruelest way imaginable.

The tragedy of it all must've been so bad that he just... turned the switch off.

Abuse has a way of breaking people. Some escape it through death, like Grant's mom. Some run, like my mom. And others become the very thing they despise.

Grant chose the latter.

Slowly but surely, he turned into Harrod.

Me? I bided my time. Patiently.

When I was nine, my mom finally left. She'd been planning it with Mom Jina for years, obsessing over every detail and kind of forgetting me in the meantime. She'd be so out of it sometimes, hiding the bruises covering her body like a walking battlefield, that she didn't see *my* bruises.

Then, one day, she took me, and we fled. The three of us. All the way to Switzerland.

For three months, we lived like the happiest family in the world. But even at nine, I knew it wouldn't last.

Harrod would find us. And he'd kill my moms.

So I called Grant and asked for help.

He traced my call and handed our location to Harrod. Because by then, Grant wasn't just Harrod's son; he was Harrod.

But before he hung up, Grant told me to wait outside when

Harrod arrived. Said if I went with him willingly, the moms would live.

I struck a deal with Harrod.

I'd be his perfect son. The opposite of Grant. I'd give him everything he wanted—power, profit, status. *Everything.*

To this day, I don't know why he agreed. Maybe he never wanted my mom. Maybe he feared losing me completely.

Whatever the reason, I had to call my moms and tell them I chose him.

Then I cut contact.

For years, I became Harrod's golden child. Straight A's, star athlete, problem solver. Everything Grant wasn't.

And I thrived on it.

The control. The resources. The killing.

Especially the killing.

Slaughtering for Vencor became second nature—hunting, executing, then sharing a smoke with Julian and the others. Not all of them loved the bloodshed, but we all got off on the power. The knowledge that one day, we'd own everything.

I was riding that high when I met Cassandra on a blind date.

Our dads arranged it—typical rich people shit.

She was smart, confident, persistent. A Senior Vencor member and an executive in the Davenport company. She liked me immediately and decided I was the man for her.

I didn't argue. I liked her, mainly because I could be open with her since she was a Senior member—the highest position attainable for a non-founding family.

Since I was expected to get married anyway, I thought Cassandra was a perfect fit. My father loved her, and Grant liked her fire. His own wife, another arranged marriage, was meek and he hated that.

Cassandra was a free spirit who didn't conform to social norms. Despite the marriage, she was anti-monogamy and loved threesomes a lot. I didn't mind. But we both got bored a few months into our marriage, so we agreed to have an open marriage. She also preferred dishing out orders during sex, and her streak of dominance clashed with mine, so six months after the marriage, we admitted we just weren't sexually compatible and stopped having sex altogether, opting to satisfy our preferences with other people. But aside from that, we were an ideal couple.

A perfect match. No deep feelings, no mess.

I think that's part of the reason my moms never liked Cassandra. They wanted someone to love me and for me to love them back, but they're hopeless romantics, and I don't do love.

Our marriage was a practical, harmonious partnership. We were close friends who told each other everything and had the same goals and aspirations.

It worked.

Until it didn't.

When Cassandra was taken from me, I didn't feel heartbreak. I felt rage.

Rage at the audacity that someone dared to touch her. I needed revenge, to kill every single person who hurt her.

I didn't trust the justice system, so I delivered it myself.

One by one, I made them bleed.

All except one.

Maybe it was because Alexander Carson was the last on the list. Maybe it was because I wouldn't have a purpose after he was gone.

Sandra would remain dead and I'd be alone and aimless. With nothing to tether me to life.

So I went with a different approach and decided to cut Declan from the equation. To go after Carson with needles, stabbing him slowly, until he died by a thousand cuts.

And the best way to do that? Kill his grandsons. Then his son. Then his daughter-in-law.

Break him completely before finishing him off.

The first time I met Gareth, my suspicions about his rotten blood and inherited bad habits were confirmed, and I wanted to punish him by reversing the positions. But that only planted the seed of fascination.

Because ever since then, even though I told myself I could kill him at any moment, I've only managed to grow more infatuated with him.

Enamored.

Obsessed.

Addicted.

Obviously, my original plan went to absolute hell, because I'm in the back of a van, heading straight to where that cockroach Declan is keeping my little monster.

While staring at a selfie he took of us the other day.

He's lying on my lap, grinning at the camera, dimples deep in his cheeks, blond hair messy, and Moka curled up on his shoulder.

I wasn't even looking at the camera. My hand was in his hair, stroking absentmindedly while I watched the game.

LITTLE MONSTER

Looking hot.

ME

Me?

No, me. You're not so bad yourself, though.
We kind of look good together.

We do.

We *did.*

Now, I keep staring at his face, wishing he'd sent me more pictures of him. Especially since I know he always takes pictures of us when he thinks I'm not paying attention.

I slide the back of my fingers on the screen as if it's his face.

You better be safe, little monster.

He can hate me all he wants. I know I deserve it and more considering what I planned to do to him and his family.

But he *has* to be safe.

The image of his blood and what that degenerate Declan could have been doing to him in the thirty-six hours it took me to find him has been causing pressure on the inside of my skull.

"We're twenty minutes out from the target," Simone's voice echoes in the van as she speaks in the earpiece to my security team in the other vans.

She's sitting opposite me in full combat gear, holding her rifle down.

Her braided hair is held in a bun, special night vision glasses resting on her head as her dark eyes silently shoot a laser in my direction.

"You'll kill him with those eyes, Simone," Jethro says from his position beside me while tapping on his computer. "Not that he doesn't deserve it."

Jethro is tall but lean and wears frameless glasses that sit low on his nose. As a typical nerd, he usually dresses in hoodies with anime characters or metal band logos, but Simone forced him into combat gear today. Something he hates more than getting his prim, soft hands dirty.

I met Jethro—then Eduard—in college. Soon after, he got arrested for breaching some Pentagon security. I knew I needed his services, so I arranged his murder during the transfer, made him a ghost, and gave him a new identity. Ever since then, he's been my right hand.

He's the one who found Simone a year later. She quit the army and was wasting away in a mid-range security firm and he said she'd be perfect for our team.

Cassandra never liked them. Neither of them. I think the feeling was mutual. She didn't appreciate how they expressed their opinions and didn't mince their words. And they didn't like how she treated them like servants—the only thing I clashed with her on.

Jethro and Simone are, in a sense, the siblings I never had —Grant doesn't count—and I never liked how she disregarded them.

But while I appreciate their input, they really don't know when to shut up.

Like right now.

"Be quiet, both of you." I pocket my phone. "Go faster, Sal."

"Yes, Boss!" the driver says.

"With all due respect," Simone says, throwing a quick glance at her watch. "We wouldn't be in this situation if you'd just stayed in the States."

"And miss fucking around with a college kid?" Jethro whistles. "And being the cause of his death?"

"He's not dying." I pull at the collar of my combat gear.

Jethro lifts a shoulder. "He wouldn't have if you hadn't gotten into his life."

"I'll knock your teeth out," I snap.

"No, thanks. That will probably hurt, and I don't like that shit."

"Jethro's right." Simone, who's usually less argumentative than Jethro, is still glaring at me. "Gareth doesn't deserve this. No matter what his grandfather did."

"Save the I-told-you-so moment." I pull harder on the collar, nearly ripping it.

Of course, they were both against it. Even Jethro has been saying there's proof Alexander was there that night, not that he was present when Cassandra was violated and killed.

Lately, they've both been trying to get me to come back. Abandon the whole thing. Leave Gareth alone.

Simone even saved all the money Gareth paid her for the PI side gig in a different bank account, intent on giving it all back.

Unless I'm imagining it, I'd think they both like him. Which is ironic since they don't even like *me* most of the time.

"Let's get this over with first." Simone jumps out of the van before it properly stops. "One and two, with me!"

A few other men jump from the vans and I follow suit, a gun in my hand.

We're surrounded by trees on all sides, their dark branches stretching upward, cutting into the sky. The air is thick with the earthy scent of moss and damp soil, muffling the world beyond the wilderness. In the distance stands a large, brutalist-like structure, its sharp angles and imposing concrete facade looking lifeless against the natural chaos of the forest.

"All security disabled," Jethro says. "Fifteen minutes."

We rush into the formation Simone devised with the little knowledge we have on Declan's house in the forest.

Which isn't much since I didn't even know he had this place. It's more like a compound.

Declan and his men only carry untraceable phones, especially since they knew I'd try to find him through them.

We only managed to locate this place through the tracker I had Jethro insert in Gareth's bracelet. We lost the signal when Declan took him on a plane, but we got it back again once they landed in Chicago and then they headed all the way here.

It took us time to arrange the plane and the plan, but we finally made it—without a wink of sleep on my part. I couldn't do that when Gareth's fate is unknown.

Declan's men start shooting at us immediately, but Simone and the others cover me as we kill our way in.

Simone's presence is like a wall of steel at my back. The air is thick and suffocating inside as she shoots and wrestles men twice her size with brutal efficiency, tossing one of them into the wall.

I grab one by his hair and slam his head on the concrete, watching as it cracks open.

Jethro gives me directions to where Gareth is, and I follow, letting Simone and the others take care of the men.

The floor beneath me thuds with each step, but I barely hear or see anything. Not the shouts, the alarms, the gunshots.

As I shoot open the door to the room where Gareth is, my heart pounds so violently in my chest, I feel the sickening sound of it in my throat, like it's trying to rip its way out.

Gareth's arms are bound in a straitjacket as he bangs his head on the wall.

Again.

And again.

The thuds are a disturbing silent scream.

Blood spatters across the wall, splashing over a projected video, and drips in jagged lines, carving small veins that trail down to the floor, pooling beneath him. It stains his bare feet, and his white pants, and there's a red blotch on the arm of his straitjacket—messing him up.

You messed him up.

I rush toward him and pull him back by the shoulders. There's a gaping wound in his forehead, blood trickling over his nose, his eyes, his entire face.

Fuck.

I wipe it with the back of my sleeve, keeping the gun out of reach.

His eyes stare at nowhere, his pupils are so dark and blown up, he looks like an entirely different person.

My little monster, who often takes pride in his unearthly beauty, is now all bloodied.

Because of me.

"Gareth?"

He pulls from my grip with inhuman strength and bangs his head harder on the wall. It's so powerful, I think he'll crack his skull open.

"Shut up, shut up, shut up," he mumbles. "Stop laughing, shut up."

I press my hand against the wall, and he slams against it as I shoot the projector in the ceiling, making the video stop.

Gareth stays still, his bloody forehead resting on my palm. His breathing is so low, it causes my skin to prickle.

"Gareth? Can you hear me?"

No reply.

Goddamn it.

I pull him up straighter and he stands on unsteady feet, swaying as if he can't feel his legs while still looking at the wall with those blown-up eyes.

Eyes that used to only look at me.

Following me everywhere.

Even when he pretends he doesn't care.

Now they're not seeing me.

"Gareth?" I stroke his face, beneath his eyes, his cheek. "Say something."

The wound in his head is still bleeding. I need to have that looked at—

"Sir, we're leaving!" Simone growls from the door. "Now."

I gather Gareth in my arms, and he's so stiff, his limbs resemble a rigid cord. I manage to lean his head on my shoulder.

"I'm getting you out of here," I whisper, but he's not responding, his lips trembling, his face pale, his eyes still staring nowhere.

Like they're dead.

No.

Simone covers me as I rush back to the van and then we speed away, Declan's men still shooting at us. The man himself wasn't there, but I'll find him and rip his head off his shoulders for what he did.

I cut through Gareth's straitjacket with a knife as Simone forms a makeshift bandage for his forehead.

My molars grind when I see the long slashes along his arm, and the sloppy stitches Declan probably did to torture him further are mostly ripped open. Bruises on his torso, his collarbone, his chest.

I'm going to torture that motherfucker Declan before I kill him. A week for every goddamn wound he put on my Gareth's previously perfect body.

You ruined him, not Declan.

It's you.

"Gareth." My lips tremble around the word. "Talk to me. Say something, baby, please."

He blinks twice, and I think he sees me, even for a fraction of a second, but then his eyes stare up.

At nothing.

No. At something.

Anything.

Just not at me.

33
KAYDEN

"Alexander Carson speaking."

I release a long breath at the sound of his voice. Not too long ago, I wanted to kill this motherfucker with everything in me, but now, I don't wish him harm—just because he's Gareth's grandfather.

The grandfather he wouldn't stop talking about. Grandpa this and Grandpa that.

I don't know when my animosity toward Alexander stopped, but it was probably around the time Cassandra started appearing in my nightmares trying to kill Gareth.

And I wanted to kill *her*, in the nightmare, for daring to touch him.

All sorts of fucked up, I know.

"Hello?" Alexander speaks again. "Who's this?"

"Kayden Davenport," I say as I leave the room where Gareth is sleeping and walk down the hallway.

We brought him to one of my family's safe houses in Chicago's suburbs. The doctor stitched up his arm and head and said he'd lost a lot of blood, so he needed a transfusion. He also suffered a severe concussion and needs to be monitored carefully for the next twenty-four to forty-eight hours.

Per the doctor's recommendations, I'm keeping him in a dark, quiet room with no screens or loud noises. I didn't let him sleep for the first few hours, shaking him and giving him things to drink, but now, he can rest.

I'll still need to wake him up and check his responsiveness every few hours. There should be no stress, no physical activity, and just complete rest these couple of days.

The freeze-out behavior is unlikely due to the concussion according to the doctor. He recommended having a clinical psychiatrist take a look at him.

I refused.

Gareth hates those doctors. He's paranoid about being diagnosed like his brother or having people probe his brain.

And I will not be the reason for his discomfort. Not anymore.

"To what do I owe the call, Mr. Davenport?" Alexander's voice sounds more professional now.

"You know who I am?"

"Everyone does." He pauses. "If it's not urgent, can I call you back? My grandson has gone missing, and I'm flying out to help search for him."

"You don't have to."

"Pardon?"

"Your grandson's with me."

A long beat passes before he breathes harshly. "I'm not sure what this is about, but if you want something from me, there's no need to involve him or I might resort to uncivil methods."

"There's no need for threats as I'm not harming him." *Not more than I already did.* "He had a concussion and I'm monitoring him until he's out of danger. Once he's better, I'll let him call you."

"Concussion? How? Where are you? I'm coming right now to take him home."

"No, you won't. I'm only informing you because he wouldn't want his family to worry about him. Goodbye, Mr. Carson."

"Wait. What's your relationship to Gareth?"

I hang up.

What's my relationship to Gareth, really?

A couple of days ago, I thought we were in a relationship like he wanted. He was mine and I was his and that's that.

I was contemplating telling him the truth and finding a method to leave Vencor so I could be with him.

It's not really my family that are homophobes—though my dad would kill me if he were alive—it's the whole goddamn thing.

Gay members aren't allowed, and if you're found out to be frolicking with men, you're killed Middle Ages style.

That's the end of that.

I don't give a fuck about myself, but no one is allowed to come near Gareth.

Not anymore.

I'm still racking my brain about the possible options when my phone vibrates.

DECLAN

You blew up my whole house for that rat? You truly fucked up, Davenport.

I ignore him because he's a dead man walking. Simone and

Jethro are tracking him down and will bring him to me so I can slash his face open.

My shoulders are hunched and my movements are lethargic as I walk back to the room. I need to sleep, even if only for twenty minutes, before I wake Gareth up again.

Simone and Jethro offered to watch him on my behalf, but I can't possibly leave his side. Besides, he doesn't know them and might get violent. He's not himself—far from it—and that makes him dangerous.

So I need to personally make sure he's okay—

A crash comes from the bedroom and I run, throwing the door open. Arm and head bandaged, Gareth stands in the middle of the room, looking pale in my big white shirt and black shorts. The side lamp's shards are scattered all around him as he bends over at an unnatural angle.

Then he grabs a piece of glass in his hand and brings it to his uninjured arm.

"Gareth, no!" I snatch his hand, twisting it to the side with little force so as not to open his stitches.

"Let me go." He speaks so low, sounding far away, then shouts, "Let me the fuck go!"

The glass digs into his fingers, and blood bubbles out of the wound and drips on the carpet. I've seen his blood way too much these past couple of days.

I want that to *stop*.

His pupils are still wide, but not as wide as earlier, and he's looking at me, those eyes a mixture of rage, disappointment, and hate, but what pierces me open is the sadness.

The pale color of his face and the chapped lips are unnatural and nothing like my Gareth. He looks so depressed, so down, I want to kick myself in the fucking gut.

I try to reach for the piece of glass, but he digs it deeper into his hand, blood oozing in rivulets.

So I stop.

Fuck.

"Gareth, please give me that piece of glass," I say in my softest tone.

"Why?"

"So you don't hurt yourself."

"I have to, so I can remove you." His voice sounds rough in the near-dark silence, his eyes almost glowing.

And I feel as if I've been stabbed.

"You want to remove me?" I ask.

"Yeah. I want you gone once and for all, so let me go."

I pull his hand with the glass and push it against my chest. "Then remove me. Don't hurt yourself. Hurt *me*."

He cocks his head to the side, slowly, manically. "Hurt you?"

"You said you'd rip my heart out. It's all yours, so do with it as you please, baby."

His hand doesn't tremble, doesn't lose its steadiness. I suspect that even if he were to take a life, which is a matter of when, not if, he'd be very methodical about it and not question it.

He wouldn't think twice about it like he is now.

All of a sudden, Gareth rips my shirt down the middle with the glass, splashing his blood all over the fabric. He cuts my side, and I let him, watching how his eyes darken upon seeing my tattoos.

Then he stabs me over the lily tattoo. No, not stabs. He scratches it over and over again with the shard of glass, erasing it, completely removing it from my skin.

Because he now knows I got that tattoo for Cassandra. He must've seen it on her wrist in all those videos.

I rein in my grunt of pain, letting him do what he pleases. I don't think I'd move even if he slit my throat open.

His shoulders shake and so does his hand. It's full of blood now—his hand, my abdomen, my ripped shirt, and my pants.

It's everywhere, our blood, messing up the carpet, and him.

And I need to bandage his hand.

He keeps losing blood and I'm unable to put an end to it.

It's like he's slipping from between my fingers with each drop of blood.

His movements come to a halt, his lips wobbling as he looks up at me with shiny eyes. "I can't remove it."

He lets the glass fall to the carpet and I immediately take off my shirt and wrap it around his hand, squeezing against the wound.

He's dazed as I drag him with me to the bathroom, sit him on a padded bench, and retrieve a first aid kit.

He doesn't move as I sit across from him and drench his fingers and palm with antiseptic. Thank God the wounds are not that deep, but he fucked up all his fingers, with multiple cuts on every digit.

"Why can't I remove it?" he whispers in a detached tone as I dab his injuries with alcohol pads.

"Remove what?"

"Her soul from your blood." He reaches out his free hand and squeezes my wound with trembling fingers. "I hurt you, but she still wouldn't go away."

"Gareth, listen to me." I grab his jaw and wrench him closer. "I never had her soul in my blood. I know you're hurt and in pain, but I want you to know I never cared about her like I care about you, okay, baby?"

He shudders, his hand trembling on my lap. "Do you lie to everyone you care about? Use them for revenge against their grandad? Make them fall for you just to pull the rug from beneath their feet? Is that what caring looks like?"

"No, and I'm sorry." I release his face and wrap Band-Aids around each of his cuts. "I admit that I approached you for revenge in the beginning, but my vision blurred along the way and things changed. Every single moment we had was genuine,

Gareth. I truly care about you, more than I thought possible. Seeing you in pain is worse than being stabbed."

"Why would you care about my pain after you caused it, Professor? Oh, wait. You're not a professor. That was part of the image you crafted so well to draw me into your web." He laughs, the sound a bit unstable and unhinged. "Was the PI your work as well? Must've been. You're filthy rich and come from an influential family, apparently. God, you must've thought I was a pretentious prick trying to impress you with all that expensive stuff."

"No, I was thankful for everything, Gareth. I mean it."

"Don't fucking lie to me!" He wrenches his hand from my wound and then grabs my hair, tugging hard. "If Declan hadn't told me, would you have kept me in the dark my whole life?"

"Of course not. I was planning to tell you the truth."

"The truth that I'm only a means you're using to avenge your wife?"

"I told you that changed, Gareth."

"How can it change? If you loved her so much to go ballistic after her death, to tattoo her on your body and keep her soul beneath your skin, how can it fucking change?!"

He's becoming agitated again, his pupils dilating, his breathing growing all chopped off, and his grip tightening on my hair.

I gently hold his bandaged hand in mine. "I never loved Cassandra, Gareth. Not like you think."

"Liar!" He jerks up, releasing me as he paces back and forth, back and forth, biting his finger until blood coats his teeth, lips, everywhere. "Liar, everything is a lie...you're a goddamn liar... you've *used* me...*played* me... I need to remove you like I did with all of them."

"Gareth, baby, please calm down."

"Don't..." His head snaps in my direction, his eyes glittery. "Don't fucking call me that!"

"Okay, I won't. Would you sit down? You have a severe concussion, and this will make it worse."

He comes to a halt, cocking his head to the side, his eyes manic. "Do you care if I'm hurt?"

"Of course I do."

"Will you go crazy if I die like when she died? Will you start hunting people down and going into a loop of nothingness?"

"Gareth, fuck." I rush toward him and hold his shoulders. "Don't say that, please. Don't...don't make me lose you. I will do whatever you want me to do."

"*Whatever* I want?"

"Yes. You name it and I'll make it happen."

"Leave Grandpa alone." His voice trembles before it becomes steady again. "I don't know what evidence you have or don't have, but he'd never assault a woman and kill her. Not after he saw me kill my girlfriend's rapist. He doesn't...doesn't even take rape cases. He's not that type of man."

I pause. His girlfriend's rapist?

What girlfriend?

And he's killed? He took a life before?

While I'm not surprised, I have so many questions. But this isn't the time to ask them, so I nod. "I won't go after your grandfather. I've abandoned that for a while now."

"Because of guilt? Can you feel that?"

"If it's toward you, yes, I do feel all sorts of emotions I thought I was incapable of. And it's not guilt per se. I would never hurt someone you care about." I stroke his shoulder. "What else do you want, Gareth?"

"I want to kill you." His hand shoots up to wrap around my throat, but he's not squeezing. "I want to carve your heart out and erase her from it. I want to leave a hole in your chest shaped like me. I want to hurt you so deeply, you'll *never* move on. You'll become a ghost of yourself, haunted by me in your dreams and nightmares, waking up screaming my name, only to realize I'm gone. I want to *possess* you, to make sure you die with my taste on your tongue and my soul coursing through your veins."

"Gareth—"

"Shut the fuck up. Don't call my name, don't make me hear your voice or your fucking lies." A puff of air blows out of his trembling lips. "I can't stop thinking about you with her. I can't stop thinking that your expression, your smile, your everything was *hers*. The very thought fills me with revulsion. You were married to someone before me. You gave your heart, your body, and your soul to someone else. You touched someone so deeply, and it wasn't *me*. And I don't give a fuck that she came before me. It still makes me *fucking sick*."

He sounds so broken and lost.

And for the first time, I can't stop it. Can't mend his wounds or smooth out his emotions.

And now, I wish I'd never known Cassandra or married her. Maybe she'd be alive and happy, and I'd naturally find my way to Gareth, because I would have.

He's the one I share a soul with, not her.

Gareth drops his bandaged forehead on mine, as if he's tired, and inhales sharply, sniffing me in that way he usually does.

I inhale, too, sucking him into my lungs. The scent of him binding me to reality.

His touch.

His breaths.

The way his upper lip twitches, how his eyes soften.

I'm obsessed with every inch of him, his joy, his anger, his body, and every word out of his mouth. Forget about making a hole the size of him inside me. That's already done.

Along with him coursing through my veins.

But he's not letting me speak, and I don't want to agitate

him any further. He doesn't seem ready to believe a word coming out of my mouth.

"I shouldn't have let myself be captivated by you, addicted to you, *used to you.*" His harsh breaths fan my dry lips. "I should've avoided you from the start. I sensed the obsession right away, and obsessions aren't good for me. They consume me. *You* consumed me, Kayden. And the thought that you're in my life because you were consumed by someone else makes my vision red. It provokes my murderous side—the one I swore to suppress so I wouldn't get caught. But it's too late. You've already caught me, hook, line, and sinker. And the only way to escape is for you to rip my head off."

"Gareth, no, don't hurt yourself. Hurt me. Okay? Shoot *me.* Cut off my arm. Break my legs. Do whatever you want with me."

"I can't." He releases me, his fingers trembling as he chuckles softly. "I can't hurt you. It hurts me, too."

"I will do it, then. I'll mutilate myself."

"No. I want you to live, Kayden. I want you physically healthy but mentally fucked up—just like you made me." He turns on his heel, his voice sharp enough to slice through the tension. "I'm ending the obsession and amputating you."

"Gareth..." I take a step toward him, but the look he throws over his shoulder stops me cold.

It's a look that promises he'd destroy himself just to make me watch.

He's that hurt. That confused. That suicidal.

And the last thing I want to do is provoke him.

So I let him go.

But as he walks away, I say softly, "My life is yours to take whenever you wish, little monster."

He doesn't pause. Doesn't turn. Doesn't even look back. But his voice is hollow when he speaks.

"It's not about taking your life; it's about wiping you out of mine."

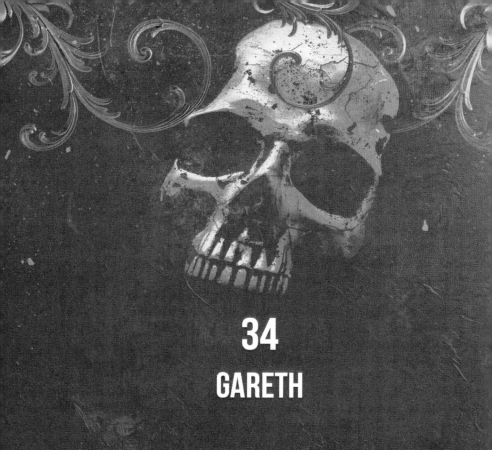

34
GARETH

For as long as I can remember, there's been a void inside me.

An emptiness that can't be filled, sustained, or eliminated.

It's like a hole of nothingness, stretching wider and deeper every day, every month, every year.

At first, I despised it. That thing that made me different from my parents. That thing that made me different from other kids my age.

But then I saw Kill embrace it. He had a void, too, but he called it a superpower. He was proud of it—proud of his brain, his perception, his ability to crush others under his heel.

He didn't hide it. He flaunted it, doing whatever he wanted, whenever and however he wanted.

But not me.

Because, unlike Kill, I care what Dad thinks.

I need his approval. I love his approval. I *crave* it.

The thought that he might one day look at me with disapproval like he did with Kill is my worst nightmare.

So I stitched that void up with pieces of my soul and shoved it into the darkest corner of my mind.

The closest I've ever come to filling it was when I killed David. When I felt his essence flow into my hands. When his wide, lifeless eyes stared up at me, knowing I was his god at that moment.

A rush of life poured into me in the form of his blood. It filled that void to the brim, and I think I sighed in relief as I stared at his jacked-up body lying on the bed.

The same bed where he assaulted Harper for years, until she took her life to escape him.

Maybe I smiled. Maybe I laughed, like a madman, because for the first time, that void felt full.

I was euphoric.

Deliriously elated.

Floating on a peaceful cloud, sitting in my quiet, beautiful white room.

Until I remembered Dad.

Until I imagined that frown on his face.

And all my joy crashed and burned.

The same frown he's wearing now as we sit in my room. The walls are painted black-green, a muted color that matches the rest of the decor. I keep staring at the sheets—black silk.

Like in the apartment.

I hate silk. It reminds me of my bloodied white room. The one I can never clean up.

It's been two days since Kayden had his bodyguards take me

on a private jet from Chicago to New York, then drive me to my parents' house.

Nadine—his chief of security or whatever she calls herself —made the arrangements. Or, rather, *Simone*. That's her real name. Nadine was the alias he made her use so he could lie to me.

Mom's been crying and fawning over me nonstop since I got here, and it's making my head throb.

I hate how emotional she can get. Maybe because I don't have that switch in my brain, so I can't relate.

And while I usually understand her love, her over-whelming emotions are like nails on a chalkboard right now, worsening the pounding in my skull that hasn't stopped since I left.

She said she'd make my favorite dishes for lunch, and honestly, I'm relieved she's gone. Mom's a good person. She's dedicated her life to us and to charity. I shouldn't be an ungrateful little cretin.

But with my mood swings, I need her gone. The last thing I want is to snap and hurt her.

It's not her fault she gave birth to two monsters.

But that leaves me with Dad.

And Grandpa, who hasn't left my side since I got here.

Dad—Asher Carson—is basically a younger version of Grandpa. Jet-black hair slicked back. A strong jawline. Deep-green eyes. The only thing I inherited from him.

He's calm and collected. Not emotional like Mom. The only time I've seen him lose his cool was when Mom was in the hospital and we thought she had cancer. It turned out to be benign, but for those few days, he was aimless. Distraught.

I remember watching him and thinking, *This type of love is dangerous.*

Because the strongest man I know would crumble if he lost her.

And I remember thinking, *I'm glad this kind of love will never find me.*

But, boy, was I fucking mistaken.

"Are you going to tell me what really happened now?" Dad asks, his voice soft, though tension cuts through the undertone like a blade.

"Leave him be," Grandpa replies, his tone firm but measured.

Grandpa's frown is less pronounced than Dad's, his upright posture defying his age. Wisps of white hair brush against his forehead, settling into the deep lines etched on his face. Those lines, carved by time and experience, lend him an air of quiet authority, even when his expression softens.

He doesn't need to shield me from Dad. He *shouldn't* have to.

I needed to do this a long time ago.

"Dad, I'm trying to have a conversation with my son," my father snaps, his frustration spilling over. "I'd appreciate it if you stayed out of it."

"It's my grandson, so I'm not staying out. You leave."

"Can you not fight?" I sigh, rubbing the back of my neck. "I was kidnapped and tortured, Dad. That's what happened."

The room falls into a weighted silence. Both of them stiffen, their reactions like opposite sides of the same coin.

Dad inches closer to the bed, his face caught between fear and fury. "Who was it? Is this because of the mafia connections?"

"No."

"Then who? Who hurt you like this, Gaz?"

"Oh, this?" I gesture at the bandage on my forehead, then lift my arm. "I did these myself."

Grandpa closes his eyes, his expression twisting in quiet pain.

I brace myself.

Stop breathing.

Wait for the disappointment to surface on Dad's face.

But it doesn't come.

Instead, his expression is unreadable, and I hate that more.

"Why?" he asks, his voice soft but sharp enough to cut me deep.

The word rips through the tendons holding my sanity together.

I shrug, feigning indifference. "Because I wanted to get rid of something in my blood. It was poisoning me, and it hurt. So I decided to take it out."

"Then you should've hurt them, not yourself."

Heat floods my face, and I shift uncomfortably on the bed. "You...you'd be okay with that? Me hurting others?"

"If they hurt you, why not? Why the fuck would you hurt yourself instead of them, Gareth?"

I stay silent, my heart hammering so loudly it drowns out his words.

Dad's okay with me hurting others.

He said it's *okay*.

"Son." He takes my hand—the one not covered in little Band-Aids. The ones I refused to let Mom replace because I can still feel Kayden's touch when he put them on.

I stare at Dad, probably looking lost as hell. "Yeah?"

"I want you to tell me why you hurt yourself and not them. You're not someone who'd hurt himself. Ever."

"Leave the kid alone," Grandpa says.

"Be quiet or get out, Dad," my father barks, the tension between them sparking like static electricity.

"Why are you so sure I wouldn't?" I ask, my voice barely audible, even to myself.

"Because you're outward, not inward. That's why I got you into hunting, archery, and shooting. I wanted you to channel your energy at a target instead of yourself, or..." He trails off. "... people."

"Christ," Grandpa mutters under his breath, the weight of Dad's words sinking into the room.

My teeth dig into my lower lip. "Y-you...you knew?"

"That you wanted to kill people?" His lips tug into a faint, almost bitter smile. "Sort of."

"H-how?" My voice cracks before I can rein it in.

"My suspicion started early."

"How early?"

"When you were eight. Nine, maybe. You've never been the type to let things slide, especially when it came to what you considered yours."

"And that made you think I wanted to kill people?"

Dad leans forward, his green eyes locking with my identical ones. "My suspicions were confirmed after the fight with Gilbert in school. You were both ten, and you beat the crap out of each other until a teacher intervened. It seemed over after that. But then at Killian's birthday party a month later, you asked Gilbert if he wanted to see the toy he'd been begging his parents for. A toy you asked your mom for two weeks prior. You took him to the indoor pool, pushed him in, and held his head underwater. If I hadn't followed you out of suspicion, you would've drowned him. And you had a poker face the whole time."

"He pushed Kill down the stairs," I snap, clenching my fists. "He twisted his ankle and almost broke it. He needed to pay."

I purse my lips, stealing a glance at Grandpa, who gives me a sad smile.

The words tumble out before I can stop them. It's the concussion talking—or maybe it's the aggression that's been festering in the void for years.

Gilbert was the first person I wanted to kill.

The demons in the void whispered that the world would be

better off without him. When I was holding Gilbert under the water, I heard a noise, so I ran off. When I came back, I saw Dad pulling the waste of space out of the pool and helping him, but I hid from his view, then called Grandpa to pick me up, and I spent a whole week at his place.

I was terrified Dad would have me diagnosed like he did to Kill. That he'd hate me, reject me, and stop liking me. But when Dad picked me up from Grandpa's, he took me and Kill hunting for the first time.

I believe that's when I became self-conscious about the image I needed to portray in public. To ensure that I'd never be caught in a Gilbert-like incident again.

"Is it because Kill is your brother or because you think of him as something that belongs to you?" Dad's tone remains soft, almost clinical. "Tell me the truth."

"Both. But more because..."

"Because?"

"Kill belongs to me. No one is allowed to hurt what belongs to me."

Dad's jaw tightens. "Is your brother an object to you?"

"Kill, an object?" I laugh, though the sound comes out hollow. "He'd throw a fit if he heard that."

Neither Dad nor Grandpa laughs.

My voice drops, more serious now. "I know he's a person—a massive headache of one—but...I've always felt like you brought him into the world for me. To keep me company. So I wouldn't be alone. In a sense, he exists for me, so no one else gets to hurt him."

"And Harper?" Dad presses. "Did you feel the same about her? That she belonged to you? Is that why you killed her father?"

My head snaps toward Grandpa. "You told him?"

"No," Grandpa sighs, leaning back. "He figured it out a couple of years ago."

Dad's expression sharpens. "After a little altercation with Senator Baltimore."

The air thins around me. My ears ring as the senator's name stirs the truth I uncovered.

Baltimore—the man who assaulted and killed Cassandra. The senator Kayden wiped off the face of the earth after her death.

I've done my research since yesterday, getting sucked in to reveal the truth. That's the senator who was dealing with the Davenports a couple of years ago, around the time of her death, and then a few months later, he died.

And so did the governor and a whole bunch of people.

Because Kayden was so heartbroken about his wife, he wiped out people like they were flies. And I was on his list, too.

"What about the senator?" I ask, my throat dry.

Grandpa rubs his temple. "He was the police chief and an old friend at the time you killed that scum. I called in a favor to clean up the scene, but Baltimore kept some evidence—DNA, fingerprints—for leverage."

"Did he blackmail you?"

"Once. He was at the peak of his career and made a mess by raping and killing a woman with his friends." Grandpa's voice lowers, his words measured.

"Were...were you there?" My voice barely rises above a whisper.

"No, I left as she was walking in. But I pieced it together later. He threatened to use the evidence against you if I didn't stay quiet. Said, and I quote, 'Just bury your head in the sand if you don't want your psychopath of a grandson thrown in jail for all the inmates to use as a warm hole. As you know, pretty faces like his are popular.'"

Dad's grip tightens around my hand. "I was in the room when he made that threat. Your grandpa told me everything afterward."

"You knew?" My stomach churns.

"Yes, Gareth." His voice softens. "I only wish you'd trusted me then."

"It wasn't that. I just didn't want to wake you up," I mumble, unease eating at me.

"It's okay, Gareth. I know you didn't trust me. Not after Killian."

"W-what?"

"You hated me a little after Kill was diagnosed."

"No, I would never hate you, Dad."

"But you did, and that's fine. You couldn't help it. Because Kill is like you and part of you, so you felt like I let you down by letting him down, and you hid your true nature from me. So I would never find out."

My jaw nearly hits the floor. "You... Is that why you never had me diagnosed even though you suspected it?"

"I didn't want to lose another son. It was hard enough being despised by Kill."

"D-Dad, I...never despised you or anything of the sort. I was scared that you'd...you'd see the real me and find me disturbing."

"Never, Gareth." He strokes my cheek. "You're my son, I'd never find you, or your brother, for that matter, disturbing. But I understand I went about explaining that the wrong way."

"Hotheaded, more like," Grandpa mutters.

"Can you not add fuel to the fire?" Dad throws him a glare. "We wouldn't be in this mess if you weren't friends with that snake Baltimore."

"So it's my fault I saved my grandson from prison?"

"No, but it would've been smarter to let us use the mafia connections instead of him."

"Would that be before or after you throw a bitch fit?"

I can't help the small smile that stretches my lips, because Dad said he's not disturbed by me. Or worse, scared.

"At any rate," Grandpa says after they're done fighting. "Your father managed to have the evidence stolen and burned after Senator Baltimore died, so you don't need to worry, my boy."

"You did that for me, Dad?"

"Of course," Dad replies, his voice steady. "I'd never let you go to prison."

"Even if I kill again?"

Dad's eyes darken, but his answer is firm. "I'd prefer you didn't. But yes, even then."

"It's not like I'm a serial killer or anything, don't worry." I pause. "Though I think I would've become one if I didn't have a loving family, so there's that. I also found something to fill up the emptiness..."

The words linger as a realization punches me in the gut.

Oh.

The void hasn't plagued me in months.

Because of Kayden.

I was so obsessed with him, so distracted by his sheer presence, bursting at each of his praises that not only did the void shrink, I also forgot about it.

He filled it, saturated the emptiness with his existence, his touch. He took me to that peaceful white room.

But now, knowing I was just another stand-in for *her*, the void is back. Ten times worse than before.

Wider.

Deeper.

Emptier.

"Something?" Dad prompts, his tone expectant. "Is this about the numerous calls we received about wooing a certain girl?"

I gulp. "I...it's not about a girl."

His brows knit together.

"It was a man," I admit, my voice faltering.

The silence is deafening.

Yeah, this isn't how I wanted to come out—if this even counts as coming out.

Well, fuck it. Who cares?

Obviously, my dad and grandpa do, because they're just staring at me.

"Doesn't matter anyway. We're not together anymore," I grumble, sinking into the bed like it might swallow me whole. "And before you ask, I don't think I'm gay. Maybe bi. Not entirely sure, and honestly, I don't want to box myself in. What I do know is that he's the only man I've ever been attracted to. You know I've only dated girls, so this might be...a surprise."

"There's absolutely nothing wrong with being gay or bi," Dad says, his eyes narrowing like he's trying to read my mind. "I'm just trying to figure out who this guy is. Someone we know?"

"He's not important," I mutter, avoiding his gaze.

Grandpa's chair scrapes back as he bolts upright. "Gareth Anthony Carson!"

"What?" I jerk my head toward him, my heart thudding.

Dad's glare shifts to Grandpa. "Why are you yelling at my son?"

Grandpa pinches the bridge of his nose. "This someone...he wouldn't happen to be the same man who called me to say you were 'under his care' and then hung up in my face, would he? No, that's not possible. Right, Gareth?"

My lips part, and the room tilts slightly.

Kayden called Grandpa? To let him know I was okay?

"It's true?" Grandpa's face turns red, his voice rising. "God fucking dammit, Gareth! He's your father's age!"

"Actually," I cut in, holding up a hand, "he's thirty-three. Dad is forty-seven. So you're way off the mark."

Grandpa's shoulders stiffen, his jaw tightening. "That's not the point here."

"Then what is the point? That I fell for someone who happens to be older?"

"Yes!" Grandpa's voice booms, his frustration palpable. "He is *old*, Gareth. Why didn't you tell us? We could've protected you from him."

"I didn't need protecting!" My voice slices through the tension, sharp and biting. "I'm not some fragile doll. I can handle myself."

"Clearly," Grandpa grits out, leaning forward. "Until you end up kidnapped and injured. You're still a child—"

"I'm twenty-two!"

"And he's in his thirties!"

"Can we not make this about the numbers?" I groan, dragging a hand down my face. "You're acting like I brought home someone on Social Security."

Grandpa's lips twitch, betraying the faintest hint of amusement before his scowl returns. "Gareth, this isn't just about his age. It's about the dynamic. Did he manipulate you? Use his position to—"

"*No*," I snap, cutting him off. "I threatened to kill him if he left me. Happy now?"

Silence stretches between us, thick and suffocating.

Grandpa finally exhales heavily, rubbing his temples. "Threatened to kill him or not, you're my grandson, and I don't like the thought of anyone taking advantage of you."

"Noted," I reply dryly. "But maybe trust me when I say he didn't."

Dad, who's been quietly observing the whole exchange, leans back, his expression unreadable. "Can someone fill me in?"

Grandpa scoffs. "Well, your dear son thought it was a *fantastic* idea to go out with Kayden Davenport."

"*The* Kayden Davenport?" Dad's brows shoot up.

"The one and only," Grandpa mutters darkly.

"I didn't even know his last name was Davenport," I add with an awkward shrug. "Does that help?"

"Age aside, he obviously played you to try to get to me." Grandpa sits back down. "Fucking bastard. I will send people to kill him. Don't worry, Gareth. It's not your fault for falling for that snake's tricks."

"So let me get this straight," Dad says slowly, his voice even. "Kayden Davenport, whose wife was raped and murdered by Senator Baltimore and his friends, and who definitely killed or had them killed over the past couple years, is the same person you've been...in love with?"

"I haven't been in love!" I shout, my face heating.

"He hasn't been in love with him," Grandpa yells simultaneously, his voice laced with denial.

Dad's lips twitch, but his gaze sharpens. "All right. I *definitely* believe you. Was he the one who kidnapped you?"

"No," I mumble. "He saved me. It was his wife's brother."

"Is the brother dead?" Dad's tone hardens.

"I...don't know."

"Probably not," Grandpa interjects, crossing his arms. "Considering the two guards stationed outside since you were dropped off."

My brows knit. "Two guards?"

"Yes," Dad confirms. "The woman who drove you here and another guy built like a brick wall."

Nadine didn't leave? Or Simone—whatever her name is. Not my fault she has two identities.

"Don't send people to kill him, Grandpa," I say, flicking my thumb on the corner of my lip. "We're nothing to each other now, and he promised not to hurt you. We don't owe each other anything."

"Like hell we don't!" Grandpa snarls. "He used you. Lied to you. Asher, we need to do something about this."

"He did it for his wife," I argue softly, my chest tightening. "I think you'd do the same, Dad."

Dad's gaze hardens, but his voice is calm. "Gareth, you're far from okay if you're hurting yourself instead of him."

"I'll blow his head off if he comes near you again," Grandpa adds with a growl.

A bitter smile tugs at my lips. I guess we're safe since I'll never see Kayden again.

Even if he's still in my blood. Even if I can't remove him unless I rip myself apart.

But I won't do that—not when it'll make Dad and Grandpa look like this. Distraught. Torn.

Grandpa feels guilty for involving Baltimore, but he shouldn't. He had nothing to do with Cassandra's death. Nothing to feel guilty about.

Dad, though, is another story. He's regretting not handling Baltimore himself. In his mind, if he had, none of this would've happened.

But that means I wouldn't have met Kayden.

And that's a reality I hate more than this feeling.

———

AN HOUR LATER, THE DOOR TO MY ROOM BANGS OPEN, AND MY brother strolls in with Glyn trailing behind him. He looks slightly disheveled, like he just rolled out of bed, which is rare for Killian.

Dad and Grandpa exchange glances before standing up and leaving the room. Not without first giving me a look, though. Not sure what it's supposed to be. Concern, maybe?

Do they think I'm fragile or something? That I'm breakable? Please. I don't do feelings, so this...*thing* isn't affecting me.

At *all*.

It's not like I'm itching to go back to him. Or that I keep

glancing at my fingers because he bandaged them. Or that I'm fighting the urge to call him just to hear his voice.

I haven't smelled him in more than a day, and I'm pretty sure that's the reason for the headache.

Morbid withdrawal. That's it.

That's *all*.

"Oh my God, are you okay, Gaz?" Glyn rushes to my bedside, her eyes glistening with unshed tears.

Her messy bun wobbles as she sits, dressed in casual jeans and an oversized sweater. Judging by the dark circles under her eyes, she hasn't slept well. Probably fretting over Killian, who's standing a short distance away with both hands stuffed into his pockets.

"We were so worried about you when you disappeared." Her voice wavers slightly.

"I'm fine." I grin at Kill, ignoring her mushiness. "Were you also worried about me, brother dearest?"

"She dragged me here against my will." He juts his chin toward Glyn, but his eyes are locked on me, scanning me up and down like he's taking inventory. His expression is as unreadable as ever, but his gaze darkens slightly upon seeing my bandages, betraying him.

Kill might pretend he's indifferent, but I know better. My brother is someone who thinks I belong to him, just like I think he belongs to me. Sure, he gives me shit, but if anyone dared to touch me, he'd raze their entire existence to the ground.

Guess that's our warped way of showing care.

"He's lying," Glyn pipes up, giving him an exasperated look. "He lost his mind when you went missing. Made everyone look for you, including my brother Lan—whom he *never* talks to. Can you imagine? He actually said, 'You, stop being a waste of space and use your skills to do something useful for once in your miserable life.' He even stormed the Serpents' territory and nearly killed everyone just to confirm you weren't there. It was terrifying, honestly."

I bite my bottom lip to keep a smile from breaking through. "I'm touched."

"I did it for Mom and Dad," Killian grumbles, his gaze snapping to Glyn in warning. "They'd start crying, and I didn't want to deal with the drama."

"I appreciate it anyway," I say with a shrug.

"He's still lying." Glyn rolls her eyes dramatically. "He was agitated the entire plane ride."

"Motion sickness, not agitation," Kill corrects her without missing a beat.

"You don't get motion sickness." She glares. "Would it kill you to admit you were worried about Gareth?"

"Who did that?" he asks, completely ignoring her, his gaze zeroing in on my bandages. "Do we have a name?"

"Why? So you can kill them for me?" I quirk a brow.

"It can be arranged." His tone is matter-of-fact, like he's offering to pick up groceries.

"Thanks, Kill, but I've got this under control."

Because I'll get over the man who gave me a lifeline, only to cut the rope.

And when I do, I'll kill him with my bare hands.

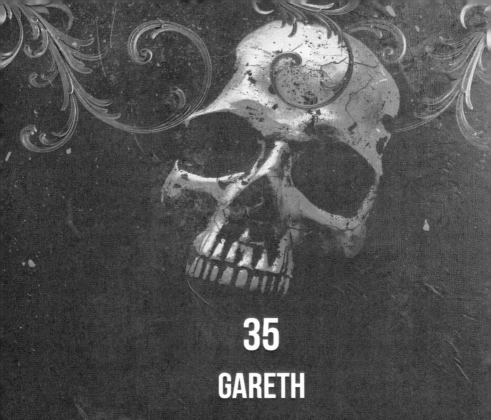

35

GARETH

"How long will you keep following me?"

Simone and the guy stop in their tracks as I turn around to face them.

I mostly ignored them over the past few days when they shadowed me on my walks or errands or when I was shooting arrows.

But now, I'm annoyed.

Or too stuffed.

Or just murderous.

At any rate, I'm in desperate need of a distraction.

The wind blows along the edge of the lake near my parents' house, pushing strands of hair into my eyes. I should cut it.

And maybe carve out my goddamn heart while I'm at it.

The guy takes a few steps back, clearly deferring to Simone, signaling she's in charge. It's not like I'd get much out of him anyway.

They delivered Medusa to the Heathens' mansion, conveniently missing the dashcam memory cards—likely Declan's doing, covering his tracks. Not sure why he took the interior camera's card, though.

Simone also asked if I wanted to see Moka. As much as I want to, she's with Kayden, and I've made a vow never to see that man again.

And I won't.

Because I'm moving on.

I *have* to.

Next week, I'll be back on the island for school. With an ocean between us and his absence as my professor, I'll be fine.

I have to be.

"Join me, Simone." I motion to the bench overlooking the lake and sit on the hard wood.

The fact that I no longer wince when sitting should bring some comfort. It doesn't. It only stretches the emptiness wider.

Sure, I can go to some BDSM club and find someone to get me off. But I don't think it's necessarily about the pain for me. It's the person who inflicts it.

Besides, I would never, and I mean *never* give someone else power over me.

Kayden was the exception, and he stomped all over me.

Simone hesitates before joining me, standing a few feet away with her hands clasped behind her like a soldier.

"Can't you stop following me?" I sigh.

"No. I'm under strict orders to ensure your safety. Declan is still out there, and until we find him, you're a target."

"My family can afford bodyguards."

"Not as good as me, Mr. Carson."

"Call me Gareth. The 'Mr. Carson' thing gives me PTSD from when you pretended to be my PI."

Her expression falters, and something like guilt flashes in her eyes. "I know it doesn't mean much now, but I'm sorry for lying. And for what it's worth, Boss only kept up the pretense because he wanted to hold on to the illusion a little longer."

My chest tightens, and I fix my gaze on the lake, where couples paddle boats as the sun paints the water in fiery hues of orange and red.

I exhale slowly, the breath dragging out of my lungs like a curse. "Pretty sure he just wanted to extend the torture. To make me pay for your mistress's death."

"Mrs. Davenport was never my mistress, and I'm positive he gave up on revenge not long after he met you."

Mrs. Davenport. Cassandra. The woman who had his last name.

My skin prickles as I stare ahead, willing the smiling couples to distract me. But all I want to do is drown them in the lake. Hold their heads under the water like I did Gilbert. Feel their struggles, their gurgling screams, until they go still.

Why the fuck are they smiling so much?

"You don't have to believe me," Simone continues. "But he never looked at her the way he looks at you."

"Naturally. He loved her, and I was just a toy."

Her head shakes. "It's the other way around."

I laugh, sharp and bitter. "Do you get a bonus for trying to sell me on his bullshit?"

"Mr. Carson...Gareth." She hesitates. "Deep down, you know it's not bullshit. He killed all his previous targets immediately, after torture. He would've never kept you around—let alone been...intimate with you—if he planned to kill or hurt you. He's been a wreck since you left, burying himself in work and smoking himself to an early grave."

Didn't he quit smoking? He had, after I told him I hated the smell.

"Has he been in pain?" I run a finger over the bracelet I should've thrown away but couldn't.

"Immense pain."

"More than when Cassandra died?"

"He wasn't in pain then. Just enraged."

"He'd have to feel pain to be enraged."

"Not him. For him, they're distinct emotions." She pauses. "He flew to the UK to retrieve your cat and some of his belongings. One of my men said he found a bowl of rotting strawberries and stared at it for twenty minutes."

I tighten my fingers around the bracelet, then release it.

Fuck him.

I haven't touched a strawberry since I left. Can't swim, watch TV, or even study without seeing him everywhere.

In *everything*.

He's like a curse, embedded in my bloodstream.

And because I can't help myself, I ask Simone more questions, probe further, and dig deep into Kayden Davenport, who's entirely different from Kayden Lockwood but somehow the same.

She tells me about his parents, his dad, in particular, about his moms and why they were banished and what he had to do to protect them. She talks about Grant, the slimy bastard, and Cassandra. About their open, arranged marriage, which surprises me a bit, because he kind of loses his shit when he sees me with someone else.

I listen to Simone talk in a steady voice, not mincing her words but apologizing when she curses. She tells me about Vencor and what he had to do to be in it. I'm not sure why she feels confident enough to tell me about some sort of a secret society, but maybe it's because she feels guilty for lying, and now, she wants to make up for it.

Or maybe this is a ploy from Kayden, but I doubt he'd ever
want me to know about this. That man is like a vault, really. He
keeps all different compartments of his life separate.

His resistance to the Taser and the drug I injected him with
makes sense now that I hear about all the poison and pain-
endurance training he had while growing up.

And I'm having this tingling urge beneath my skin, the one
I always had about others hurting what's mine. I have it toward
his dad and Vencor.

And this Julian, who's the reason why Kayden's vision grows
bad sometimes and why he had that fever and was coughing.
It's why he had that 'accident' after which his moms visited. In
reality, he had a major immune system attack. Apparently,
Kayden's been doing these off-the-record drug experiments for
his pharmaceutical company.

Apparently, the lavender I remember smelling in his apartment in the first few weeks I knew him is Cassandra's scent. I
don't know whether I should laugh or cry that he did stop
having that scent in the house right after the time I walked in
on him in that ice bath.

I think I fall asleep with a frown between my brows after
Simone tells me Vencor is the reason he can't be in a relationship with a man. That they'd kill him if they found out
about me.

Who the fuck are they to decide whether he should be with
a man or an alien?

Fucking assholes.

A part of me wants to scream. Another wants to kill them
all, one by one, and fill the void with their blood.

Long, lean fingers thread through my hair, their touch
familiar, deliberate. His amber scent fills the air, curling into
my lungs, and his warmth seeps into my bones, warding off the
ever-present chill in my chest.

He always feels so warm in my dreams. His touch soothing.

His presence grounding. It's as if I can almost feel his heartbeat under my fingertips, steady and alive.

For someone desperate to get over him, I surely sleep a lot, as if chasing fragments of him in the recesses of my mind. To lose myself in the echoes of his touch. To steal fleeting moments where I lay my head on his lap and watch TV, back when things felt simpler.

"He's lost weight."

His voice, hoarse yet deep, slices through the haze of sleep. His fingers feel more solid, more real. Careful, hesitant.

My heart jolts.

But I don't move. I remain still, breathing evenly, holding on to the fragile figments of my dream.

"Are they even feeding him properly at home?"

The tenor of his voice rings in my ear and rushes to my starving heart.

His fingers burn against my scalp, not in a painful way, but in a way that ignites every nerve in my body. The *good* kind of burn. The kind I've been fantasizing about every night when I close my eyes.

"Are you going to pick a fight with his parents if they aren't?" Simone's voice cuts through the moment.

And that's how I know.

It's not a dream.

She's never in them.

Only him.

So he's here. Right *here*. Sitting beside me, my head resting on his thigh. My fingers twitch involuntarily, and he catches them, lifting my hand to inspect the Band-Aids covering them.

I should open my eyes and tell him to leave. To stop invading my space, my mind, my everything.

But then he brings my hand to his cold lips, pressing a kiss to each finger. My entire body shivers, and I know that if I open my eyes, I'll fall back into bad habits.

Namely, *him.*

"You better not pick a fight," Simone says, her tone sharp. "Pretty sure his dad, grandad, and brother want to kill you on sight."

"And what did Gareth say?"

He keeps kissing my fingers, the roughness of his voice warming me along with the heat radiating from his body.

"He told them not to," Simone replies dryly. "Said he'd do it himself."

"I knew he loved me."

"Loves to kill you, more like," Simone mutters, and I want to high-five her from across the bench.

"They're one and the same with him," he murmurs, his lips brushing against my fingertips one last time before lowering my hand to my chest.

The absence of his touch leaves my skin cold.

"Is he hurting himself or showing signs to?" he asks, his voice dipping into something darker, quieter.

"Not that I noticed," Simone replies.

A slight tremor passes through his hand, still buried in my hair. It's so faint, I wouldn't have caught it if he weren't touching me.

"Pay more attention, Simone. Nothing happens to him, clear?"

"Worry about yourself. You look like the walking dead."

I want to open my eyes and see him. The last image I have of him is the sadness in his eyes and the resolve to die as he offered me his life.

And I hate that image.

It's not *him.*

Not my Kayden.

Not that he's mine. Or anything.

My body stills, as if time itself holds its breath when his lips meet my forehead.

The soft, lingering press is a quiet invasion, tender and almost reverent. His shaky breaths and the gentle careful touch speak louder than words ever could.

His breaths are warm against my skin, ghosting over me in shallow whispers, like the slow exhale of a reality he couldn't maintain.

That ache returns to my chest, and the weight of what he made me lose hangs between us like forbidden fruit.

"I'm sorry, my little monster." The deep rumble of his apology slides over my skin, barely touching the air and pressing against my chest.

And then he's gone.

Taking my heart with him.

———

Today, I'm going back to the island.

For the pesky thing called school.

I've kind of lost interest in that. I've lost interest in many things, actually.

I think I underestimated how disruptive the void can be.

How it can deepen and widen and demand vengeance.

I also haven't been able to stop thinking about when Kayden held my head on his lap and kissed my forehead.

That was five days ago.

I've been wondering how many times he came over when I was asleep. And I've been beating myself up for not opening my eyes and talking to him.

I should've given him a piece of my mind. Asked him if I made him feel sick whenever he touched me, knowing he should've killed me.

Cursed him.

Choked him.

Just...*looked* at him.

Because I'm starting to hate my life without him in it.

And for some reason, I don't recall how I used to be before he came along. Or don't want to recall.

The crisp air bites at my face as Mom adjusts the collar of my jacket, her hands trembling slightly. "You should stay with us a little longer," she insists, her voice soft but resolute. "You're not completely healed yet."

"I'm fine, Mom."

My injuries are now hidden beneath Band-Aids, and though the stitches remain, they'll come out soon enough. And then I'll be left with scars the shape of fucking Kayden.

"My point still stands." Mom hugs me and I have to lower myself so she can wrap her arms around my neck. "I love you, darling. You know that, right?"

"I do." I pat her back. "Love you, too, Mom."

She steps back, dabbing at her eyes, and Dad instinctively draws her into his side, his strong, silent presence grounding her. She has the kind of beauty that stops people in their tracks, a rare, ethereal kind that I inherited in its male form.

"Take care, Glyn, honey." Mom hugs Glyn. "I'm going to miss you boys," she murmurs, embracing Kill next, who, unsurprisingly, refused to leave until I do.

Clingy.

Not sure what type of conversation he had with Dad, but he's been looking at me weird. As if I'm an entirely different person that he can't wait to dissect.

Last night, he came into my room while I was going through old pictures I took of Kayden when he wasn't paying attention. What? I didn't mean to. I kind of...feel too empty. I just needed to recharge for ten minutes.

It ended up being an hour.

Until Kill interrupted me.

Mom and Glyn were in the kitchen, so without his two favorite people on earth, he probably decided to annoy me.

Kᴉʟʟ sɪᴛs ʙᴇsɪᴅᴇ ᴍᴇ ᴏɴ ᴛʜᴇ ʙᴇᴅ, ʜɪs sʜᴏᴜʟᴅᴇʀ ᴛᴏ ᴍɪɴᴇ ᴀs ʜᴇ *stares at the large window overlooking the garden.* "Do you really resemble me more than you resemble Dad?"

"Dad told you?"

"Yeah. But Grandpa hinted at it several years back. He said something like 'Remember, you always have your brother. You're more alike than you realize.' I thought he was trying to build some stupid brotherly shit. I never thought it was because he knows you better than anyone else does."

"He helped cover up murder for me."

He tilts his head in my direction, his eyes lighting up. "How did it feel?"

I lift a shoulder. "Euphoric, but only for a few minutes, though. Then it was just...the void again."

"Is that...why you never killed again? Because the void came back so fast?" There's a strange deepness to his voice, an eagerness almost. This is the side I share with Killian. If he hadn't been such an outward person who loved advertising his neurodivergence, I would've been more comfortable talking to him.

It's not really about the threats he regularly made. That was his way to demand my attention since I usually ignored him. It's that, despite our similarities, I'm more private than he is and don't enjoy having others' noses in my business. I also despise how he can hurt Dad.

I don't like that.

But now, the words just spill out. "It's because I knew I wouldn't be able to stop if I started, and someone as beautiful as myself isn't made for prison."

He bursts out laughing. The sight is so curious. He looks so *happy. Ecstatic. His shoulders vibrate, and he even wipes the corners of his eyes.*

I've honestly never seen Kill this happy, not even when we were kids.

"What?" *I pout.* "I am *beautiful.*"

"*I knew it.*"

"*Knew what?*"

"*That you thought yourself to be more beautiful than me.*"

"*That's because I am. You might be the mama's boy, but I'm the one who got her looks.*"

"*And I got Dad's.*" *He wiggles his brows.*

I slam a hand to his face and push it away. "Fuck off, asshole."

"*Wow. Were you always* this *petty?*"

"*Damn straight. I'm* the *petty king, so shut the fuck up, Kill.*"

"*I've been missing out. Pity*" *He chuckles again, then ruffles my hair like I used to do to him when we were young.* "*I feel the same, though.*"

"*About?*"

"*Not killing because I wouldn't be able to stop.*" *He grins.* "*Lucky for me, I found Glyn. She tames my demons and fills up that void.*"

"*Ha. No need to brag. I found someone too—*" *I bite my lower lip because I didn't.*

I haven't.

Kill has Glyn by his side, and I have no one to calm the raging emptiness gnawing at my insides.

I'm glad Kill doesn't push. Instead, he kept talking. Which is the most I've heard him talk, and that kind of distracts me. Even if only for a while.

BACK TO THE PRESENT, AFTER PROMISING DAD AND GRANDPA that I'll keep in touch, Kill and I head to the car. Glyn walks ahead, chattering on the phone with her mom. She's been hovering ever since I got back, either out of worry or because Kill won't let her out of his sight

I glance around, frowning. Simone is nowhere to be seen.

She's always by the door.

Isaac, her silent shadow, is also missing.

Weird. I've grown used to them tailing me, and I don't entirely hate it. Simone, at least, has been apologetic about her PI stint and answers every question I throw at her.

Over the past few days, I've learned more about the Davenport side of Kayden. About his dual life—balancing working from the London office, trips to the States, and teaching.

Because he didn't want me to get suspicious.

Simone says it's mostly because he wanted to be close to me, but she's biased.

"So you're going to let him get away with it?" Kill's voice cuts through my thoughts as he stops near the car.

I drag my gaze to him.

Aside from last night's conversation, he's been asking all sorts of stupid questions. Like, when am I going to punish the asshole for messing with me? When do we start?

He said he'd help since he has time now and can consider it.

Hot and cold kind of runs in the family.

"It's unlike you to let things go," he continues. "Just saying."

"What do you know about what's like or unlike me?"

"Not much, admittedly," he says, leaning casually against the car. "But I'm relearning. I should've known when you gave me that tip about emulating others. You always had that disgustingly fake smile. I had my suspicions, but you fooled me for years. I'm impressed."

"Impressing you is not on my to-do list." My eyes sweep the area again. Where the hell are Simone and Isaac?

Does their mission end today now that I'm leaving? Though that doesn't really make sense.

I'm under more of a threat on foreign soil, right?

"It should be," Kill retorts. "As should making sure Kayden doesn't get off easily."

"Seriously, why do you care?"

"He's the *girl*"—he air quotes—"you were humming about, right? Except he's not a girl."

My jaw tightens. "And what if he is? Are you about to drop some god-awful gay joke?"

"Nah, I'm all about fluidity. Though I am a little bummed you're a bottom."

"Who the fuck says I am?"

"So you *are*?" He sighs dramatically. "RIP, my ego. Dad and Grandpa would have a stroke."

"Killian, I swear to fuck I'm going to cut you—"

"My point is." He grips my shoulder. "If you want him, keep him. And if something stands in the way, simply eliminate it."

He walks ahead of me to the car and I stare for two beats. My phone vibrates and I pull it out.

SIMONE

Declan is taken care of. You're safe, Gareth.

What does this mean? That they'll stop being here?
All of them?

I press Call and put the phone to my ear, then speak as soon as she picks up. "You could've at least said goodbye."

"I apologize. I left in a rush."

My fingers twitch. Her voice sounds off.

My teeth graze my lips. "What's wrong, Simone?"

"Nothing."

"Don't lie to me." I breathe harshly. "Something is wrong. Tell me. Now."

"It's that... Screw this. When we captured Declan and tortured him, he managed to have one of his men send a video to a Senior member of the organization. And although Kayden killed Declan, he couldn't stop the footage from spreading."

"What footage?"

"From your dashcam. It captured the two of you...kissing. Among other things."

My fingers tighten around the phone. "Is he... Did they..."

"He's fine. We managed to send him into hiding, but we're not sure how long we can be on the run. I'm looking into options to get him off US soil for now." She pauses. "Fortunately, your face wasn't visible, so you're safe, Gareth. Kayden forbade me from telling you anything. He wants you to go back to school and live your life normally."

My chest expands in painful breaths.

Fuck what he wants.

Fuck *him*.

As Simone keeps talking, her words blur together. All I can hear is the truth staring me in the face.

I'll never have a normal life again.

Not after Kayden Davenport tore my delusions of normalcy to shreds.

36
KAYDEN

I should've tortured Declan more.

Scalded him alive.

Cut his skin slower.

Melted him in acid, piece by piece.

I did spend fucking hours torturing him, making him pay for every single cut he inflicted on Gareth's body, but it still wasn't enough. I could still smell his rotten flesh and see the smirk on his goddamn mouth when Jethro came into the basement and told me we had to go.

"My little parting gift for you, motherfucker." That's what he said.

He put Gareth in danger again. Because of me.

It's always because of *me*.

The stitches, the wounds, the internal and external hell he's been going through are all because of me.

Declan laughed out loud as blood dripped all over his body, his face unrecognizable. One of his eyes was shut, but he still glared at me with the other one.

"You're right, Davenport, I did torture that little psycho, but he was unresponsive, no matter how much we kicked and punched and threw him around. He had this unperturbed look and it pissed me the fuck off, but he got so angry when I said ye fucked him just because he has similar eyes to Caysie. Ah, you should've seen the rage and bloodlust in his eyes. Damn cunt would've killed me with his bare hands if he could. Since he seemed so jealous of her, I made him watch you happy together, playing with his mind, making him crazy because ye betrayed her with him. Ye tarnished her memory by being with her rapist's grandson. Since ye couldn't respect her in death, you should join her. See if ye can look her in the fucking eye!"

That's when I put a bullet in his fucking head.

Silenced him for life.

I sit on a rock overlooking the ocean's violent waves. The late afternoon sun casts a golden reflection on the water.

Cassandra never liked water since she couldn't swim. It's ironic that she was thrown into a lake, almost like a last fuck you of sorts.

"I'm sorry," I whisper, imagining her sitting beside me.

She's stopped appearing in my nightmares now, replaced by Gareth being all bloodied and refusing to talk to me.

"Declan was right," I murmur, my voice barely audible over the crashing waves. "I did grow fond of your rapist's grandson. A boy I intended to kill, only to find myself captivated by him in ways I never thought possible."

I exhale slowly, the sea breeze carrying a bitter chill that seeps into my bones. "You'd understand, wouldn't you, Sandra? You were my friend, after all. You always understood me. Ma Jina says he's changed me, and she's right. He has. In ways I didn't consent to, in ways I didn't even realize until it was too late. I wanted..."

A small smile tugs at my lips, bitter and fleeting. "At some point, I wished I could be someone ordinary. A simple professor, free from the weight of the Davenport name, free from the chains of legacy and expectation. Just a man who could be with him without all of this hanging over us."

The wind lashes against my face, and I close my eyes. "Sandra...what happened to you made me angry and vengeful. I wanted to give you justice, to give you closure. I made it my purpose. But maybe it wasn't just for you. Maybe it was for me —a distraction from my own life, my obligations, from Grant's ceaseless demands.

"But losing him..." My voice cracks as a violent wave hits the rocks, sending icy water splashing against my legs. "It's unbearable. I haven't been able to breathe, as if I've been walking around with a fireball lodged in my chest, suffocating me every moment of every day."

I turn my gaze to the horizon, where the water meets the sky in a vast, endless expanse. "I'm sorry, Sandra. Truly. I can't harm his grandfather, and I can never harm him. I killed your brother because he hurt him, and I would do it again without hesitation.

"I know it's selfish. I know it betrays the purpose I claimed to have, but I'm letting you go. For good. If you can't forgive me, I'll accept that. Because the truth is, he's my priority now. He's the only thing that matters. Even if it costs me my life. Even if it costs me my soul."

The wind howls, carrying my words away, but there's no response, naturally, but I like to think she's at peace now—at least one of us is.

Standing, I dust off my pants and trek down the jagged rocks. Jethro arranged our transport to one of my coastal safe houses, a location Grant has no clue about.

For now.

According to Jethro, Grant's obsessive need for control means he'll find us eventually, so we need to move soon.

Still, my thoughts stray to Gareth. I wonder if he's made it to the island by now. A quick trip to check on him wouldn't hurt.

Not that Jethro will agree. He's hell-bent on getting us out of here and taking us all the way to South Africa.

He'll just have to pick somewhere closer to the UK, maybe North Africa or Southern Europe, because I will go to the island. Regularly. Without drawing attention, of course. Because I can't *not* see him.

The medium-sized house is quiet when I enter. Jethro is sitting at a desk near the entrance, dressed in a worn Metallica hoodie. His hair is a mess, sticking out in every direction. He's typing furiously with one hand and holding a half-eaten sandwich in the other.

It's clear he didn't sleep last night, busy arranging meetings with directors and shareholders.

My banishment from Vencor might've come with a bounty on my head, but I still own half of the Davenport corporations. If Grant thinks my influence will dwindle just because I've been shunned, he's in for a rude awakening.

I *am* Davenport Corp.

My father always favored the way I did business over Grant's methods. I've built the empire stronger, handled threats more efficiently, and amassed a loyal following.

It doesn't matter where I am. My power remains mine, and I won't relinquish it to Grant.

Standing by Jethro's desk, I pull out a cigarette, lighting it with a flick of my lighter. The first drag burns my lungs in a way that feels both wrong and familiar. I'd quit since Gareth hates it, but his absence shoved me back into my bad habits.

"Where's Simone?" I ask, exhaling a plume of smoke.

Jethro doesn't even glance up. "She said she had to run an errand."

"We're leaving tomorrow," I say, blowing out another cloud. "Passing by Brighton Island."

This gets his attention. He lifts his head, a smear of mustard clinging to his chin. "No way in hell. Grant knows that was your last stop before coming back. He'll have people watching."

"Since I already returned, he won't suspect it."

"He might."

"Then we'll take the risk."

Jethro glares, swallowing the bite of his sandwich. "The fuck is wrong with you, man? You'd risk getting killed just to see him from a distance?"

"I suppose."

"You could just have one of the men take pictures and send them to you."

"It's not the same." I turn and head toward the stairs. "Arrange it."

His curses and muttered empty threats to quit follow me as I climb the stairs. I ignore him, entering my room and shutting the door behind me.

The room is sparsely furnished—functional but not homey. Definitely nothing like the home I had on that godforsaken gloomy island.

It's ridiculous how one person's presence can either light up the darkness or snuff out the light.

Shaking off the thought, I sit at the desk, the wood cool beneath my palms, and retrieve my laptop. I power it on and focus on the screen.

Moka jumps into my lap, her soft meow breaking the

oppressive silence. I stroke her sleek black coat, my fingers moving absently. "You miss him, too, huh?"

She meows again.

"I know," I whisper.

The cat leaps onto the brown leather sofa and lets out another haughty meow, her tone dripping with attitude. Just like a certain someone.

I should be working, replying to correspondence, and smoothing a few connections. But instead, I open a video file.

The video Declan sent to the Osborns so they'd have me kicked out. He probably figured that if he sent it to my brother, he would sweep it under the rug just to keep me around.

But in that case, Grant would've found Gareth and killed him. Just like our father did to his college sweetheart.

So, in a twisted way, I owe Declan.

The clip is short, grainy, and soundless. Gareth isn't visible, tucked in the seat as I climbed on top of him. That was after he called his car, Medusa, his "baby" again. Irrational jealousy over a car—how fucking absurd.

The memory is vivid, sharper than the video. The surprised grunt he let out when I shoved him back. The mischievous sparkle in his green eyes. Those damn dimples creasing his cheeks as he wrapped his arms around me.

"Am I going to be punished, Professor?" His voice had been a low, rough murmur, heavy with arousal.

I see it in the clip—our bodies pressed together, his mouth beneath mine. Even soundless, I can almost hear him, feel the rasp of his breaths against my skin. "K-Kayde...more...fuck yes..."

I can still feel the way his muscles softened beneath my hands, his heartbeat thundering against mine, and his ears turning red. The small, needy noises he only ever makes for me.

The ghost of his scent fills my senses, and I'm instantly hard, the ache sharp and all-consuming. I can feel him even now—the heat, the tension, the way his hips aligned perfectly with mine.

I'm about to reach into my pants and relieve the ache when Moka jumps from the sofa to the table, scattering chess pieces across the table.

Voices filter in from downstairs, dragging me back to reality.

I slam the laptop shut to stand and open the door for Moka, who's meowing loudly. Tension coils in my body as I stride to the top of the stairs.

Then I freeze.

At first, I think he's a figment of my imagination, just like all the other times.

When I sleep, I picture him wiping me down and stroking my hand.

But he never speaks to me. No matter what I say, he just stares at me with those empty eyes.

Eyes I turned dead.

But then I blink, and he's gone.

And I go back to sleep, but he's not there again.

But this time, he's real.

I'm blinking and he's still standing there, holding Moka in his hands as she headbutts his chin.

My lungs seize, the air thick and heavy as though it's been sucked from the room. The sight of him is a punch to the gut, a heavy, raw wave crashing into me.

His golden hair is longer now, falling messily over his fore-head. His sharp jaw and cheekbones seem even more pronounced, but the rest of him...

He's hollowed out.

My little monster has lost weight, rapidly, his muscles no longer stretching along his arms like they used to. His white T-shirt clings to his body, his jeans hanging low on his hips, hinting at the frame I used to worship daily.

But now, he seems distant. Untouchable, even.

The Band-Aid on his forehead is a stark, glaring reminder of what I've done and why I shouldn't touch him.

Even though I can't see them, I know jagged stitches are hidden beneath his jacket sleeve. I see them every time I close my eyes. The sight of him back then, his own blood that he didn't think twice about spilling, haunts me.

I can almost feel the cold sting of his blood beneath my fingertips, in my veins, and carved in my chest.

Still, seeing him expands my lungs. For the first time in what feels like forever, I can breathe. His presence fills the space like a storm, leaving me both paralyzed and desperate to reach him.

But I can't.

A burning tightness twists my stomach, but I say in a clipped, detached tone, "What are you doing here?"

Simone's and Jethro's bickering fades as Gareth's green eyes meet mine. My grip tightens on the railing to stop myself from descending, from pulling him into my arms, from touching him.

"That's what I was asking!" Jethro snaps, his voice cutting through the tension. "Why the fuck did you bring him here, Simone? You trying to get him killed?"

She shoves him away. "He said either I bring him or he goes to Grant. What do you think was the smarter option, genius?"

He was on his way back to school, but he demanded Simone bring him here? To me?

"You should leave," I say coldly, though my grip on the railing threatens to crack the wood.

Gareth's brow furrows, his gaze darkening as Moka jumps from his arms. Then his upper lip curls into a snarl. "The fuck you just say to me?"

"Leave, Gareth. Go back to school." I aim for firm, not harsh, but I see the anger ignite in his eyes.

Then I turn, climbing the two steps again, and head back to my office. I barely sit down before the door hits the wall as he barges in, his shoulders crowding with tension and the lines in his face harsh.

He rounds the desk and grips me by the collar of my shirt, turning me in the chair so I'm looking up at him.

The brush of his knuckles against my neck sends a zap down my spine, and I want to touch him, to grab his waist and pull him into me, but I can't.

I *won't.*

He needs to leave before I lose control.

I flex my hands on either side of me to stop myself from reaching up.

"Who the fuck are you to tell me what to do?" The bite in his deep, slightly husky voice rolls off my skin and settles in my gut.

Fuck. I missed his voice.

"Whether I go to school or sabotage my whole fucking life is none of your goddamn business." He tightens his grip on my collar, his rage mounting, but so does the pain tucked underneath.

Gareth has always been mentally strong. I know because I attempted to break him in the beginning, but he kept bouncing back again.

And again.

But now, he's in pain and it rips at my chest.

"You shouldn't throw your future away for me." My tone remains neutral.

"It's not for you!"

"Then why are you here, Gareth?"

His beautiful defined lips set in a line, and I want to press my mouth to them, taste him.

Just...for a moment.

But I force myself to drag my gaze to his eyes. "Because you feel sorry for me? Pity my pending death?"

A flash of darkness strikes his pupils again, blowing them up, his voice dropping to a dangerous whisper. "Your life is mine, remember? You're not allowed to die without my permission."

"Ah. So it's that."

"Yes, it's *that*! Are you not going to keep your promise?"

"Of course I will."

"Then...you won't die?"

"I won't."

His chest rises and falls faster, his lips parting just the slightest bit, the smallest opening that will allow me to slide my finger in—

"Are you mine?" His voice wavers, a crack of vulnerability slipping through.

"Always."

I reach for his hip—I can't help it—and a rough breath spills out of me as his breathing stutters. Just the slightest bit, telling me how much he also missed my touch.

I sneak my fingers beneath the hem of his T-shirt, and a shock of electricity bursts between us. Gareth's chin wobbles and he sinks his teeth into his lower lip until it's discolored.

"Since you're mine..." His fingers wrap around my throat, squeezing hard. "I'm going to fucking erase her from under your skin. Piece by piece, I'll carve her out and sink myself so deep, there will be no one but me."

His lips crash against mine, biting, splitting the skin. Blood coats his tongue as he thrusts it into my mouth, letting me taste his fury and pain.

His longing and despair.

His rage and anguish.

I take it all.

His anger. His torment. His insatiable hunger.

I let him consume me, devour me, and light me on fire.

I grab his face and kiss him deeper, pressing him harder against me, fusing him further into me until I can't discern his groans from mine.

Until all I can do is feel alive.

For one last time.

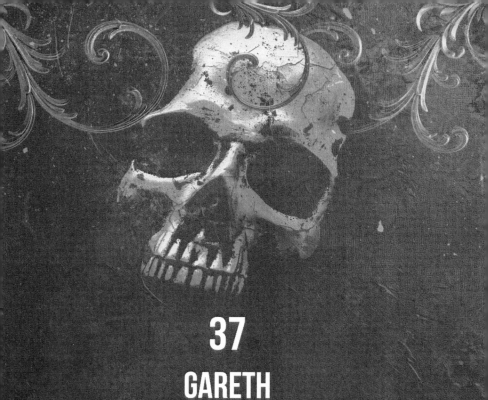

37

GARETH

I free fall into the kiss, melting into his arms.

His touch.

His scent.

His breaths.

Everything.

I'm falling and rolling and unable to hit the ground.

My kiss is pain and frustration and bloodlust. It's the only cocktail my fucked-up brain can conjure, and yet he's *welcoming* it.

Grunting into it.

Into *me*.

Because he meant it when he said he's like me. It's why his

darkness spoke to mine from the very beginning. Why his touch electrified me to the core and still does.

It's beating in the hollow of my heart. Filling up the void slowly but surely.

I'm sitting on his lap now, sucking his face, drinking his blood, not wanting this to end.

Needing this not to end.

God, I missed him.

And I need him.

And I want to erase fucking Cassandra from him. I don't care if that seems deranged, but I want her gone. Completely.

His erection nudges against my ass and I rub myself all over him, my own cock straining and shoving the fabric of my pants, gliding against his abs. A strangled noise leaves me when he digs his fingers into my ass through the jeans.

"Mmmff..." I moan in his mouth, biting on his tongue because I still want to hurt him.

Still want to sink my teeth into his skin and cause him pain, make him pay for the hole he dug inside me. Or more like for tearing the stitches he slowly but surely closed the void with.

He rips his lips from mine, and I jerk forward, my mouth chasing his.

Kayden drops his forehead against mine, his harsh breathing mingling with my own. Then he inhales me deeply, as if he wants to engrave my smell into his memory. As if, like me, he built me a shrine in his mind that he visits every day for a hit.

Like a goddamn junkie.

But my shrine has been lacking smell lately, meaning, life, touch...everything.

So when Kayden's eyes close as he inhales me in reverence, my breath stutters and my chest hurts.

"Fuck, I missed you, baby." His gruff words are low and charged, and it makes the pain in my chest stronger.

Because he called me baby and said that he missed me, and I think I'll burst.

My breath is stuttering, and he must feel how much I'm shuddering against him, but I don't care as I seal my trembling lips to his and kiss him again, slower this time but deeper, digging my fingers into the back of his head, reveling in how loudly his heart beats against my chest.

Almost as erratic as mine.

Almost.

Kayden grabs me by the ass as he stands up, and I wrap my legs around him, not wanting to break the kiss. It must be awkward to hold a tall guy like me this way, but he's taller and broader, and I like it.

I like how he kisses me while carrying me. As if, like me, he can't touch me enough.

Press his body into me enough.

He walks down the hall and into a room. Then he throws me on a mattress and he's on top of me, ripping my clothes away, and I do the same until we're both naked.

I'm on my back while he kneels in front of me, pulling lube from the drawer.

"Why do you have that here?" I ask, glaring at the lube.

"It's a habit. I started stocking all my safe houses with lube about a month ago."

"Wanting to get lucky?"

"With you, yes."

"You...thought you'd bring me to one of your safe houses?"

"In case Declan or Grant finds you, yes. But enough about that. I'm having withdrawals and need to touch you." He kisses me softly before pulling away to unclasp the bottle.

I reach for him to kiss him again, not wanting to waste one second without his mouth on mine or his blood in me—and mine in his.

That's when I notice something, and my chest tightens with a scorching burn.

The lily tattoo I mutilated has stitches all over it, the whole thing gone. But that's not what makes me stop and stare.

It's a new tattoo.

Right in the middle of the snake's scales, near his heart, there used to be a circle formed by its undulating form. But right now, there are crossed arrows in the middle of a compass.

My fingers shake as I touch the slightly red skin, tracing the small serif, two neat words written on either side of the arrow.

Little Monster.

"Why..." My lower lip wobbles, and I don't know what to say.

Why get my nickname tattooed on your skin?

Why did you lie to me if you care enough to do this?

"Why a compass?" I ask instead.

"Because you helped me find myself, baby." He takes my arm and peppers gentle kisses along my stitches, his lips shaking. "I'm sorry I couldn't do the same. I'm sorry I hurt you enough to make you self-destruct. Seeing you in pain eats me alive."

The skin he touches burns, his lips burn, my heart burns.

And even my eyes burn, because why the fuck is he being like this when I only planned to fuck him out of my system and leave?

Well, I wouldn't leave until he's safe, but still.

I came here with jumbled thoughts and fear. Lots of terrorizing fear at the thought of never seeing him again. I didn't know what I want and I still don't.

But when he touches me, I realize that the pain of being with him, knowing everything he did, is better than the dark void I felt without him.

My throat closes when he kisses my neck, nibbles on my

earlobe, and then drops several kisses to my nose as his chest rubs against mine.

His hard nipples cause mine to bunch up and ache like crazy as he kisses my nose again and again.

"S-stop that," I whine because he's humping my cock and it'd be embarrassing if I come from just his kisses.

"Shh, let me worship your freckles."

I lift my hand to hide them, but he slams it above my head on the pillow, intertwining his fingers with mine. "They're beautiful, all nineteen of them." He nibbles on my jaw. "So is your mole here." He kisses the shell of my right ear. "And the twenty-two freckles here." He bites my left ear. "And the twenty-seven here." He slides down my chest, then kneels between my legs. "Because you're a goddamn masterpiece, baby."

And then he takes my cock in his mouth.

My toes curl and I'm panting, my head is dizzy, and my face is so warm, I'm going to explode.

Literally.

"Fuckfuckfuck..." I blurt in one breath as I sink my unsteady fingers into his hair as he deep-throats me, taking my cock so far inside, my eyes roll to the back of my head.

I'm so starved, so wound up, I'm riding his mouth, falling into the scorching pleasure he's giving me.

"Jesus Christ, Kayde...your mouth feels so fucking good, I'm gonna, I'm gonna..." My hips jerk, and Kayde takes my cum deep in his throat as I empty my load.

I keep watching him, mesmerized, just the view of him between my legs giving me butterflies. God damn. Am I even able to get butterflies?

But as I watch him gathering my cum off his chin and licking it off his fingers, I can't help but feel them multiply, the butterflies.

I don't think it's sexual gratification. I've gotten that with many people before, even if it wasn't as intense.

It's all him. The person behind the sexual gratification and the feelings that come with that make his touch searing.

"Mmm. I missed your taste." His gruff words pierce my chest and settle into the void, filling it drip by drip.

"I missed my pussy, baby. I want to spank your little ass, but I need to be inside you first." He squirts lube all over his cock, but before he can work himself, I reach over and wrap my fingers around his girth.

"Let me do it."

"You'll make my cock nice and wet so I can stuff it inside my pussy?"

"Yeah." I release a choked sound when he rims me with two lubed fingers and then thrusts them inside me.

"Fuck, you're so tight." He curls his fingers against my walls and I slump over, still jerking his throbbing cock. "Did you let someone else touch you, Gareth?"

"You know I didn't. You had Simone with me at all times."

"True. I wouldn't have been able to stay away if you did." His voice darkens.

"What about you? Did someone touch what's mine?"

"Baby, I couldn't breathe properly without you, let alone be able to look at anyone else."

"Good. I would've killed them."

He chuckles. "Always a menace."

"I mean that."

"I know you do," he says, but he's still smiling, almost like he's proud of me. "Did you touch yourself then? Did you touch my cunt?"

"Mmm, once."

"Once?"

After the time he kissed my forehead and I couldn't take it anymore. It's insane how I never considered myself a sexual person before, but being with this man made me horny at all times, as if I couldn't get enough.

"Yeah, I...couldn't get off by jerking off, so I...put two fingers in."

He thrusts against my sensitive spot and I groan, my cock thickening in an instant as if I didn't just come. "Like this?"

"Mmm...fuck...yeah...like that."

"Did you imagine it was my fingers?"

"I closed my eyes and imagined it was your...your cock."

He goes still and I peek at him through my lashes and his nostrils are flaring. "Fuck, I need to watch my cock slide into you."

He pulls out his fingers and grabs my hand around his cock, then makes me guide him inside me.

I can't look away, watching him disappear inside me slowly, surely, and my cock leaks onto my abs.

"That looks so good," I moan as his hand tightens around mine.

"*You* look so good, baby. You take my cock so well. God, I missed this. I missed you." He kisses my forehead over the Band-Aid, my lashes, my eyes.

And fuck.

Why do I feel like I'm coming again?

"You're so goddamn beautiful." He removes our hands and pushes me onto my back. His hand falls on my hip, pulling my legs up, and the other wraps around my throat as he kisses me.

I'm moaning and groaning and speaking nonsense in his mouth as he gives a delicious shove and pushes all the way in, his pelvis slapping against my ass.

My arms wrap around his neck and my legs around his thighs, pressing him closer, needing him nearer.

Everything in me roars to life. My brain, my body, my heart, my soul.

Everything.

He stimulates me in ways no one else can. No one else will ever be able to.

And I crave it.

I crave *him*.

Because he tames my demons.

He's removing the blood from my white room with every thrust, every shaky breath against my mouth. Every glide of his abs against my cock.

"I could stay inside you forever," he pants against my face, kissing my nose again, my lips, my jaw. "You're my goddamn home, baby."

My entire body shudders because I believe him. I believe his thundering heartbeat against mine, his stuttering breaths on my lips, the way he touches me as if I'm sacred.

The fact that this stoic man is trembling against me, unable to get enough of me, does things to me.

But it also makes the pain and stupid thoughts rush to the surface.

"More than her?" I strain, my chest burning.

"More than anyone," he grunts, going faster but still deep, and not as hard as usual. The way he fucks me today sets my entire body on fire.

"Really?" I'm mumbling against his lips, digging my fingers into his muscular back.

"You're my one and only, baby."

I'm coming then.

I don't even feel it.

A choked noise rips out of me as I spray cum all over his abs and the sheets.

But I keep rocking, keep pulling him into me, and he curses and kisses me as he pulses and throbs inside me.

My walls clench around him as he fills me up.

"Mine," he growls. "You're only fucking mine."

"Mine," I bite his lower lip, then suck it into my mouth.

We kiss until I go numb.

Every inhale fills me with the sharp tang of him as he

consumes me, devours me so entirely, that I become part of him.

It's a heady, dizzying rush, and my whole body hums in delirious bliss. I feel high, not from anything physical, but from the way his entire existence seems to orbit around me.

I'm still dazed as he pulls out of me and then cleans me up with a wet towel.

I lie there, my eyes following his movements. I can't help but notice that he's lost weight, his legs look thinner than usual, his face has definitely sunken, and his stubble is longer.

For someone who wanted him in pain, I sure am not enjoying this.

And my chest twists whenever I see his new tattoo.

Something he got even with the possibility of never seeing me again.

Kayden lifts me up and slides me on top of him as he sits against the headboard. His big arms wrap around my waist as my back rests on his chest, my legs between his and my head pressed to his shoulder.

For just a moment in time, it feels like we're in the apartment, just existing together, being peaceful.

Happy.

But that's not the case.

And the silence is strained, which is an anomaly, because we often existed perfectly well in silence together.

Before I knew everything.

"You were never her replacement," his quiet voice carries through the room, sucking all the air out of it.

"What?"

"Declan mentioned telling you that you were her replacement and that made you snap. He was just provoking you. That was *never* the case."

"It doesn't matter."

"It does, Gareth. You're entirely different, and I never saw her in you. Are we clear?"

"Even though you married her?"

"Is that what this is about? Marriage? It's a business transaction in my world."

"I don't care. I don't even believe in the institution, okay?"

Well, I didn't before. Not sure now.

Now, I'm battling with a disgusting taste at the back of my throat.

"I never intended to rape Yulian," I whisper.

"What?"

"I think you were so mad that first time we met because you thought I wanted to rape him, and that I was a piece of shit like those men who drugged and raped your wife, but I just wanted to mess with him. I had semen-like lube and wanted to take a picture, and that's all. I swear."

"I believe you. You don't need to explain, Gareth."

"But I want to. I don't want you to think I'm like those men."

"I *know* you're not."

"My grandfather isn't either." I stare at the door opposite us. "I talked to him and he said he was there, but he left when Cassandra came along, not knowing what would happen. He stayed quiet afterward because the senator threatened to expose the murder I committed when I was fifteen. Baltimore was the police chief at the time, and he kept evidence and blackmailed Grandpa."

He stares down at me, the gray similar to a storm. "What happened to that evidence?"

His question catches me by surprise, but I still say, "Grandpa and Dad got rid of it."

"Good."

"That's all you have to say?"

"I want to ask why you murdered someone, but I don't want to push you."

I tell him about Harper and David and how it felt euphoric. For some reason, I don't feel like I'll scare him anymore.

He's quiet by the end, and I clear my throat. "So what I mean about this whole thing is, you should blame me, not Grandpa. He was blackmailed to stay silent because of me."

"Doesn't matter."

"It doesn't?"

"Not anymore, no. Even if he did it, I wouldn't hurt him."

"Why not?"

"I told you. Because he's your grandfather and I won't hurt someone you love."

But you're okay hurting yourself?

I pause at that thought, my eyes widening. I don't want him to hurt someone I love and that's him, because he seems tired and is not taking proper care of himself.

And I do love him.

Fuck. I *think*?

It's love if I can't live without him and can feel this peaceful in his arms, right?

The realization crashes into me harder than a hurricane. The reason I nearly lost my goddamn mind isn't because I'm so obsessed with him that I can't tolerate someone else having him. It's because I was hurt, so deeply, thinking he never reciprocated the magnitude of the feelings I have for him.

Feelings I had for the first time in my life, and they scared me because I was giving up control to him.

His lips meet my forehead, over the Band-Aid, lingering for a few long beats. "I'm so sorry."

I reach a trembling hand for his cheek, stroking the stubble on his jaw. "It's not your fault I hit my head on the wall or slashed my own arm open. I'm just...weird and very intense when I'm obsessed with someone, which is why I only had two serious romantic partners in my life. You shouldn't want me this much or tattoo me on you. If you let me in, I will consume you."

"Too late." He strokes my hair. "You already are."

My heart feels like it'd burst, enlarging and engraving each of his words inside its walls.

"Who are the two serious romantic partners?" he asks with a note of apprehension.

"You and Harper. Isn't that obvious?"

"Harper, whose father you killed to avenge."

"Yeah. I just told you that." I pause, my fingers twitching. "Do you feel bad for her prick father or something? Am I a monster if I kill a monster? I mean, I am, but at least I don't stoop that low."

I'm blabbering now because he's not saying anything, and the silence is deafening.

It's true that I don't care if others see me as a monster. But will he be scared of me now?

"Did you love her?" he asks in a low voice.

"Who?"

"Harper."

"I don't know. Maybe." The words taste hollow, like I'm grasping at memories that don't quite fit anymore. "My perception of love is skewed. She was pure, and I liked that, I guess. I liked her company."

But even as I say that, it sounds weird. What I felt for Harper was quiet, soft, like a ripple in a pond. But what I feel for him? It's a storm. Relentless, all-consuming chaos that's burned its way into my very core.

He literally flipped my world upside down. Took everything I thought I knew about myself and smashed it into a million unrecognizable pieces.

But I can't say that. I'm still jittery and in pain.

I'm also terrified that if I lay my heart on the table, he won't take it. And I'll be left picking up the pieces all over again. So I bite my tongue, keeping the words buried where they can't hurt me.

"I never loved Cassandra," he says out of the blue, the rough timbre of his voice vibrating against my back, sending shivers down my spine. "I liked her as a friend, but it was never love."

"H-how do you know for sure?" I whisper, my voice cracking under the weight of his words.

"Because you're the one who ripped my heart open and made yourself a place inside, Gareth. You're the one who makes me irrationally mad and hurt because a dead teenager had your heart before me, and I can never be pure enough to compete."

His words crash into me like a tidal wave, and my heart soars, rising like it's been untethered from the ground. It's dizzying, overwhelming. My chest feels impossibly full, bursting with his presence, his scent, his touch, his voice—they flood my senses, leaving no room for anything else.

I open my mouth, my lips trembling with the words I want to say. To tell him that no one—absolutely no one—has my heart but him.

That, as obsessive and unusual as it is, my heart beats only for *him*.

But before I can utter a word, a sharp, piercing sound rips through the moment.

Gunshots.

38
KAYDEN

Well, this is inconvenient.

And annoying.

And all manner of frustrating.

I'm going to slice open whoever interrupted what Gareth was about to say.

While looking up at me with bright eyes the color of a tropical island and all the beasts lurking within.

But guess we have no choice but to get past this pesky problem.

We dress in record time as the chaos downstairs crescendos. Gunshots rip through the air, sharp and deafening, followed by the sound of shattering glass and splintering wood.

The violence isn't slowing—it's accelerating.

While I'm confident Simone and her men can hold their ground for a while, I can't stay here. Not when the situation is escalating by the second.

I'm the best-trained fighter in this house aside from her, and my presence down there could mean the difference between survival and a bloodbath.

Gareth doesn't seem fazed by the loud noises as he slides on his T-shirt. Normal people would at least be apprehensive, even with security in place, but he just looks at me with those slightly wide eyes. An expression he has when he tries to figure me out, read the emotions on my face.

"Give me a knife," he says. "Actually, that's useless. I want a gun, though I've never shot at people before, but there's a first time for everything."

He's grinning, practically bouncing in place with excitement. Goddamn menace would be murdering people left and right if given the chance.

"You're not coming with me, Gareth," I say in my firmest tone, the one I usually use when he's being a brat.

A frown appears between his brows, and I can't help but look at that bandage. This is the first time I've felt remorse in my life—because of him, because he hurt himself for me—and I don't know how to stop this feeling.

One would think I'm immune to that, considering I slowly but surely killed my father using one of Julian's undetectable drugs.

Years.

It took fucking years for his lungs to fail, but we got there. People thought it was because of the smoking, and we left it at that.

Yes, I became his favorite, and I honestly didn't care for the fuckery he put me through with Vencor. The dark part of my soul enjoyed that shit. What I didn't enjoy, however, were childhood images of my beaten-up mother curled up in depression and Ma Jina hiding in a room to cry so my mother didn't see her.

I never forgave him for that.

After he helped me establish myself in the corporation and Vencor, he had no use being alive.

So off he went.

And I never regretted it. Not once.

But looking at Gareth's Band-Aid and stitches sends a burn of discomfort through my bones.

"What do you mean I'm not coming along?" Gareth's voice is low, controlled, but the tension threading through it is unmistakable. His anger simmers just beneath the surface, threatening to spill over.

Before I can answer, the door flies open, and Jethro stumbles inside, clutching his laptop like it's a lifeline, shielding his eyes with Moka's cage as she hides inside. "I better not see any dicks, lovebirds. Are you covered up?"

"Yeah."

"Thank fuck." He puts down the cage and straightens. "Simone's out there fighting for her life shounen anime style." He whistles, shaking his head. "I disabled their communications, but your brother sent an army, Kayden. Goddamn, he really hates your guts."

I grab Gareth's wrist, pulling him toward Jethro. "Take him through the tunnel. I'll meet you at the port."

Jethro grins, already edging toward the door. "Don't mind if I do. Fighting isn't my thing, so let's get out of here, Blondie."

"I'm not going anywhere." Gareth yanks his wrist free and faces me, his jaw tightening. "I'm coming with you."

"I said you're not."

"And I said I am."

"You want to die or something?"

"Do you?"

"Sorry to interrupt this touching moment of overprotective

banter," Jethro interjects, inching toward the far-right door leading to the tunnel. "But the fighting is getting closer, and I'm not staying to be collateral damage."

I shove Gareth toward the tunnel, my hand firm on his back. His muscles tense beneath my grip, rigid and defiant.

"Kayden, I said I'm not going—"

"Listen to me." I grab his shoulders, forcing him to face me. My voice drops, firm and unyielding. "Your presence will put me in danger because I won't be able to focus on anything but you. I can protect myself better if I know you're safe. Do you understand me, Gareth?"

His lips part, trembling for a moment before he presses them into a thin line. "Am I your weakness?"

"Not a weakness," I say, my voice softening. "But you're the most important person to me, and I need you on your way to the port. Now."

"Then come with me."

"I can't abandon Simone. I'll get her and follow you. All right?"

I see the resistance in his eyes, the stubborn refusal to leave. Or maybe it's his fixation, that all-consuming need to keep me within reach.

That's why he came here in the first place. Gareth doesn't like the thought of someone else ending my life.

But I've already made my decision.

"I won't die." I brush my lips against his forehead, and he goes still, a faint shiver rippling through his body. I step back, meeting his gaze. "You didn't allow me to, remember?"

"You better not," he murmurs, his hand sliding up to wrap around my throat. His chin quivers, his grip firm but hesitant. "I didn't forgive you yet."

"All right, we really need to go." Jethro reaches for Gareth's arm, casting me a wary glance.

"Protect him," I tell Jethro, my tone brooking no argument.

Jethro gawks at me. "Pretty sure it should be the other way around. I'm the nerd in this situation."

Gareth steps toward me, but I turn, pushing the door shut.

And lock it.

As I walk out, a gun in hand, I send Jethro a text.

> Take him the fuck out of here. Drop him at his parents' and tell them to ask their mafia connections for protection.

So maybe I lied.

Pretty sure I'm dying today.

Even if my brother's men don't manage it, the other founding families will. In their eyes, I'm an anomaly—a dangerous precedent that needs to be wiped out. And as a high-ranking member, they'll want to make an example out of me, a gruesome one at that.

But at least Gareth is safe.

A long breath escapes my lungs as I move through the chaos, firing at anyone in my path. Each shot is a message—a dent in Grant's little army for daring to come at me at the worst possible time.

"The fuck are you doing here?" Simone shouts, swinging her knife at a guy's throat. Blood splashes across her face, matting her hair, and I notice her jacket is ripped and soaked with red.

"Helping?"

"Fuck, Kayden, you should've left!"

"And let you die alone?" I grin, reloading. "Am I that much of a monster?"

I raise my gun and shoot a guy aiming his rifle at her, right between the eyes. The crack of the shot echoes, but I'm already running low on ammunition.

Simone takes a hit in the leg, and she stumbles.

"Shit," she grits out, blood streaming down her thigh as I rush to her side.

I sling her arm over my shoulder, half carrying her as the men under her command create a shield around us, returning fire.

We barely make it outside when I see Grant.

He stands with a few of his men, his posture rigid, his face as stoic and impassive as ever.

"Take her," I order Isaac, shoving Simone toward the car as she twists in my grip, shouting.

"Kayden, don't be fucking stupid!"

"Just protect them for me, yeah?" I wave her off, ignoring the way her bloodied fists pound against the window as the car screeches out of the driveway.

Her muffled screams echo as I turn to face my brother.

"Let her go, Grant." My voice is steady, calm, the finger on my trigger unwavering. "It's the least you can do after your shitty timing."

He doesn't move, doesn't order his men to detain me or shoot.

But his eyes—those silver eyes that are identical to mine— glint with something dangerous, something calculated.

All I can see is Harrod.

The resemblance is uncanny. Same cold stare. Same dark hair. Similar facial features.

And it disgusts me.

Grant isn't just a carbon copy of our father—he *is* him, to the very core.

And we all know how much I loathe that man.

Looking at Grant makes my blood boil, those same murderous thoughts bubbling to the surface, thoughts I harbored for Harrod.

Funny thing is, I much prefer Grant's son over him.

Though, I'd have preferred a cute little niece instead.

But anyway.

"You're not going to shoot me?" I ask, leaning back slightly.

"I don't like killing my family members," Grant replies evenly, his calm exterior betraying the storm brewing underneath. "You know that."

"Oh, so this is just to scare me a little? You sure love theatrics. Must be because you were never loved. Your mom abandoned you, and I ranked first on Dad's list."

I'm provoking him. Need to wipe that calm off his face and keep him talking—anything to buy me more time.

Jethro and Gareth should've reached the open water by now. They have to be out of Grant's reach before he realizes what's happening.

Grant's face contorts, his mask of composure slipping just a fraction. "I can always make an exception for you."

"Actually, you should've done that a long time ago, back when your mom died. If you'd killed Dad then, he wouldn't have forced Mom into marriage, and I wouldn't exist. You could've been king of the world. But no, you craved his approval too much to come up with that plan, didn't you?"

I glance at my watch. Five more minutes. Maybe ten—to be safe.

"Not all of us engage in patricide, Kayden." His words are laced with something deeper than hatred.

Rage.

So he's known all along. My grin widens. "You knew?"

"That you'd been poisoning him? Slowly, methodically? Of course I knew. Though by the time I figured it out, it was too late." He exhales sharply, his breath heavy with bitterness. "I even told him you were killing him. You know what he said?"

"That he didn't believe you because he loved me too much?"

Grant's laugh is low, cold. "He said, 'At least he has the balls to.'"

Well, that's one way to look at it. Dear old Dad always did admire my mind. He loved that I wasn't squeamish, that I didn't flinch when taking a life, and that I used everything to my advantage—including my marriage.

Harrod always said I reminded him of himself. He was wrong. I'd never be the disgusting abuser he was.

Still, I'm a little bummed he wasn't hurt by my betrayal. I wanted him to die bitter and broken, not resigned.

"Don't be jealous you were never his favorite." I sit on the step across from Grant, resting the rifle on the ground. Blood smears the cigarette I pull from my pocket. "Lighter?"

One of his men hesitates, looking at Grant. When he doesn't object, the guy lights my cigarette.

"You think you'd still be his favorite if he knew you were gobbling cock?"

"It's one cock, actually." I exhale a stream of smoke. "But no, he wouldn't approve. Not that it matters."

"You're not even ashamed?"

"Of what?"

"Being a lesser fucking man."

"For preferring dick?" I chuckle, slow and deliberate. "You actually believe Vencor's bullshit about how being gay makes someone 'imperfect'? Oh, Grant. I hate to say it, but Dad was right—you really are an idiot."

Grant grabs a gun from one of his men's holsters and points it at me.

"My." My grin widens. "Poked the daddy issues?"

"You know, I never liked you, Kayden." His voice is low, simmering. "You always had things easy. Rachel was abused. So fucking *what*? She wasn't driven to her death like my mom. And you always had her, didn't you? Her *and* another mom. Meanwhile, Dad liked you for some reason I'll never fucking understand. No matter what I did, he always put you first. *Always*. I should send you to join him."

"Wouldn't you be jealous if Dad and I reunited in Hell without you?" I let the smirk stretch across my face. "Though even if you joined us, he'd still like me better. Want to know why? Because, unlike you, I never begged for his attention like a desperate little bitch. I *earned* it. Till the day he died, Harrod respected me. He never respected you."

The click of the gun echoes, and I close my eyes.

I guess Gareth and Jethro are far enough now.

Still, I doubt Grant will pull the trigger. He knows he can't control my side of the business if I'm gone.

But then again, maybe I pushed him too far.

And his daddy issues aren't adorable like Gareth's, they're destructive. Like the way he raised his son to be ruthless, as if Harrod's ghost is still on his shoulders telling him exactly what to do. So, just in case, I don't want to have my last thoughts filled with Grant or Harrod.

Bright eyes rush through my mind, ethereal green eyes that pierce through me with every look, full of life and something I could never quite reach. I picture his smile with the dimples that always tightened my heart, like he was a force I couldn't control but couldn't stop wanting.

I fall into the memory of how his breath would catch, a soft sigh escaping him when I ran my fingers through his hair, the way he'd close his eyes in a kind of surrender.

I picture him asleep in my arms, his face relaxed, his breathing even, holding me close like he never wants to let me go.

And I feel peace.

"Kayden!"

For a brief moment, I think I'm conjuring up his voice, but then again, he doesn't sound this frightened in my head.

Never frightened.

I open my eyes and, sure enough, Gareth is running toward me.

What the—

My eyes stray to Grant, whose gaze shifts between us, his lips curling into a smirk as realization dawns.

He knows.

And he'll kill Gareth, not because he has to, but to teach me a lesson. To make me feel the same anguish he endured when Dad killed his girlfriend.

"I knew you were lying! I fucking knew it!" Gareth screams, his voice raw and thunderous as he lunges for a gun on the ground.

I don't think. I don't hesitate.

I run toward him at full speed, my focus narrowing until there's nothing but the need to shield him. My body crashes into his, my back to Grant as the shot rings out.

The sound is deafening, a sharp crack splitting through the chaos.

Pain blooms in my side like an explosion, radiating outward in jagged waves.

But Gareth is fine.

I'm on top of him, and he's fine.

It's fine.

This is fine.

My ears ring, muffling the world around me. I hear Simone's distant voice—panicked, shouting orders. That's good. Maybe she brought more men. She'll protect him. She likes Gareth, enough to spill everything about me if it means earning his forgiveness.

He'll be fine.

Gareth's frantic tears grip my face, and salty droplets slip into my mouth as they stream down his cheeks.

"Kay...Kayde...no...no...you fucking idiot. What have you done?" His voice cracks, filled with anguish I've never heard before.

I love his voice. But not like this. Not when it's laced with so much pain.

"Kay...please...fuck! You said you wouldn't die. You promised...you *promised* me!"

His hand presses tightly against my side, futilely trying to stop the flow of blood. He's shaking all over like a live wire.

"Please...don't go...I'm begging you...please...don't leave me. Baby, *please*..."

I lift a hand to his face, smearing his beautiful skin with blood as I try to wipe away the tears.

Don't cry, I want to tell him.

But no words come out.

The world blurs, darkening at the edges as the pain dulls into a distant throb. All I can do is let the darkness swallow me whole, carrying me away from his broken voice, the tremor in his hands, and the tears that feel heavier than the bullet in my side.

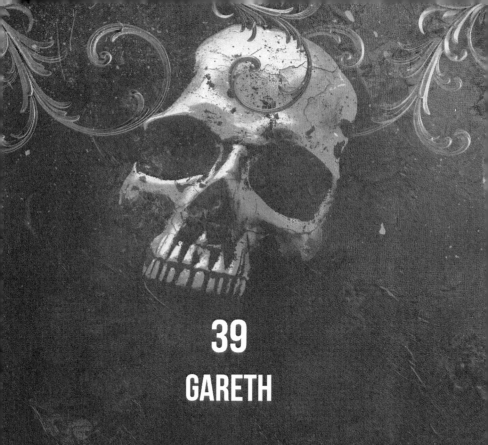

39

GARETH

I'm staring at the red on my hands.

At the blood.

His blood.

My Kayden's blood that flowed out of him persistently no matter how much I tried to stop it. I removed my shirt and pressed on it. I used both my hands, but it still soaked everything and escaped him.

Escaped *me*.

The crimson red is dry now and etches into the creases of my palms, tinting my fingernails, slipping under the skin, lodged there.

My hands are shaking uncontrollably.

My hands have never shook before. Not when I held Gilbert

underwater. Not when Mr. Laurent died before my eyes. Not even when I killed David in cold blood.

But now, I can't stop the trembling, not after I felt the sticky liquid against my fingers.

It was warm, but now it's cold.

Because it's no longer inside him.

It's on me. My hands. My chest. My jeans. Everywhere but in *him*.

I grab onto the sink in the hospital's bathroom and turn on the faucet, then scrub at the blood, harshly, incessantly, until I'm sure I'll scrub the fucking skin off.

A flicker of fear slams into my throat and widens the void as I watch his blood diluting and trickling down the drain.

What if... What if that's the last time I touch him?

No.

I squeeze my eyes shut and breathe deeply. Inhale. Slow exhale. Count to ten like he always tells me to do when my thoughts spiral.

My lips quiver, and my eyes sting with unshed tears.

If...if he's not there anymore, who's going to keep my twisted personality in check? Who's going to pull me back down when I get too high? When the impulses grow too deep?

Who's going to fill the void and carry me to my white room?

The white room is closed now, locked. Not even bloodied like it used to be. I don't have access to it anymore, because Kayden has the keys. And Kayden is fighting for his life on a surgeon's table

For six hours now.

Six hours I spent staring at his blood on my palms until Simone brought me a shirt and told me maybe I should go wash up.

I didn't want to, but if I stayed there one more minute, I'd barge in there and threaten the doctors to save him. And I don't think that's a good idea.

I open my eyes and pause as I stare at my reflection in the mirror. I reach a trembling finger to the streak of red on my cheek. From when he last touched me, wiped my cheek before he lost consciousness.

The pads of my fingers burn when touching the dry streaks of blood, and I jerk my hand away, refusing to wipe off his last imprint.

No, it *can't* be his last.

It won't be.

I refuse to think he'd just...leave me.

If he does, I'll follow him.

If he thinks death will make him escape me, he has no idea how far my madness can reach.

I step out of the bathroom, pulling out my phone. It's time to stop wallowing in desperate scenarios and make myself useful.

My first phone call is to my aunt. She picks up despite the time and assures me that she'll try everything in her might.

The subject of my second call picks up after a few rings. Vaughn's groggy voice greets me. "G? It's three in the fucking morning, man."

"I need your help."

"Hold on." There's shuffling on his end before I hear footsteps and a door closing. "I'm listening," he says, his voice now entirely sober.

I stare at the cracks in the hospital tiles, tightening my grip on the phone. "Not sure if you figured it out by now, but we've been talking on Reddit."

He groans. "Did you have to shatter the illusion?"

"Kind of. He's dying, V." My voice catches, and I have to bite my lower lip to keep from breaking.

I've always been friends with Jer and Niko. Maya and Mia, too. Vaughn as well, but I've kept them all at arm's length, never allowing any of them to get too close or see inside me.

But talking to V anonymously allowed me freedom and a sense of companionship and friendship I didn't know I needed.

I was always a loner anyway. Even in a group, I was alone. Even when laughing and talking and being surrounded by people, my outer layer kept me in a bubble. One that Kayden snuck into, and I want to keep him there.

In my bubble.

Not outside or on an operating table or bleeding out.

But V is actually the first person whose friendship I appreciate. The one who listened to me bitch the entire time and kind of did the same about Yulian.

"Fuck, man." He releases a long breath. "What can I do?"

"I already called Aunt Rai, but I want to double my efforts. Kayden..." My voice chokes on his name and I exhale slowly. "That's his name. Kayden. He's become a target of this stupid-ass organization because of me. Because he's with...me. And I want to kill his brother and all of them, but Simone and Jethro tell me that would be hard and I'd become a target and so would Kayden if he..." *survives.*

I *can't* say it.

The words taste like acid, burning my throat and boiling in my veins.

"He will." Vaughn's voice comes out calm and steady. "From what you told me, he'd never leave you, right?"

"I want to think he wouldn't, but he...he went into the bullet's path to protect me. He didn't think about it, he...he ran straight toward death like a fucking idiot."

"I don't think he wanted to die per se. He just didn't want *you* to die." He pauses. "He's a keeper, G. I like you much better when you're with him."

"Hey, does that mean you never liked me before?"

"You were always just fucking shit up while you were being a golden boy. Now, you're all right, I guess."

"Gee, thanks."

"Anytime, my bro."

"Will you talk to your dad about protection?"

"I'll make it happen." His voice softens—as much softening as V is capable of. "I've got your back, man. Always."

"Thanks. And, V?"

"Yeah?"

"You deserve better."

He blows out a breath. "I know."

"I'm always here. Until you figure your shit out."

"Thanks, G."

I'm about to insist on him talking to his dad when I see Simone hobbling toward me on a crutch, Jethro supporting her.

If it weren't for Simone, I would've probably died. She called the police, so Grant and his men fucked off from the scene as soon as they heard sirens.

And Jethro, well, I don't like him that much because he tried to stop me when I decided to go back.

If it weren't for him, I wouldn't have left Kayden, and he wouldn't be in this predicament right now.

But I have no right to blame him when Kayden took that shot for me.

He's dying because of *me*.

I meet Simone, my legs barely carrying me. "What's...what's wrong?"

"He made it." She speaks through tears. "He's alive. He lost a lot of blood, but he fought, Gareth. He's alive."

A strangled noise fills my throat as she hugs me, and Jethro calls us dramatic as he hugs us, too.

I wrap my arm around her, hiding my face in her shoulder, spitting out a shaky exhale.

He's alive.

He didn't leave me.

And I can breathe.

———

I spent the next few days by Kayden's side.

He was in the ICU, but this morning, they moved him to the general ward, and he's looking better.

I asked Jethro and Simone not to tell Rachel and Jina. They can't travel to the States anyway, so telling them would only worry them to no end. Rachel actually has severe depression, and she tends to get too worried about him, so I chose to hide the truth. Something Kayden agreed with, then said we'd visit them when he's better.

Even though the threat of his organization still looms, I have more security than a president around the hospital. Not only did Aunt Rai and V's dad, the Russian mafia leader, come through, but my dad and grandpa were also extra and hired their own security.

Pretty sure they'd buy the whole hospital if we spend one more week here.

Grandpa can't stand Kayden, even when he's sick. Said he's a goddamn leech and I was almost shot because of him, and he still insists he's Dad's age.

Not sure what Dad feels, but he's at least thankful that Kayden saved my life, so silver linings, I guess.

Ever since Kayden was moved to this room, I've been cutting him apples and strawberries. He said he doesn't really have a favorite fruit, but he grew fond of strawberries, so I got him those.

And I've been giving him lots of massages since he's been lying in bed for a long time. I had one of the nurses teach me the technique, and since I'm a fast learner, I got it right away.

Now, they can get their greedy hands off my man.

What? They've been giving him heart eyes, and this one nurse keeps calling him Mr. Handsome.

I'll cut her throat. Not even kidding.

A couple of days ago, I found this tall, buff guy talking to him in the ICU and, thankfully, I didn't reach for my knife first and ask questions later, because, apparently, it's his nephew, Kane.

Can you imagine the complications that we would be dealing with if I'd let my impulses win?

I did tell Kane I'd kill his dad, though, to which he simply smiled.

So, anyway, that's who Kayden is currently watching on the laptop—his nephew playing in a college hockey game—while I press on his leg to help with blood circulation.

He releases a grunt and I look up, only to find him observing me as the commentator's voice fills the hospital room.

Kayden's jawline is more defined, his stubble not as long—because I shaved him earlier—and his waist is wrapped in this godforsaken bandage that reminds me he could've slipped between my fingers, like the blood.

His color is slowly coming back, but his lips are still pale, and there's a sheen of something unreadable in his stormy eyes.

I ease the pressure. "Does it hurt?"

"It does." He taps his chest. "Here. Because you're not talking to me."

"I am talking to you," I grumble as I resume the massage.

So maybe I've been in too much pain to be completely sappy, and I don't know how to direct these emotions.

"But you're mad at me." He closes the laptop, cutting off the thrill of the game, and grabs my hand. "Baby, look at me."

I lift my eyes and he pulls me closer, making me sit on top of him. I straddle his waist, careful not to touch the bandage. My senses fill with him—his warmth, his scent, his breathing.

Damn, I love the sound of his breathing.

He's here. He's alive.

He didn't leave, because I didn't allow him to.

And I'll *never* allow him to.

Kayden's big hands land on my waist, and I suck in a large gulp of air as his silver eyes bore into me. "I know you still haven't forgiven me, and while I can't go back to the past and change my marriage or history, I promise you the rest of my life."

"What's the point if you're going to shorten it?"

A frown appears deep in his forehead. "What do you mean?"

"I'm not mad about that, asshole. I'm mad because you threw away your life without any thoughts of me! Of us! How do you expect me to live on without you, Kayden? You injected yourself in my bones and you're flowing in my veins, my head, my soul. You're *in* me. How can you not see that if you remove yourself from inside me, I'll just wither and die?"

He strokes my cheek, the pad of his thumb gliding beneath my eye. "The last thing I want is to hurt you, baby. But I'm physically unable to watch you being hurt. That just won't happen, but I promise to be more careful. I'm not done with you yet, and I never will be. I want to show you how much you mean to me, my little monster."

"You already did." I punch his chest with no actual strength. "Took a bullet for me like a goddamn idiot, remember?"

"I'd take ten and however many it takes to erase your pain."

"Don't you dare." I slide my hand to his face, trembling with all the emotions vibrating through me. "Please don't leave me. Or I swear I will kill you."

He chuckles, the sound soaring through my chest, expanding my lungs. "Never, baby. I might have entered your life with thoughts to break you, but you're the one who broke me. You cracked me open, tore me apart, and molded me back together in your image. Now, I'm incapable of existing without you. The absence of your voice, your scent, your tough love, and even your impulsiveness and spoiled-brat behavior painted my world black. I was fine with that color before you, but I can't stand it now. Will *not* stand it. You gave my life meaning after years of aimlessness. Your chaos soothes my calm, your darkness is a mirror of my own, and that beautiful soul of yours is a figment of mine and a torch that burns in the depths of my blackened heart. I didn't know what love was before you, but I'm certain that's what I feel for you, my little monster."

My chest aches with every inhale, his words incinerating me alive, and I grab his face with both trembling hands. "You're not allowed to leave me. Ever."

"I won't."

"I mean it, Kayde. If you do, there'll be no me without you." I lean closer, *needing* him closer. "There's this void inside me. A black hole I lived with my entire life. I thought I'd filled it up once when I killed for the first time, but that high only lasted for a while. I'd always had this insatiable urge for more and more and *more*. But then you came into my life and filled me up. Not the void, *me*. So I mean it when I say you're inside me. You tame my darkness, calm my chaos, and quiet the voices. I don't only love you, but I'm physically unable to live without you. It hurts to even think about it."

"Good." He drags me closer so that his breaths skim my lips. "Because I refuse to think about it."

"You should probably think about it, not that I'll let you go, but I'm kind of toxic."

"I'm toxic, too."

"I get jealous easily. I'll keep thinking about the years you were married."

"I'll give you the rest of my years instead."

"I might act like a brat sometimes."

"Only sometimes?" He lifts a brow.

"Okay, all the time."

"You'll be my brat, and you'll be punished accordingly."

A jolt rocks through me, and I whisper, "What if I get the urge to kill? Will you hate me?"

"I'll bring you a waste of space and hold your hand while you do it."

Fuck, that sounded hot.

Should it sound hot?

"What if—"

"Gareth," he cuts me off. "Shut up so I can kiss you."

I close my eyes, shifting closer, but his lips don't come, so I peek at him and he's watching me with a slight frown.

"What?"

"I'm trying to think if you actually called me baby while I was dying or if it was a figment of my imagination."

I laugh. "I did, baby."

"Fuck. Say that again," he growls.

"I love you, baby—" My words end with a moan because he's devouring me.

And I'm consuming him.

We're so toxic, it's unhealthy but also right.

Because we're each other's darkness and light.

I'm his.

And he's so fucking mine.

EPILOGUE 1
GARETH

THREE MONTHS LATER

"Can you pass me the salt?"

Kayden slides it across the table toward Grandpa, who just asked for it.

But upon seeing it came from Kayden, not Kill or Dad, he scowls. "Lost my appetite."

Mom and I release a collective sigh.

She and Glyn went all out for this dinner. Like, no kidding, they were shopping and micromanaging the catering and even cooking. Kill was jealous—which made me smug—because, apparently, Glyn doesn't really cook, but she did for this.

Anyway, they went all out just to make this family dinner special. Since, well, it's the first time I've officially brought Kayden home.

He had to recover, and I went back to school on his insistence. So you can bet that I took him with me. Either that or I was staying with him in the States.

That led to me sort of coming out to my friends, and that was a shitshow. The only mature one was Jeremy, who just patted my shoulder.

Nikolai laughed out loud and said, "I knew it for months, you bitches, and kept all these secrets. You never would've seen it coming from me, right? *Right?* Also, Jer, you're like the only straight dude around here, so maybe experiment a little. No offense to Cecy."

I reminded him that there was still Vaughn, because I'm not letting his secret out until he's comfortable doing so—that is, if he's ever comfortable. And Niko replied, "Jer and V should form the *Boring Dick Alliance.*"

His words, not mine.

Anyway, Niko was so quick to introduce us to his own boyfriend, his enemy's twin brother, if you believe it, and kept saying, "Lotus flower this and lotus flower that."

Kill said, "You do realize you're kind of fucking Landon, right?"

"Fuck no!" Niko shouted. "They're entirely damn different."

"They're literally identical twins," I said.

"Shut up, Gaz. They're totally worlds apart. Don't go comparing a diamond to a swamp."

Anyway, I swear to fuck I don't know how Brandon, a very well-mannered, quiet artist, not to mention a British guy who's allergic to violence, could ever be with my unhinged cousin Niko, but I guess no one would expect someone like me to be with someone like Kayden, yet here we fucking are.

Together.

And following each other everywhere.

Though Kayden made the island his home base for me—

and apparently owns the entire building we live in—he still travels for business.

Diva Jethro hated the island; I mean, he completely loathes the UK and its depressing weather, so I told him it's not like he goes out anyway, which made both Kayden and Simone burst out laughing and Jethro transform into a bigger diva.

Seriously, we flew here two days ago, and he's just cooped up in one of the houses Kayden owns nearby, being a major nerd. I know he's been basically running the business with Kayden, but he's weird, and I've honestly never seen him without a laptop.

Like, never.

The other day, I caught him spying on the Serpents' mansion, and I don't know what's up with all that.

He's strange, end of story.

Simone is amazing, though.

I wanted her to join us for dinner, but she vehemently refused to leave her post. No, seriously, we have more body-guards than a mafia leader, and she's still always obsessing about our security.

Which now leaves Kayden in unfriendly territory, sitting between Dad and Kill while Grandpa glares at him from the head of the table.

"Grandpa," I say with a knowing look.

"What?" He cuts into his steak. "I don't like my grandson dating someone his dad's age. Call me old-fashioned."

"I told you he's thirty-three, definitely not Dad's age."

"Close enough," he grumbles. "Right, Asher?"

"I have to say," my father takes a sip of his wine, "I'm not thrilled to share a table with someone who made my son hurt himself."

"Asher," Mom scoffs. "Forgive and forget, you've heard of that?"

His eyes soften when looking at her, but he still says, "I don't believe in that nonsense."

"I agree to an extent." Kill looks Kayden up and down, which he's been doing since he first met him. On the island, he barged into our apartment, interrupting a little romantic dinner I planned, to meet 'the prick,' as he likes to call him. On the whole, ever since Kill realized I'm more like him, he's been demanding that we spend time together.

But that night was bad timing. To say Kill looked horrified upon seeing me wrapped around Kayden would be an understatement.

I've never seen him with that wide-eyed expression before, almost as if he was seeing his life flash before his eyes.

I don't care.

After I almost lost Kayden, I'm touching him all the time, appreciating every second I spend with him.

"You don't have other young boys to take your pick from? Why did it have to be my brother?"

Glyn must kick him under the table, because he grunts, smiles at her, then glares back at Kayden.

My brother's girl, who I truly appreciate for taming the motherfucker, touches my arm and gives me an apologetic look, mouthing, "You know how he is."

Both—and I mean *both*—Kayden's and Kill's eyes zero in on her hand on my arm.

I can't help the smile that creeps up my mouth.

Kayden has been generally unruffled by all of the questioning, taking a few bites of food and complimenting my mom and Glyn, but just her hand on my arm is darkening his gray eyes, the black flecks turning sharper.

He catches me smiling at him, and he squints the slightest bit. Which is his silent, "Watch it." Or, "Behave." Or, "Don't be a brat."

God, I love how alive he looks right now.

The color has slowly returned to his gorgeous face, a warm flush that softens the harshness from when he was shot. The cut lines of his stubbled jaw are even more prominent now, sharper and alive.

The smooth lines of his tailored shirt are so tight around his biceps and chest, it feels like if he takes a bigger breath, he might burst out of it.

My gaze shifts unwillingly to his hands gripping the fork and knife, the veins along his fingers stretching and flexing with each movement. They look so strong, an urge fills me to reach out, to touch them, to feel that pulse beneath my fingertips.

I think I'm a lost addict at this point. I spent a few minutes not touching him, and I feel as if something is missing.

He only slides his gaze to Kill when Glyn removes her hand and goes back to eating, completely unaware of the small moment of camaraderie Kill and Kayden just shared.

"He's neither young nor a boy, he's your older brother," Kayden says with a firm but confident edge. "And no, I couldn't just go for someone else, so while I respect all your objections and your roles in his life, I'm here to stay, and none of you can change that."

His words burn the fire he's been igniting in my chest. I think it's the light he's bringing into my life, but, anyway, no matter what it is, I can't have the flames go out.

Ever.

"Not if you end up in a little freak accident," Kill muses while stabbing his steak, making a show of gliding the piece of meat through the blood, because, of course, his steak is rare.

"That won't stop me." Kayden's lips curve in a small smile. "I assure you."

Not sure if they believe him, but I do, wholeheartedly. I won't say I'm a saint or that I've stopped being a petulant jealous fool, but over these past few months, I've become categorically sure of the feelings he has for me.

Like, no kidding. Kayden's entire confident and untouchable demeanor cracks when he sees the smallest injury on my body. The other day, I accidentally cut myself with a knife while I was cooking, and he had this frightened look in his eyes while he sucked the blood.

I was more hard than anything, really. The feeling of my fingers in his wet, hot mouth kind of made it impossible to concentrate. But I could see that he was apprehensive about my being hurt in any shape or form. He said he couldn't get the sight of my blood out of his mind, and that he never wanted to see it again.

And I relate to that.

I still have nightmares about all the blood that escaped him when he was shot.

Kill opens his mouth, to threaten him again, no doubt, while Grandpa and Dad seem content with him doing so, but I pointedly glare at him. "Don't you dare play that game. Cut it out."

"I'm just laying some ground rules. Like no one will find his body if he ever makes you bleed again."

I smile at Glyn. "He shouldn't threaten others at a family dinner, don't you think, Glyn?"

"Absolutely." She gives him a look. "Stop it."

He merely releases a grumble, and I flash him a grin. He knows Glyn and I are friends, and she always puts a leash on that side of him, and he despises that.

Good thing he'll never be friends with Kayden and can't pull it off. Kayden is not able to be charmed, and Kill kind of dislikes him.

Win-win for me.

"He's not my family," Grandpa says with a glare. "I still don't approve."

"Alex, please." Mom speaks in a gentle tone. "I love and respect you and I'm glad my sons have you in their lives, but with all due respect, your approval or the lack thereof doesn't matter. This applies to you, too, Ash and Kill." She gives them a pointed look. "Gareth chose Kayden, and I know it seems odd from the outside looking in due to the age gap and whatnot, but you've seen them together throughout the night. I didn't notice any age difference or genders, I just saw two people in love. I saw my son smile genuinely and often for the first time in a long time. I'd rather my son be happy than focus on what irrelevant society or others think. So I'll be taking real offense to anyone threatening my son's man. Are we clear?"

Dad and Kill go quiet at that. Of course they would. Dad kind of worships her, and Kill is a mama's boy. Grandpa grumbles under his breath, but he doesn't say anything out loud.

Kayden thanks my mom with that blinding smile that kind of gives me butterflies. It's insane to still have them when we've been together for some time. It's like at the beginning when I was crushing on him and becoming full-blown obsessed while denying it.

"Thanks, Mom." I side-hug her and she kisses my cheek.

"I want you to be happy, hon."

"I am, Mom. Truly."

And I mean it.

I don't think I knew what happiness was before, but now, just being in the same room as Kayden is happiness.

Happiness takes many forms. It can range from comfortably existing in silence while playing chess to watching Moka eat Jethro's cables while he tries to wrestle her away. It's listening to Kayden's steady heartbeat when I fall asleep and knowing he's here with me.

It's how he smiles upon seeing me after a whole day of being apart, how he hugs and kisses me as if he can breathe only when I'm around.

It's hearing Rachel and Jina's stories about a younger, mischievous, but incredibly smart Kayden and seeing his baby albums. I might have even made them give up a few pictures so I could frame and keep them in that shrine I have of him.

Happiness is Kayden and Kayden is happiness. They're one and the same in my mind.

Maybe they shouldn't be, but me and my mind never conformed to normal anyway.

The rest of the dinner is less tense, and Kill keeps trying to be a little shit. He gets kicked by Glyn every time, and I think he's doing it on purpose at this point.

But Dad is warming up a little to Kayden. They have a pretty similar levelheadedness, so maybe that helps. I do want Dad to like him, I really do, and perhaps that's an aftereffect of those times when I always craved his approval to the point that I invented a public personality so as not to disappoint him.

But over the past few months, I realized that I like my dad better when he knows exactly what I'm capable of. When I don't have to hide my true self just to please him.

After dinner, Kayden is swept away by Mom with bribes to show him my photo albums and all the awards I've won.

"Mom, stop. That's embarrassing," I say then narrow my eyes on Kayden. "Why would you want to see those anyway?"

"The same reason you begged my moms for pictures of me." He gives an evil grin. "Please lead the way, Reina."

Kill catches up to them. "I'll join for commentary."

I grunt. "Please don't."

"I'm going to enjoy this." He pulls Glyn along. "Come on."

"I'm sorry," she mouths. "I'll defend you!"

"No one will be making fun of my grandson on my watch." Grandpa all but storms to the sitting area.

I groan. "Fuck my life. I don't want to go in there."

"Then don't." Dad squeezes my shoulder and leads me out

to the balcony. The night's chill doesn't manage to cool down my grumbly mood.

"Kill will definitely have his revenge for the time we showed Glyn pictures of him in a dress." I rub my eyes with the heel of my palm. "That prick never forgave me for that."

"On the bright side, you don't have a picture in a dress." Dad smiles with nostalgia. "Your mom really wanted Kill to be a girl. She was devastated to be only a boys' mom. I believe that's why she dotes on Glyn so much—she's the daughter she always wanted."

I lean against the railing, listening to the laughs filtering in from the other room, mostly my mom's. "I hope she doesn't hate me for not giving her another daughter-in-law."

"Nonsense. You heard her earlier. Your happiness is what's important to her, no matter who you choose to be with."

"What about you, Dad?"

"Your happiness is important to me, too. You know that, Gareth."

I perk up, looking at him with blinding expectations. "So... you'll accept Kayde? With time, I mean."

"It's not that I don't accept him." He lets out a sigh. "I just don't like how you looked when he hurt you or that he used you. I suppose I'm having trouble moving past that, but I also get your mother's point. You look more like yourself with him, and he did take a bullet for you, so I respect that. I also like that he contains your impulsiveness, and you actually listen to him."

"I listened to you, too."

"No, Gareth. You didn't really listen. You hid away from me to fit the image you thought I wanted of you. But I get it. You were nervous about my reaction, and that's my fault. Point is, " he grabs my shoulders, "I'm happy you're happy. That's all."

I wrap my arms around him. "Thank you, Dad. Really."

He pats my back and when we break free, I catch a glimpse

of Kayden standing by the door, patiently waiting with a hand in his pocket.

And his eyes soften upon clashing with mine.

The eyes that were so dead the first time I saw him. The eyes that are indifferent, polite, or downright dismissive when talking with others only soften for me.

Dad smiles at me before he leaves.

I all but throw myself at Kayden when he walks in, wrapping my arms around his neck and pressing myself into him so suddenly, he grabs my waist to steady us.

God, I feel so complete when I touch him.

When he's gone, I lose the part of myself that's anchored by him. The air feels thinner without the feel of his skin against mine, and the quiet I usually enjoy with him is deafening without him.

Now that I'm all over him, I can breathe properly.

"I assume that was a good talk." He strokes my dimples, smiling softly. "You look like you'll burst."

"Dad likes you. I mean, not fully, but he's getting there."

"And that makes you happy."

It's not a question, but I nod. "You know how much his approval means to me."

"I do. And now, I'm starting to think you're only with me for your little daddy issues."

I mock gasp. "Oh my, you figured me out? Whatever am I going to do now?"

He laughs, the sound like music to my ears. Honestly, he's so serious outside, I feel like the chosen one for making him laugh.

I swear to God, Jethro and Simone gawk every time he does.

"As long as I'm not your *daddy*, we're good." He raises a brow. "Unless you're into that?"

"Nah, not my thing. I like baby better." I brush my lips

against his jaw, licking and biting slightly. "You smell so good and look so hot, baby."

He groans, his hand sliding from my waist to my ass, squeezing the marks he left there last night. "You better stop that, or your family's going to get a front-row seat to me bending you over this balcony and fucking you right here, right now."

I moan, growing hard as the pain ignites the pleasure and rushes throughout my skin. "Mmm, don't threaten me with a good time."

"Fuck, baby. You're driving me insane." He squeezes my ass, pressing me against him. "Your grandpa will have a stroke."

I can feel the contours of his cock through the clothes, and it makes my mouth water and my own dick harden. "He'll live."

"Not for long. I assure you." He grunts and pushes me away, grabbing my waist again, then says in an austere voice, "Stop. Rein it in until I have you all to myself."

I release a whine but don't try to seduce him again. He really can make me fold with those firm orders of his.

"Speaking of having me all to yourself," I muse, sniffing him. His scent kinda calms me. Better than the sight of blood—weird, I know. "What do you think about having a threesome? Like sharing me with another guy or girl?"

Something curious happens then. Something that literally sets the butterflies ablaze in my stomach.

Because not only does Kayden stiffen, but his eyes darken like I've never seen before, lighting up, becoming frightening, even.

His hand tightens around my waist, the pads digging into my muscles as he speaks in that firm, nonnegotiable tone. "Listen to me, Gareth, I don't know where that came from, but I will *not* be sharing you with anyone. Are we fucking clear?"

"I'm just asking. No need to look murderous."

"Would you be open to sharing me with someone else?"

I grab his throat. "No way in fuck. I'd kill them, you know I would."

"Then you know exactly how I feel." He pulls my hand from his throat, frowning. "What made you think that anyway? You can barely walk after I'm done with you, so I like to think you're thoroughly satisfied."

"Damn straight I am. I definitely don't want a threesome."

"There's a reason you brought that up." He strokes my cheek again. "Tell me."

"It's not important."

"I'll be the judge. Talk to me, Gareth."

"It's just Simone said you often shared Cassandra and had an open marriage, so I wanted to see if you felt the same about me."

"I told you, I never loved her, so I went along with what she wanted. But with you, I get downright murderous at the thought of someone else touching you. It makes me fucking unhinged. I don't even like thinking about all the girls who had you before me."

"Because you love me and are possessive of me and can't live without me?"

"Correct on all accounts." His lips brush against my forehead, and it's my favorite kiss. It's like he's worshipping me every time he does it. "So don't bring up this subject again."

"I won't. I'm as possessive as you, and I get all stabby and shit at the thought of someone else."

"I love your violent brain."

"Because you can tame it?"

"Because you let me inside it."

"Well, you let me inside yours, too."

"You happen to be my favorite little monster."

"And you're my favorite villain, baby."

———

"WAKE UP, SLEEPYHEAD."

I groan, burying my face deeper into Kayden's neck. "Five more minutes."

A soft chuckle rumbles through his chest, the sound floods my ears and ripples through me. "As much as I love watching your sleepy face, your cousin will be here any minute."

I groan harder, tightening my arms around his shoulders. It's not like I *meant* to take a nap or anything, but it's the weekend, and I haven't seen much of him this week because he's been busy with work. And by "much," I mean I've only been seeing him in the evenings, which is far from enough in my book.

Anyway, he was sitting on the sofa, going through his tablet, and I kind of climbed into his lap like a koala, wrapping myself around him, my head resting on his shoulder. I'd meant to recharge for a bit—just a moment of peace—but then I fell asleep.

And he let me.

I love how he always lets me attach myself to him whenever and however I please. He doesn't even flinch when I jump on him out of nowhere or hug him from behind while he's doing the most mundane things. Or when I get on his lap when he's working or something.

Truth be told, I know I'm a goddamn clingy pest sometimes, but he never complains.

If anything, he always gives me this little smile, like I've somehow made his day better. Sometimes, he'll kiss me softly, stroke my hand, or ruffle my hair. It's those small touches that make me come back for more, like a hopeless addict.

I still crave him in ways I can't even explain, and I can't seem to stop touching him—whether we're alone or in public. I want to make up for all the time I couldn't muster the courage to.

Lifting my head, I stare at him, my arms still framing either side of his neck. My fingers find their way to the back of his hair, stroking it lightly.

Goddamn. Why does he keep getting more beautiful? His sharp features and those piercing eyes that seem to see straight through my soul are a lethal combination.

His hand rubs slow circles on my back, and his lips tilt into that soft smile that could undo me on the spot. "There you are. Feeling better?"

"How do you always know when I'm feeling off?"

"Your eyes, baby." He sets his table aside and cups my cheek. "They get a bit lifeless when something's bothering you."

I pout, my lower lip sticking out. "That's because you haven't been around enough."

Before he can respond, Moka meows and jumps onto the sofa beside us. I reach out to scratch behind her ears, grinning. "See? My sidekick agrees with me."

"I'll rectify that." His lips quirk, his hand sliding down to my ass giving it a firm squeeze. "Although, I wish I could charge you differently since you're being so adorably clingy."

"Mm." I grind my ass back against his cock, deliberately slow. "You *totally* should."

"We have guests coming over, remember?"

"I can kick Niko out," I grumble. Honest to God, I don't know why I agreed to this whole dinner thing in the first place.

Just kidding. I *do* know. I wanted to show off Kayden, and Niko wanted to show off his boyfriend.

"No, I want to meet your family one by one," Kayden says, tightening his grip on my ass to make me stop moving. "That's what I promised you, remember?"

"Fine, fine." I roll my eyes. "Still don't know how you managed to fascinate Mia and Maya the other day. They keep texting me to say hi to you."

"I'm charming."

"Pfft. *I am* charming. Not you."

"I can be charming too."

"I guess that's true." I press a quick kiss to his cheek, then pepper kisses along his jaw and mouth. "But you can only be charming with me, or I'll cut someone."

"There's my little violent psycho."

"Not my fault you're *kind of* hot."

"Kind of?"

"*Really* hot," I admit with an exaggerated eye roll.

He chuckles, the sound wrapping around me like a peaceful cloud. God. I love his laughter, his smell, his voice, his face, his body, but mostly, I love his little gestures, how he knows things about me without me having to say anything, how he looks out after me, how he recognizes my uneven edges and smooths them with care.

I love him.

And I keep falling further in love every single day.

I'm about to get on my knees and drink his cum dry when the doorbell rings.

My groan of displeasure only makes him laugh harder as he gently pushes me off.

"Can we not?" I whine, grabbing onto his hand like a child.

"Don't be a brat, Gareth. If you behave tonight..." He slides two of his fingers into my mouth, and I suck on them hard, taking them in deep like it's his cock.

His eyes darken, and I put on a show, lapping at his fingers with my tongue. But he pulls them out too soon, leaving me aching. "I'll reward you later."

I'm about to argue, but he's already walking toward the door with Moka trailing after him. Grumbling, I follow, trying to will my very inconvenient erection away.

A few moments later, Niko walks in, dressed in jeans and a leather jacket, his long hair tied in a bun. Brandon follows close behind, carrying a bottle of wine and looking like he just walked out of a British *Vogue* cover.

"So you're the motherfucker who got our Gaz hurt, huh?" Niko says, balling his hand into a fist. "Should've killed you in that alley, but maybe that can still be rectified."

I dart forward, wrapping an arm around his neck in a head-lock just as Bran steps in. "You *already* have the best fucking timing, and the last thing you want to do is threaten my man, bitch."

He taps my arm, wheezing. "Kill especially told me he has to pay."

"Kill can go fuck himself. Behave or I'm kicking you out."

"Let me punch him once."

"No."

"Just a tiny bit."

"I said no, asshole."

"How about—"

"Nikolai," Brandon interrupts, his calm, commanding voice cutting through the chaos. Niko immediately stops struggling, going still like a chastised puppy.

I let him go, and the strangest thing happens. My cousin, the certified chaos machine, grins apologetically at Bran, walking toward him with stars in his eyes.

"You promised not to start any fights," Bran says with a small frown. Unlike my cousin, he's dressed in a cardigan and khaki pants, and his accent is that of British royalty.

He's the exact opposite of my cousin, but somehow, they work.

"I'm sorry, lotus flower." Niko wraps an arm around his waist. "Won't happen again. Cross my heart and hope to die."

"It's nice to officially meet you, Nikolai," Kayden says, step-ping to my side, now clutching the bottle of wine Bran must've offered him.

My cousin narrows his eyes. "While I'm glad you introduced Gaz to the *Fun Dick Alliance*, Kill specifically told me not to like you."

"And what did *I* tell you?" Bran asks

Niko grins. "Not to be violent, to form my own opinion, and be happy for my cousin who's finally not a fake little bitch. The last part is mine, but anyway, my lotus flower's opinion is definitely more important than Killian's. Kill who? Don't know that guy."

Bran just smiles, and I release a breath I didn't know I was holding.

"I officially like you, Bran," I say, shaking his hand. "Didn't think anyone could tame Niko, but here we are."

Bran smiles, the corners of his mouth quirking in that polite, British way that somehow feels more genuine than a full grin. "I wouldn't say I'm *taming* him."

"You totally are," Niko and I say in unison, earning a soft laugh from Brandon.

"Gaz, I know you've met him before," Niko says, standing taller and tugging Bran closer. "But this is Brandon—my lotus flower and the love of my life. Bran, this is my cousin Gaz. He's *slightly* less insufferable now."

"This is Kayden," I say, pulling him into the fold with an arm around his waist. "My man. Also, yeah, the love of my life, so you better not give him any trouble, Niko. I mean it."

Kayden strokes my hair, his fingers gentle as he looks down at me with that softness that could melt the Arctic. If he keeps looking at me like that, I might spontaneously combust.

Dinner is chaotic in the way only my family can manage. Niko oscillates between being an absolute menace and a lovesick idiot, while Bran calmly keeps him tethered, offering quiet smiles and soft touches that make my cousin settle in ways I didn't think possible.

Kayden and I exchange a glance a few times throughout the evening and he strokes my thigh every now and then. He knows what I'm thinking, that I can't stand not touching him even for a while. I can see it in his small, knowing smirks.

Watching Niko being tamed by Bran is like watching myself through someone else's eyes. The clinginess, the chaos, the need to show off—yeah, that's me.

After dinner, Niko is bickering with Kayden over dessert. Something about how "macarons are superior to whatever boring shit you brought." I leave them to it, grabbing Bran and pulling him toward the sitting room.

Moka is curled up on Bran's lap not five minutes later, purring like a spoiled queen as he strokes her fur.

"She usually doesn't like strangers," I say, narrowing my eyes at my little traitor. "She's not this friendly with anyone but Kayden and me."

Bran shrugs, his smile soft. "Animals and children usually like me."

I lean back, arms crossed. "Makes sense. Niko *does* have the personality of a hyperactive toddler. Kudos to you for keeping up with him."

Bran laughs, his blue eyes bright as he steals a glance at my cousin, who's still loudly debating Kayden in the kitchen. "He's the one who kept up with me, really. This is nothing. If anything, I'm happy to see him happy."

"He's been over the moon since he started introducing you to us."

A flicker of sadness crosses his face, dimming the light in his eyes for a moment. "That's because I insisted we stay a secret for too long. I wish I'd been more courageous earlier and came out sooner."

"You shouldn't blame yourself for that. Coming out is a different experience for everyone. I don't have the best track record myself."

He tilts his head, studying me. "Niko said Kayden was your professor, so you had a *viable* reason to keep things quiet."

"There's no such thing as a *viable* reason. Coming out is personal, and it depends on the person, and this is coming from someone who had a massive struggle with my sexuality in the beginning."

"Me too, for years, actually. If Niko hadn't come along, I have no idea where I would be."

"Honestly, same. Kayde kind of pulled me out kicking and screaming."

"Wow. We have that in common, too." He grins. "I think, aside from Mia, you're my new favorite from all of Niko's entourage."

"Former *Confused Dick Alliance* not to be mistaken for Niko's *Fun Dick Alliance*?"

He chuckles, but before he can respond, Niko bursts into the room.

"What's making my lotus flower laugh?" he demands, wedging himself between us on the sofa.

"Me, obviously," I say, smirking.

Niko narrows his eyes and then does the most *Niko* thing ever—he shoves me off the sofa and wraps his arms around Bran like a possessive octopus.

"Only *I* get to make him laugh," he declares, pressing a dramatic kiss to Bran's cheek.

"Stop being dramatic," Bran mutters, though his smile suggests he doesn't mind one bit.

They're still tangled together when I make my way to the kitchen, where Kayden leans against the counter, arms crossed and a faint frown tugging at his lips.

I slip my arms around his waist, pressing against him. "What?"

"Don't be so charming with others," he murmurs, his voice low and rough.

I grin, leaning up on my tiptoes. "Jealous?"

"You know I am."

"Mmm." My grin widens. "I guess I'll try to tone it down."

"*Gareth.*"

"Yeah?"

"Behave."

"No promises." I press my lips to his ear, my voice dropping to a sultry whisper. "Feeling cute, so I want to turn that reward into a punishment, baby."

He's kissing me then, groaning in my mouth because he loves how I call him baby.

And I love that I'm his baby.

Now.

Forever.

And beyond.

EPILOGUE 2
KAYDEN

SIX MONTHS LATER

"That was fucking sick!"

Gareth punches the air as we sit in a bougie restaurant in Manhattan.

His treat.

And it's not for me.

That statement that's bursting with excitement is also *not* for me.

It's for the third party that's joining us for the dinner—upon Gareth's invitation. As I said, *his treat.*

And he's standing out like a sore thumb in the midst of all the smartly dressed people because he's still wearing the hockey jersey he bought at the game earlier in the evening.

No one would refuse to let him in, though, because one of

his mafia friends owns this place, and he just walked in like it's his house.

I know I was the one who introduced him to hockey and promised to take him to his first game, but I'm starting to have regrets.

Maybe dragging him to my nephew's college away game in New York wasn't the best idea, because he's been annoyingly cheerful all evening.

And it's not because of *me*.

Okay, so he said he loves me and thanked me for bringing him while kissing me in the stands, but still.

And no, I don't *really* hold a grudge against my nephew.

Or maybe I do, because now, he's smiling at Gareth as he eats a bite of his food.

Kane is tall, almost as tall as me—little fucker wouldn't stop growing up—and he has a lethal broad and muscular body, which is a product of a decade and a half of rigid hockey—and Vencor—training.

I made the decision to leave that shitshow, even if I don't get to step a foot in my hometown and the state ever again. Aside from the mafia protection Gareth managed to summon, I made a deal with Grant. I willingly banish myself from town, and I keep his profits going. He doesn't want to kill me anyway, not when I'm better at business than he'll ever be.

As for Vencor, they can try. It's impossible with the amount of security we have. Besides, New York is the Russian mafia's turf, and they wouldn't dare come here.

Grant also made the other families promise to stay away from me. At least, for now.

Unlike me, however, Kane wants to own that style of life. Breathe it. Drown in it, even.

You wouldn't think he could be so cunning and intense looking at him.

He has a welcoming expression, a polite smile, and deeply

unreadable light-blue eyes. Like Prince Charming or the good-looking guy next door, but like Gareth, what you see is *not* what you get.

Annoyingly, Kane's also about Gareth's age, but he's always seemed older in mannerisms and character. Being born as Grant's son isn't a tragedy I would wish on anyone, but he's passing it with flying colors.

Anyhow, he has a lot of things in common with Gareth, and it's making me kill half a bottle of wine in no time.

I wish I had a cigarette, but my strict little monster made me quit again.

And I would rather break my own arm than hurt him with that nonsense, so cigarettes and I are officially done.

Gareth grins at something Kane says, his hand going back and forth on my thigh.

I guess that's the only good thing about this. At least he always wants to touch me, and I mean *always*. Whether in public or not. It can be as subtle as right now or downright sucking my face with his mouth.

He says I charge him, so if we don't see each other for a few days, he's drained. Once, I was in Japan for a business deal and I had to stay for a week. On the fifth day, I found him outside the building where I was staying. In the rain, just bouncing in place and checking his phone.

Ever since then, I've made it my mission not to stay away for more than five days. That seems to be his absolute limit, and I do mean limit. He was visibly shaking with his pupils dilated and he looked depressed.

It's probably unhealthy that he's so attached to me, but I love it. I love that he loves me in this intense, all-in, no-way-out kind of way. How he can be so obsessed but also so affectionate.

And yes, he still buys me unnecessary nonsense.

But then he let me be the only one to drive his car. Not that

I'm jealous of a literal car, but if the shoe fits, yes, in your face, Medusa.

No one is more important than me. I see it when his eyes brighten to this clear green color whenever he looks at me, how he smiles wide just because he knows I'm a little bit obsessed with his dimples.

It's only fair since I also get stomachaches when he's not around. Julian said it's because I stopped testing his drugs, but Julian can go fuck himself.

I only did that when I didn't care about my body. Now, I plan to live fully. For Gareth.

And I kid you not, when Julian paid me a visit for business matters and tried to convince me to pick up with testing, Gareth pointed a gun at him and said, "Good, you're here. I've been fantasizing about killing you this whole time."

I just laughed and told Julian not to be fooled by Gareth's charming looks, because he *would* kill him without hesitation, so he'd better leave.

"That was a sick game," Gareth says to Kane. "The violence was immaculate."

I shake my head. Of course he'd like that.

"We did go a bit extra tonight," Kane says with his usual good-boy smile. "You never played?"

"No. I was more of a football guy in high school."

Now, I'm imagining him in tight football pants, and my cock jumps like an insatiable whore. It doesn't help that Gareth's hand is wrapped around my thigh, close to my dick.

Kane takes a sip of his drink. "I can teach you if you like."

"I can do the teaching myself," I grumble.

Gareth's eyes light up, his fingers pausing on my thigh. "Really?"

"I used to play, remember? And I was way better than Kane."

"I wouldn't say *way* better," Kane interjects with a grin.

I glare at the little fuck. "*Worlds apart* better."

"Whoa, relax, Uncle." He lets out a laugh. "I'm not going to steal your boyfriend."

"That's implying you could." I wrap a hand around Gareth's nape and rub the skin.

He immediately melts in my grip, gulping down his bite of food.

"I must say I've never seen this version of Uncle. What did you do to him, Gareth?"

"Lots of voodoo and a tiny bit of knives and Tasers." My little monster grins, looking so smug and proud of himself.

He loves hearing others say I'm different when I'm with him.

Often, he'll ask Simone and Jethro with a wide grin, "So you said he was *so* grumpy before me? Like absolutely insufferable? Tell me more."

The rest of the dinner is spent in relative peace. Before he leaves, Kane asks for my cooperation with his plans within Vencor.

He'll bring me back, he says.

But I don't *want* to go back. A place that doesn't accept me and my man is not for me.

However, I give Kane the green light to proceed with what he has in mind.

He'll be all right.

I *think*.

When it's time to drive home, Gareth says he wants to walk. He loves that now—just walking outside. Mostly because he likes holding hands and hugging me in public.

Must be because of all those times he couldn't do it when we had a secret relationship. I don't really care for PDA, but I'd do anything for Gareth. If people are uncomfortable, they can kindly go fuck themselves.

He used to be so peevy about touching me outside of sex, but now, it's second nature.

We're getting closer to where I want to take him, but he's underdressed in the damn jersey. I give him my jacket and wrap it around his shoulders.

"I'm not that cold." He sways on his feet, a bit drunk, as he grins up at me. "But I don't mind ogling your huge muscles. Mmm."

"Don't be a brat."

"Pfft. You love it when I'm a brat."

"Your ass will love it, too, later."

"Don't threaten me with a good time, baby."

A jolt zaps through my chest and ends in my stomach whenever he says that.

I grab his hand and drag him with me to stop my erection from growing further.

"Maybe we should take a taxi." He bites his lower lip. "I want to show you something in private."

"I want to show you something first."

"What...?" His eyes light up with intrigue, excitement, and overflowing affection.

"I'm rethinking it because you have someone else's name on your back."

He stops by the sidewalk, forcing me to do the same.

Gareth's cheeks, even his freckles, are red from the alcohol, and when he frowns with that face, he looks fucking adorable.

I can't devour him yet.

Not *yet*.

"What do you mean?" he asks.

"Kane's jersey that you bought."

He removes my jacket, then turns around on unsteady feet, and I grab his arm to keep him standing.

He points back.

"Can't you see? It says *Davenport*." He taps his shoulder and then spins around again to face me. "Last I checked, that's your last name."

"So you bought it to have...my last name on your back?"

"Why else?" He cocks his head to the side and then grins. "I've always wanted that. Your last name on me."

Fuck.

That's why he looked so exhilarated when he bought the jersey.

I grab him by the waist, all but dragging him with me because he can't keep up.

Gareth chuckles, the sound of his laughs echoing in the air as I pull him.

"Mmm, are you taking me to an alley so I can choke on your cock?"

"Quiet, Gareth."

"I would. I *so* would."

"Baby, you need to stop tempting me."

"But I want you to fuck me while I'm only wearing the jersey with your last name."

"Jesus fucking Christ." I stop and brush my lips to his, the slightest touch. "Shut up for a second."

He blinks up at me, then smiles. "You know you want to."

"I do, but first look around."

He blinks again and then studies our surroundings. It's a house we passed by before, though calling it a house is putting it lightly. It's a goddamn mansion by the hill, overlooking the city.

Gareth once said it was the perfect house, close enough to the city and his parents while also being a stone's throw away from the rest of his friends' future residences.

And while he insists on finishing his law degree on the island where his friends are and I can work from the London branch, he'll eventually want to come back.

That is, if he doesn't switch gears soon.

At any rate, this is his home. *Our* home.

Gareth steps into the lit garden, along the pool, his eyes widening. "You bought this?"

"For you."

"Just because I said I liked it?"

"A perfectly good reason to."

"But it wasn't for sale."

"Anything is for sale if I decide to buy it."

"I'm not even surprised." He smiles at me and then continues exploring the area. "Love this so much. We can get Moka a few siblings. I can set up an archery range, and you can use the pool for your morning swims. Is there another one indoor—"

His voice catches when he turns around and finds me on one knee. I've never been on my knees for anyone else. I asked Cassandra to marry me over coffee as if it were a business deal. And it was, in a sense. We toasted to it and that was that.

But this is different.

Gareth is the only one I'd get on my knees for.

"W-what's going on...?" he whispers, his eyes widening and red creeping up his neck.

"I know you said you don't believe in marriage, and you can say no if you truly hate it, but you also said you love my last name on you, so..." I reach into the pocket of my pants and pull out a ring with his name and mine carved on the inside. "I love you in ways I thought were impossible, and I want to spend the rest of my life being yours and you mine. Gareth Anthony Carson, would you marry me?"

"Fuck, oh fuck..." He drops to his knees in front of me, grabbing my hand in both of his, softly, with reverence.

He's breathing so harshly, he's almost panting.

"You'd marry me?" he asks in a murmur. "You'll give me your last name?"

"There's nothing I want more in the world, baby."

"Kayde, fuck...yes...yes...it's a goddamn *yes*."

"Thank fuck." I slip the ring on his finger and kiss his hand, and he shivers, my little monster, vibrating, against me.

"Do you have another ring?" he asks with glittery eyes.

I nod and drop the matching ring in his palm.

Gareth slides it on my finger, then holds my hand, and grins. "It looks beautiful."

"It's the only ring I'll wear for the rest of my life, baby."

"Fuck...I need you..." He's about to kiss me but then stops. "Wait."

"What's wrong?"

"There's something I want to show you. My proposal commemoration gift." He fumbles with the sleeve of the jersey and then lifts it to his elbow.

My eyes widen.

Where the scars from the knife slashes once marred his skin, a new tattoo now takes their place.

A skull is inked into the flesh, its hollow eyes staring back at me with a chilling intensity. Coiled around the jagged bone is a snake, eerily similar to mine, its sleek body threading through the cracks of the skull as if it's alive, writhing just beneath the surface.

The ink is fresh, the bold black lines still vivid against his skin, cutting through the old scars like a defiant, permanent declaration. Above it, etched with stark finality, are the words *'My Villain K.D.'* Each letter is a bold, raw shout of devotion.

"I know you always hated those scars." He smiles. "So I carved them out and replaced them with something deeper that only we can understand."

"You hid them for me?" I ask in a low voice.

"For us. So we can kill the past and just be us. I promise to never hurt myself again, and you already promised to never hurt me again." He kisses my forehead, my eyes, my cheek. "This is our new beginning."

"Now, I'll have to get some clichéd tattoo with your name on me." I pull his arm and kiss around the tattoo.

"Then I'll get one with your full name, too. We should do it together. Be clichéd as fuck because, who cares? We'll be married anyway."

I hum against his throat. "You'll be my Mr. Davenport?"

His eyes ignite like fire. "Hell yes. Mr. and Mr. Davenport sounds hot as fuck."

"I like that. A lot, actually."

"Me, too. Just thinking about you as my husband is getting me all kinds of hot and bothered."

"I'll have to take care of that immediately. Can't let my husband struggle, now, can I?"

He slams his lips to mine, and I carry him in my arms toward the start of our new life together.

As husband and husband.

Villain and monster.

Two fractured souls that fit perfectly.

Gareth is the reason and the madness.

The chaos and the calm.

The love of my goddamn life.

THE END

The Villain series continues with *Hunt the Villain*, featuring Vaughn and Yulian's story.

You can also explore the books for characters who appeared in this story:

Kane Davenport: *Beautiful Venom*

Killian & Glyndon: *God of Malice*

Nikolai & Brandon: *God of Fury*

Jeremy: *God of Wrath*

WHAT'S NEXT?

Thank you so much for reading *Kiss the Villain*! If you liked it, please leave a review.

Your support means the world to me.

For more discussion with other Rina Kent readers, you can join the Facebook group, *Rina Kent's Spoilers Room*.

You can read more about Kayden's nephew and Vencor in the dark hockey romance *Beautiful Venom*.

The *Villain* series will continue with *Hunt the Villain*, featuring Vaughn and Yulian's story.

ALSO BY RINA KENT

For more books by the author and a reading order, please visit:

www.rinakent.com/books

ABOUT THE AUTHOR

Rina Kent is a *New York Times*, *USA Today*, and #1 bestselling author of all things dark romance.

Better known for writing unapologetic anti-heroes and villains, Rina weaves tales of characters you shouldn't fall for but inevitably do. Her stories are laced with a touch of darkness, a splash of angst, and just the right amount of unhealthy intensity.

When she's not busy plotting mayhem for her ever-expanding *Rinaverse*, she leads a private life in London, travels, and pampers her cats in true Cat Lady fashion.

Find Rina Below:
Website: https://www.rinakent.com/
Newsletter: https://www.subscribepage.com/rinakent
Reader Group: https://www.facebook.com/groups/rinakent.
club/

bookbub.com/profile/rina-kent

amazon.com/stores/Rina-Kent/author/B07MM54G22

goodreads.com/rina_kent

instagram.com/author_rina

facebook.com/rinaakent

pinterest.com/AuthorRina

x.com/AuthorRina

tiktok.com/@rina.kent

Made in United States
North Haven, CT
20 March 2025